Australian
Outback
Murders

Max Barrington

Three of my favourite books, but then, they're all' my
favourites
Max............

For the love of my life,

my darling wife and my inspiration,

Lynette

First published in Australia in 2024 by Etteleah Books - Cairns Australia
This Revised Edition published in Australia in 2025 by Etteleah Books

Woolgar River Park ISBN9798304247962

Contents

WOOLGAR RIVER PARK

A Mystery Unfolds

&

A Story Retold

Max Barrington

The Call

The mobile phone burst into life with the unmistakable opening riff of the James Bond theme. It rang on and on, stopped abruptly, and then started again, insistently. Gus groaned, fumbling in the dark. The ringtone stopped again, only to restart with determination. Finally, he snatched it up.

"Hello, this is Gus," he answered, his voice groggy with sleep.

"Good morning, is that Angus Teague?" came a crisp voice on the other end.

"It is. And who's calling?" Gus replied, still half-asleep but beginning to wake up.

"This is Malcolm Davies, Mr. Teague. I'm a solicitor at Wedderburn & Holt. Could you please confirm your date of birth for me?"

Gus frowned, rubbing his eyes. "Well, Mr. Davies, if that's who you are, you'll have to tell me what this is about first. And make it quick, I'm seconds away from hanging up."

"Please don't hang up, Mr. Teague," the voice implored. "It's regarding your uncle, Lachlan Teague."

"My uncle?" Gus replied, confused. "Is he sick?"

"Mr. Teague," Malcolm said gently, "your uncle passed away. It actually happened some time ago, but it took considerable effort for us to locate you."

Gus's mind worked to conjure up an image of Uncle Lachlan. Ah, yes, Dad's younger brother, the family outcast no one ever spoke about!

"Oh," Gus stammered, still trying to process the news. "I wasn't aware. I haven't seen him since I was a kid in Scotland. Last I heard, he bought a property near Richmond, Queensland. That must've been... sixteen years ago, maybe longer."

"That's correct," Malcolm confirmed. "Mr. Teague, to get straight to the point, you're the sole beneficiary of your uncle's estate, according to his will."

The words hung in the air, heavy with surprise.

Angus Teague was no stranger to sudden twists in life's plot. Born in Canonbie, Scotland, the only child of Alisdair and Eileen Teague, he had immigrated to Australia with his parents in 1950. They'd started out in a transitional hostel near Sydney before settling in Yass, New South Wales, where Alisdair had taken over a 300-acre Romney sheep breeding property.

Angus completed his education partly in Yass and then in Canberra, where he trained as a carpenter before pursuing further studies in applied science. A stint as a building inspector followed, but the harsh Yass climate eventually drove him north to the sunny shores of Cairns in Far North Queensland. His parents, meanwhile, retired in Canberra and passed away the year Angus turned sixty. Their inheritance had allowed him to retire early, a decision he never regretted.

Life in Cairns suited him perfectly. It was there, in the idyllic suburb of Clifton Beach, that he met Lynette under unusual circumstances. His unit had been broken into one evening, and after dealing with the theft of his cash, a broken camera, and his fridge's contents, including a treasured stockpile of beer, he'd gone out to drown his sorrows at the Reef Casino. A chance encounter at the bar with a striking woman named Lynette led to a surprising revelation the next morning: she was one of the police officers assigned to investigate his break-in.

From that serendipitous moment, their story unfolded into a life together, filled with shared adventures and a quiet retirement in Cairns City.

Gus checked the time: 7:30 a.m. After a quick trip to the bathroom, he wandered onto the balcony, where Lynette was enjoying her breakfast.

"You're up early," she said with a smile. "What's the occasion?"

"I got a call," Gus replied, sitting down beside her. "It's about Uncle Lachlan. Turns out he died. Some solicitor found me, said I'm the sole beneficiary of his estate."

Lynette's fork clattered onto her plate. "Are you serious? Did he say how much it's worth?"

"No," Gus admitted, shaking his head. "Just that it's substantial."

Lynette's eyes lit up with excitement. "Substantial? Oh, Gus, this is incredible! Let's go celebrate, drinks on the Esplanade tonight!"

Gus chuckled, watching her enthusiasm bubble over. "Let's see what the solicitor says first," he said, though a grin was already spreading across his face.

A new chapter had begun.

The offices of Wedderburn & Holt were located on Denham Street in Townsville. Since Gus and his wife Lynette lived on the Esplanade in Cairns City, an appointment was scheduled for the following week to handle the necessary formalities. Gus needed to finalise the transfer of the estate, including the title of the late Mr. Lachlan Teague's property and $692,000 in cash that would be deposited into Gus's account.

During the meeting, Malcolm Davies informed Gus that Sonia Teague, Lachlan's wife, had attempted to challenge the will. Her efforts, however, were unsuccessful unless the named beneficiary, Gus, could not be found or was deceased.

"The bottom line," Malcolm explained, "is that Mr. Teague specifically excluded Sonia from his will. The land titles were solely in his name, with no shared ownership or communal claims."

"Interesting," Gus thought with a smirk, "but who cares? It's all mine now." He later shared this blunt sentiment with Lynette, who laughed at his unapologetic reaction.

While waiting for a full inventory of the estate to be prepared, Gus asked Malcolm if he had known Lachlan personally. To his surprise, Malcolm revealed that he had met Lachlan only once, six months before his death, when Lachlan came in to draft his will. Lynette, curious as always, casually asked if Malcolm knew the cause of death. Malcolm shook his head. "I assumed it was natural causes," he said, "but I don't have the details."

After some formalities, Malcolm finally announced, "All done!" The title to the sprawling property, 'Woolgar River Park,' was officially transferred to Gus.

The property, approximately 30,000 hectares (73,000 acres), was located in the County of Yappar and the Parish of Saxby, about 150 kilometres northwest of Hughenden. Its features were nothing short of impressive:

A two-story, five-bedroom homestead with verandahs on three sides

A cool room adjacent to the residence

A four-car garage

Additional accommodations, including:

A three-bedroom, two-bathroom manager's house, 160 meters from the homestead

Two self-contained staff quarters, each with two bedrooms, one near the manager's house, the other about four kilometres from the homestead

The property boasted numerous bores, each roughly 300 meters deep, and riparian water rights along the Woolgar River. Shaded cattle yards with a capacity for 6,000 backgrounder cattle further added to its value.

While the will mentioned no livestock at the time of drafting, Malcolm explained that any cattle found on the property, unless owned by a lessee, would form part of the estate. The property's description dated back to its purchase by Lachlan in 2003.

However, there was one hitch: there were no keys to the buildings. Malcolm's office had secured the front gates to deter trespassers, but whether Sonia Teague had vacated the property remained unclear. She had been served a notice to vacate, allowing her to take only her personal belongings. Even her car, registered in Lachlan's name, had to be left behind.

When the inventory arrived, Malcolm handed a copy to Gus. It listed the property details, furniture, machinery, tools, and vehicles:

A 2012 BMW X5

A 2018 Honda Accord Euro

A 2006 Toyota LandCruiser Cab/Chassis with a steel tray

Malcolm emphasised that his firm was responsible for verifying the inventory before Gus signed the acknowledgment. He offered to accompany Gus to the property and suggested they stay overnight in Hughenden to break up the 560-kilometre journey from Townsville.

Grateful for Malcolm's help, Gus proposed dinner that evening to discuss travel plans. Malcolm declined with a smile, explaining, "I'm hosting a BBQ this afternoon with my parents, who are visiting. Why don't you and Lynette join us? We can talk dates then."

That afternoon, Gus and Lynette arrived at Malcolm's house in North Ward. They were warmly greeted by Malcolm's wife, Ros, and his parents. Gus brought along a carton of xxxx Gold stubbies and a bottle of Port Phillip Estate Chardonnay, which he had chosen at random.

The BBQ turned out to be a relaxed and enjoyable affair. The conversation ranged from retirement to the joys of unit living. Malcolm and Ros shared their thoughts on downsizing, while Gus and Lynette offered anecdotes about their life in Cairns.

By the end of the evening, Gus and Malcolm had agreed on a date to visit Woolgar River Park. For Gus, the reality of inheriting such an expansive estate was slowly sinking in. It was more than just a financial windfall, it was the start of a new adventure.

Neither Gus nor Lynette asked Malcolm and Ros why they didn't have children, respecting their privacy. Soon after, Malcolm's parents excused themselves, declaring it was their bedtime. This left the four of them to continue chatting and getting better acquainted.

It didn't take long for Ros to bring up the inheritance. "You must be so excited!" she exclaimed. "I wish we could get a call out of the blue like you did." Her comment sparked a lively conversation, accompanied by another drink, or four.

Malcolm leaned back in his chair and revealed, "My firm receives all death notices, and we check our records accordingly. When Lachlan Teague's name came up as a registered client of Wedderburn & Holt, the file was flagged with my name, so it came straight to me."

As the others listened intently, Malcolm continued, "I remembered him immediately. Lachlan came into the office out of the blue one day. He walked up to the receptionist and asked if he could have a will drafted on the spot."

The group chuckled at the idea, but Malcolm explained further. "The receptionist told him it wasn't that simple, he'd need to book an appointment and bring three types of ID, including one with a photograph. If real estate was involved, he'd also need a current rates notice and an electricity account in his name."

"What happened next?" Lynette asked, intrigued.

Malcolm smiled. "Lachlan said he had everything in his bag and mentioned he was from out of town. But when the receptionist explained she couldn't guarantee an appointment that day, he shrugged and was about to leave. Luckily, I had a cancellation. She called me, and I decided to squeeze him in."

Ros, fascinated, got up to fetch more drinks, exclaiming, "This is getting good!"

Malcolm chuckled. "Well, when he came into my office, he was quiet and direct. He said he wanted to draft a simple will with one sole beneficiary. Naturally, I asked for his details and what he intended to include in the will.

That's when he opened his bag and handed me a full inventory of his estate. He wanted everything, property, assets, and all, to go to his nephew, Angus Teague of Australia."

Malcolm paused, glancing at Gus. "That's you, of course."

Gus nodded, his expression thoughtful. "So he came in, prepared and determined."

"Absolutely," Malcolm confirmed. "He knew exactly what he wanted, and we drafted the will right then and there. It was all very straightforward, almost too straightforward, if you ask me. But that's Lachlan for you, I suppose."

The story lingered in the air as the group sipped their drinks. For Gus, it added a new layer of intrigue to the mysterious fortune that had unexpectedly fallen into his lap.

Lachlan Teague had also produced a detailed inventory of his estate, accompanied by copies of original documents, including the land title and deed to his property, as well as deeds for goods, chattels, and vehicles, all in his name.

Malcolm explained that he had advised Lachlan he would need more information about Angus's address. However, Lachlan admitted that all he knew was Angus's name and a vague reference to his location in Australia. He did, however, provide Angus's birthdate and the name of Angus's father, suggesting that might help in the future.

The will was completed promptly, and Lachlan signed it in the presence of Malcolm's secretary, who acted as the witness. Lachlan then paid all required fees, including an additional fee for potential travel and accommodation expenses.

Gus, intrigued by the peculiar circumstances, volunteered to fetch more drinks. As he handed them around, he couldn't help but think how strange it all seemed.

Malcolm resumed the story as everyone settled back into their seats. "The really odd part," he said, "is that when we were notified of Lachlan's death and moved to register the execution of the will, we discovered that another will had been registered just two hours before the one in our possession. Naturally, this raised a red flag. However, after verifying the details, it was confirmed that our will was valid, while the other one was void."

Malcolm paused, glancing at Gus and Lynette for their reactions. "And then, as we mentioned earlier today, Mrs. Sonia Teague stormed into our office. She was demanding details about the will, clearly upset. She challenged it but lost outright on currency dates. When that failed, she insisted she was entitled to at least half of the estate. Unfortunately for her, when we presented the inventory, titles, and deeds, everything showing Lachlan's sole ownership, she was, well, pardon my French, 'completely screwed.'"

Lynette chuckled, while Gus nodded with interest.

Malcolm continued, "The other strange thing is what she said when I told her who the beneficiary was. She claimed she'd never heard of you, Gus. Not even once."

This revelation gave Gus pause, but he didn't comment. Malcolm then turned the conversation practical. "So, what day would you like to head up to the property for a look?"

"Any day works for us," Lynette said. Gus nodded in agreement. "The sooner, the better, we're really eager to see it," he added.

Gus then suggested, "Why don't we all travel together and make a little holiday out of it?"

Ros perked up at the idea. "That sounds great! Malcolm's parents are visiting, so they can stay here and look after the dog while we're away."

"Perfect," Malcolm said. "How about the day after tomorrow? That's Thursday. We'll spend Thursday and Friday in Hughenden, then head back Saturday. Done deal!"

"Done!" Gus agreed enthusiastically.

Malcolm raised his glass. "Another round?"

On Wednesday morning, Gus and Lynette woke up at the Townsville Casino, feeling the thrill of newfound wealth. Overnight, the substantial inheritance had been transferred into their bank account. With a few extra days in Townsville ahead of them, they decided it was time to treat themselves.

Having initially planned to stay only one night, they had packed minimally and now needed a wardrobe refresh for their extended trip. They headed to Castletown Shopping Centre to indulge in some retail therapy.

By Thursday morning at eight o'clock, Malcolm and Ros arrived at the casino to collect Gus and Lynette in Malcolm's LandCruiser 200 VX. As they stepped out onto the casino's steps, Ros shifted from the front seat to the back to sit with Lynette, allowing the men to discuss business. Ever prepared, Ros handed out cold bottles of water to everyone.

As they settled in, Malcolm asked Gus, "Is your car okay in the casino's car park for a few days?"

Gus chuckled, "It's insured."

The conversation soon turned casual as they began the long drive. Malcolm inquired about Gus and Lynette's life in Cairns and their past professions.

Lynette shared with Ros, "Gus was a building surveyor until his early retirement last year, at the grand age of sixty. He still gets called in occasionally by his former workplace when they need an expert hand."

Ros smiled, impressed, as Lynette continued, "As for me, I was a detective sergeant with the Queensland Police until I decided to retire alongside Gus last year. We figured it was time to enjoy life while we could."

Ros nodded. "Sounds like you've earned it. And now, with everything going on, it must feel like the universe is rewarding you!"

Lynette exchanged a knowing glance with Gus, both quietly acknowledging how surreal recent events had been.

As the LandCruiser sped along the highway, the promise of adventure loomed ahead, with plenty of stories yet to unfold.

Malcolm asked Gus how well he had known his uncle Lachlan. Gus replied with a chuckle, "It's a long story, Malcolm. I haven't seen him since I left Scotland when I was ten years old, that's exactly fifty years ago this year. Lachlan was fifteen years younger than my dad and from a different mother. Let me think… Dad died at eighty-six, and that was six years ago. So, Lachlan would've been seventy-seven when he passed, which means he was twenty-seven years old the last time I saw him."

Gus continued, "My father, Alisdair, had an adjoining property in Canonbie with his father, Campbell Teague. Lachlan, my father's younger half-brother, owned another adjoining property on the other side of my father's land." Gus paused and laughed. "Have I totally confused everyone yet?"

He went on, "Anyway, my dad's property was a gift from his father, as was Lachlan's, and they all worked well together. They made good money. But then Dad got fed up with sheep farming and decided to switch to producing Aberdeen Angus cattle on his property. My grandfather wasn't happy about that, he was furious. The fight they had was so bad that Dad gave in and went back to sheep farming.

"But by then, Dad had lost all interest. He decided to migrate to Australia and asked his father to buy his property from him. That didn't go over well. My grandfather lost his temper and told Alisdair that if he left, he'd disown him and cut him off completely."

Gus shrugged as he concluded, "There was no need for the old man to act like that, but that's how things went back in Scotland."

The group stopped in Charters Towers for morning tea before continuing their journey. As they drove on to Hughenden, Malcolm mused aloud, "I wonder if Mrs. Sonia Teague is still at the property?" He glanced at Gus. "She shouldn't be. The court order to vacate was hand-delivered and receipted. But if she is… well, things might get interesting."

They stopped in Hughenden for lunch and then checked into the Royal Hotel-Motel on Moran Street. After settling in, they set out toward Richmond. Just beyond the town, they turned onto the Richmond-Woolgar Road and drove about thirty-five kilometres before taking another right turn that led them six kilometres further.

Eventually, they arrived at a cattle grid in the road with a gate beside it. Adjacent to the grid was a large, double gate, likely for road trains, flanked by a timber fence. The faded lettering on one side of the fence read Woolgar River Park. It was clear the sign was in dire need of repainting, but this was unmistakably the property they had come to see.

Both the large gates were secured with chains and padlocks, and the single gate on the grid was similarly locked. Malcolm rummaged through the console of the car, eventually producing a set of keys. He joined Gus at the grid gate.

"What beautiful country," Gus remarked to no one in particular as Malcolm struggled with the padlock.

"No luck," Malcolm said, frustrated. "The key won't work. Let me try the double gates." He moved over, but after a few minutes of trying the other lock, he shook his head. "Same issue. The locks must've been changed again since we last had them replaced. Both locks were supposed to use the same key, but these are completely different."

While Malcolm fiddled with the locks, Gus inspected the grid gate. The hinges were simple pins welded to the gate, fitting into sockets on the steel post. With a bit of effort, Gus lifted the gate, pulling the pins out of the sockets. Using the chain and padlock as a makeshift hinge, he swung the gate away from the grid.

"You ripper!" Malcolm exclaimed, noticing the fresh tire tracks leading through the grid and continuing in both directions.

They drove slowly along the track toward the house, about two kilometres ahead. Rounding a long curve, the house came into view. Its full-length verandah and grand porte-cochere at the centre were striking. Gus and Lynette stared in awe.

The porte-cochere framed an elaborate set of double doors with extravagant moldings, but they were securely locked. A walk around the perimeter revealed that all the doors and windows were also locked. Standing beneath the grand entrance, wondering what to do next, Ros noticed a large, empty concrete plant pot. She tilted it to one side and revealed a hidden key. The discovery earned her applause from the group.

They were about to try the key when the sound of an approaching car caught their attention. They turned to see a white Land Cruiser ute pulling up beside Malcolm's vehicle. A large, dark-haired man sat in the driver's seat, silently observing them.

The passenger door opened, and a woman stepped out. She moved to the front of the vehicle and began shouting, "Who are you? What do you want? Who are you?"

Gus, a little startled but somewhat prepared for a confrontation, took a steadying breath and replied firmly, "I beg your pardon, Madam, but who, may I ask, are YOU?"

His measured response seemed to catch her off guard. She froze for a moment, then snapped, "I am the OWNER of this property!"

"NO, MADAM, you are NOT," Gus replied, his voice calm but authoritative. "This is my property, and you are trespassing."

Before the woman could respond, Malcolm stepped in. "Excuse me, but are you, by any chance, Mrs. Sonia Teague?"

Her demeanour shifted slightly, though her tone remained defensive. "What concern is it to you if I am? Who are you people, and what do you want? What do you mean, this property belongs to you? It's mine!"

Malcolm introduced himself and then gestured to Gus. "This is Mr. Angus Teague. We're here today because this property legally belongs to him. As of now, Mrs. Teague, you are trespassing, and Mr. Teague is here to formally take possession of his property, today, in fact."

This was the last straw for Mrs. Sonia Teague. Turning sharply, she called out to the driver of the ute, demanding he come inside the house with her. She reached toward the concrete plant pot by the entrance, only to find the key missing. Her frustration was evident.

"Can we please discuss this sensibly?" Gus attempted, his tone calm but firm. Sonia glared at him, her expression filled with disdain. Gus, who had initially approached the situation with patience, thought to himself, You… bitch. He was done with her antics.

Turning to Malcolm, Gus said with growing frustration, "I've had enough of this. I'm not putting up with her behaviour. What do we do now? I want her off this property now." His voice betrayed both anger and disappointment. Earlier, he'd looked forward to meeting Sonia, his aunt by marriage, despite the circumstances. Now, that sentiment had evaporated entirely.

Hearing his words, Sonia snapped back defiantly. "No one, and I mean no one, is going to move me from my home. I know my rights. I could call squatters' rights and stay right here!"

Malcolm, keeping his composure, replied, "Mrs. Teague, unfortunately for you, this situation is not in your favor. You've been served a court order requiring you to vacate the premises. Refusing to comply could lead to your arrest."

Sonia crossed her arms, her stance unchanged. She scoffed at the notion and refused to budge.

Seeing her resistance, Malcolm turned to the others. "We're not getting anywhere with this. Let's go back to Hughenden and involve the police. They'll handle her removal."

The group piled back into Malcolm's Land Cruiser for the tense drive to Hughenden. They arrived at the police station, a large brick building on Brodie Street, at around 2:30 p.m. Malcolm and Gus went inside, Malcolm armed with the court order and the receipt proving it had been served to Sonia.

Sergeant Trevor Strawn, the acting officer in charge, reviewed the documents carefully. "You're saying she's still on the property?" he asked.

"She is," Malcolm confirmed.

"Well," the sergeant began, "we'll need assistance for this. These situations can get physical. I'll request a policewoman from Charters Towers to accompany us, just in case."

Trevor made the necessary calls, and Charters Towers Police confirmed that a WPC (Woman Police Constable) would be available to assist the following morning at 10:00 a.m.

That evening, the Teague's and the Davies dined at the Royal Hotel. Over a few drinks, they reflected on the day's events. Disappointment lingered in the air, they'd all been eager to explore the property, but Sonia's behaviour had soured the experience.

"She didn't have to act so aggressively," Malcolm commented. "This could have been sorted out amicably."

"Agreed," Lynette chimed in. "Why escalate things unnecessarily?"

"Well," Gus said, sipping his drink, "my bet is that she'll end up in handcuffs tomorrow."

"We'll see," Ros replied, though the group largely shared Gus's sentiment.

The next morning, everyone regrouped at the police station. The WPC had arrived from Charters Towers and was in deep conversation with Sergeant Strawn. Another male constable joined them as part of the team.

At precisely 10:00 a.m., the sergeant addressed the group. "We'll meet you out at the property," he said, departing in his police sedan. The WPC and the constable followed in a HiLux paddy wagon, with Malcolm's Land Cruiser bringing up the rear.

Upon arrival, they found the gates over the grid locked once again. Gus repeated his trick, lifting the gate off its hinges to allow access. They proceeded toward the house, where Sonia's white Land Cruiser was still parked under the porte-cochere.

As they approached, the front door swung open, and Sonia appeared in the doorway, arms folded and face defiant. The tension in the air was palpable as everyone exited their vehicles and approached the house.

"Let's hope this goes smoothly," Malcolm muttered under his breath as they prepared for the confrontation that lay ahead.

Mrs. Sonia Teague emerged from under the porte-cochere with a surprisingly warm and cheery demeanour. "Well, hello! How nice to see visitors. What on earth is the occasion for this?" she said, smiling broadly.

Sergeant Trevor Strawn, however, was in no mood for pleasantries. Ignoring her greeting, he addressed her curtly. "Are you Sonia Teague?"

Sonia blinked in surprise. "Well, yes, of course, I am. What is this about, "

Strawn cut her off sharply. "Mrs. Teague, you are hereby required to leave this property immediately, in accordance with court order number XXXXXX issued by the Townsville District Court. If you do not vacate of your own free will, you will be escorted off the property. Should you resist, you may be placed under arrest."

Sonia's expression changed instantly. The welcoming smile vanished, replaced by a cold glare. She stood silent for a moment before responding indignantly. "Fine. I'll gather my things and be out by this evening."

The sergeant shook his head firmly. "Too late for that. Any items not removed by the date stipulated in your court order to quit are now legally considered the property of the rightful owner. You must leave now."

Gus, taken aback by the harshness of the exchange, stepped forward. "Really, Sergeant, is this necessary? Surely she can at least collect some of her belongings…"

The sergeant turned to Gus, cutting him off mid-sentence. "Sir, you requested the Queensland Police to act upon an issued court order. We are bound by the protocols set by the courts. This is not a negotiation."

Malcolm interjected, trying to mediate. "At least let her pack a bag, Sergeant. Surely that's reasonable."

After a brief pause, Strawn relented. "Fine. She may pack one bag. Officer Riley," he gestured to the policewoman, "please accompany Mrs. Teague into the house. Make sure she packs only personal essentials. Mrs. Teague," he addressed her directly, "you may also write a list of any other personal items you wish to request from the legal owner. He will decide whether or not to return them."

Sonia huffed but complied, marching toward the door with Officer Riley in tow.

It wasn't long before she emerged from the house, a small suitcase on wheels trailing behind her. There were no tears, no visible sadness, only seething hatred in her eyes. Without a word, she placed the suitcase under the porte-cochere and strode purposefully toward a garage at the end of the house.

Sergeant Strawn called after her, his voice sharp. "Mrs. Teague, where do you think you're going?"

She turned briefly, her expression filled with indignation. "To get my car," she snapped, disappearing into the garage. Moments later, the sound of an engine echoed as she reversed a silver Honda Accord out of the garage and parked it in front of the porte-cochere.

As Sonia exited the car to retrieve her suitcase, Malcolm stepped forward. "That's not your car to take," he said firmly.

Before Sonia could reply, Gus waved him off. "Let her take it, Malcolm. I just want her gone from here."

Malcolm hesitated, clearly frustrated. "Gus, don't be so quick to give things away, "

"I don't care," Gus interrupted. "Let her have the car. She can deal with the registration later."

Strawn nodded in agreement. "It's reasonable. She'll need transportation to leave the property. You can arrange the transfer of registration at Hughenden when convenient."

Sonia wasted no time. She threw her suitcase onto the back seat of the Honda, slammed the door with unnecessary force, and turned to glare at both Gus and Malcolm. "You'll be hearing from me," she hissed venomously before getting into the driver's seat.

With a screech of tires, she sped off down the driveway, leaving a trail of dust in her wake.

Everyone stood silently for a moment, the tension finally dissipating.

"Well," Sergeant Strawn said, breaking the silence, "that was almost too easy. Watch your backs with that one, she's not done yet." He gave a nod to his officers, and the police vehicles departed soon after.

Malcolm let out a long exhale, glancing at Gus. "Thank heavens that's over. She's a piece of work, isn't she?"

"Tell me about it," Gus muttered.

The group slowly walked to the front door, anticipation replacing the earlier stress. Finally, they could start exploring the property without interference.

"Let's see what's inside," Malcolm said with a small smile, holding up the key they'd discovered earlier. The day, it seemed, was finally theirs to enjoy.

Woolgar River Park

The entrance to the homestead of Woolgar River Park is nothing short of impressive. As you step inside, you're immediately greeted by a grand formal vestibule. The rich, polished timber floors gleam beneath the soft lighting, while a striking staircase of gleaming stainless steel and polished wood spirals gracefully from the centre, commanding attention as it leads to the upper levels of the house.

To the left of the entrance lies a spacious open reception room, where the soft hum of elegance fills the air. The room is designed for both comfort and business, with a long, rectangular table positioned centrally, surrounded by six sturdy, timber and leather office chairs. Two large office-style three-seater lounges sit along one side, offering a place to relax or converse. A door at the far end of the reception leads into a more private office, where a simple but functional desk and chair sit beneath a window that overlooks the outbuildings scattered around the expansive property.

On the opposite side of the vestibule, double doors open into a grand lounge room that invites both relaxation and entertaining. The lounge area is expansive, with a comfortable dining area at its rear and a set of double doors leading into the enormous kitchen beyond. Adjacent to the dining room is a serving area, ideal for entertaining guests. The space is well-appointed, with high ceilings and expansive windows that offer sweeping views of the plains stretching out beyond the property.

In the far-right corner of the lounge, beside a large bay window, a curved bar commands attention. Six sleek bar stools are arranged around it, inviting conversation and socialising. Nearby, a round low table with four lay-back chairs offers a more casual seating arrangement for guests to relax. A restroom conveniently sits beside the bar, easily accessible without interrupting the flow of the space.

At the heart of the lounge is a magnificent open fireplace, its hearth encircling a metal base with a large, circular copper chimney flue rising above it, anchored by a striking circular flange. The warmth of the fire adds a cozy ambiance to the room, enhancing its inviting atmosphere. Flanking the fireplace are two three-seater, square-design lounges, placed to face one another, perfect for gatherings and conversation. Another pair of similar lounges rests in a cozy corner, adding further comfort and seating. A wall-mounted television hangs above one of the lounges, offering modern convenience in an otherwise traditional space.

Across from the bar, a three-quarter size pool table occupies an adjacent corner, further elevating the entertainment options within the room. The pool table is complemented by an impressive cue rack, standing proudly at the corner of the room, adding a touch of sophistication to the leisure area.

Woolgar River Park's homestead is a harmonious blend of luxury, functionality, and comfort, designed to be both a place of relaxation and a space for formal business. The layout thoughtfully connects living, entertaining, and working areas, making it as practical as it is impressive.

They decided to check out the other house, which was located a short distance from the main homestead. The front door on the wide verandah was unlocked, and as they entered, it was immediately clear that someone had definitely been living there recently, or perhaps still was. The house appeared to be the station manager's residence, based on its layout and location.

Inside, the atmosphere was markedly different from the pristine, almost sterile environment of the main house. The lounge area was comfortably furnished, featuring a combined kitchen and dining room that flowed seamlessly into one another. The space had a lived-in feel, with a certain warmth that contrasted the empty and impersonal rooms of the larger homestead. The house boasted three bedrooms, all of which had built-in robes, though none of the wardrobes contained any clothing.

The main bedroom was modest but functional, complete with an ensuite bathroom, while a separate bathroom and toilet were located near the back of the house. There was a laundry situated on the back verandah, where a few items of clothing were left in a laundry basket, suggesting someone had been doing chores just recently.

Despite the lack of personal items in the wardrobes, the kitchen was a different story. Unlike the immaculate emptiness of the larger homestead, this kitchen bore signs of recent use. The cupboards were stocked with items of food, though there was no sign of anything fresh or perishable. The sink held a few dirty plates, and in the drawers, there was some crockery and cutlery, including saucepans and frypans, items that were clearly in regular use. The presence of everyday items, such as a knife block on the counter, stood in stark contrast to the bare and sterile environment of the main homestead.

The lounge area had a green tracksuit top casually draped over one of the chairs, and next to the laundry on the verandah, there were a pair of very old sneakers, worn and weathered from frequent use. A half-empty dog food bowl sat nearby, further confirming that someone, or something, had been living here. The presence of an ashtray with several hand-rolled cigarette butts scattered inside it added to the feeling of a more relaxed, lived-in atmosphere.

It was clear that this was a house where someone had been making themselves at home, but there were still strange discrepancies. Despite the signs of life, the lack of personal clothing and the overall disarray of the place left an odd sense of ambiguity in the air. It seemed like someone had left in a hurry, or perhaps was still staying here, but there were no clear answers yet.

The garage, a spacious four-car structure with four roller doors, housed only the X5 Beamer. There were no other vehicles in sight, and oddly, there was no access to the house from the garage. Adjacent to it, what appeared to be a workshop contained nothing but a solitary workbench, no tools, no equipment, just an empty concrete floor.

The machinery shed, once thought to be a storage area for equipment, was entirely barren, nothing remained. The chicken shed was empty. The dog kennels? Also devoid of any life. It was as if the property had been stripped of everything.

Gus scanned the adjoining paddocks and muttered aloud, "I suppose there's no stock on the property either." Everyone exchanged uneasy glances, their suspicions growing. It was bizarre, everything had been cleared out since Lachlan's death. But why? What was really going on?

As Malcolm and Gus continued to cross-reference the property's inventory with what they could see, the discrepancies were glaring. Numerous small items were missing: wall decorations here and there, a piano that should've been in the lounge, and a gun cabinet containing two rifles, a .222 Stirling and a .308 Sako, along with a five-shot pump-action shotgun. A printer that had been in the office was also gone, as was a wall-mounted key cabinet, complete with keys. The second two-door filing cabinet was nowhere to be found either.

But it didn't end there. The inventory also listed high-value items like a John Deere Gator, a John Deere 6430 tractor with a front-end loader and attachments, a John Deere 2420 with a centre mower, and a Husqvarna 542X front mower. All of these items were missing, along with smaller equipment such as hand tools, power tools, chainsaws, whipper snippers, and hedge trimmers.

Oddly, the inventory made no mention of livestock or other animals, which was consistent with what Lachlan had said before his passing, that the property had not been trading for over a year.

Malcolm's frustration was palpable. The missing items amounted to thousands of dollars, and he was determined to speak with Sergeant Trevor Strawn about the theft the following day.

However, Gus was less concerned. "It doesn't matter," he said with a grin. "I'm over the moon with the property as it is. I couldn't care less about the missing gear. And I definitely don't want the police involved."

Lynette echoed Gus's sentiment. She was equally thrilled with the property and had no interest in the missing items. "Let's lock up what we can and head back to Hughenden for a drink," she said, chuckling. "Before I die of boredom in this place!" The group agreed, and they made their way around the property, locking up what they could before heading back to town.

It was still only 2:30 when they arrived back at the Royal Hotel in Hughenden. Gus immediately called around for a locksmith, but there was none available locally. The closest one was in Charters Towers, and he said he could make it there around 9:00 the next morning. Gus confirmed the appointment and asked Malcolm if they could extend their stay for another day.

"We'd love to!" Ros replied enthusiastically. "I'll call Malcolm's mum now and let her know." Gus confirmed the locksmith for the following morning.

Over drinks, the group discussed what to do next. Should they stay and try to get the property up and running again? Should they start fresh with cattle? The questions swirled, but no clear answers emerged. Malcolm suggested that Gus should hire someone immediately to watch over the place. He didn't trust Sonia, and everyone agreed.

While the group debated their next steps, Lynette headed to the bar to grab more drinks. While chatting with the bartender, a young woman with a distinctly British accent, Lynette asked if she knew anyone who might be interested in a caretaking job on a farm out of town.

It seemed like luck was on her side. The bartender revealed that her girlfriend and her male partner were leaving town the next day. They hadn't been able to find any suitable work in Hughenden, and they were planning to leave. The bartender said she'd ask them if they were interested in the job.

Lynette eagerly inquired, "How soon could you ask them?"

The bartender replied that they usually came in for a drink around this time, so she'd keep an eye out for them. Lynette's excitement grew, this could be exactly what they needed to keep an eye on the property.

Lynette returned to the table, distributing the drinks as she began recounting her conversation with the bartender. Before she could finish, the girl from the bar appeared, followed by two other people. "These are the people I was telling you about," she said, glancing at Lynette. "Do you want three caretakers? I've had enough of working behind a bar. I came to Australia for the sun and to get a tan, not to be stuck behind a bar."

Lynette didn't hesitate. "Yes! Absolutely!" she replied, eager to move things forward. "Let's all talk."

The bartender, whose name they learned was Janice, introduced her girlfriend, Hailee, and Hailee's partner, Willem. Janice explained that she couldn't talk much more until her shift ended in about an hour, but she was clearly keen to get started.

Lynette had to bite back her concern. Bloody hell, she thought. We don't even know what we're paying these people or what the arrangement is, and here we are, hiring them on the spot.

She introduced Hailee and Willem to the group. Malcolm quickly fetched more chairs, while Gus asked them what they'd like to drink and went to grab more drinks.

Willem was a big, strong-looking man with fair hair, originally from Valkenswaard, a small town near Eindhoven in the Netherlands. His parents bred goats. Hailee, a woman with a warm smile and an easy laugh, hailed from Bramley, south of London. They'd been in Australia for six months and had their own transport.

Malcolm took over the conversation, his solicitor instincts kicking in. He explained the available position at Woolgar River Park. "At this stage, there's not much work to do. We just need someone to keep an eye on the house and outbuildings, make sure no strangers come on the property. No need to worry about checking the paddocks or anything like that."

When they mentioned the accommodation, a three-bedroom house, Hailee and Willem lit up, clearly delighted. The idea of living in a house while earning a wage was appealing.

Lynette quickly added, "There will be a lot of cleaning, some painting, mowing, and gardening as well. Nothing too heavy, but it will keep you busy."

Gus chimed in, "We'll pay cash, of course." Malcolm shot him a disapproving glance, but Gus didn't mind.

They explained that they needed the caretakers to start the very next day, which was fine with Willem and Hailee.

Once Janice finished her shift, she came over with drinks for everyone. The job details were reiterated, and they agreed that Janice could join them in a week's time after finishing up her work at the pub. Willem and Hailee would come to pick her up in a week, and they would head to the property together.

With everything in place, directions to Woolgar River Park were given to the new caretakers, and they agreed to meet the following morning at nine o'clock.

As they said their goodbyes to Janice, Hailee, and Willem, things started to feel more settled. The uncertainty was beginning to fade, and they headed off for dinner.

Over dinner, the conversation turned to Woolgar River Park and the increasingly strange situation surrounding Sonia Teague.

"It's obvious Sonia wasn't living in the house," Lynette remarked. "So, where is she living? And why did she show up at the property on the first day we arrived?"

"And who was the bloke with her in the Landcruiser?" Ros added, her brow furrowed.

Lynette continued, "And why was the house so completely devoid of anything? It's like no one has lived there for ages. Didn't Lachlan die in that house, in his bed? So where are all his belongings? Where are his clothes? This doesn't make any sense."

"Should we sell it, or should we live in it?" Lynette asked, glancing at Gus. "What do you think it's worth?"

Malcolm took a moment to consider, then shrugged. "Well, off the top of my head, I'd say four million, maybe five. But it wouldn't be too hard to find out," he said.

Lynette quickly shot down the idea of selling. "No, no, not yet," she said, shaking her head. "Let's think it through. There's no rush. Once we get our caretakers in place, it might be nice to live there. It's a beautiful house."

Gus interjected with a smirk, "But it's a hell of a long way from anything."

They all laughed, but the unease about the situation lingered.

The following morning, they set out at 7:00 AM, arriving at Woolgar River Park by 9:00 AM. On the way, they overtook an old Subaru Outback with Willem and Hailee inside. The two waved as they passed.

When they reached the property, they noticed that the gate at the grid was still closed, just as Gus had left it the day before. There were no fresh tire tracks, but it was hard to tell for sure.

As they pulled up to the house, Malcolm had a sudden thought. He remembered that Sonia had emerged from inside the house when they arrived yesterday, but they had taken the key from the plant pot and hadn't given it to her. Sonia couldn't have had a key. "How did she get in?" Malcolm asked, turning to Gus. "We need to figure out how she broke in."

Gus nodded, a frown crossing his face. "Good thinking, Malcolm. I'll ask the locksmith to look for signs of a break-in when he changes the locks this morning."

The mystery deepened, and the sense that something was very off about the property grew stronger with every passing moment.

They all looked up the driveway with apprehension as another vehicle approached, a Landcruiser Troopy with sign writing. It was the locksmith. Not far behind him were Willem and Hailee.

Gus greeted the locksmith and his assistant, who had come along in case the job turned out to be more complicated than expected. The locksmith, Dave, extended his hand toward Gus. "Dave," he said with a firm handshake. "And this is my number one man, Grant."

Gus nodded and began walking them both toward the house. "I need a master key for every lock on the property," he said. "And separate pass keys for the main house, the manager's house, the machinery shed, the equipment shed, and the entrance gates."

He continued, outlining the security measures he wanted. "I also want a restricted key system to control the number of keys produced, two keys each for all pass keys, except for the manager's house, which will require three keys. And three master keys for the property as a whole."

He added, as an afterthought, "Can you also check for signs of a break-in around the main house? I suspect someone may have broken in recently, but I'm not sure how."

The locksmith nodded thoughtfully. "I'll take a look while I'm at it."

Gus paused, then asked, "By the way, can you make a key for the BMW? It's got a transponder, but I'd need the code from the owner's logbook to get a new one made."

Dave replied, "I can get a transponder for it sometime next week, as long as we can get the code. If you find the logbook, that should do the trick."

"I'll check for it," Gus said, feeling a little more at ease knowing there was a solution in sight.

Meanwhile, Lynette and Ros were showing Willem and Hailee around the manager's house. They were clearing out old, expired food from the cupboards and tossing broken or useless items. When they opened the refrigerator door to air it out, they noticed a faint musty smell.

"We've got enough food to last us until next Thursday when we head into Hughenden to pick up Janice and do some shopping," Hailee said, smiling as she sorted through the cabinets. "We'll be fine until then."

The caretakers had bedding and pillows packed in their Outback, which would be perfect for their bedroom. However, they figured Janice would need to buy some sheets and blankets once she arrived.

As they unpacked their car and made themselves at home, it was clear they were pleased with the job and the accommodation. They were eager to settle in.

Gus and Lynette had already agreed that they couldn't leave until the locksmith had finished his work and handed over the keys. The locksmith had estimated he'd be done by around one o'clock, though the BMW key would take longer.

"Malcolm," Gus said, turning to his friend, "since we're going to be waiting around for a while, how about we take a drive around the property? We could get a better sense of the land."

Malcolm frowned slightly. "We could, but the parish plan only shows the outline on a larger map, no details. We wouldn't really know where to go."

"Fair point," Gus replied. "But I'll see if I can get some topographical maps when we get back to Cairns. Maybe we can spend a few days here and explore the property properly."

Ros and Malcolm both agreed that it sounded like a great idea. Lynette, however, had already started thinking ahead. "I'll bring up the linen for the beds, along with some crockery, cutlery, saucepans, food, and drinks," she said, clearly excited. "I'll make sure we've got everything to make this place feel like home."

Gus nodded, impressed. "Sounds like a plan. We'll be ready for a real homestead soon."

As the locksmith worked, Gus suggested to Malcolm, "If you and Ros want to head back to Hughenden, instead of waiting for the locksmith, Lynette and I can bring the Landcruiser into town and leave it there for Janice to pick up."

Malcolm considered the idea, then nodded. "Sounds good. But are you sure the Landcruiser's all right to drive? We should probably double-check it before you head off."

Gus smiled. "We'll take care of it. Don't worry."

With the plan in place, they continued to enjoy the calm morning at Woolgar River Park, though the sense of anticipation for the future lingered in the air.

It was a 2006 model, so the Landcruiser was getting on in years, but it was in excellent condition. The exterior was covered in dirt, but the interior was immaculate and well-maintained. The vehicle was registered for another four months, but, there was one catch, no keys.

The locksmith, having already completed several tasks, wandered over to the Landcruiser. After a brief search, he opened the glove box and, to his delight, found the owner's manual still in its plastic cover. Inside, he discovered the key number, and within minutes, he had produced a new key. Gus felt a sense of relief; if the Landcruiser's logbook was intact, surely the BMW's logbook would be as well.

As the locksmith worked, he suggested, "You might want to recode the Landcruiser's locks. Someone could have keys, and they might come back for it."

"Great idea, Dave," Gus replied. He was starting to feel like things were finally falling into place.

The Landcruiser roared to life without hesitation, but it only had a quarter tank of fuel. Malcolm pointed toward the fuel tank on the stand. "Let's check it out," he said.

The tank was located beside the machinery shed, out of sight. The visigauge showed that it was over three-quarters full. A brand-new padlock was now on the delivery handle, installed by the locksmith. Things were finally looking good.

At 11:00 AM, Ros and Malcolm prepared to leave Woolgar River Park to head back to Hughenden. Gus and Lynette waved them off, saying, "We'll be there about three o'clock, just in time for afternoon drinks."

Both Gus and Lynette were excited to be alone for a while to take another look at the house, make plans, and create a long list of things to bring on their next visit. They had briefly discussed moving into the house within the next couple of weeks, leaving their Cairns unit behind for long weekends and holidays. The idea was exhilarating.

Lynette had initially thought about asking Hailee and Janice to clean the house while they were away. But after another look, she decided against it. The house wasn't dirty, and she didn't want others in there while they weren't around.

They went to see the caretakers to let them know that they would leave the Landcruiser in Hughenden for Janice to drive back. Gus assumed she had a license, but if not, Willem or Hailee could drive it. He also told Willem that he'd arrange for a ride-on mower to be delivered in Hughenden, along with fuel drums for the mower, which Willem could pick up with the Landcruiser on Thursday.

Gus also informed Willem and Hailee that he would go to an ATM in Hughenden and leave a couple of weeks' pay for each of them in cash with Janice. "Is that alright?" he asked. Hailee nodded. "That's cool. I trust Janice with my life."

Gus mentioned that he and Lynette would be back in about two weeks and gave Willem his and Lynette's mobile numbers. "Don't hesitate to call either of us if you need anything." He also asked for Willem and Hailee's numbers and promised to send them Malcolm's number later that day.

By the time the locksmith had finished, Gus had received all the keys he had requested. He also gave Dave his home address to send the new BMW transponder key once they found the code in the car's logbook. The locksmith's portable EFTPOS machine was with Telstra, which had the only mobile reception in the area, so Gus was able to finalise the payment for the locksmith's services.

Before leaving, Dave asked if he and his mates could come out pig hunting in the future. Gus grinned. "Anytime. Just give me a call," he said, as the locksmith drove off.

Gus and Lynette said their goodbyes to Willem and Hailee, who were busy cleaning the fridge and oven in the manager's house. The caretakers were thrilled when Gus handed them two keys to the manager's house and one key each for the machinery shed and gates. "Take it easy," Gus told Willem. "We'll see you in two weeks. In the meantime, just watch the place, keep it neat, and enjoy yourselves."

He reminded Willem that the locksmith had put the grid gate back on its pivots and that he could leave it open during the day, locking it only at night if he wished.

With that, Gus and Lynette waved goodbye to the caretakers and drove off in the Landcruiser, heading toward Hughenden.

The trip in the Landcruiser ute was far from comfortable. It was the worst ride they'd experienced; every bump seemed to throw them off the seat. They speculated it could be because the back was empty, or maybe the tires were pumped up too high. Either way, it felt like ninety-five to a hundred kilometres per hour was the maximum speed they could manage without being jolted around.

They arrived in Hughenden at 3:30 PM, parked at the hotel, and headed straight for the bar. Janice was working behind the counter, and she wasted no time asking about the property. "What did Willem and Hailee think? Are they happy?" she asked. After a few more questions, she brought them their beers.

Gus had the third key for the manager's house, a gate key, and the Landcruiser key in his pocket. He handed them over to Janice while telling her about the Landcruiser parked in the motel car park. Janice's excitement grew, and she mentioned she would call Hailee once she finished work.

Gus made a quick stop at the hotel ATM, withdrawing two weeks' pay for Willem and Hailee, and one week's pay for Janice. He handed the money to Janice, instructing her to pass the other two's pay along when she saw them on Thursday. "We'll see you in a couple of weeks. Have fun," Gus said.

He then called the mower center and arranged for a Zorro zero-turn mower and two twenty-liter fuel drums, which he paid for using his credit card.

Afterward, Gus and Lynette went to their room to enjoy a well-deserved shower before meeting Ros and Malcolm for drinks and dinner. They would be heading back to Townsville the next day.

Dinner at the hotel was filled with conversation about Woolgar Creek Park and, of course, Sonia Teague.

Ros asked, "Did anyone notice on Friday, when the police were out there, how Sonia didn't seem upset about having to leave the house? And what about her luggage? It was barely a small suitcase, there was no way it could hold sheets, blankets, and pillows."

"I think," Ros continued, "she had only just arrived that morning. And who was that guy driving the Landcruiser on Thursday?"

Everyone agreed with Ros. Sonia hadn't appeared upset; in fact, she looked full of anger as she left the house on Friday. But how did she get in?

Gus reminded them that the locksmith had found no signs of forced entry. However, there were marks on the pavers near the laundry door, suggesting a large pot had been moved. "Another key?" suggested Malcolm.

Lynette then commented, "The Landcruiser was parked in the Porte-cochère when we returned. It wasn't there when we left on Thursday, and the man driving it wasn't around on Friday. I think Sonia must have arrived that morning to take something from the house, and was about to leave when we turned up."

"I'll bet the keys to the Landcruiser were in her pocket," Ros said, putting the pieces together.

Malcolm shifted the conversation. "When we walked around the house, did anyone try lifting the garage doors?"

"I did," Gus answered. "I remember now, definitely tried all four doors, thinking the garage might be another entrance. But they were all locked."

Malcolm nodded. "But Sonia didn't unlock the garage door she used to get the Honda. It was already open."

More pondering followed, accompanied by sips of drinks. Finally, Lynette broke the silence. "And you know what?" she asked, with Gus grinning to himself. She had a habit of saying "And you know what" before every question.

"No! What?" Gus responded, unable to resist.

The group chuckled, except for Lynette, who continued, "Why was the place cleaned out of everything, other than furniture?"

Everyone stopped to think. "Hmm…" they all mused. If Lachlan's body had been in the house for any length of time, surely everything would've been contaminated. But the mattresses were still on the beds, which would've been the first thing to go if that had been the case.

"Maybe Sonia had too many memories of Lachlan and had to remove items," Gus suggested.

"But pots and pans? Really?" Lynette countered.

"What about the machinery?" Malcolm added. "Sold? Stolen?"

The questions hung in the air, unanswered, as they all took another sip of their drinks.

Despite all the questions and confusion, the group agreed that it had been a great weekend. However, the more drinks they had, the more bewildered they became about the mysteries surrounding Woolgar River Park. With no answers in sight, they all said goodnight.

Sunday morning arrived, and as they drove back to Townsville, the car was filled with silence. Each of them had their own thoughts about the strange events of the past four days at Woolgar River Park.

Lynette was mentally running through her extensive shopping list for the new house.

Ros was reflecting on the lovely new friends they'd met and hoping that their friendship would last.

Malcolm, on the other hand, was thinking, "Screw work tomorrow," wishing he were retired like Lynette and Gus.

Gus was asleep!

Back in Cairns, Lynette and Gus were busy shopping for their new home. It was an exciting time, though the shopping list was growing by the day. They considered whether it might be better to buy some items in Townsville, as it was 360 kilometres closer to the property than Cairns. Traveling via the

Bruce and Flinders Highways would take them a total of 730 kilometres. Alternatively, there was State Route 62, which went from Cairns to Ravenshoe, then Greenvale to Hughenden, covering only 590 kilometres, 140 kilometres less, but it was a rough road, about 60% dirt.

Since they only had one car these days, a Subaru 2.5 Outback, they were starting to fill it with gear. The Subaru was great, but not ideal for carrying large loads. They decided to take the bush route via Route 62, despite the rough road, as it would save them some distance.

As they were packing, Lynette received a phone call from Hailee. "A well-dressed gentleman is at the property, wanting to speak with you. He's asking for your mobile number. Should I give it to him?"

Lynette asked what the man wanted, but Hailee said he wouldn't talk to her, only to Mrs. Teague. "Okay," Lynette said, "Give him my number and tell him to call me. I'll talk to you soon. We should be up there next Monday. Did Janice get there okay? Great, talk to you later. Bye."

No sooner had she hung up than her phone rang again.

"Hello?" she answered.

"Mrs. Teague?" the voice on the other end asked.

"Speaking," Lynette responded.

"It's Jason Strange, Mrs. Teague. I've been trying to contact you. Your other number has been ringing out, and I've left messages."

"I'm sorry, who did you say you are?" Lynette asked, confused.

Jason Strange introduced himself again, explaining that he was from Richmond Hill Real Estate at Charters Towers. "I've been trying to contact you since last Friday. The buyer wants to do a final inspection before settlement this Friday, which is in two days."

Lynette's head spun. What buyer? What settlement? She tried to regain control of the conversation. "I think you have the wrong person, Mr. Strange. I'm Lynette Teague. Who do you need to talk to?"

After a long pause, Strange awkwardly responded, "I need to talk to Mrs. Sonia Teague. Is that your mother?"

He then went on to explain that they had sold Woolgar River Park on Sonia's behalf and that the settlement was due in two days. The buyer had flown in from Horsham, Victoria, to do a final inspection.

Lynette was shocked and interrupted him. "I don't have a mother or a mother-in-law named Sonia. My husband and I own Woolgar River Park. The property hasn't been sold, nor is it for sale."

Strange was persistent, claiming to have a binding contract signed by both Lachlan and Sonia Teague. Lynette, now even more confused and hurt, asked for his mobile number, saying their solicitor would call him back.

At that moment, Gus walked in and could tell something was wrong by the look on Lynette's face.

After hearing the details, Gus was also deeply concerned and tried calling Malcolm in Townsville. Both his personal and mobile numbers were busy, so Gus left urgent messages asking for a call back.

Lynette brought Gus a beer, and he sat on the balcony, staring at his phone, wondering what to do next. "This is unreal. It can't be happening," Gus muttered, more to himself than anyone else.

Gus then called Willem at the property to ask if the man was still there. Willem informed him that the man had left a few minutes earlier. He had asked for a key to the main house, but Willem had told him he didn't have one. The man then left in his car.

"Have you got the grid gate open?" Gus asked.

Willem replied, "It's open. I haven't closed it since we came back with the mower last week. But, actually, I was going to call you today about something."

Willem continued, explaining that Janice had gotten a cattle dog pup in Hughenden and brought it to the property last week. The dog had started barking the previous night. Willem went outside to check and heard something near the Landcruiser. As he walked over in the dark, he thought he heard someone running away.

This morning, when Willem checked the Landcruiser, he found the quarter window on the driver's side open. It had been forced open, as if someone had tried to break in. He thought it might have been an attempted theft. Willem planned to lock the grid gate that night. Gus suggested that they keep it locked for now until things settled down, and mentioned they'd be back on Monday.

Not long after Gus spoke to Willem, his phone rang. It was Malcolm, asking if they were still on for the weekend after next.

"Problems," Gus announced, his voice tense, "weird problems." He then proceeded to recount everything that had transpired, laying out the entire situation as he knew it.

Malcolm listened intently, his voice growing serious. "I'll give Jason Strange a call and see if I can meet him this afternoon in Charters Towers. I need to have a look at that sale contract in person. I'll let you know what I find out." There was a brief pause before Malcolm continued, "Don't worry, Gus. The sale won't go through, not on my watch."

Gus let out a relieved breath. "You really think so?"

"It just doesn't make sense," Malcolm replied. "Lachlan wouldn't have set up a will and then gone and sold the house. But even if the sale does go through, all the money will belong to you, Gus. I'll call you as soon as I know anything, probably later this evening. Just hang tight, alright?"

Lynette, sitting across from Gus, gave him a curious look as he hung up. "Malcolm's going to see Strange, if he can, this afternoon in Charters Towers. He says not to worry."

"Not to worry?" Gus muttered, shaking his head. "We don't need these kinds of dramas in our life, Lynette. What the hell is going on?" He sighed, frustration clear in his voice.

By the time Malcolm called them around 6:30 that evening, Gus and Lynette had come to terms with the fact that the property would most likely be sold. They had resigned themselves to the idea, feeling it wasn't the worst outcome. The sales price was likely to be in the $5 to $6 million range, which, though disappointing, still put them miles ahead financially.

But still, there was a nagging feeling in the back of their minds. They had fallen in love with the property in the short time they had spent there.

Malcolm's first words when he called confirmed their worst fears, "It's a fraud case."

"What?" Gus blurted out.

"I took a copy of Lachlan's signature from his will, the one I witnessed," Malcolm continued, "and compared it to the one on the sale contract. It's a complete forgery. Same goes for the bank details that were submitted to me. And then I spoke to the seller's conveyancing solicitor, those signatures were nothing like Lachlan's either. The whole thing's a setup."

A wave of relief washed over Gus and Lynette, but the gravity of the situation still hung heavy in the air.

"I've made copies of everything, the contract, the conveyancing authority, the bank details, and I've handed it all over to the Townsville police for their review. They'll be taking it from here. So, there's no sale. It's all a scam."

Gus exhaled deeply, the tension lifting from his shoulders. "Well, we had sort of resigned ourselves to the fact that it was probably going to be sold."

"I don't think you'd have been too happy if it had gone through, though, would you?" Malcolm chuckled.

Gus smiled bitterly. "No, I guess not. But still, that sale price, $2.1 million? It's about $4.5 million short of the property's actual value."

"Exactly," Malcolm agreed. "Our Mr. Strange is going to have a lot of explaining to do, as will some of the so-called witnesses to those signatures."

"Well, bottom line is, the buyer gets his deposit back, the agent's got some serious questions to answer, and the conveyancing solicitor will have a lot to explain. As for Sonia Teague…" Malcolm trailed off, clearly exasperated.

"Well, thanks again, mate," Gus said, his voice full of gratitude. "We can't thank you enough. We'll see you at Woolgar River Park on the long weekend, next Saturday."

"You bet," Malcolm said. "We'll see you then. Just get on with life, and don't worry about this mess anymore. We've got it covered."

After hanging up, Lynette wasted no time. She quickly reached out to an old friend in the police force, Detective Inspector Graham Jamison.

"A blast from the past! It's been too long, Gazza," Lynette greeted warmly, the familiar tone of old friendship evident in her voice. They exchanged pleasantries for a few minutes, reminiscing about old times before Lynette got down to business.

"By any chance, are you on the Sonia Teague case?" she asked.

"Never heard of it," Graham replied, sounding genuinely curious. "Should I know about it?"

Lynette filled him in, explaining the inheritance, the fraudulent sale, and all the chaos that had followed. Graham's interest piqued, and he promised to look into it. "Let me make a few enquiries, Linnie, and I'll get back to you. It's good talking again."

Meanwhile, the next morning, Gus and Lynette packed up their Subaru Outback for the long drive to Woolgar River Park. The car was jam-packed with pillows, sheets, doonas, pots, pans, cutlery, foodstuffs, basically everything they needed for a comfortable stay. Among the essentials were six cartons of **XXXX** Gold stubbies in the back and another two cartons packed in ice in their massive esky.

By 3:00 PM, they reached the grid gate at Woolgar River Park. Gus got out to unlock it, drove through, then relocked it behind them. They made their way down the dirt road toward the house and onto the porte-cochère.

The three caretakers were already there, waiting for them with smiles and greetings. "Welcome home!" they said as Gus and Lynette stepped out of the car.

"First things first!" Gus said with a grin, opening the back of the car and pulling out five stubbies. "Beer all around!"

They all gathered on the verandah, cracking open the beers and settling in for a relaxed afternoon. The caretakers filled them in on the latest happenings, though there wasn't much news to share, other than Janice finding a mobile phone behind the seat of the Landcruiser.

"I'll grab it later," Gus said casually. "No rush."

Lynette told the caretakers that she had enough steak for a BBQ that evening if they wanted to join them. "Come by around six," she added with a smile.

"That sounds perfect!" they agreed, waving as they headed back to the manager's house.

Gus and Lynette exchanged a look, the weight of the previous days' events still lingering in their minds, but for now, they were home, and the evening promised a moment of peace before they had to deal with anything more.

The sound of unpacking the car was drowned out by the urgency of the task at hand. It wasn't glamorous work, but it was necessary. First things first, Gus and Lynette set to cleaning out the fridges and freezers, five fridges, two freezers, and a cool room to be exact. The job was tedious, but it had to be done before anything else could be unpacked. The fridges were cleared of old, spoiled food and wiped down until they were spotless. By the time they'd finished, it was around five-thirty in the evening, and things were starting to feel a bit more like home.

Their bed was made and ready for a good night's sleep, though Lynette wasn't in any rush to make up the second bed just yet, she had all week to get that done. The fridges were stocked with cold beers, drinking water, and Coca-Cola, so at least they were set up for the evening.

Gus moved on to the BBQ, a task that was more to his liking. The BBQ was sparkling clean, which was no surprise considering the property had recently been on the market. The thought crossed his mind that the house was likely kept immaculate to make it presentable for prospective buyers, but now, for the first time, it felt like their place.

As he was tending to the BBQ, the caretakers, who Gus had started calling "the kids", arrived just before six, carrying drinks and chips in hand. Gus had noticed a fridge next to the BBQ, which he hadn't seen before, and he opened it to find it fairly clean inside. He flipped it on and found a carton of XXXX Gold stubbies, along with cider, Jack Daniel's and Coke, and a few stubbies of Great Northern. It seemed the kids had made themselves at home.

They all settled around a large round teak table on teak chairs with leather cushions, the setting perfect for the evening. Janice had brought the mobile phone she had found behind the seat of the Landcruiser. It was an iPhone, but unfortunately, it was dead. Janice explained that none of them had an iPhone, so they didn't have the charging cable. Gus, ever the problem solver, took the phone inside and plugged it in.

When he returned, Janice was telling Lynette about her interaction with the estate agent, Jason Strange. "What a creep he was," she said with a laugh. "He wanted to look everywhere, and we kept telling him no. And he kept asking questions about Mrs. Teague, at first, we thought he meant you, Lynette." She chuckled at the thought. "Strange, alright," she added, her voice full of disbelief.

Willem, who had been quietly listening, chimed in next. "We've been going into Richmond for supplies. It's only about a forty-minute drive, much shorter than going all the way to Hughenden, but it's not as good. A lot smaller, and more expensive, but they have a good butcher, a supermarket, and of course, a pub and a bowls club."

Willem also mentioned that he had fixed the quarter window on the Landcruiser. The catch had only been bent, but he was sure it hadn't been like that before. He was equally certain he had heard someone running away the night before, not a kangaroo as they had initially assumed.

As the night wore on, the conversation drifted, and they all continued to enjoy the drinks and snacks, the warm evening settling around them. Gus and Lynette retired for the night, the sound of the night's wildlife filling the silence, punctuated only by the occasional kookaburra call.

The next morning, they both woke at the same time, startled by the quiet. The only sounds were the distant calls of birds, until a pair of kookaburras started their signature laughter. Gus stretched, his mind still hazy with sleep. The bed had been incredibly comfortable, though strange in the way the mattress didn't seem to budge when they tried to flip it earlier. It was an odd feeling, but one they'd both appreciated as they lay there, enjoying the comfort.

They were staying in the second large bedroom while Lynette planned to paint the master bedroom before they moved into it. She was eager to start today, perhaps with some paint samples, if not the actual work.

Lynette glanced at the clock. "It's already nine-thirty."

Gus blinked at the clock, surprised. "What? You've got to be joking." He groaned and rolled over, hoping for a few more minutes of sleep. But before he could settle in, Lynette disappeared into the ensuite to freshen up. Gus, still half-asleep, pulled the covers up and tried to doze for a few more moments.

When he finally roused himself and made his way to the kitchen, the delicious smell of bacon greeted him. Lynette was standing by the stove, trying out one of her new frypans. "Won't be long," she said with a smile.

Gus walked over to the breakfast bar, his hand reaching for the mysterious iPhone that was still charging. He picked it up, inspecting it more closely now that it was powered on. "Wonder who this belongs to," he muttered to himself, still puzzled by the discovery from the night before.

"Unreal, it's still connected!" Gus exclaimed, staring at the phone in his hand. "But it's locked."

He wandered out to his car and brought in his laptop. Sure enough, the Wi-Fi was showing up, but it was locked and required a password.

Lynette brought over the breakfasts they'd prepared and set them on the table. As they dug in, the conversation drifted back to the mysterious phone. "I wonder where the Wi-Fi is," Gus mused, scanning the room. Neither of them had spotted a modem or router anywhere in sight.

"Might be the kids?" Gus suggested, glancing at Lynette. She nodded in agreement. "Of course. They would have some sort of internet device."

Gus turned his attention back to the phone. "How can we unlock this thing?"

Lynette thought for a moment. "There's a place in Cairns called 'King It.' They can probably unlock it for us. We should take it there when we're back next week."

Just as they were finishing their conversation, there was a knock at the door. "The kids, I suppose," Gus remarked as he stood up to answer it.

Lynette, a little more focused on the day ahead, replied, "I was expecting Janice and Hailee this morning for house cleaning. And maybe some painting too, a big day ahead."

"Right," Gus said, "Well, I'll head into Richmond and check out the butcher. I'll also take a look at the price of beer at the pub."

He grabbed the keys to the Landcruiser ute and set off for town.

When Gus walked into the butcher shop, he was surprised by how busy it was. Four men were working behind the counter and in the backroom, prepping orders and slicing meat. The shop had a great reputation, and from the looks of it, the beef was top-quality, though Gus knew better than anyone that it's not until you actually taste the meat that you can tell whether it's good or not. Most of the beef around this area was Drought-master, known for its tough texture, but Gus had learned to appreciate the flavour, even if it was a bit more resilient to the knife.

Drought-master cattle were an Australian breed developed in the early 20th century, a hybrid of Zebuine cattle and British breeds like the Beef Shorthorn. While it had great flavour, Gus knew it could be a bit tough, an acquired taste, so to speak.

As he scanned the display, Gus asked the butcher, "You got any Hereford or Lowline? The kind of Angus?"

The butcher nodded, pointing to a few cuts. "Got whole rumps of both, and some whole porterhouse of Hereford."

Gus decided on two large whole rumps of Lowline and one large whole rump of Hereford, all cut into 19-millimetre steaks, with a roast piece from each of about two kilos. He also ordered six kilos of sausages, both beef and thin varieties, packed into separate two-kilo and six-kilo bags.

As the butcher passed the order to his younger workers, he glanced outside at Gus's ute. "Are you driving Barry's ute?" he asked, pointing towards the white Landcruiser parked outside.

Gus turned to look. "Do you mean the white cruiser ute?" he asked, confirming.

"Yeah, it looks like Barry's. I'm sure of it."

"Who's Barry?" Gus inquired, intrigued.

The butcher paused while packing up the meat and gave Gus a quick look. "Barry was the manager at Woolgar Creek Park, a big cattle property just west of here. The old bloke who owned it got crook and sold off all the cattle, so Barry ran out of a job. But the old guy kept him on, just to keep the place neat and tidy and to keep an eye on it."

"Where does Barry live now?" Gus asked.

"Lives out at the station with his father," the butcher replied, handing Gus the meat. "Haven't seen him around for about a week though."

Gus took the package of meat, paying with EFTPOS. As two of the young fellows carried the heavy bags out to the ute, Gus thought about the conversation. He thanked the butcher and headed for the drive-in bottle shop at the pub. The mention of Barry intrigued him. He didn't know if it meant anything, but it was a curious detail that stuck in his mind as he continued his errands for the day.

Gus drove down Harris Street, turning into the driveway that led to the bottle shop. The shop was quiet, but he could hear voices coming from the bar. A moment later, a female voice called out from inside, "Be right with you, Barry!" Gus raised an eyebrow, starting to get the impression that Barry was a pretty well-known guy around Richmond. But, then again, with only about six hundred people living here, it wasn't hard to be recognised.

The lady, who had come out of the bar to the bottle shop, quickly realised her mistake when she saw Gus. "Oh, it's not Barry, sorry, I thought you were someone else," she said with an apologetic smile.

"No problem," Gus replied. "Good morning. Can I get six cartons of xxxx Gold and three cartons of Great Northern Super Crisp?"

"Sure," she nodded, "but I'll have to warn you, they're all hot, mate. I don't have that many cold ones left."

"That's fine," Gus said, pulling out his card to pay.

She helped him load the cartons into the back of his ute, and as she grabbed the EFTPOS machine, she dialled in the price, five hundred and sixty dollars. Gus held up his card to pay.

"Having a party, mate?" she asked casually as she swiped the card.

"No, just stocking up. Got some visitors arriving soon," Gus replied.

As she handed him the receipt, she asked, "So, do you live around here?"

"Yeah, just moved in," Gus said.

"Well, my name's Alice," she said with a smile. "And I always welcome thirsty new customers. Whereabouts are you living?"

Gus nodded and introduced himself, adding that he was living at his uncle's place, about thirty kilometres down the river road.

Alice's eyes lit up as she connected the dots. "Ah, Lachie's place. That's why you're driving Barry's ute." Gus didn't correct her. "Yes, it is Lachlan's place, and it was Barry's ute," he said, deciding it was easier to leave it at that. "I have to get back soon, though," he added, hoping to end the conversation.

But Alice wasn't done. "Such a shame about Lachie, he was a great bloke. You must get along well with Sonia if you're living there."

Gus felt a twinge of unease but kept his expression neutral. He wasn't ready to get into any conversation about the people at the property just yet. "I'll catch up with you later," he said, as politely as he could manage, "but I really have to get going."

As he made his way back to the ute, Gus couldn't shake the strange feeling gnawing at him. Barry seemed to be a popular name around here. Everyone assumed Barry still lived at the property, along with his father, no less. That was an odd bit of information that Gus filed away in the back of his mind.

He stopped at the manager's house on the way back and grabbed a couple of the Lowline beef rump packs and a two-kilo pack of sausages from the passenger side of the ute. Willem was just coming out of the front door as Gus walked up to the verandah.

"Here's the meat," Gus said, handing it over. "And there's a carton of Great Northern for you too."

Willem took the meat inside and set it on a table just inside the door before coming back out for the beer. "How much do I owe you?" he asked.

"Nothing," Gus replied. "Just a little thank you gift. I won't make a habit of it, I promise."

Back at the main house, Gus worked quickly to sort the meat into the fridges and load the beer into the cool room. He then grabbed a cold stubbie from the fridge, sat down on the front verandah in the shade, and took a long drink.

It wasn't long before Lynette came out, bringing two more stubbies with her. She sat down beside him, and Gus took one with a grateful nod.

"Cheers," he said. "What's new?"

"Loads," Lynette replied, raising an eyebrow. "What's new with you?"

Gus echoed her question, "Loads, such as…?"

"Well," Lynette began, "we were up in the master bedroom this morning, as you know, to get the walls ready for painting. The second coat's on now, and it looks great. But while Hailee was removing the left-hand drape from the right-side window, we all heard something fall to the floor. It sounded like a coin or something small, and Janice called out, 'Look, it's a bullet!'"

Gus felt a chill run through him. Lynette continued, "I went over just as Janice was about to pick it up and told her not to touch it. It was a spent cartridge case, a .22."

"A bullet?" Gus repeated, still processing what she was saying. "You're sure?"

Lynette nodded gravely. "I went down to the kitchen, grabbed a small freezer bag and a toothpick, and picked it up with the toothpick. Then I placed it in the freezer bag."

Gus was still trying to catch up. "So, what are you saying? A bullet was stuck in the drapes?"

Lynette's face grew serious. "Gus, I think that bedroom might be a murder scene."

Gus's mind raced. "No way," he muttered, but Lynette wasn't finished.

"Think about it, Gus," she said, her voice intense. "If I were to fire a rifle through that bedroom window, the shell casing would be ejected to the right if it were an automatic rifle, or if it were a manual rifle, I'd have to work the bolt, but it would still eject to the right. But the cartridge case was stuck in the left-side drapes of the right-hand window. Are you starting to get the picture?"

Gus sat back, trying to process everything. It was starting to make sense in a way that he wasn't quite ready for. But Lynette wasn't done.

"I made Hailee and Janice write and sign a statutory declaration about the discovery of the cartridge case and their opinion that it was dislodged from the left-hand drape. It's that important, Gus."

Gus, still shaken, stood up and went inside to grab two more beers. He returned with them, trying to process what Lynette had said. "So, what do you think?" he asked her.

"I think there's more to this property than meets the eye," she replied. "And I think we need to figure out what happened in that bedroom."

Gus sat, trying to process Lynette's theory, but the more he thought about it, the more baffled he became. "Not really. Are you suggesting someone fired a rifle into the wall, just to the left side of the window?" he asked, genuinely confused.

"No, Gus, not really," Lynette replied, trying to stay calm. "Even if a rifle barrel was hard up against the wall, the casing would most likely be ejected well away from the window drapes and would probably end up on the bed." She paused for a moment, then added, "That's not what I'm suggesting."

"Well, you've certainly lost me this time, Lynette," Gus said, rubbing his forehead in frustration.

Lynette sighed and looked him squarely in the eyes. "What I'm suggesting, Gus, is that someone shot an automatic pistol into the bed, close to the wall. The spent casing would then be ejected from the right-hand side of the handgun and could possibly lodge in the left-side drapes."

Gus blinked, trying to make sense of it. "And are there any holes in the mattress, Lynette?" he asked sarcastically, though the thought was nagging at him.

"No, Gus," Lynette snapped, now visibly annoyed. "No holes in the mattress. You're not getting it!" She stood up and walked into the kitchen, returning shortly with her notebook. She sat back down at the table on the verandah and began sketching something.

Gus watched, still trying to piece everything together, as Lynette finished her drawing and slid the notebook over to him. It was an aerial view of the master bedroom. The bed was situated between two windows. There was a person lying on the right-hand side of the bed, and another person standing beside the bed, holding a gun. A line indicated a possible trajectory of a spent casing, pointing toward the left-hand drapes of the right-side window.

Gus's mouth dropped open. "What? What the fuck… are you suggesting… fuck me… no way."

Lynette leaned in, her voice calm but firm. "Come up with a different scenario, Gus. Otherwise, this is the only explanation."

Gus sat back in his chair, stunned. "No way..."

Lynette added, "No one is going to throw a spent cartridge case at the drapes or place it inside the folds of the heavy fabric, Gus. It's doubtful. This is what makes sense."

A tense silence followed. Gus couldn't shake the disturbing image that Lynette's drawing had painted in his mind. He took a deep breath, then noticed that the fridge on the verandah was empty of cold beers. Lynette went inside to the kitchen fridge to grab more, while Gus set to work filling the verandah fridge with more cold beer from the cool room.

Once the beers were sorted, Lynette turned to Gus, a more serious tone in her voice. "Gus, we need to figure out where Lachlan died and what caused it. Was there an autopsy?"

Gus hesitated, then suggested, "Maybe we should call the police."

Lynette shook her head. "They'll probably just laugh at us. I remember cases from back in my police days when people would come in with crazy theories, thinking they'd watched too many detective shows."

Lynette leaned in closer and lowered her voice. "I've already contacted Graham Jamison at the Townsville police station. He's looking into Sonia's activities for us, and I might tell him about the spent .22 casing and my theory. He can find out Lachlan's cause of death and where it happened."

"Too late for today," Lynette added. "I'll give him a call tomorrow." She paused for a moment, then asked, "What do you want for dinner, Gus? Did you get some steak from Richmond?"

"I certainly did," Gus said, glad for a change of topic. "Two lots to choose from: Lowline or Hereford."

Lynette smiled, the mention of beef making her eyes light up. "I'll go with the Aberdeen," she said, referring to a cut she loved. Being a beef connoisseur herself, she knew exactly what Lowline beef was all about.

Gus went to work on the steaks, cutting and trimming two perfect-looking pieces from the Lowline rump. He salted them generously on both sides and let them come to room temperature for about an hour. Then, he added a little avocado oil and black pepper, cooking the steaks in one of Lynette's new Tefal skillets at a high temperature. He sealed each side, lowered the heat a little, then turned the steaks over and finished them off with a dash of Hanford Port.

For the sides, he slowly cooked some chat potatoes in just boiling water, finishing them off with butter, and served them with fresh (ish) green beans. No wine with this meal, just cold beer. And it was delicious.

"What a busy Monday," Gus mused, sinking back into his chair after finishing his meal. He hadn't even had time to tell Lynette about his trip to Richmond and the odd conversation with Alice. There was always tomorrow.

Who is Barry

Neither Gus nor Lynette had slept well that night, despite having consumed a large number of stubbies between them. The unsettled feeling lingered, and by Tuesday morning, they were both groggy but determined to get things done. The girls arrived around 8:30, eager to begin work on the master bedroom. Meanwhile, Gus and Lynette were having a light breakfast in the kitchen when Gus brought up his trip to Richmond the day before, particularly the conversation he'd had about Barry.

He explained that the butcher had asked if he was driving Barry's ute, then went on to tell Gus that both Barry and his father lived at Woolgar River Park. The woman at the bottle shop had made a similar assumption, believing it was Barry behind the wheel. When Gus mentioned that they'd moved into Woolgar River Park, she automatically assumed that he and Sonia were on good terms.

Lynette frowned. "It's like everyone's still stuck in the past," she said. Gus nodded, his thoughts turning over the peculiarities of his visit.

They agreed it would be wise to spend some time at the pub in Richmond. The locals there could hold more information about Barry and his father, and it might help them piece together the mystery.

Meanwhile, Lynette had a productive conversation with Graham Jamison at the Townsville police station. He confirmed that Sonia Teague had hired Jason Strange, an agent at Richmond Hill Real Estate in Charters Towers, to sell Woolgar River Station for $2.1 million. However, Strange had advised her that the asking price was far too low, suggesting it should be closer to $4 million. He also recommended getting a valuation before putting the property on the market. But Sonia was insistent on the lower price, citing her husband's declining health and the urgency of a quick sale.

Lynette's voice lowered as she relayed the next piece of information. "But here's the kicker, Lachlan Teague's signature on the contract to sell the property was a fake."

Graham confirmed it. "Yes, it seems it was. According to Jason Strange, Lachlan was present when the engagement form was signed, and he received his signature then. Later, when the sale to the Horsham buyer was finalised, Strange returned to the property with the contract, and again, Lachlan signed."

The situation grew even murkier. "And now?" Lynette asked.

Graham sighed. "We can't find Sonia. No one knows where she is."

Before Graham hung up, Lynette mentioned the spent cartridge case they had found in the master bedroom. Graham was intrigued, and after hearing her theory, he found it plausible, especially coming from someone with her background as a former detective sergeant.

Graham promised to gather more information and mentioned that he would like to see the room where the cartridge was found. Lynette suggested he visit the property next weekend, bringing his wife Stefanie along, as it was a long weekend. Their solicitor, who was also a friend, would be there too. Graham agreed, "Sounds good. Book us in, we'll be there Friday afternoon."

Lynette quickly briefed Gus on the phone call with Graham. Gus, who had been listening intently, added, "It sounds like the signatures are the only proof we have in our favour when it comes to the sale."

As she told him about Graham and Stefanie coming out for the weekend, Lynette suddenly realised they didn't have enough bedding for their guests. "Shit, we don't have any queen-size sheets, pillows, or a doona," she exclaimed, running her hand through her hair in frustration. "Charters Towers is over four hundred kilometres away. How are we going to manage?"

Gus suggested, "Why don't you call Ros? She can pick up the bedding for you and have the store call you for your credit card details."

Lynette's face lit up. "Brilliant idea," she said, dialling Ros's number immediately.

"When you're done, how about we head into Richmond?" Gus suggested, his tone upbeat again. "I need to talk to the stock and station agent about cattle agistment, and we can check out the Palace Hotel while we're at it."

The Subaru, as always, handled the dirt roads far more comfortably than the Landcruiser ute, making the journey to Richmond much more pleasant. They stopped first at the stock agents on Goldring Street, just a couple of doors up from the pub.

Inside, the receptionist greeted them warmly. "Good morning, oh, wait, it's afternoon already. But I'm forgiven for that, right? What can I do for you today?"

"We'd like to speak with someone about cattle agistment," Gus replied.

The woman informed them that Peter was away but would be back in about half an hour. "If you leave your name and contact number, I'll have him call you as soon as he's back."

"Sounds good," Gus said, giving her his mobile number.

With their contact details left behind, they walked to the pub, ready for lunch, drinks, and hopefully some information about Barry.

Lynette raised an eyebrow. "Gus, why didn't you give her our last name?"

He shrugged. "I'm not in the mood for too many questions just yet."

Lynette didn't push it, and instead, she walked up to the bar while Gus headed for the gents. Alice, the bartender, greeted her with a smile. "What can I get you?"

Lynette ordered two stubbies of **XXXX** Gold and asked for a lunch menu. As Alice went to fetch their drinks, Gus returned from the restroom, and the two of them settled into the cozy corner of the pub.

Gus couldn't help but glance around the room, wondering if anyone here might have more insight into Barry and his father's whereabouts. Maybe, just maybe, the answers were waiting to be found in this small town.

As Alice returned to the bar with their drinks, Gus smiled and greeted her. "You're right, Alice. I was here yesterday," he said. "This is my wife, Lynette."

Alice looked over at Lynette, offering a warm smile. "Pleased to meet you, Lynette. I'm Alice."

Lynette returned the smile, her tone friendly. "And you too, Alice."

They placed their order for the classic 'T' bone steak, chips, and salad, with two more stubbies of Gold. Alice, nodding approvingly, remarked, "Good choice!" before walking off towards the kitchen. A moment later, she returned with the beers and asked, "Cash or EFTPOS?" Lynette raised her card, and Alice quickly processed the payment.

As Alice set down their drinks, she turned to Lynette. "How are you getting on with Sonia?"

Lynette furrowed her brow. "Hmm, Sonia Teague?"

Alice's expression shifted. "Sonia Teague, is it now? The last time I saw her, she was still Sonia Harris," she spat out, clearly unimpressed. She then turned back toward the kitchen at the sound of the bell, only to return with their meals shortly after.

There was no one else at the bar, so Gus and Lynette decided to settle in and enjoy their meal there, making small talk with Alice, who, it seemed, had a lot to say about Sonia. Her tone clearly indicated a strong dislike for her.

"Did that bitch tell you she was married to Lachie?" Alice asked, her voice dripping with scorn. "That'd be a laugh, poor old Lachie, God bless his soul." She shook her head, her expression hardening. "Lachie wouldn't have had her there unless she was good at cooking and cleaning. Didn't you know Lachie was the other way?"

Lynette looked at Alice, stunned. "The other way? What do you mean?"

Alice didn't hesitate. "Yeah, I think most people around here think that. Don't get me wrong, Lachie was the best. He was always pleasant, kind, and helpful to anyone who needed it. It didn't bother me in the slightest that he was queer... or gay, as they call them now."

Lynette, still processing the new information, glanced at Gus, who remained quiet, taking in Alice's words.

Alice, noticing the empty stubbies on the counter, asked, "Another two?"

Lynette exchanged a glance with Gus, who gave a slight nod. "Yes, thanks," Gus said. As Alice moved to get their drinks, Lynette's mind was already racing, the new revelations about Lachlan Teague adding more confusion to the already tangled situation.

"Yes, thanks Alice," Gus replied, his voice carrying a hint of disbelief. The revelation Alice had casually shared in that one sentence had left both of them reeling.

"So, Sonia was the housekeeper?" Gus ventured, trying to piece things together. But the conversation was quickly interrupted as more people began filtering into the bar, making it difficult to continue. Gus and Lynette finished their beers, exchanged glances, and decided to leave, heading back to the stock agent's office.

As they approached the door, Gus's phone rang. "Hello, this is Gus," he answered, recognising the caller. It was Peter Lansky, the stock agent. As soon as he realised Gus was standing just outside, he quickly hung up the phone and called out, "Gus and Lynette!"

They entered together, exchanging smiles and introductions. This time, Gus mentioned their surname, Teague. "Any relation to Lachlan Teague?" Peter asked, raising an eyebrow.

"He was my late uncle," Gus replied. "Lynette and I decided to stay on at the property for a while and see what transpires. Hence our visit today."

Peter nodded, seemingly pleased to meet them. "I knew Lachlan quite well," he said. "We did business together for the past seven years. Mostly buying and selling cattle." He then turned to Gus and asked, "Are you in the market for yearlings?"

Gus and Lynette exchanged a glance. They weren't in the financial position to purchase any cattle, so Gus politely declined.

"I was more interested in agisting the land," Gus explained. "What do you think about that?"

Peter gave a thoughtful nod. "Agistment's in a good spot right now," he said. "Your location's solid. Road trains can get in easily. But, the area doesn't exactly demand high agistment fees. For Woolgar River Park, I'd say it's a good fit for around five thousand head. The water's great, and the place is well-grassed, Buffel Grass, Curly Mitchell, Flinders Grass, Seca Stylo. You've also seeded various Buffel varieties. Fencing's in good shape too."

Gus took note. This was sounding promising.

Peter continued, "Barry and his crew do a good job maintaining the fencing and pumps. Based on current conditions, you'd be looking at something between three and four fifty per head for agistment."

Lynette frowned, confused. "What does that mean?" she asked. Gus shrugged, not wanting to admit he wasn't sure either, but not wanting to appear uninformed.

"I'll Google it when we get back," Gus muttered under his breath.

Peter added that he'd need to visit the property to assess it more thoroughly before giving a final estimate, but he seemed optimistic. They thanked him for his time and said they'd be in touch later in the week.

On the drive back to the homestead, Lynette couldn't resist asking again, "So what exactly is this three to four fifty thing?"

Gus, still avoiding the question, smirked and replied, "I don't have a clue, but I'll figure it out when we get back. And about the internet… we still need to sort that out."

Lynette raised an eyebrow. "Right, the internet! Don't forget about that. And what about Sonia? And your uncle being gay? This whole thing is getting weirder by the minute."

Gus let out a short laugh, shaking his head. "The plot thickens. I can't wait for Malcolm and Graham to get up here. It's going to be one hell of a discussion."

Lynette agreed. "Yes, and we still need to find out more about Barry. He could be important for the cattle agistment thing."

By the time they returned to the house, it was still early afternoon, but Gus was already determined to solve the internet mystery. Their devices, iPhones, iPads, and Gus's MacBook Air, all showed a strong Wi-Fi signal when near the house. But as soon as they moved further away, the signal dropped, meaning the modem/router was somewhere inside.

"We need to find this modem," Gus said, frustrated. "Once we get the password, we'll finally be able to join the Wi-Fi service."

They knew the internet antenna was on the roof, so Gus decided to follow the cable inside to see where it led. However, the two Mac desktop PCs in the house were locked with passwords, rendering them useless.

Gus decided to ask Willem, who had also noticed the Wi-Fi and was planning to ask Gus for the password. "Willem, do you know anything about the internet here?" Gus asked.

Willem nodded, confirming that he'd also found the Wi-Fi signal and had been meaning to ask about the password. Together, they climbed to the small landing at the top of the rear staircase, where they discovered an access panel.

Gus asked Willem if he had seen any step ladders around. Willem replied that he hadn't, so Gus sent him off in the ute to buy a two-meter aluminium ladder from the hardware store in Richmond. Gus asked him to have the store call for payment details.

With Willem gone, Gus retreated to the verandah, which he had dubbed the "beer garden." He grabbed a stubbie from the fridge and settled in. It wasn't long before Lynette, accompanied by Hailee and Janice, joined him.

"I'm shouting the girls a drink," Lynette announced. "They've done a fantastic job on the master bedroom. We should be able to move into it tomorrow. Then they can start on the other King room and one of the Queen rooms. Hopefully, everything will be ready by Friday for the visitors."

As they were finishing their third or fourth beer, Willem returned with the ladder. He handed it to Gus, who waved him off, saying, "No rush, we can deal with it tomorrow. Here, Willem, have a beer."

Willem looked puzzled. "Why didn't the hardware store call for payment?" he asked.

"They said they've opened an account for us," Willem replied. "They know who you are."

Gus chuckled softly. "Small towns, huh? Two visits to town and everyone already knows who I am and what I'm up to."

"Well, happy days, then," he said with a wry grin.

While they were chatting and drinking, Gus had casually mentioned the two Mac desktops, prompting Hailee to pipe up. "I might be able to reset and reload the MacOS on them," she said with a smile. "I used to work for an IT company in London, specialising in Macs."

Gus blinked in surprise. He hadn't even thought to ask these guys what their skills were beyond the obvious. "For fuck's sake," he muttered, more to himself than anyone else.

Lynette, ever the practical one, interrupted with a grin. "Remember, we're painting tomorrow, not playing with computers!"

Hailee laughed. "I'll just take one of the Macs to our house with me and work on it at night. It'll be easier that way."

The next morning, around eight-thirty, the girls were ready to work. Willem had gone back to Richmond to fetch more supplies, roller covers, paint, and whatever else Lynette needed. Hailee was carrying one of the Mac desktops, and Gus suddenly remembered that she had taken it with her the previous afternoon.

Hailee waved her hand dismissively. "It's all good and connected to the Wi-Fi now. I can't get the password from it though, so you'll still have to track down the modem. But it's as good as gold, very quick." She paused, then giggled. "It had its hard drive erased by someone who must know just enough to be dangerous. They didn't empty the trash can though."

Gus looked at her, a little confused. "What kind of shit do you mean?"

"Just files and stuff," Hailee replied with a shrug. "Banking, stock valuations, that kind of stuff. Some of it's probably protected."

Great, Gus thought, mentally noting this new complication. As he googled cattle agistment rates, he discovered they were charged weekly. He did a quick calculation, five thousand head at four dollars per head came out to just over one million dollars a year. The figures were looking good, but it depended on how many cattle they could actually find to agist. It was promising, though, and Gus felt a bit more optimistic.

By Friday morning, the girls had finished painting the master bedroom, the king room, and one of the queen rooms. The drapes and curtains had been cleaned, and the rooms looked fantastic. The queen room was still waiting for bedding, but that was due to arrive this weekend with Ros. Gus and Lynette had moved into the master bedroom, and things were starting to fall into place.

Lynette was eager for their visitors to arrive, Malcolm and Ros from Townsville. They would be staying in the king room, while Graham and Stefanie would take the queen room. She was looking forward to catching up with everyone.

Gus had been busy preparing dinner. He'd trimmed and seasoned three porterhouse steaks, cut in half to make six 300-gram portions. He also made a spicy peppered potato and cheese casserole, with mushrooms on the side. He had pulled two cartons of Gold and one carton of Super Crisp from the cool room and placed them in the fridge on the verandah, along with the bar fridge. Lynette had just returned from Richmond with two bottles of Paringa Estate Riesling, a carton of Jacobs Creek Classic Sauvignon Blanc, and two bottles of Johnny Walker Black Label. She also picked up two kilos of mushrooms for dinner.

Malcolm and Ros arrived at four-thirty that afternoon, having left Townsville at eleven in the morning. Ros had brought the pillows, pillowcases, two sets of 400-count sheets in pale pastel grey, a doona with a dark grey cover, and a matching dark grey bathroom set. "I hope the colours are what you wanted," Ros said as they went upstairs to make the queen room.

Lynette and Ros were both amazed by how much of a difference the paint had made to the rooms. Once they finished making up the queen room, they went downstairs to find the men enjoying drinks in the bar.

"Beer, Ros? Or something else?" Lynette asked, opening the bar fridge and grabbing two Gold stubbies for Malcolm and Gus. Ros, deciding to keep it simple, took a stubbie as well, not wanting to get too tipsy before the other guests arrived.

Just as it was getting dark, Graham and Stefanie pulled up. After the introductions, Gus had to rack his brain to remember where he'd seen them before. It clicked after a moment, at their wedding.

"Looking good, Gus!" Graham said, offering a handshake. "It's been a while, huh?"

Stefanie echoed the sentiment. "Nice to see you both. Has it really been that long?"

After some catching up, everyone migrated to the bar for a drink. Three drinks later, they moved onto the verandah for dinner, which Gus had been busy preparing. It was about seven by the time they sat down, and the conversation was a bit more subdued. The long drive had taken its toll on their visitors, and everyone was visibly tired.

They briefly touched on the fraudulent activities and other mysteries, but all agreed to save the discussion for tomorrow.

It was an early night for everyone except Gus and Graham, who stayed up late into the night, playing pool and drinking beers. By the time they finally called it a night, it was around two a.m.

The warm sunlight cast a golden glow over the verandah as Ros and Lynette laid out a delicious breakfast spread the next morning. Malcolm, ever the adventurer, pulled out a topographical map of Woolgar River Park, which he had brought along on their trip. "Why don't we take a drive around the property today?" he suggested, his eyes scanning the map. "There are some fascinating places to explore, like this gorge in the river, some buildings in the centre of the property, and another house that's supposed to be around here somewhere."

Gus, always up for a good time, chimed in, "And we can pack some drinks and snacks in my esky to keep us fuelled along the way!" His large portable esky was quickly filled with as much ice as they could scrounge up from the house, and soon it was stocked with an assortment of refreshing beverages.

Malcolm's trusty VX Landcruiser, with its seven seats, was the obvious choice for their excursion. As they set off, the group was filled with excitement and anticipation. The scenery was breathtaking, with rolling hills and vast expanses of open land stretching out as far as the eye could see.

Their first discovery was the remnants of a six-stand shearing shed, accompanied by a shearer's quarters and cookhouse. It was clear that this property had once been a thriving sheep station. As they continued their journey, they marvelled at the sheer size of the property, clocking up an impressive twenty-seven kilometres before reaching the far boundary.

Turning left, they drove for another thirteen kilometres, eventually reaching the northern boundary. From there, they headed south, making their way back towards the homestead. The sun beat down on them, but the Landcruiser's air conditioning kept them cool and comfortable.

About twenty kilometres from the homestead, they stumbled upon the fourth residence on the property. As they approached the house, everyone's eyes widened in surprise – someone was sitting on the verandah, waving at them! The person stood up, walked to the edge of the verandah, and greeted them warmly as Malcolm brought the Landcruiser to a stop.

The group piled out of the vehicle, curiosity getting the better of them. As they walked towards the verandah, the person shouted out, "Good day all! I suppose I'd better put the kettle on!" The group exchanged amused glances, intrigued by this unexpected encounter.

As they approached the entrance, it became clear that this person was no stranger to the property. The verandah was cluttered with personal belongings, and the air was thick with the scent of years of habitation. Whoever this person was, they had clearly been living here for a long time. The group's curiosity was piqued, and they eagerly awaited the opportunity to learn more about this mysterious resident.

"Angus Teague, I presume," said Owen Harrigan, his arm outstretched as he walked towards Gus with a warm smile

"I'm Owen Harrigan, nice to finally meet you." Gus acknowledged Owen with a firm handshake. "G'day Owen, nice to meet you too."

Owen gestured towards the group. "Tea, anyone? Please, come on up and take a seat here at the table. I'm sure we've all got a bit to catch up on."

The group politely declined the offer of tea, but Gus suggested, "How about a cold beer instead? It's been a long day."

Owen chuckled. "Sorry, can't help you there, Gus. I'm afraid I don't have any beer on hand." Just then, Malcolm called out from the cruiser, "Will you have a beer, Owen?"

Owen's face lit up. "Love one, thank you, Malcolm. And please, everyone, take a seat. Make yourselves at home."

As they sat down, Gus turned to Owen and asked, "So, Owen, should I know you? I mean, you're living in my house, after all."

Owen laughed. "I've been meaning to come up to the homestead and introduce myself, but I thought I'd let you settle in a bit first. I've been on Woolgar River Park for nearly thirty years, you know. First as the station manager, and then... well, let's just say I'm getting a bit long in the tooth. My son Barry's taken over from me now."

Gus's eyes lit up with interest. "Thirty years? That's amazing. I'm sure you've got a wealth of knowledge about this place. I'd love to hear more about it."

Owen smiled, seeming to relax into the conversation. "Well, I've seen a lot of changes over the years, that's for sure. But I'm happy to share some stories with you, Gus. You're welcome to ask me anything you like."

Gus grinned. "How about coming up to the homestead for dinner tonight? You can tell me – tell all of us, actually – about the history of Woolgar River Park. I'm sure we'd all love to hear it." Owen's face lit up with pleasure. "I'd love to, Gus. Thank you for the invitation. What time should I come up?"

As the evening approached, Lynette busied herself in the kitchen, preparing a delicious meal for their guest. She had found two old camp ovens on the property, which she used to cook two perfectly roasted two-kilogram rump pieces. The aroma wafting from the ovens was incredible, and everyone's stomach was growling in anticipation.

To accompany the roast, Lynette had prepared roast potatoes and pumpkin in the kitchen oven, and microwaved Brussels sprouts and green peas to perfection. Owen took a sip of his beer, a faraway look in his eye, and began to spin a tale that would captivate them all...

Owen Harrigan made his entrance in his 1949 Land Rover Series 1, accompanied by a bottle of Chivas Regal. The distinctive sound of his vehicle could be heard from quite a distance, with the transmission's noise overshadowing the motor's. Rather than being greeted warmly, people strolled to the porte-cochère, drawn more by curiosity about the source of the commotion. The Land Rover was a magnificent original specimen, appearing to have been meticulously maintained. Owen explained that it was his sole vehicle since his son Barry had taken his other car for a ride. Afterward, they all gathered in the bar to enjoy a drink together.

This evening marked the inaugural use of the dining area, a space that housed a stunning table with six legs. These legs were meticulously crafted from Australian Corymbia Maculata, a timber more commonly referred to as spotted gum, which also adorned the tabletop. The choice of this particular wood was deliberate, as it was a recurring element in the home's design, including all the floor timbers. The table was complemented by ten chairs, arranged symmetrically with four placed on each side and one at each end. However, for tonight's gathering, Lynette had thoughtfully set three chairs on each side and one at the end, creating an intimate and inviting setting for their guests.

Both roasts were partially sliced and elegantly arranged on a large stainless steel serving tray, which was then placed on the matching dining buffet. This buffet was positioned in front of the dining table, creating a sophisticated separation of about two and a half meters. The roast potatoes were presented on two separate trays, while the pumpkin, Brussels sprouts, and peas were combined on a single serving platter. To complement the meal, two gravy boats were placed on either side of the platter, adding a touch of elegance to the presentation. The arrangement looked impressive and very inviting.

There were no disputes about the quality of the meal, as the beef and its accompaniments were quickly consumed. Owen, seated at the head of the table and sipping a glass of wine, declared it the best meal he had in years. Everyone at the table agreed, and soon the plates and cutlery were cleared away. In their place, more wine bottles were arranged, along with Owen's bottle of Chivas Regal. Gus, with a keen eye, discovered some glasses of unusual shapes and sizes behind the bar. Graham, ever resourceful, assembled a bucket of ice. Ros, meanwhile, found two additional bottles of sauvignon blanc, and all these items were brought to the dining table. Gus ensured that everyone had a drink in hand before turning to Owen and asking when he had first arrived at Woolgar River Park.

Do you know it was once referred to as the 'Woolgar River Curse' by the locals around Richmond for a period? Everyone fell silent and just stared at Owen as if he had fired a gun.

Owen had arrived in Richmond at the impressive age of forty, taking on the role of the new bank manager for the ES&A Banking Co. He had previously been employed as an accountant with Esanda in Brisbane and had managed to secure a promotion to Bank Manager. Promotion, my arse, he would tell everyone. No other fool wanted to leave Brissy to come out here to woop woop, except for muggins here, who thought it might be quite an adventure. Owen's wife, Jenny, was also eager to leave Brisbane.

Owen's son, Barry, was nineteen years old and was just completing his apprenticeship as a mechanic. He only had three months left until his training was finished and had stayed back in Brisbane with his employer. He planned to join Owen in Richmond once he was done.

While working in the bank in Brisbane, Owen went on, if you looked out of the seventh-floor window where he worked, you could only see other buildings across from you. It was a much better view inside, looking at the walls. But in Richmond, when he looked out of the window from his office, he saw sunshine, hills, people walking around in shorts and navy blue singlets. And here he was, stuck inside the bank. A fellow named Curtis Southwell would occasionally come into the bank, generally to withdraw a bit of money. I didn't really get to meet him or to get to know him. But one day, I went for lunch at the Palace Hotel and had a meal there and a couple of beers. I started talking to the guys in the bar and had a few more beers. I never went back to the bank. They gave me the boot, of course, and I couldn't care less.

They granted me a month to vacate the bank's property. I was uncertain about my future plans, but I was resolute in not returning to the city. We had relocated there just under three months ago, and Barry was expected to arrive in town soon. However, while there were numerous options and strategies available for mechanics, the situation was quite different for bank managers, who faced more limited alternatives.

Curtis Southwell was a curious character in Richmond, known by most locals for his genial demeanour and willingness to share a yarn or two. He had a rugged charisma, the kind forged by years under the scorching Australian sun, and an inviting smile that made you feel like you'd known him forever, even if it was your first meeting. Owen had seen him around, particularly during his brief tenure at the bank, but they had never exchanged more than a nod of recognition.

On this particular day, as Owen sat nursing his pint at the pub, he felt somewhat adrift, contemplating his future now that he was no longer chained to the monotonous rhythm of banking life. Curtis approached with the casual confidence of someone who had nothing to prove and only kindness to offer. His offer of a beer cut through Owen's thoughts like a beacon, a small gesture that felt monumental in that moment.

"How are you doin', Owen?" Curtis asked, his voice carrying the warmth of genuine concern. "I'll buy you a beer, have a seat."

Owen was taken aback by the familiarity and friendliness in Curtis's approach. He accepted the offer with a nod and a grateful, "Cheers, mate." Curtis gestured to a booth in the corner of the room, away from the clinking glasses and bustling chatter that filled the pub.

As they settled into the worn leather seats, Owen couldn't help but feel the weight of his recent decisions lifting slightly; there was comfort in the company of someone who seemed to understand the challenges of adjusting to life in a small town far from the metropolitan hustle. Curtis, with a knowing look in his eye, leaned back and cracked a joke about the bank's loss being Richmond's gain, sparking a smile from Owen.

For the first time in weeks, Owen felt at ease, no longer preoccupied with the uncertainties that lay ahead. He found himself lost in conversation, discussing everything from the local footy team to the best fishing spots along the river, all the while sipping their frothy pints. As the sun dipped below the horizon, casting a warm glow through the pub's windows, Owen realised that perhaps Richmond held more promise than he had initially thought.

Curtis's easy laughter and the genuine camaraderie they shared over those beers marked the beginning of a new chapter for Owen. It was a moment that signified more than just a casual drink; it was an unspoken invitation to embrace this unexpected turn in life's road, with new friendships and opportunities waiting to be discovered in the most unlikely of places

The Curse

Curtis's offer to Owen was simple yet enticing. He laid it out plainly: a monthly salary that was reasonable for the position, a comfortable two-bedroom house, and provisions that included meat, which was a significant perk in this remote setting. The use of a utility vehicle, or ute, added further appeal, as it would give Owen the flexibility to manage his duties around the station with ease. Most importantly, Curtis required a commitment of at least twelve months, ensuring stability for both parties and giving Owen enough time to settle into the role.

Owen, despite his initial reservations due to his lack of experience with livestock or rural life, found the proposition intriguing. He pondered the benefits of this new lifestyle, freedom from the monotony of banking and the chance to learn something completely outside his comfort zone. His wife, Jenny, had been enthusiastic about embracing a new, quieter way of living away from the hustle and bustle of Brisbane, and this seemed like the perfect opportunity.

The thought of managing a station, albeit with little direct involvement with the animals, was both daunting and exciting. Owen considered the skills he had honed over the years, management, organisation, and a knack for problem-solving, realising these could be quite valuable in his new role. Furthermore, the prospect of a supportive community and new friendships, such as the one he was already forming with Curtis, made the decision easier.

As Owen weighed these factors, he realised the offer was not just a job change but a chance for a fresh start, an adventure he and his family had unknowingly craved. With a final sip of his drink, he looked at Curtis and nodded, "I'm in. Let's do this." The agreement marked the start of a bold new chapter for Owen, one filled with promise and the potential for personal growth.

The evening continued with everyone at the table engrossed in Owen's tales, hanging onto his every word. He had captivated the crowd, and as he lifted his glass to finish his last sip, Graham sprang up to replenish the drinks. Malcolm, in the meantime, topped up Owen's glass with more ice and Chivas Regal, ensuring the storytelling flowed as smoothly as the drinks.

"Another one for the storyteller," Graham announced with a chuckle, handing a fresh drink to Owen.

"Cheers, mate," Owen replied, raising his glass to the group. "You know, it's moments like these that make you realise the beauty of good company."

"Too right, Owen," piped up Lynette from across the table, a warm smile on her face. "So, about this Curtis fellow, did you ever take him up on that fishing offer?"

"Well, as a matter of fact, I did," Owen said with a grin. "And let me tell you, it was quite an adventure. We ended up catching more yabbies than fish!"

This prompted a round of laughter, with Ros adding, "Sounds like you might have found a new hobby, Owen."

"Maybe so," Owen chuckled, taking a sip of his drink. "Richmond's starting to feel like home, thanks to folks like you lot."

"Here's to new beginnings and old friends," Malcolm toasted, lifting his glass.

As the evening wore on, the conversation shifted from stories of the past to plans for the future, with everyone sharing their hopes and dreams. The camaraderie and laughter continued well into the night, filling the room with warmth and a sense of belonging.

Owen Harrigan sat back and savoured the moment, as the laughter slowly subsided and everyone resumed their conversations. It was an evening of camaraderie, of shared stories and the forging of new friendships, a balm for his soul after the whirlwind of changes in his life.

Owen continued his memory of the day at the pub with Curtis; As the night wore on, Owen and Curtis continued talking, their conversation punctuated by shared laughs and memories of their earlier escapades. Eventually, the two decided it was time to leave the warmth of the pub for the cool night air outside. Owen, still buzzing from the evening's merriment, was intrigued by Curtis's earlier mention of a place he might find interesting.

They left the pub and walked to Owen's trusty old Land Rover, which was parked just outside. As they drove towards Woolgar River Park, the stars above sparkled in the clear night sky, and the moon cast a gentle glow on the landscape around them. The drive was filled with the kind of comfortable silence that only new friends can share, punctuated by the occasional comment on the beauty of the night.

When they arrived at the park, Curtis led Owen to a quaint two-bedroom home, nestled behind the current Manager's residence. It was a charming little place, with an inviting feel that immediately struck a chord with Owen. "This could be perfect," Owen mused aloud, his mind already racing with possibilities.

Curtis then showed him the old Land Rover Series One, still in good condition and perfect for hauling Owen's belongings from Richmond. "This beauty will get the job done," Curtis said with a grin. "Use it to bring your things over, and once you're settled, come and see me."

Owen felt a wave of gratitude for Curtis's kindness and generosity. This was more than just a new job; it was the beginning of a fresh chapter, an opportunity to build a life in a place that already felt like home. "Thanks, Curtis," Owen said, his voice filled with sincerity. "I'll be here sooner than you think."

And so, Owen's journey at Woolgar River Park began. It was a tale he would recount many times, one that always brought a smile to his face and reminded him of the unexpected twists in life that lead us exactly where we need to be. The night, with its laughter, friendship, and promise of new beginnings, was one Owen would cherish forever.

Curtis Southwell was around fifty when Owen first met him. Curtis had a wonderful wife named Peggy, two sons named Kevin, who was twenty-five, and Dillon, who was twenty-three, as well as a daughter named Cathy, who was twenty. The Southwell family had owned Woolgar River Park since Curtis's father passed away.

Woolgar River Park was a picturesque and expansive property located near Richmond, known for its serene landscapes and stunning views of the surrounding hills. The park was a haven for outdoor enthusiasts, featuring several walking trails that meandered through lush greenery and alongside the tranquil river that ran through the property. It was a popular spot for fishing, with Curtis often inviting friends and locals to enjoy a day out on the water, catching yabbies or simply soaking up the sun.

The park was home to a quaint two-bedroom house, nestled behind the main residence, which served as the manager's home. This charming abode had a warm and inviting feel, offering a perfect blend of rustic charm and modern comfort. It was surrounded by beautifully maintained gardens, adding to the overall appeal of the property.

There was another home located towards the cattle yards for the Woolgar Park ringer.

The history of Woolgar River Park was deeply entwined with the local community. Initially established by Curtis's father, the park had long been a centre for community gatherings, picnics, and celebrations. Over the years, it became a beloved landmark, with many local events hosted on its grounds, from family reunions to community fairs. The Southwell family took immense pride in preserving the park's natural beauty and historical significance, ensuring it remained a cherished part of the local landscape.

The park played a vital role in fostering a sense of camaraderie and belonging among residents, serving as a peaceful retreat and a place where lasting memories were made. Its significance extended beyond its physical beauty, symbolising the enduring spirit of the community and its commitment to preserving the natural environment for future generations.

"But what's with the curse?" Ros asked, her curiosity piqued by the tantalising hint of mystery surrounding Woolgar River Park.

Owen grinned mischievously, savouring the anticipation he had stirred. "Well, that, my dear Ros," he began, leaning back slightly in his chair, "is a story that requires both time and a fair bit of grog, as you rightly pointed out." His words were met with a ripple of laughter across the table, the friendly banter setting a warm, inviting tone for the evening.

"It all started when Jenny and I first set foot here," Owen continued, casting a fond glance toward the window as if envisioning the early days. "We both fell in love with the sweeping landscapes and the serene beauty of the park. Jenny, always one for taking things into her own hands, decided to take charge of the chooks. She wasn't just content with feeding them and collecting eggs; she went all out, breeding them for table meat."

He paused to take a sip of his drink, the room's atmosphere vibrant with intimacy and camaraderie as the fire crackled softly in the corner. "Barry, my son, arrived not long after we'd settled in. Curtis, being the quick judge of character that he is, took one look at Barry and instantly proclaimed him the Station's Mechanic, even set him up with a wage. It was like this place was welcoming us with open arms."

The listeners, engrossed in Owen's storytelling, exchanged knowing glances, some nodding in appreciation of the warmth and hospitality that seemed to define Woolgar River Park. The room itself, with its rustic charm adorned with timber and warm ambient lighting, reinforced the sense of belonging and shared experience.

"Ah, but back to the 'curse'," Owen interjected, leaning forward to capture their full attention. "Legend has it, back in the day, there was a bit of an uproar when the locals started complaining about odd happenings in the area. Cattle wandering off, equipment going missing, things like that. It wasn't long before whispers of a 'curse' started making the rounds, mostly in jest, but still enough to give people a good laugh and an excuse to gather for a drink and some storytelling."

This revelation elicited a chorus of amused murmurs, everyone appreciating the blend of myth and reality that often characterised rural tales. "But, as you can see, it's all just good fun now," Owen reassured, raising his glass once more. "We've certainly been more blessed than cursed by this land and its people."

As the group resumed their conversations, the evening continued to unfold with stories of the past interwoven with dreams for the future. It was a gathering that, much like the park itself, embraced the spirit of community and the joy of shared experiences, ensuring that both old ties and new friendships were celebrated well into the night.

The property management was running smoothly, but Owen identified several strategies to achieve substantial financial savings. Curtis eagerly put these measures into practice, which further boosted their success. With things going well, Curtis decided it was the right time to realise his long-held ambition of building a new house. He enlisted the expertise of an architect and a builder, both from Mount Isa, to create a dream home. This remarkable house featured a bedroom for each of their children, a guest bedroom, and a grand master bedroom, along with all the luxurious amenities one could desire.

After the construction was completed, Curtis and his family moved into this stunning new residence, while we settled into their previous home. For a while, everything was harmonious. The children got on well with each other, but Owen's son, Barry, persistently pursued Cathy, which soon became problematic. Frustrated by Barry's advances, Cathy confided in her father. Faced with this issue, Curtis felt compelled to give Owen an ultimatum: Barry needed to leave, or they would all have to move out. Understanding the situation's gravity, Owen apologised and made the difficult decision to have Barry relocate.

As a result, Barry secured employment in town and found new living arrangements, allowing peace to return to both households. This development, albeit challenging, underscored the importance of maintaining harmony and respect within their close-knit community.

Owen recounts a tense and culturally loaded incident involving Kevin and Dillon, the sons of Curtis Southwell. One night, the young men were out spotlight shooting, a practice involving the use of bright lights to hunt animals after dark. They managed to catch a couple of pigs and decided to drop them off at the home of Kurrie, an Aboriginal stockman known for raising pigs on a diet of wheat and corn.

Kurrie was away at the time, so Kevin and Dillon placed the pigs in his pen. In the spirit of camaraderie and perhaps emboldened by alcohol, the young men shared a few beers with Kurrie's wife. The night took an unfortunate turn, though the specifics are lightly glossed over by Owen, hinting at a level of impropriety or misconduct that ensued.

When Kurrie returned home to discover what had transpired, he was understandably upset. His wife's account of the events, involving Mr. Southwell's boys, likely portrayed a scenario of disrespect and boundary crossing. Two days later, in a vivid and dramatic display of anger and cultural symbolism, Kurrie confronted Curtis Southwell. Early in the morning, Kurrie arrived at Curtis's residence, dressed only in his undergarments and covered in white paint, an act likely steeped in traditional significance, perhaps intended to underscore seriousness or to invoke spiritual elements. He brandished two spears, a powerful symbol of his cultural heritage and an unmistakable statement of his anger and demand for justice.

The sight of Kurrie, adorned with white paint and wielding weapons, jumping energetically and pointing the spears at Curtis, who stood defensively at his door, was charged with tension. Curtis, caught off-guard and perhaps misunderstanding the cultural weight of the gesture, simply told Kurrie to "fuck off," dismissing the display as mere aggression rather than a serious cultural grievance.

This confrontation between Curtis and Kurrie escalates rapidly, revealing a volatile mix of personal grievances and cultural conflict. Kurrie's outrage, fuelled by the alleged actions of Curtis's sons, adds a layer of tension that underscores the deep-seated animosity.

Curtis's response, refusing to let Kurrie take retribution in his own way, asserts his authority but at the cost of exacerbating an already fraught situation. The dramatic conclusion, with Kurrie cursing the land and Curtis resorting to the intimidating presence of his shotgun, leaves behind a sense of foreboding.

The curse, delivered with such intensity and theatricality, looms over the narrative like an ominous shadow, suggesting there could be lingering consequences for Curtis, his family, and the property. The description of Kurrie's ritualistic actions, dancing, pointing his spears, and wailing, adds a vivid, almost supernatural dimension to the scene. It leaves open the question of whether the curse is symbolic or if it will manifest in more tangible ways as the story unfolds.

Meanwhile, Curtis's use of the shotgun to finally drive Kurrie away shows his desperation to reassert control but also hints at his vulnerability. His brusque dismissal of Kurrie's grievance suggests unresolved tensions that might resurface later. This moment of confrontation not only heightens the drama but also sets the stage for potential fallout, whether from Kurrie's curse, Curtis's decisions, or the actions of his sons.

That seemed to be the end of the matter, and Curtis, in his gruff and straightforward way, told his boys to behave or something along those lines. But the boys, both in their mid-twenties, were a bit beyond the age of being easily reprimanded. It wasn't like Curtis could ground them or give them a clip around the ear anymore. What struck me as odd, though, was that neither of the boys had come out to back their father when Kurrie was raising hell in the yard. They'd stayed out of sight, leaving Curtis to face the confrontation alone.

It was about a week after the episode with Kurrie that tragedy struck. Cathy had gone out riding her horse, as she often did, but this time, she didn't come back. The horse returned to the property without her, its reins dragging on the ground, which immediately set off alarm bells. We all sprang into action , me, Jenny, Peggy, Kevin, Dillon, and Curtis. As night fell, we fanned out across the property, calling Cathy's name into the darkness. The air was thick with worry, and the longer she remained missing, the heavier the dread settled in our chests.

It was Curtis who found her. She was lying in the river, her lifeless body partially submerged, her head split open. The sight of her must have been unbearable, but Curtis didn't cry out or call for us right away. By the time we arrived, he was standing there silently, staring down at her, his face a mask of grief and rage.

When the police arrived, they examined the scene briefly and concluded that Cathy had been thrown from her horse. They chalked it up as a tragic accident, no foul play involved. But Curtis wasn't having any of it. "She's been murdered," he growled, his voice low and dangerous. "You're all fucking idiots if you think otherwise." He stormed into the police station in Richmond the next morning, demanding they take another look at the scene. He told them to get their arses out to the river and arrest "that bastard Kurrie."

Curtis's fury was palpable. He was convinced that Kurrie had come back to exact revenge, and he wasn't shy about saying so. "If you lot don't do your job, I'll bloody well do it for you," he spat. The officers warned him to calm down, threatening to lock him up if he kept on like that. Eventually, Curtis simmered down enough to avoid arrest, but it was clear he hadn't let it go. Kurrie, however, was nowhere to be found. He and his family had vanished, leaving no trace.

The funeral was a somber affair. Cathy had been the heart of the family in many ways, and her absence left a void that nothing could fill. Barry showed up, but his presence seemed to ignite something in Curtis. He flew into a rage, yelling at Barry to leave and making a scene in front of everyone. "You've got no bloody right to be here," he shouted. Barry left, looking utterly dejected. I felt sorry for Curtis, consumed as he was by his grief, but I also felt for Barry. He didn't deserve to be treated like that.

After the funeral, the atmosphere back at the house was heavy and oppressive. The Johnny Walker was opened because the Chivas was gone, and bottles of wine and stubbies of beer were passed around. Everyone drank in silence, the weight of Cathy's death hanging over us like a storm cloud. Owen, breaking the quiet, said grimly, "It gets worse," and we all turned to listen, bracing ourselves for more bad news.

Less than a month after Cathy's funeral, Curtis's boys were up on the top paddock doing some fencing work. They had their quads with them, Yamaha Grizzly 250s, which were perfectly good bikes in my opinion. But the boys had been complaining to Curtis for months, saying the 250s weren't up to the task. "We need 500s," they'd argued. "We can't carry enough tools and gear on these." I never bought it. The 250s were fine bikes , reliable, sturdy, and more than capable for the work they were doing. Owen chimed in, saying,

"I've still got one, and it's never let me down." The truth was, the boys just wanted the bigger bikes so they could go faster. They always had a tendency to push for more, whether they needed it or not.

Well, no one knows what happened, but the boys never came back from fencing that night. It wasn't until around two o'clock in the morning that their parents started to worry. It wasn't unusual for them to stay out until daylight, but something felt off this time.

Curtis decided to take action. At about three o'clock in the morning, he got his cruiser out and headed to where he thought the boys had been working that day. The night was moonless, the kind of darkness that makes everything seem closer and more threatening. Curtis drove up the track, his headlights cutting through the blackness, until about seven kilometres in, near where the hills begin to steepen. As he navigated a sharp corner, something in the middle of the track appeared out of nowhere. Curtis braked hard and swerved to the left, but the sudden movement sent his Landcruiser off the track and down the embankment.

At around four o'clock, Peggy came banging on our door, her fists hammering against the wood with a frantic rhythm that jolted us awake. She was screaming that something was wrong. It took her a while to calm down enough to explain, and even then, her words tumbled out in a disjointed rush. But we got the gist of it, Curtis had gone out looking for the boys and hadn't come back. I told Jenny to call the police and stay with Peggy while I grabbed the keys to the Landrover and headed out.

I didn't know exactly where the boys had been working, so I decided to follow the tracks from Curtis's Landcruiser. At a fork in the road where three turnoffs met, I plugged in my spotlight and held it out of the window to scan for tire tracks. Once I found Curtis's trail, it was easy to follow, and I hoped it would lead me straight to him.

As I reached the bendy part of the track, I noticed a faint reflection to my left, down the embankment towards the river. I stopped the Landrover and swung the spotlight in that direction. The beam caught the unmistakable glint of taillights. Curtis's Landcruiser was there, upside down.

I cursed myself for not bringing a torch. The steep embankment was treacherous in the dark, and the spotlight from the Landrover didn't reach far enough to fully illuminate the scene. It was easily more than a hundred, maybe a hundred and fifty metres down. Judging distance in the dark was near impossible, and the shadows played tricks on my eyes.

I decided to climb down, falling a couple of times as I scrambled my way to the wreck. The air was thick with the smell of oil and earth. When I reached the Landcruiser, I could see nothing clearly. I called out to Curtis several times, but the only sound was the faint hum of the Landrover idling above, its engine the only thing keeping the spotlight powered. My hands searched blindly, and at one point, I felt something warm and sticky. For a terrifying moment, I thought it was blood, but it turned out to be oil.

Realising I was ill-equipped to handle the situation in the dark, I made the difficult decision to head back up. The climb was even worse going back; the spotlight blinded me as I stumbled towards it. By the time I reached the Landrover, I was out of breath and frustrated.

I had to turn the Landrover around to return to the station. The track ahead was too narrow and unsafe for a forward drive in the dark, so I reversed carefully until I found a spot wide enough to turn. Once I was facing the right direction, I floored it, desperate to get help.

When I pulled up to the house, Jenny and Peggy ran out, their faces pale with worry. Peggy was screaming, "What's wrong? What's wrong?" but I had no time to explain. I ran straight to the phone and dialled Triple Zero. I didn't bother with the Richmond station; I knew they wouldn't answer this early, and besides, I didn't have their direct number. As the line connected, I gripped the receiver tightly, hoping help would come soon.

The operator was relentless, question after question, while I kept shouting, "Ambulance! Ambulance!" I must have repeated our location ten times, desperate for help to arrive. By five o'clock, the first hints of dawn broke over the horizon, but no one had come yet. Peggy and Jenny were beside themselves, crying and clinging to each other. I couldn't just sit there anymore. "I'm going back up," I said, but they both grabbed at me, begging, "Don't leave us! Stay here!"

Just as I wrestled with my next move, we heard the unmistakable whir of a helicopter overhead. Its spotlight panned across the property, searching for a landing zone. When it finally touched down, I bolted toward the crew, waving my arms. "The accident is about eight kilometres north!" I shouted. The loadmaster motioned for me to get in. "Show us," he said.

It took no time to reach the spot where Curtis's Landcruiser lay upside down, its red taillights still dimly visible in the early light. But then something else caught everyone's attention, a twisted mess of two quad bikes further up the track, smashed together in what could only have been a head-on collision.

The helicopter landed a ways back, near where I'd turned my Land Rover around earlier. The paramedics and I sprinted up the track, adrenaline coursing through us. In the growing daylight, the chaos became clearer. The wreckage of the quads was horrifying, and the body of one of Curtis's sons lay lifeless just off the track. A short distance away, near the embankment, the second boy's body was visible, as though flung from his bike in the collision.

One paramedic made his way down the embankment toward the Landcruiser, while the other checked the bodies on the track. The grim scene grew heavier with every step. "Call for backup," one paramedic shouted to the other as he approached the second body. The confirmation of death settled over us like a suffocating fog.

Owen paused in his recounting, his eyes glistening. Ros busied herself clearing empty wine bottles from the table, while Lynette quietly fetched another round of drinks. The rest of us sat stunned, unable to speak. Finally, Owen excused himself and stepped away to compose himself. He knew this place so well, as if it were his own home, and it was clear the memories weighed heavily on him.

When he returned, Stefanie broke the silence with a hesitant question: "Were they... all dead?"

"Yes," Owen said softly. "All three. Father and his two sons. It was... tragic."

He continued after a moment. "Poor Mrs. Southwell. Peggy couldn't take it. When they told her the news, she had a heart attack right there. The helicopter that had come for her husband was the same one that took her to Mount Isa Hospital. She didn't make it." He shook his head. "The entire family, gone. It was a tragedy that shook everyone."

The table fell silent again, the weight of the story hanging over us like a storm cloud. Lynette whispered, "We had no idea something so awful had happened here."

"Well," Owen said, "it was a long time ago. Seventeen years, give or take. It made the national news back then, 'The Accidents on Woolgar River Station,' they called it. For a while, people started referring to the place as 'Woolgar Cursed Park.'"

Gus finally spoke. "How did the boys end up in a head-on collision?"

Owen sighed, pouring another scotch before answering. "The forensic team was all over the site. They checked everything, the tracks, the wreckage, the bikes. What they pieced together was grim. One of the quads, they found, had a faulty headlight that likely went out while the boy was riding. They think he stopped to try and fix it but couldn't get it working.

"The boy in front wouldn't have known and kept going. At some point, he must have realised his brother wasn't following and turned back to look for him. They believe the two were riding fast, too fast, without seeing each other on the bendy track. The collision was inevitable in the dark."

Owen's voice tightened as he continued. "And Curtis... he wasn't wearing a seatbelt. As the Landcruiser rolled, he was thrown toward the open window. The force decapitated him. It was... beyond horrific."

The room sat in stunned silence, the reality of the story settling in. "How tragic," someone muttered.

"It was," Owen agreed. "And for some, it was enough to believe there really was a curse on this place."

Breaking the tension, someone suggested more drinks. After all, it was only half past twelve, and no one had plans to rise early. The conversation turned reflective, as they began to process the layers of loss, disbelief, and superstition tied to Woolgar River Station.

Finally, Malcolm asked, "So, with the whole family gone... what happened to the property?"

Owen leaned back, ready to continue the tale. As the group settled into more comfortable chairs and sofas, they prepared themselves for the next chapter in the story of Woolgar River Station.

 They all agreed that Owen was a fantastic narrator and very easy to listen to.

The Police Sergeant overseeing the incident advised us to carry on with life as best we could while waiting for word from the family's solicitor or another official. It seemed straightforward enough, but as the weeks passed, it became clear that things weren't so simple.

The Southwell family apparently didn't have a will, or at least one that could be found. Two months went by, and during that time, we were left in limbo. With no pay since the tragic accidents, our savings were dwindling, and we were at a loss for what to do next. Jenny and I started discussing whether we should leave Woolgar River Station and try to make a fresh start somewhere else, but the uncertainty of it all weighed heavily on us.

Just as we were on the verge of making a decision, we received a visit from an officer from the Queensland Public Trustee's office. He arrived with two other "Assisting Officers," as he referred to them. They were official and businesslike, asking a barrage of questions. Who were we? What was our role on the property? Did we have any connection to the Southwell family beyond our work here? The questions kept coming, and then they turned personal.

The officer wanted a detailed inventory of our personal belongings and asked if we had receipts to prove ownership. He even asked about the furniture in our house, who owned it? Was it ours or part of the estate? It felt invasive, but we understood they were trying to piece together the tangled web of ownership and responsibility left behind.

Then came the pivotal question: would we be willing to stay on and care for the property until it could be sold? The officer assured us we would be compensated at a rate nearly double what we'd been earning before, and the pay would be backdated to the date of the Southwell family's deaths. Given our financial situation and the lack of any better prospects, the answer was an immediate and resounding yes.

The officer explained the process. First, the property would be thoroughly surveyed. After that, crews would be sent in to perform any necessary repairs to make the station sale-ready. A team would also handle mustering the livestock for auction, a daunting task considering the sheer size of the property and the number of cattle.

Inside the home, every item would be cataloged and assessed. Anything deemed valuable would be sold, while less significant items would either be offered to surviving family members or disposed of. The officer made it clear that larger items, such as furniture, appliances, and electronics, things like washing machines, refrigerators, freezers, televisions, and office equipment, would remain in the house as part of the auction package. It seemed clinical and transactional, but I suppose that's just how these things are handled.

We had little choice but to accept the terms. The station had been our life for years, and despite the grim circumstances, staying on felt like the right thing to do, for us, and perhaps for the memory of the Southwell family. As we watched the officers begin their work, we couldn't help but feel the weight of the tragedy all over again. Woolgar River Station had been a thriving, lively place, but now it was being cataloged and prepped for sale, its history reduced to paperwork and financial transactions.

It was a sobering reminder of how fragile life can be and how quickly everything can change.

Lachlan Teague

After the tragic events, life on the property settled into a surprisingly manageable rhythm. For two months, we continued looking after Woolgar River Station under the oversight of the Public Trustee. When the property was finally sold, we were informed that the new owner wouldn't be arriving for at least three months. In the meantime, they asked if we would be willing to stay on, continuing our caretaking duties for the same pay.

We couldn't see any reason to refuse. Life had turned relatively comfortable, all things considered. The Public Trustee had hired two workers to manage the cattle, water bores, and fencing, which meant our workload was lighter than it had ever been. The best part was that one of the workers was our son, Barry, so having him nearby brought a sense of family back to the property. It was an odd mix of emotions, gratitude for the improved circumstances but an underlying sadness for the loss that had brought us to this point.

The new owner of Woolgar River Park, Lachlan Teague, came with a story as intricate as the land he was purchasing. Lachlan had been managing a family legacy of properties in Scotland. His father, Campbell Teague, had initially taken on his brother Alisdair's property after Alisdair departed for Australia years ago. When Campbell passed away at the age of sixty-one, Lachlan inherited the family holdings, eventually deciding to sell all three estates in Scotland and relocate to Australia in search of new opportunities.

Lachlan's search for a cattle station brought him to a property listing near Hughenden, in North Queensland. The proximity to Richmond, a regional hub, and the promise of a stable investment caught his eye. Through email correspondence with the auctioning agent in Townsville, he learned that the property was a deceased estate, which only piqued his interest further.

He conducted due diligence, reviewing valuations and reports, and decided it was worth pursuing. Lachlan engaged a solicitor in Townsville to act on his behalf, setting a bid limit of three million Australian dollars and entrusting the solicitor to handle all aspects of the purchase, including conveyancing and hiring interim staff. On the auction day, at 4 a.m. in Glasgow, Lachlan received a call informing him that he was the new owner of Woolgar River Park for a purchase price of 2.2 million Australian dollars.

During the interim, Lachlan maintained contact with me through his solicitor. He reassured us that our arrangement to stay on the property was secure and that we should let him know if any issues arose. He also notified me to expect a delivery of removal cartons for his belongings, requesting that we store them in the house until his arrival. His emails were polite and professional, and he promised to arrive in Australia within two weeks if everything went smoothly.

Lachlan's journey from Scotland to Australia was as seamless as it was lengthy. His flight from Glasgow to Sydney included only a single stop in Dubai, lasting 34 hours in total. After a brief overnight stay in Sydney, he boarded a direct flight to Townsville. Once there, he treated himself to a two-night stay at the local casino, taking the opportunity to prepare for his journey to the station.

His preparations included buying a vehicle suited for the rugged terrain of Woolgar River Park. Lachlan contacted the local BMW dealership and requested they pick him up from the casino. Within an hour of arriving at the dealership, he had purchased a demo model BMW X5, which the sales team assured him was ideal for the kind of travel he anticipated. The dealership arranged to deliver the car to him the following morning.

With his new car ready and his plans in motion, Lachlan was poised to begin his life in Australia and take the reins of Woolgar River Park. For us, the prospect of meeting the new owner was a mix of anticipation and hope. The station had weathered more tragedy than most places could bear, and perhaps Lachlan's arrival would bring some much-needed stability to the land and to all of us still tied to it.

The next morning, after collecting his new car and armed with a map and detailed directions from the dealership's Sales Manager, Lachlan Teague set out on his journey to Woolgar River Park. He arrived at the homestead around 4:30 that afternoon. As his sleek BMW X5 pulled into the driveway, Owen Harrigan and his wife Jenny stepped out to meet him, curious about the man who was now the station's new owner.

Owen paused his story to thank Lynette as she poured him another drink, before continuing his account of Lachlan's arrival.

"We'd been told by the Trustee that the new owner was a man named Lachlan Teague and that he'd be in touch with us about our next steps. Lachlan had emailed us a few times leading up to his arrival, and true to his word, he showed up right on schedule. When we saw that flash car pull up, we both exchanged a glance, half-expecting the worst, a high-and-mighty type who'd come to shake things up. But, as it turned out, we couldn't have been more wrong.

"The moment Lachlan stepped out of the car, we were struck by how polite and humble he was. When we addressed him as Mr. Teague, he immediately waved it off, saying, 'Mr. Teague was my father, and he's passed on. Please, call me Lachlan.' His easygoing demeanour put us at ease right away."

Jenny had gone the extra mile to prepare for Lachlan's arrival. She'd ordered a new sheet set, pillows, and a light doona from a shop in Townsville, and they had thankfully arrived just in time. She also made sure the kitchen refrigerator was running and stocked it with long-life milk, tea, coffee, sugar, and a packet of cream biscuits, simple gestures, but thoughtful ones.

"We took him over to the big house," Owen explained, "and Jenny showed him the room she'd made up for him. She told him, 'This will do until you get sorted. There's tea and coffee in the kitchen and milk in the fridge.' Then she casually let him know he was expected for dinner at our place that evening."

Lachlan had been genuinely touched by their efforts. He expressed his gratitude repeatedly, marvelling at the small comforts they had provided in the otherwise empty house. That first evening over dinner, the three of them hit it off splendidly. Lachlan, it turned out, had a taste for Scotch whisky and wasted no time helping Owen finish off two bottles of Johnny Walker Red Label, along with a dozen beers. It felt as though they had known each other for years.

Jenny, always the conversationalist, eventually asked Lachlan when his wife might be arriving. It wasn't difficult to guess his answer, but they let him say it. Lachlan replied in his thick Scottish brogue, "No wife, no kids, no worries." That line had them all laughing, and from that moment on, "Lachie," as they began to call him, was more like an old friend than a boss.

The following two weeks were a whirlwind. Lachie's arrival injected new energy into their lives. Together, they made multiple trips to Townsville, Charters Towers, and Hughenden to help him purchase everything he needed for the house, furniture, appliances, and enough food to fill the station's pantry. Their first outing even included a three-night stay at the Townsville Casino, where the Harrigan's got a small taste of luxury while Lachie handled his shopping. Each trip was a mix of work and leisure, with frequent stops at Alice's Pub for lunch and drinks. So many times, Jenny ended up driving them all back home because Lachie and Owen had indulged a bit too much.

Owen chuckled as he shared these memories. "We were having a grand time. Life felt almost carefree again, and I'll tell you this, Lachie could sure hold his liquor, but he was terrible at knowing when to stop!"

Lynette, interjecting with a grin, brought the storytelling to a close. "Speaking of, we're out of Scotch. You'll have to settle for beer if you want another drink. And, for the record, there's not much of that left either. I'm heading to bed, though, are you alright to get home, Owen, or would you like to stay here?"

Owen waved off her offer with a laugh, reassuring her. "The Land Rover knows its way home, don't you worry. Thanks for a fantastic meal, and thank you all for the wonderful company. We'll have to do this again soon."

With that, he staggered out the front door, waving goodnight as he climbed into his trusty vehicle. The group could hear the Land Rover rumbling down the dirt road, its sound fading into the night. Moments later, they shared a collective sigh of relief, confident that Owen had made it home safely.

Following a hearty breakfast of sausages, Sunday morning turned into a trip into Richmond for a much-needed "grog run." Gus, Malcolm, and Graham piled into Malcolm's cruiser around 10:30 a.m., the warm morning air buzzing with conversation. Predictably, the talk soon turned to the tragedy of the family that had perished at Woolgar River Park.

"It's such a tragic story," Gus said, shaking his head. "If I'd known about it before moving in, I might have thought twice. Hell, I still might sell the place."

Graham, intrigued, smirked and asked, "What's got you spooked, Gus? Don't tell me you believe in that 'curse' nonsense?"

"Well, Graham, how else do you explain it? A whole family wiped out in a matter of weeks? And what about Lachlan?" Gus added, his voice dropping. "You have to wonder if the so-called curse caught up to him too."

Before Graham could respond, Gus shifted the conversation with a curious remark. "Oh, I almost forgot to show you both the .22 cartridge case we found in the master bedroom. Lynette's been on about it, saying it's suspicious, and honestly, after hearing all this, I'm starting to see her point. I'll show you when we get back."

Once they stocked up on supplies, cartons of beer, bottles of sauvignon blanc, riesling, and two more bottles of Scotch, they stopped at the pub for a "dust-clearing" beer. The first one went down slow, but by the second round, the mood had lightened.

Alice, the bartender, greeted them with her usual good humour. "Morning, boys. Settling in alright? You all look a bit crook today."

Gus smiled wryly. "Crook or not, we had an interesting night. Ran into Owen Harrigan, and he filled us in on the Southwell family and what happened at Woolgar River Park."

Alice's cheerful demeanour dimmed for a moment. "Oh, that was just awful. Still hard to believe, five people from the same family gone within weeks. Some folks around here still talk about the 'curse.' They say it was an old Aboriginal curse put on the land."

"That right?" Malcolm leaned in, intrigued.

Alice nodded, her voice lowering conspiratorially. "Back then, the whole town was buzzing. We even had Sixty Minutes and Four Corners out here, reporters everywhere. Great for business, but it didn't last. The story faded, and no one talks much about it anymore. That'd be... what, eighteen years ago now? Since then, the only thing that's happened out there was Lachlan passing. But that was just old age, not curses."

The men finished their beers, their thoughts lingering on Alice's words, before heading back to the 'Park,' as she called it.

Back at the homestead, Malcolm reversed his car down to the laundry's back door for easier unloading. They carried the supplies to the cool room while the ladies lounged on the veranda, no doubt still dissecting the night's revelations, Gus figured. As they finished unpacking, Gus turned to Lynette.

"Why don't you show everyone that .22 cartridge case you found?" he suggested.

The group gathered in the master bedroom as Lynette recounted how she'd stumbled upon the used casing. Her measured tone and carefully pieced-together theory captivated everyone, eliciting audible gasps as she presented her thoughts.

"It does make sense," Malcolm murmured, his expression serious. Graham, however, seemed particularly affected. He paced the room, scrutinising every detail of the drapes, the bed, and the corners. Then, with a triumphant exclamation, he declared, "Yes! I most definitely concur, Lynette."

Still deep in thought, Graham suddenly asked, "Are there any gaps between the flooring and the skirting board in here?"

The question caught everyone off guard. As if on cue, they all began scanning the edges of the room. Graham dropped to his knees, peering under the bed. "Torch?" he called out.

Lynette fetched the flashlight from the walk-in robe and handed it to him. He slid further under the bed, carefully inspecting the floor. After what felt like an eternity, Graham finally emerged, dusting himself off with a satisfied grin.

"There's a gap," he announced. "About 7 to 8 millimetres high and 50 millimetres long under the skirting over here. Now, does that mean anything to anyone?"

The group exchanged uncertain glances, waiting for someone to respond. Lynette opened her mouth, ready to answer, but hesitated. She decided to let Graham have his moment, smiling to herself as he prepared to share his theory.

"The gap, ladies and gentlemen," Graham began, his voice tinged with playful theatricality, "strongly supports Lynette's theory. If someone fired a .22 automatic pistol into this bed and couldn't locate the spent cartridge case, they might assume it had rolled into this gap. At just over 5mm thick, the casing would easily fit, and they would likely stop searching. However, if no gap were present, they'd likely keep looking, perhaps even behind the drapes."

The group nodded in agreement as Gus leaned back in his chair. "Very plausible," he remarked, prompting murmurs of concurrence from the others.

Ros, ever practical, raised an unsettling question. "Does that mean someone murdered Lachlan?"

Graham hesitated, his usual jovial demeanour replaced by a serious expression. "It means," he began slowly, "that someone fired at least one shot into this bed, possibly more. Why would anyone do that? Typically, to harm someone lying there. And as Lynette pointed out, there are no bullet holes in the mattress, which only deepens the mystery. All jokes aside, this could be very serious."

The room fell quiet, the weight of Graham's words settling over them. That afternoon, the conversation revolved almost entirely around the spent casing and its implications. Graham mused aloud that proving the theory would likely require exhuming Lachlan's body for an autopsy. Still, he admitted, "A single spent .22 cartridge in a bedroom doesn't exactly scream 'call the coroner.' It's a Catch-22 of its own, wouldn't you say?"

During dinner that evening, Graham expanded on his suspicions. He mentioned that certain events following Lachlan's death, and perhaps even preceding it, warranted closer examination. "I'll be looking into Sonia Teague," he said, tapping his fork against his plate thoughtfully.

Gus interrupted. "Her name might not even be Sonia Teague. From what I've heard, she could be Sonia Harris."

The conversation tapered off as the night wore on, and the impending departure of their friends loomed over the gathering. Monday morning brought the inevitable: Malcolm and Ros, along with Graham and Stefanie, packed up their belongings and prepared to head back home.

Before leaving, Graham carefully pocketed the spent .22 casing. "I'll run some tests," he assured them. "First for fingerprints, and then to identify the firearm's manufacturer through the firing pin indent. Let's see if this leads anywhere."

Despite their reluctance to leave, everyone agreed they'd enjoyed the weekend and proposed another gathering soon, perhaps even a longer stay to fully enjoy the countryside and each other's company. As they hugged their goodbyes, plans were already forming for a future visit.

Gus and Lynette stood on the verandah, waving as their friends' vehicles disappeared into the distance. When they finally settled into their favourite chairs, Gus noticed the faraway look in Lynette's eyes. "What's on your mind?" he asked gently.

"Oh, Gus," Lynette began, her voice tinged with uncertainty. "I don't even know where to start. I do know I wouldn't have moved in if I'd known about all the tragedy tied to this place. This morning, when I walked down the hallway, I could almost see the Southwell children, grown children, emerging from their rooms, heading downstairs for breakfast. It was... haunting."

She trailed off, staring into the horizon before continuing. "When I first saw this house and the property, I thought it was beautiful. Even knowing it was for sale didn't bother me. But now, with the cartridge case, the possibility of a murder in our bedroom, and all the history here... it's hard to reconcile. I love it here, but I can't shake the feeling that this place holds secrets we're not meant to uncover."

Gus reached out and took her hand, offering a reassuring squeeze. "We'll figure it out, Lynette. One step at a time. But no matter what's happened here before, this is our home now."

Lynette nodded, though the look in her eyes suggested she wasn't entirely convinced. Together, they sat in silence, the late afternoon sun casting long shadows across the verandah.

The knowledge that an entire family had died here within a matter of days, three of them on one single night, gave Lynette an overwhelming sense of unease. The "curse" the Aboriginal man had placed on the family, was it tied to the property itself? Was the "curse" truly responsible for the tragic deaths of all the family members? The questions gnawed at her, a constant echo in her thoughts.

Had you read about the tragic events leading to their demise, everything seemed, well, possible, fluky, but possible; uncanny, but not entirely out of the realm of reason. Add to that the story of the black fella's "curse," and the whole thing began to feel absurd. "I don't know if I can keep living here, Gus," Lynette confessed, her voice tinged with uncertainty. "I do want to find out more about the place, though, especially about the mystery of that spent casing. I think there might have been a murder here. But honestly, I think the bottom line is, I need to get to the truth of all these little mysteries that keep popping up."

Gus nodded in agreement, his mind unsettled as well. Now that he knew what had transpired in the house all those years ago, he couldn't help but feel a strange sense of foreboding. But there was a comforting thought, too, it had all happened seventeen years ago. Aside from the passing of Lachlan, he didn't recall any other tragedies, save for the mess Sonia had made. He was determined to uncover what exactly had happened there, and he was sure they'd get to the bottom of it together.

They both agreed to stay and figure it all out. Gus decided to call on Willem to bring the step ladder to the laundry stairs, where the access panel to the ceiling was located. "We'll sort out this wifi," Gus told Willem, trying to keep his mind focused on the task at hand.

While Willem fetched the ladder, Gus retrieved his LED torch. They met at the access panel, where Gus, despite being a seasoned Building Surveyor, was still not a fan of ceiling spaces. He always found them a bit unnerving.

With a deep breath, Gus climbed the steps and flipped open the access panel, carefully setting it on a batten. Standing at the top of the ladder, he grabbed hold of a truss strut and slowly pulled himself up into the ceiling. He cast his light around, taking in the neatness of the space. The 50-millimetre planks spanned the roof trusses, placed at 900-millimetre centres, stretching the full length of the roof, in line with the hallway below.

Gus knew roughly where the satellite aerial was located, so he directed the beam of his torch in that direction. He immediately saw the cables hanging down from the aerial. He moved carefully along the full length of the plank walkway, then crossed over to his right, stepping gingerly along the truss chords as he followed the cables.

There were two cables, one a power cord, the other an ethernet cable. Gus continued to follow the cables with his light until he saw them disappear behind the brick chimney. He made his way along, tracking the cables until he reached their terminus: a modem fixed next to a power point on a strut. He took out his mobile phone and, squatting down next to the modem, carefully photographed the password on the bottom.

As he began to stand, preparing to make his way back to the walkway, he couldn't help but notice the overall condition of the roof structure. The trusses, roof chords, and ceiling battens were all made from hardwood, while the partition stud framing was pressed metal. A solid choice for this area, he thought, especially with the termites that seemed to wreak havoc on gates and fences nearby. From where he stood, the roof looked solid, the entire structure in sound condition.

As Gus made his way back to the access panel, he glanced to his left at the partitions. He could make out the void areas where the dropped ceilings of the wardrobes in the queen rooms lay at the far end of the building. He was almost at the access panel when something caught his attention. There was no dropped ceiling void in the last queen room.

Shining his light in that direction, he could see clearly that, from the ceiling's perspective, there was no wardrobe in that room. But he knew there was. Confused, he thought about the room again. It seemed strange, as though the ceiling height in that area should be much higher, almost as if there had been an error during construction. Maybe it had something to do with the partitioning or the linings. Gus squinted, trying to make sense of it all. It was an odd detail, one that seemed too curious to ignore, but it was just another mystery, another enigma to add to the growing list.

Getting down from a ceiling was always a relief. Gus was glad to be back on solid ground. Willem was standing patiently nearby, and Lynette had joined him. "Well, what treasures did you discover up there?" Lynette asked with a curious smile. Gus shook his head, a deep breath escaping his chest as he responded, "It's as clean as a whistle up there, just one odd thing that I'm about to check now." He gestured toward the hallway and started walking toward the first queen room, both Willem and Lynette following closely behind.

As Gus entered the first room, he made a beeline for the wardrobe. The wardrobes in this room were positioned on the left-hand side. As you walked in, there were two wardrobes on each side of the ensuite entry. The mirrored doors of the wardrobes faced into the bedroom, creating a spacious and elegant look. The 900-millimetre-wide walkthrough between the two wardrobes was framed with a transom above, measuring 2100 millimetres in height and 600 millimetres in width, perfectly matching the depth of the wardrobes.

From inside the room, the architectural effect was striking. On either side, there were large mirrored doors, and in the centre, a painted sliding door that, when opened, revealed the ensuite. It was a clever design, making the room appear neater and tidier by hiding the ensuite from view when the doors were closed.

Gus's attention shifted to the ceiling above the walkthrough. It was framed with white timber, a clean and simple feature that complemented the space.

Next, Gus moved to the second queen room. Here, the wardrobes were positioned to the right side of the room, and they appeared to be identical in layout. However, as Gus looked up at the ceiling above the walkthrough, he noticed something different. The ceiling was flush set plasterboard, no timber framing. Gus checked the wardrobe in the last queen room, and the same flush set plasterboard ceiling was present there as well.

Lynette, noticing Gus's deep concentration, asked, "What the hell are you doing?"

Gus looked over at her, offering only a cryptic "you'll see" look before heading back to the first room. He moved the chair from the desk and placed it under the walkthrough. Standing on the chair, Gus gently pressed up on the ceiling between the white timber framing. To his surprise, the ceiling shifted away from the frame with a faint creak, almost like an access panel. Gus carefully lifted the panel and moved it to the side, placing it by the right-hand wardrobe. He shone his light into the space above, revealing that plywood had been laid on the dropped ceiling framing, creating what appeared to be a hidden shelf.

"Anything in there, Gus?" Lynette asked, her voice tinged with curiosity.

Gus paused for a moment, his light scanning the hidden space. "It might be the missing rifles," he said, reaching in to grab one.

"No! No, Gus, don't touch anything!" Lynette exclaimed. "There could be prints on those. I'll get you some rubber gloves." She hurried off to the kitchen but returned a moment later, her brow furrowed. "Actually, it might be better to leave them there until I talk to Graham."

Reluctantly, Gus stepped back, shining his light on the other side of the shelf. There, tucked away behind the rifles, he saw a small timber box. He called down to Lynette, describing the box's dimensions, roughly 350 millimetres long, 200 millimetres wide, and 100 millimetres deep, and the name written on its top. "It's got a name on it. M-A-R-G-O-L-I-N M-C-M," Gus read out, though he couldn't make out the full details since the box was upside down.

Lynette, eager to note the name, pulled out her mobile phone and typed it into her memo app. Gus continued, describing other items he could see in the box: a shot shell belt, some Winchester X shot shell boxes, and several smaller boxes. But the lighting wasn't good enough for him to get a clear view of everything.

"Interesting," Gus muttered to himself as he climbed down from the chair and turned to face Lynette.

"So, I wonder who Margolin, MCM is?" Gus mused aloud. "More mysteries to unravel."

Willem, who had been silently observing, turned to Gus with a grin. "Did you get the Wi-Fi passwords or not?" he asked, half-joking. Gus laughed and nodded, pulling out his phone. "I'll text it to you," he replied.

Lynette, still processing what they had found, said, "I'll contact Graham tomorrow, let him know what we've discovered, and ask for his advice. I'll also ask if he can come up and take prints from the rifles and that mysterious box."

The next day, Tuesday, Gus took a moment to call Peter Lansky at the stock agents' office in Richmond. "Sorry I didn't get back to you last week," Gus said, his tone apologetic. "You know how things turn out, I just ran out of time. But I wanted to check in and see if you could come out to assess the property this week. We need to get things moving."

Peter's response was encouraging. He was already in contact with a company that was looking to agist around three thousand head of cattle and could likely make it out tomorrow afternoon. "I'll look forward to seeing you then," Gus replied, relieved that things were finally falling into place.

Gus decided to take a drive down the track to see Owen, figuring it was a good time for a chat. As he arrived, he found Owen tinkering under the bonnet of his old Land Rover. The sound of the Landcruiser's engine caught Owen's attention, and he emerged from beneath the bonnet with a grin. "If you've come for a cold beer, then you're in luck," he said.

"Sounds like a plan to me," Gus replied, following Owen up to the verandah. Owen disappeared inside for a moment and returned with two ice-cold XXXX Gold stubbies. They settled onto the verandah, the warm afternoon sun casting a relaxed glow over the scene.

Owen took a long sip from his bottle and nodded, reflecting on the previous night's dinner. "That was a great evening, Gus. Thanks for the food and drinks. I promise we'll return the favour, get you and Lynette around for dinner before too long."

Gus nodded, his mind already moving on to business. "Actually, Owen, I wanted to run something by you. I'm thinking about cattle agistment for the property."

Owen raised an eyebrow. "Agistment, eh? Sounds like a good way to go, but you'll need some solid people to look after the cattle, pumps, and fences."

Gus gave a wry smile. "That's exactly why I'm here. I'd like to offer you the job."

Owen's face darkened a little, and he shook his head. "I'm too old for that sort of work now, Gus. But I can organise a crew for you. In return, I'd want rent here at the house. I've got my son, Barry, in mind. He'll take care of the bulk of the work, and I know two of his mates who'd be keen to help as well. Barry can stay here with me, and the others can camp out at the other house near the Homestead."

Gus listened intently, impressed by Owen's resourcefulness. "That sounds like it could work, Owen. What do you think about scaling up the agistment herd? Six or seven thousand head would need only one extra hand, right? More money in the bank, too."

Owen grinned. "Exactly. The more cattle you've got, the easier it is to manage. A good-sized herd and the right crew, and you're set."

Gus nodded in agreement, his thoughts turning to the practicalities of the operation. "Peter Lansky's coming out tomorrow afternoon to assess the property."

Owen's expression soured. "That thieving prick Lansky? You'd be better off with Dillons at Hughenden. They're straight shooters, but if you've got to deal with Lansky, just steer him toward me before you let him look around. I'll sort him out for you."

Gus chuckled. "Alright, Owen, you're on. But I insist on a wage as well as the house. No one's working here for nothing."

Owen gave a half-laugh, his tone matter-of-fact. "At my age, I won't be doing too much of the heavy lifting, Gus. That'll be the boys' job. But I'll make sure everything gets done properly. If you insist on paying me a wage, well... I don't want to be on the wrong side of you, so you pay me whatever you think's fair."

He held out his hand for a handshake. Gus took it firmly, sealing the agreement. They cracked open two more beers, chatting more casually about the future, before Gus finally headed back home, feeling a sense of relief. "Forget the curse," he thought to himself. "This could be a good business. Owen's the right man to look after the agistment side of things. And maybe Willem can help out too as the extra hand Owen mentioned."

Meanwhile, back at the house, Graham Jamison was listening to Lynette as she explained the discovery of the rifles in the hidden storage area. She suggested that it might be a good idea to have Graham fingerprint the rifles. But Graham's interest seemed to be waning. The test results on the cartridge hadn't yet been revealed, and he was still waiting on the lab to get back to him. Besides, his job wasn't officially on the books, so he didn't want to stir up too much attention.

Half-listening, Graham's interest piqued again when Lynette mentioned the mysterious box. She could tell something had caught his attention when he straightened in his chair and asked, "Spell that again."

"Margolin," she said, repeating the name written on the box.

Graham's eyes widened. "Margolin? That's the make of a Russian target pistol. Was there a pistol in the box?"

Lynette hesitated, then said, "We didn't open it. It's still up in the ceiling space. We didn't want to disturb anything in case there were prints on it."

Graham's voice became more urgent. "Alright, listen. I want you to get the box down. Wear gloves, just in case, but check if there's a pistol inside. If there is, I'll arrange for a police courier to take it to Townsville for ballistic testing. We'll see if the spent casing matches. I'll also send a print kit with the courier. You can dust for prints on the rifles, take photos of everything, and email them to me."

Lynette agreed, and Graham added, "When's a good time for the courier to come by?"

"Anytime, as long as they call me first," Lynette replied.

"Great," said Graham. "Call me back as soon as you've got the box down and checked."

Later that day, Lynette donned disposable kitchen gloves and carefully took the steps up to the first queen room. She retrieved the box, its weight confirming her suspicion that it likely contained the pistol. She took it downstairs to the office, placing it gently on the desk. With steady hands, she undid the clasps on the leather carry handle and opened the lid.

Inside was an elegant black target pistol, strikingly similar to a Luger at first glance. The pistol was nestled securely in its compartment within the box, alongside two magazines, one of which was loaded, and various accessories, including a cleaning rod, barrel weights, an oil bottle, and a small screwdriver.

Lynette carefully closed the box and called Graham back, her heart racing as she shared the discovery.

The following day, as Gus was preparing for Peter Lansky's visit, he received a call from Constable Kathy Green. She needed to arrange the collection of an item for Townsville Ballistics, the same time Peter Lansky was on his way to assess the property. Things were moving quickly now, and Gus couldn't shake the feeling that everything was about to take a sharp turn, one way or another.

The constable was the first to arrive, pulling up in her brightly coloured highway patrol car just before midday. She had driven the five hundred kilometres from Townsville that morning, and despite the long journey, she seemed upbeat and efficient. After introducing herself, she handed Lynette the fingerprint kit, a small, professionally packaged set of tools, and explained how to use it to dust for prints.

As she spoke, it was clear that she was already familiar with Lynette's background, word had obviously spread about Lynette's previous role as a police sergeant. The constable seemed comfortable in Lynette's presence, and they quickly settled into a relaxed conversation. The constable asked about Lynette's life since her time in the force, and Lynette was happy to chat, though always with one eye on the task at hand. It was a welcome distraction from the tension building around the mystery of the rifles and the pistol.

After a few minutes of friendly banter, the constable asked if Lynette was in need of anything else. When Lynette mentioned she could use a bit of a break, the constable offered to make a coffee. They enjoyed a quiet, shared moment, sipping their drinks and nibbling on toasted sandwiches that Lynette had prepared earlier. The casual exchange was a brief respite, a moment of normalcy in what had become an increasingly strange and tense situation.

Once they had finished their meal, the constable packed up the fingerprint kit, checked the contents of the box containing the Margolin pistol, and carefully secured it again. "I'll take this back to Townsville with me," she said, her tone professional but with a hint of understanding that this was no ordinary case. "I'll make sure it gets to Ballistics as soon as possible. I'll also get a courier to pick up the rifles. You've got a good handle on things, Lynette. I'll let you know what we find."

Lynette nodded, grateful for her calm and capable presence. The constable then made her way back to the car, and after one final glance at the property, she drove off toward Townsville. Lynette watched her go, feeling the weight of the case growing heavier. There was no telling what the results would reveal, but one thing was clear, this mystery was far from over.

As the constable's car disappeared down the track, Lynette's mind turned to the next steps. She had the print kit, and now it was time to carefully examine everything that had been found. She wasn't sure where all of this would lead, but there was no going back now.

Peter Lansky arrived just as the marked police car was pulling away, giving Gus a quizzical look as he approached. Gus, always quick with an explanation, shrugged and smiled. "Just one of Lynette's police friends dropping by," he remarked, not bothering to elaborate further. "Hop in the cruiser, and I'll take you over to Owen's place."

"Owen?" Peter asked, raising an eyebrow. "I thought Barry would be the one to show me the grazing conditions."

Gus nodded, but clarified, "Barry will be handling all the grazing, watering, and welfare of the agistment cattle. He'll be in charge of the day-to-day operations. But Owen's overseeing the whole operation, agistment conditions, costings, and logistics. He's got the experience for that." Gus could tell that Peter wasn't too keen on the arrangement, but there was no time to dwell on it.

They drove to Owen's place, where the two men exchanged pleasantries before heading up to the verandah. Gus had hoped to use the homestead's newly acquired office for the negotiations, it was professional and impressive, something he thought would be more fitting for a deal of this scale. However, Owen had other ideas. "Lansky doesn't rate high enough for the office," Owen had said with a grin. "Banker's psychology. We'll keep it simple here."

Owen wasted no time getting to the point. He looked at Peter and said, "We're aiming for a minimum of six thousand head. If we can't settle on four dollars and fifty cents per head, plus any vet bills, minus the stock transport by road, and in accordance with the Animals Care and Protection Act 2001, then this trip's a waste of time. And that's straight to the point," Owen added firmly.

Peter seemed slightly caught off guard but responded, "I don't have six thousand head right now. It's just over four thousand."

Owen nodded, unfazed. "Then we'll need around five dollars fifty per head for less than six thousand. I'm not interested in anything less than that. For six thousand, we'll drop it to four-fifty, but not a penny less."

Peter Lansky, now looking a little more perturbed, agreed to the five-fifty price for the current four thousand head. He added, "I'll have the numbers up to six thousand within a month, and then we'll drop the rate to four-fifty."

Owen wasn't having any of the "almost six thousand" talk. "It'll need to be six thousand," he said firmly. "Not five thousand nine hundred and ninety-nine, mind you. It has to be six thousand, no exceptions."

Peter, a bit flustered, agreed and pulled out the contract form. The terms were quickly discussed, and when it came to the duration of the agistment, it was agreed upon as six months with an option to extend. Owen noted that agistment availability would start in two weeks.

Peter, eager to get the ball rolling, mentioned that he hoped to begin next week with the first road trains, each carrying one hundred and ten bullocks. He explained that he could get five road trains per day, so it would take almost two weeks to transport the four thousand head to the property. Owen nodded approvingly, saying they'd be ready. "We'll just have to lay down some extra road base in front of the yards after the last wet," he added casually.

The deal was sealed. Peter signed the contract, and Owen made a quick call to his son Barry, telling him to come out the following Saturday to meet Gus. The BBQ at Owen's place was planned, and though Gus and Lynette hadn't been informed ahead of time, they agreed it would be a good chance to meet Barry and catch up.

Later that morning, Lynette received an urgent call from Graham Jamison. His voice was serious as he told her the news. "The spent cartridge you found in the bedroom? It was fired in the Margolin pistol you discovered in the house," he said, his tone now taking on a darker edge. "The police are seeking a court order to exhume Lachlan Teague's body."

Lynette felt a chill at the news, the weight of the situation growing heavier. Graham asked her not to share the information with anyone yet, as the investigation was still unfolding. He also asked about the fingerprinting progress, to which Lynette replied that she planned to get them done that day.

Graham offered a solution, suggesting that the forensics team would be in Richmond for the exhumation and that they could assist with the prints if Lynette preferred. She agreed, grateful for the expertise. She hadn't worked with prints in years, certainly not since her training days. She promised to have everything ready for them.

When Gus heard the news, he just shook his head, a mix of disbelief and frustration written across his face. The situation had escalated from strange to something far more sinister, and he could feel the tension growing by the day. There was definitely no turning back now.

Dinner on Saturday night at Owen's place was a memorable BBQ and an evening full of good food, laughter, and conversation. It was also the first time Gus and Lynette had the chance to meet Barry, Owen's son. Barry, despite being a large and imposing figure, had a gentle, almost slow demeanor. His kindness and warmth were immediately apparent, and it quickly became clear that he was a deeply humble person. He seemed grateful to be back in his old job, and his sincere appreciation for the opportunity made a strong impression. Though he was quiet, his pleasant nature stood out, and everyone enjoyed his company.

After dinner, the evening unfolded as it often did in these parts, with drinks on the verandah. The warm air, the laughter, and the stars overhead created a relaxed atmosphere that encouraged people to linger. While most everyone enjoyed a drink or two, Barry, being a non-drinker, stuck to a steady supply of Coke cans throughout the evening. He seemed content with his soft drink of choice, nursing the cans as the conversation flowed. Eventually, when the night drew to a close, Barry retired early to bed, where he was staying with his father Owen.

During the evening, Lynette brought up the topic of Sonia Teague. It was something that had been weighing on her mind ever since the mysterious woman had entered the scene. Owen's response was less than flattering. He explained that Sonia was not actually married to Lachlan, nor had she ever been. In fact, she had seemingly taken the name "Teague" on her own initiative, perhaps to align herself with Lachlan in some way, though they had never been a couple.

Owen's recollections painted a picture of a woman who had woven herself into Lachlan's life in a way that seemed both opportunistic and manipulative. Lachlan had often confided in Owen, saying he regretted ever employing her. Despite Sonia's efficiency as a housekeeper, Owen said Lachlan had always felt she had overstayed her welcome. She had never lived in the main house, instead residing in one of the smaller two-bedroom homes on the property. Lachlan had been clear about not wanting her in the main house, though Sonia frequently came up with excuses to stay there.

As Lachlan's health declined, Owen explained, Sonia had gradually taken control of everything. It was during this time that she began referring to herself as "Sonia Teague" when placing orders for goods or coordinating with tradespeople. Owen had heard through the grapevine, from locals in the Richmond pub, that Sonia had been telling people she and Lachlan had secretly married a couple of years ago, something that seemed to be more of a fabrication than a reality.

Over the last year of Lachlan's life, Sonia had become increasingly difficult. Owen, who had often been a regular visitor at the big house, used to stroll in unannounced for breakfast with Lachlan or to share a drink. But soon, the house was always locked. When he would knock, Sonia would answer the door and shush him, explaining that Lachlan wasn't well and needed rest. Owen said it became a regular occurrence, with Sonia turning him away more and more. By the end, he could count on one hand the number of times he actually saw Lachlan before his death. When he did see him, Lachlan was in terrible shape, coughing painfully and unable to finish his sentences.

Lachlan had told Owen that the doctor had diagnosed him with ulcers and wanted to perform surgery, but Lachlan had refused. Instead, the doctor had prescribed a medicine that would supposedly clear the ulcers over time, though Owen was skeptical of such a treatment. Lachlan's condition worsened, and one morning, Sonia arrived at the Manager's House to announce, almost casually, that Lachlan had passed away. The coldness of her delivery stuck with Owen, and he muttered to himself, "Fucking bitch."

The next morning, just before the first cattle were due to arrive, Barry came up to the house to speak with Gus. He explained that one of the workers who was supposed to start that day had failed to show up, and it seemed unlikely that he ever would. Barry mentioned that his father had suggested Gus might have someone he could use. Gus, always ready to help, agreed and took Barry down to meet Willem, who had been somewhat idle since arriving.

While Hailee and Janice were busy every day, helping Lynette with cleaning, painting, and various jobs around the house, Willem had found himself without much to do. He'd occasionally run errands to Richmond for the girls, but that was about the extent of his tasks. Gus was confident that Willem could step up and help Barry with the cattle, so the two of them would make a good team. It seemed that everyone had their place, and the morning's events had only reinforced Gus's belief that the agistment operation was on the right track.

Barry approached Willem early in the morning, explaining that he needed help with bore runs and maintenance on the fences. Willem, eager to contribute, was more than happy to have some work to do. It had been a slow start since his arrival, so this was exactly what he needed. Barry then turned to Gus, adding that he would require a station vehicle for himself, as well as one for Willem. He also mentioned that once the cattle arrived, they would need a few quads for managing the herds. Barry seemed to assume that Owen had already discussed this with Gus, but it was news to Gus.

Gus had initially thought about suggesting that Barry get his old ute back but quickly reconsidered, realising he had grown rather fond of it. Instead, he assured Barry that he would arrange for some additional vehicles for the property that afternoon. He also asked Barry what kind of quads they would need. Barry responded with a very specific request: Yamaha 250 Grizzly 4WDs. He explained that these were perfect for the wet conditions around the property, especially when it got greasy after rain. Gus nodded, making a mental note of the model.

Later that day, Gus set off to search for the vehicles. He called around for used Landcruiser ute's and found two options at Charters Towers Toyota. One was a nearly new 2018 model, a top-of-the-line version with a steel body, bucket seats, and extra features like electric windows, air conditioning, and cruise control. The other was a 2000 model, much older but still functional. Gus decided to take both of them. A deal was struck, and Gus transferred the funds to the dealership, planning to pick them up on Wednesday.

Next, Gus contacted a local dealership in Charters Towers that sold quad bikes. They had several Yamaha Grizzly 250 4WD bikes in stock, and Gus worked out a deal for three. He transferred the funds for the bikes, which were ready for pickup on Wednesday as well.

That evening, Gus informed Barry that he would be able to get his old ute back. Barry was thrilled at the news, visibly excited to have his vehicle restored to him. Gus also told him that the three of them, Gus, Barry, and Willem, would be heading to Charters Towers the next day to pick up the vehicles. Barry was impressed with how quickly things were progressing and remarked that it was good to see some real action happening on the property again.

Wednesday morning arrived, and Gus, Barry, and Willem packed into the front of the Landcruiser for the long drive to Charters Towers. It was a cramped journey, but they were all in good spirits, eager to get the new vehicles. They left at six in the morning, aiming to return by three that afternoon. After a four-hour drive, they arrived at the Toyota dealership. Gus and Willem stayed behind to pick up the ute's, while Barry headed to the Yamaha dealership just down the road to collect the quad bikes.

Gus met with the salesman at the Toyota dealership, completing the registration paperwork for the two ute's. The salesman, recognising the Teague name, expressed his condolences for Lachlan's passing. It was clear that Lachlan had been a loyal customer, having purchased a 2006 model from the dealership not long before his death. Gus thanked the salesman and moved on, ready to collect the vehicles.

Willem, meanwhile, took the 2000 model Landcruiser and drove to the Yamaha dealership to meet Barry and load the quad bikes onto the ute's. Gus had to purchase six pairs of ratchet tie-down straps at the Yamaha dealership to secure the bikes. When the dealer asked if they had a loading ramp, Barry explained that they had one at the property, which was a relief. Gus couldn't understand why the dealer couldn't have thrown in the tie-down straps, given he was purchasing three new bikes from him. Instead, Gus grumbled about the extra cost, twenty-four thousand dollars for three quad bikes, and the dealer couldn't even offer a small courtesy like that. At least the Toyota dealership had filled both utes with about two hundred dollars' worth of diesel, which helped soften the blow.

As they made their way back, Gus couldn't help but be impressed with the nearly new cruiser ute he'd acquired. The ride was noticeably smoother than his 2006 model, and the comfort level was much higher, especially with the added bonus of air conditioning.

They arrived back at the homestead around three-thirty in the afternoon. Gus and Willem followed Barry to the loading ramp behind the cattle yards, where they unloaded the quad bikes. They ferried two of the bikes back to the shed at the homestead and then returned to the loading ramp to grab the last bike. Afterward, they took the utes to their respective places, with Gus feeling satisfied with the progress made. The day had been long, but the vehicles and equipment were now in place, and the property was ready to tackle the upcoming agistment operations head-on.

After a long day of driving, Gus finally returned to the house, exhausted but satisfied with the progress made. He found Lynette in the bar, and the two of them settled in for a quiet moment together, each with a cold beer in hand. The stress of the day began to melt away as they chatted, but soon, Lynette raised a question that had been on her mind.

"Where is all the money coming from to buy all these new ute's and quad bikes?" she asked, her brow furrowed in curiosity.

Gus, taking a sip of his beer, smiled and pulled his laptop closer. He opened up the spreadsheet he had been working on for the agistment herd. The numbers on the screen were still in the early stages, but they were already impressive. Gus pointed out the projected turnover for the incoming stock, his eyes widening as he explained, "At this rate, we're looking at an annual agistment turnover of about one point four million dollars."

Lynette's eyes widened as she took in the figure. Gus continued, "I'm still setting up the spreadsheet, so I don't have exact costs yet, but even if we factor in sixty percent in expenses, which is likely on the high side, we're still looking at a profit of around six hundred thousand dollars. And those expenses, like the ute's and quads, will be tax offsets."

Gus leaned back, looking thoughtful. "I also plan on asking Malcolm if he can recommend an accountant to help us with the books. It's not really my area of expertise, and we'll need someone to keep everything in order as things get busier."

Lynette nodded, impressed with the clear plan Gus had laid out. She could see how the operation was growing, and while it was still early days, the future seemed bright. The cattle had begun arriving, everything appeared to be running smoothly, and the tension that had been building for weeks seemed to be lifting.

With the day's work done, and the major purchases now in place, both Gus and Lynette found themselves relaxing more. The weight of uncertainty had begun to lift, and the pieces of the operation were falling into place. It felt like the beginning of something substantial, and the signs were all pointing toward success.

They chatted for a while longer, both of them savouring the sense of progress and relief. There was still a long road ahead, but for the first time in weeks, they allowed themselves to enjoy the moment and look forward to the future with renewed optimism. Things were looking good, and both of them could sense the promising changes ahead.

Graham Jamison had called Lynette with some chilling news that sent a wave of disbelief through her. "Lynette," he began, his tone serious, "we've found a projectile in the skull of Lachlan Teague. It's a .22 calibre round, and the ballistics team has confirmed that it matches the ammunition from the Margolin target pistol you found."

Lynette's stomach tightened as Graham continued. "The ammo is designed for target shooting at 25 meters. It's a low-velocity round, and it seems the pistol was placed in Lachlan's ear and fired. The round likely killed him instantly, though it didn't exit, which is why we didn't find an exit wound or bloodstains on the mattress."

Graham paused for a moment before adding, "I'll be heading up there tomorrow with the forensic team to take prints and photographs. We'll get to the bottom of this. But, Lynette, I should let you know, though you and Gus are not suspects, it's better that you stay clear of the scene, just to keep everything above board. If I do happen to stay for dinner and a few too many drinks, well, shit happens, right?"

Lynette's heart sank as she absorbed the gravity of the situation. While it was a shock, it wasn't entirely unexpected. She'd suspected a shooting from the moment she found the casing, and the discovery of the Margolin had only confirmed her theory. Graham had just solidified what she already suspected.

But there was more. "That's not all, Lynette," Graham continued. "While they were exhuming the body, they ran some tests that were still possible given the stage of decomposition. They found a strange substance in Lachlan's system, 'Brodifacoum'."

Lynette frowned, puzzled. "Brodifacoum? That sounds familiar. Isn't it something in rat poison?"

"Yes, it's very common," Graham confirmed. "It's found in rat poison, probably in every house, but the level found in Lachlan's system was far beyond what anyone would normally ingest. It's not something you just consume by accident."

Lynette felt a chill run down her spine. Not only had Lachlan been shot, but he'd also been poisoned. The thought was staggering. "Well, that's just great," she muttered. "I'll have plenty to discuss with you tomorrow when I see you."

After the call, Lynette was left in a daze, the weight of the information settling heavily on her. She knew she had to tell Gus. He was most likely out at the cattle yards, but she didn't want to delay the news.

She hopped into the Subaru, parked next to the BMW, remembering that the new key with the transponder had arrived the week before. She'd been too busy to try it out, but now seemed like a good time. Locking the Subaru, she went back inside to grab the key.

The car started instantly. It had been sitting for a while, but the fuel gauge was almost full, and the tan leather seats felt luxuriously soft and comfortable. She put the car into reverse and was impressed by how smoothly it handled. The vehicle purred like a kitten as she reversed out of the driveway. "Very nice," she thought, noticing the all-around camera system that switched off once she selected drive. "This car's got all the bells and whistles."

As she headed toward the cattle yards, about six kilometres away, Lynette couldn't help but enjoy the power of the dual-turbo engine. She pressed the accelerator just a little, and the car shot forward. "Woo woo!" she laughed, easing off the gas as she got a feel for the car. "This little baby wants to boogey," she said aloud, impressed by how smooth and powerful it felt. She smiled to herself. My machine now, she thought.

When she arrived at the cattle yards, she saw two road trains waiting to unload. There were at least two hundred head of cattle already in the yard, with a road train just pulling out. She spotted Gus's new Landcruiser parked next to Barry's and headed over to him. Gus, who hadn't been able to get out of his new ute all day, was clearly enjoying it.

As she pulled up, Gus walked over, his eyebrows raised. "I wondered who the hell it was when I saw that car," he said with a grin. "Nice wheels you've got there, miss."

Lynette smiled mischievously. "Well, don't look too hard, brother, because these wheels are mine. You've got your ute, and I've got my Beamer." Then, with a more serious tone, she added, "You'd better come home. I've got some big news."

They sat on the verandah with icy beers as Lynette began to tell Gus about the murder investigation. She left nothing out of Graham's phone call, detailing everything from the bullet to the poison. "He'll be here tomorrow morning," she concluded.

Gus leaned back, his eyes wide with astonishment. "Well, fuck me. You were onto that from the moment you found that casing," he said, shaking his head in admiration. He leaned across and kissed her. "You're a fucking legend, Lynette. I mean, if anyone else had found that casing, it would've just ended up in the bin, and if you weren't here, I'd probably be out there shooting with that damn gun. Good on you."

Despite the grim circumstances, Lynette couldn't help but feel a little proud of herself. But Gus's tone turned somber as he added, "It's sad, though. His life got cut short by that bitch."

Lynette quickly interrupted. "We don't know who killed him yet, Gus. You can't go around making accusations like that."

He sighed. "Well, who else could it have been?"

"You'll just have to wait and see what comes out," Lynette said, trying to remain neutral. "But I bet you London to a brick it's that bitch."

Gus raised an eyebrow, a small smirk playing on his lips. "Would you bet your new ute on it?"

Lynette laughed. "Not my new ute, but I still bet it's her."

"Well, we'll find out soon enough. Now, it's your shout," Gus said with a wink.

Graham had arrived alone in his unmarked police car just after 10 a.m. the next morning, his forensic team following about half an hour later. Quick hellos were exchanged, and then they all got straight to work, beginning with the concealed area above the queen room's ensuite entry. The forensic officers were stunned by how Gus had managed to find it, with some of them casting suspicious glances at him, as though they couldn't fathom how he had discovered the hidden space.

When Gus led them up into the ceiling and pointed out what he considered a clear anomaly below, the forensic team was completely baffled. They couldn't see anything that appeared suspicious. Gus, feeling a mixture of frustration and disbelief, thought they were as "dumb as dog shit" for failing to spot such a glaring mistake in construction. He showed them how the ceilings of the wardrobes in the other queen rooms had been designed as "dropped" ceilings, then pointed out that this particular robe ceiling wasn't dropped.

"How do you know there's a void underneath if you can't see it?" asked a Senior Sergeant, clearly skeptical.

Gus couldn't believe the question. Did they really think he had known about all these hidden spaces beforehand? "You must have known there was a place to hide things," the Sergeant pressed, "how would anyone know just by looking? It's impossible."

Gus, feeling exasperated, just let it go. He wasn't sure whether the officers were genuinely confused or if they were just trying to cover up their own lack of knowledge. Either way, he was done trying to explain.

The forensic team proceeded to take around 3,000 photographs of the ceiling area and the concealed space above the walkthrough. They meticulously photographed the rifles at least twenty times before carefully moving them to their special police van. They dusted for fingerprints on every surface, the access panel, the removable ceiling section, and the surrounding areas.

Next, they went to the bedroom where Lynette had found the cartridge casing. Lynette had to recount the entire sequence of events at least nine times, each time more patiently than the last. The forensic officers took photos of the drapes, the bed, and the window frame. Lynette was asked to pull back the bed sheets to expose the mattress, where the casing had been discovered.

When Gus and Lynette thought they were finally finished, the forensic team requested to inspect the kitchen. They dusted for prints in the kitchen, the butler's pantry, the dining area, and even around the front entry and the house perimeter. The investigation felt endless, with every inch of the house thoroughly examined. After about five hours, the forensic team packed up and left, heading back to Hughenden where they would be staying. They informed Gus and Lynette that they had concluded taking any further evidence and didn't anticipate returning.

Once the forensic team had departed, Graham suggested a meeting on the verandah to discuss what had transpired. Lynette, aware that Graham was officially working, offered him a Coke. He looked at her, his face weary but amused. "Please tell me you're joking, Lynette," he said with a dry laugh. "After driving up here for five hours and dealing with those boffins for another five, I think something a little more substantial might be more beneficial."

With a grin, Lynette handed him a cold beer and asked Gus if he was ready for another, passing him one as well.

Graham took the beer and leaned back in his chair, stretching his legs out. "I'd like to interview Owen tomorrow regarding Sonia, whatever her name might be," he said, his tone thoughtful.

Lynette brought over more beers as Graham dug a file out of his laptop bag. He passed it to her, saying, "Have a read of this. It's Jason Strange's statement and declaration."

Lynette flipped open the file and began reading aloud for Gus and Graham to hear. Her voice was steady, but the contents of the statement seemed to carry a weight that made the air feel heavier. As she read through it, both Gus and Graham listened intently, the gravity of the situation sinking in with every word.

Jason Strange's statement was a significant piece of the puzzle. It painted a picture of events and people that Gus and Lynette hadn't fully understood until now. The more she read, the clearer it became that they were dealing with something much larger than they had initially thought. This wasn't just about the murder investigation anymore, it was about unraveling a web of lies, betrayal, and manipulation that reached further than they could have imagined.

Once she finished, Lynette looked up, her eyes meeting Graham's. "Well," she said, her voice low but resolute, "looks like we have a lot more to figure out."

Queensland Police: Statement from Jason Strange

Mrs. Teague first contacted me on a Tuesday in March 2021 regarding the sale of her property. She provided a brief description of the property and mentioned she could email me a more detailed description along with photographs of the four dwellings on the land. She was looking for a quick sale and was asking for exactly $2.1 million, then asked if I would broker the sale.

I explained that things were not quite that simple. Before we could discuss numbers, we needed to gather some basic facts. I suggested she send me the information she had, including a description and any photographs. Once I received the details, I would arrange a time to visit the property, bringing with me a sales engagement contract for her to sign.

I also asked if the property was solely in one name, and she told me it was jointly owned with her husband, Lachlan Teague. She then sent me the email with the details and photographs, and I was genuinely impressed. In fact, I couldn't wait to get it listed. As an estate agent, the goal is always a quick sale, and this property looked like it had a lot of potential.

After reviewing the photos and description, I knew this place would sell fast. I reached out to a friend of mine, Richard Kemp, who's a solicitor specialising in conveyancing. I told him about this opportunity where we could potentially make millions. We discussed forming a company with both of us as directors, buying the property as soon as it was listed, holding onto it for two years to avoid capital gains tax, and then selling it for $7 to $8 million. It seemed like a golden opportunity. If all went to plan, I could pocket a million or more, and Richard would do the same. We decided to move forward with the idea.

Richard's office is in Firebrace Street, Horsham, Victoria.

I made an appointment with Mrs. Teague to meet her at the property and went out there to see it firsthand. She had one of her workers, Barry, drive me around the property, and then she showed me the Manager's Cottage and a two-bedroom cottage, which were both tenanted. She mentioned that there was another identical two-bedroom cottage a bit farther from the homestead, but I didn't get to see it on my tour with Barry.

Next, Mrs. Teague showed me the main house. We toured the downstairs areas first, and then she took me upstairs. There was one room that I couldn't view, as her sister was staying there for the month and wasn't feeling well. Mrs. Teague assured me that the room was almost identical to another "king" room in the house.

She explained that the property would be sold without stock or machinery, though the furniture would be negotiable. We sat at the table on the verandah, where she handed me a Coke. I pretended to do some calculations on my laptop, confirming various details. She seemed a bit anxious, so I reassured her that while $2.1 million might be pushing it, $1.8 to $1.9 million should be an acceptable offer. I wanted this deal, though, and I could see the potential for a huge profit, so I suggested, "Let's go for $2.3 million and see what we get."

Mrs. Teague was thrilled with this suggestion and agreed to it. She said she would have Mr. Teague come over from the cattle yards to sign the contract while I prepared the sales and marketing documents. I saw her walk over to the Manager's House, where she spoke to Barry, who drove off and returned a few minutes later with Mr. Teague.

To be honest, he didn't look like I expected. He appeared a bit scruffy, especially compared to Mrs. Teague, who was very well-dressed. She warned me, with a lovely smile, not to engage Mr. Teague too much in conversation as he was suffering from Alzheimer's, and it would only confuse him. "Just point to where he needs to sign, okay?" she said.

Mr. Teague walked up to us, looked at the paperwork, and asked, "Where do I sign?" I showed him the five places to sign, and he did so without question, flipping the pages as I indicated. When he was finished, he asked if that was all, then turned around and walked back to Barry's ute, getting in and being driven away. Mrs. Teague sighed next to his signature and I witnessed all of it.

It struck me as a bit strange, but honestly, I didn't care. I had the listing, and I knew it would make me a lot of money.

A week later, I called Mrs. Teague to let her know I had a contract for the sale of the property. She seemed a little confused, responding, "Yes, you were here last week." I explained that the property had sold, and we had a contract for $2.1 million. She confirmed that was the price she wanted, and I told her I would come out the next day to get the contract signed. She mentioned that no one had visited the property yet, but I assured her I would explain everything when I arrived.

I was eager to get the sale finalised, so I drove out the next day. Mrs. Teague offered me another Coke, and this time, she called Mr. Teague on his mobile. Soon after, he arrived at the verandah and signed the contract, just like before. He was in and out quickly. Mrs. Teague signed as well, and I witnessed the entire process.

When I asked her for the name of her solicitor, she said she would need to call me back with that information. Seizing the opportunity, I suggested I could refer her to Richard, the solicitor I knew who specialised in conveyancing. I mentioned that he was a straightforward professional, didn't fuss with unnecessary formalities, and would accept most things by email.

Mrs. Teague agreed to use Richard, thinking it was just conveyancing after all.

As we know, everything came crashing down just a week before settlement. The entire deal fell apart, and I was exposed for insider trading. I am now awaiting charges for that and several other criminal offences.

Richard, my friend in Horsham, has also been arrested and is facing similar charges.

I, Jason Strange, of Charters Towers, Queensland, do solemnly swear that the above statement is true and accurate to the best of my knowledge. This statement was signed at the Law Courts of Australia, Townsville, in 2021.

"Wow, you've been busy, Graham," Lynette said, genuinely impressed by the progress so far.

"Well, that's why I need to talk to Owen," Graham replied, his expression turning more serious. "We think he may have been impersonating Mr. Teague and signing these documents. We know Barry was involved in getting the signatures for the initial signing, but before we bring him into this mess, I'd like to give Owen a chance to come clean."

Graham glanced at Gus, who had been unusually quiet. "Are you alright there, Gus? You've gone a bit quiet."

"No, Graham," Gus said with a sigh, frustration lacing his words. "I'm far from alright. I've just brought in four thousand head of cattle and am expecting another two thousand next month. And the only thing I know about cattle is how to cook and eat them. You're about to arrest the only two guys on this property who know how to handle six thousand head of cattle!" Gus paused, his voice thick with anxiety. "And Graham, I'm really starting to worry here. Hell, I'm starting to think the worst thing that ever happened to me was that damn phone call from Malcolm. I really don't think I can handle this anymore... maybe this 'curse' everyone talks about is real."

Graham's face softened with understanding. "Sorry, old chap, I didn't even think about that. Shit, yeah, I was so wrapped up in the hunt that I didn't consider the fallout for you. This could leave you in a real bind."

"It's just me, Graham," Gus muttered, his shoulders slumping. "Things tend to pile up on me, and your guys rubbed me the wrong way today. I almost lost it with that Sergeant. But, I'll come good." Gus tried to brush off the disappointment, though it was clear how much it was eating at him.

Lynette, seeing Gus' tension, walked over and put her arm around his shoulder in a supportive gesture. "I'm on your side, darling," she said softly, offering comfort.

They spent some more time discussing Owen. Gus speculated that Owen might not have realised what he was signing, perhaps thinking he was merely witnessing something. It sounded plausible until Lynette interrupted, raising a valid point. "Gus, have you forgotten? Owen was once a bank manager. He would have recognised a real estate document, surely, at least once, maybe twice. Sonia must've prepped him for what was happening."

It became clear to everyone that Owen's involvement was far more questionable than they had initially hoped. Despite Gus' suggestion that Owen might not have known what he was signing, Lynette's insight brought a sobering reality to the situation. Graham was resolute; although he could delay the interview with Owen for a bit, he knew that sooner or later, Owen would have to be questioned. And once that happened, it would only be a matter of time before Owen faced charges.

"Well, what has to be done, has to be done," Graham concluded. "I'll talk to Owen first thing tomorrow. But in the meantime, let's enjoy some beers and have a late night. Maybe we can figure out a way to get poor old Owen off the hook, but I'm not optimistic."

The group tried to unwind, but despite their best efforts, there was an undercurrent of anxiety that lingered as they shared a few more drinks late into the evening. As the night wore on, it became clear that no one would be able to find an easy solution for Owen.

The next morning, after a slightly hungover breakfast on the verandah, they said their goodbyes. Graham was heading to Owen's place, and Lynette and Gus had their own tasks to attend to. Graham would go directly from there to Townsville, bringing Owen in as a prisoner, sadly, the outcome they had all feared.

Gus headed off to the cattle yards, and Lynette went to Richmond for a few errands. Hailee and Janice took care of the breakfast cleanup before moving on to making the beds and tidying up the house.

When Graham arrived at Owen's property, he immediately knew something was off. Despite the Landrover being parked in the shed, Owen was nowhere to be found. Graham was aware that Owen had another vehicle, which Barry had been using since Owen's Landcruiser ute had been temporarily out of commission. But Owen's car was nowhere to be seen. Graham figured Owen must have been at the cattle yards, where cattle were being unloaded that morning, so he made his way there.

But as he approached the yards, a thought struck him, he realised Owen wouldn't be at the yards. He could ask Barry about Owen's whereabouts, but

Graham dismissed the idea, thinking, No, screw it. This is a job for the boys in blue. He turned his car around and headed back to Townsville, knowing it was time to let the police handle it from here.

Neither Gus nor Lynette had spoken about Owen for a couple of days. They both felt the weight of knowing that Owen would soon be behind bars in the Townsville watch house. Despite everything, they had grown quite fond of Owen and had hoped he might be able to turn things around.

Barry didn't mention anything about his father, and there was no sign of distress in his demeanour. He was fully absorbed in his work, alongside Willem, as if nothing out of the ordinary had happened. Gus and Lynette didn't bring up Owen either; it was clear from Barry's behaviour that he wasn't going to volunteer any information.

A few days later, Graham called Lynette with an update. "No prints were found on any of the firearms taken from the property, including the pistol," he said casually. "The only prints we found were on the spent casing and the cartridges in the magazine of the Margolin pistol. By the way, has Owen turned up?"

Lynette asked if Owen had been released, but Graham's response was unsettling. "He never got locked up. I went to interview him, but when I arrived, Owen wasn't there. The police now have a lookout for two suspects."

Graham paused for a moment. "We also found the car that Gus gave to Sonia. The Honda Accord turned up in Mount Isa. She sold it privately, and the new owner hasn't changed over the registration yet. As for Sonia's whereabouts, we've got nothing. And Owen's location is still a mystery. We've got his vehicle description and registration numbers out there, but we're drawing blanks."

Graham then asked if Lynette had come across anything at the house that might have Lachlan's fingerprints on it. "It could help us eliminate any prints on the cartridges," he explained.

Lynette thought for a moment. "I'll have a look around, but I don't think there's anything of Lachlan's lying around the house. Wait…" She paused as realisation hit her. "Why would all his things have disappeared? I didn't really think about it until now, but why would that happen?"

Graham suggested that Lachlan's belongings might still be hidden somewhere in the house. "They could be stashed away," he said.

"I'll let you know if I find anything," Lynette promised, ending the call.

Just then, Gus walked into the bar and called out, "Make it two, my darling."

Lynette, her mind still racing with the information she'd just received, looked up and asked, "How's the cattle arrivals going?"

"Busy as always," Gus replied, cracking open a beer. "But we've got bigger problems now."

"A bit slow since Owen's been gone, but we're getting there," Gus said, looking thoughtful. "Barry's a great worker, and young Willem's a fast learner. But I think we could use another hand. I'll have a word with Barry later about finding someone." He passed Lynette a stubbie and continued, "I'll head into town tomorrow to get some more beer, and I'll see Peter Lansky too. I'll ask if he knows anyone who might want a job out here. Want to come with me?"

Lynette smiled but shook her head. "Love to, Gus, but the girls and I are setting up a veggie garden tomorrow. But there is a parcel you can pick up for me at the Post Office, if you don't mind."

"Sure thing," Gus replied, holding up the six-pack of stubbies. "Another?" he asked, offering her one.

"Don't mind if I do," Lynette replied, accepting the beer with a grateful smile.

After their brief exchange, Gus grabbed the six-pack of gold stubbies, popped one open, and drove down to Owen's property. Well, now it was Barry's property, he supposed. Gus didn't want to step on any toes or get on Barry's bad side, after all, Owen was no longer around, and Gus was relying heavily on the younger man.

When Gus arrived, both Barry and Willem's Utes were parked in front of the house. They had just gotten back from the cattle yards and had settled down for an after-work beer. Barry waved as Gus approached, and Gus raised the six-pack in a friendly gesture. Bush sign language for "I've got one here."

"Gus!" Barry greeted him warmly, "Grab a beer, mate."

Gus sat down with the two younger men, cracking open a beer. The conversation quickly turned to the cattle. Barry informed him that all the cattle had been brought onto the property now.

"I'll go see Lansky tomorrow and ask if he knows anyone available to help us out here," Gus said. "I think a team of three would be a good number now that we have about six thousand cattle to manage. It would certainly make things easier, especially with the three herds. Trying to keep them separate is a real hassle."

Barry agreed. "Yeah, a third person would be a big help, especially with three herds, one at a thousand, another at three thousand, and one at two thousand. Keeping them all apart is a pain in the arse."

He also mentioned that there were six cleanskins among the last cattle shipment. "They don't have any tags, so we've got them in the old lambing paddock for now. If no one claims them, they'll become our meat supply."

Gus raised an eyebrow. "How does that happen?"

Barry shrugged. "It's a mix-up. Sometimes the owners don't draft properly, or they just can't be bothered getting them off the truck. It happens more often than you think."

As they continued chatting, Willem finished his second beer. "I'd better get going," he said, looking toward the horizon. "Hailee will be waiting for me. See you guys in the morning."

Barry nodded. "Be here around seven, and we'll move the big herd up to the top."

Once Willem left, Gus turned to Barry and got straight to the point. "Where's your old man, Barry?"

Barry hesitated, his expression turning serious. "I'm not sure. I told him not to do anything that damn Sonia was asking him, but she was offering Dad a lot of money just to help her out. I think I know where he is, but I'm not saying anything, because I know the cops will be chasing him."

"I don't want to know where he is," Gus replied firmly. "Don't even give me a hint. I can't afford to be caught in the middle. I just hope he's okay. I actually liked your dad. We were getting along well."

Barry looked at Gus and nodded. "He'll be fine. I reckon he'll hand himself in to the cops eventually. It's not like he wanted to get mixed up in all this."

Barry went on to explain that Owen had turned down the money Sonia had offered him to sign the real estate contracts. "She offered him a hell of a lot, Gus, but Dad didn't want anything to do with it. I don't think it's him, really. He's not a bad guy."

Gus breathed a sigh of relief. "If Owen didn't take the money, then maybe it'll go easier on him. He might not even end up with prison time. I'm glad to hear that."

Curious, Gus asked, "How well did you get along with Sonia?"

Barry's face darkened, and he took a long swig of his beer. "I wish she'd never come out here, Gus. Life was good before she showed up. If Mum hadn't gone missing, Sonia would've never come into the picture."

Gus raised an eyebrow, his curiosity piqued. "I was wondering where your mum was. I didn't like to ask Owen about it."

Barry sighed deeply. "About five years ago, my mum's sister Kath, Auntie Kath, was really sick. She had bowel cancer, and her husband, Uncle Jim, was struggling to look after her. It didn't look like Kath had long to live, so Mum decided to go to Brisbane and help out.

"Dad took Mum to the airport in Townsville. He said goodbye, and she went through the boarding gate. That was the last time we saw her. The taxi she was in was involved in a head-on collision on the Warrego Highway, about nine kilometres east of Ipswich. Mum was sitting in the back and wasn't wearing a seatbelt. They think she died instantly, and the cab driver walked away without a scratch."

Barry paused, taking a breath. "Ironically, Auntie Kath passed away that morning, before Mum's plane even landed."

Gus listened intently, his heart heavy with the story.

Barry went on, his voice tinged with pain. "The taxi driver was in a rush to get back to Brisbane, apparently. They don't like driving out to Ipswich, so he was speeding. The whole thing destroyed Dad. I honestly don't think he would've survived it if it weren't for Lachlan. He was in a bad way, suicidal even. Lachlan took him on a holiday to the U.S. for over three months, Route 66, Miami, a cruise to the Bahamas, then they drove to Las Vegas in a Ford Mustang. After that, they went to New York, and then to Scotland. Lachlan even took Dad to his old farm in Canonbie. They spent time in London too, Lachlan's first time there. I think it did Dad a world of good."

Gus nodded slowly, trying to absorb the weight of the story. "Sounds like Lachlan really pulled him out of a dark place."

Barry smiled faintly, remembering his brother's efforts. "Yeah, he did. And when Dad asked Lachlan why he hadn't travelled much around England, Lachlan just laughed and said, 'Och laddie, they do na moove aroond here mooch. Ye may as well be a fooking tree, laddie!'"

Gus chuckled, imagining Lachlan's thick Scottish accent. "Sounds like Lachlan, alright. He's got a way with words."

"Yeah, he does," Barry said, a slight smile tugging at his lips. The pain of his mother's death was still there, but the memories of Lachlan's support were a source of strength for both of them.

Even when they returned from their trip, it wasn't for long. Lachlan and his father went straight down to Sydney, where they stayed at the luxurious Star Casino. They visited Darling Harbour and took in all the major attractions, just soaking up the city's vibrancy and spending some much-needed time together. From Sydney, they traveled to Melbourne, enjoying the city's culture and the quiet escape it offered. Then it was off to Perth for a few more weeks of downtime before finally heading back home.

Barry's voice hardened when he spoke next. "Sonia was fuming the whole time. She told everyone that she'd been feeling sick, and that's why Owen went away with Lachlan instead of her." His bitterness was palpable. "The thing is, she wasn't sick. She just didn't like being left behind, so she made up that story."

But when Owen and Lachlan returned, it wasn't long before they left again, taking another brief trip for a change of scenery. That was when, according to Barry, Sonia began spreading a vicious rumour. "That's when she started telling people that Lachlan and my father were gay," Barry said, his eyes narrowing with anger.

"I tell you, that fucking bitch Sonia is a real piece of work," Barry concluded, his voice thick with disgust. "She'll do anything to make people believe whatever story fits her agenda. I'm just glad Dad and Lachlan didn't let her get to them."

The air around them seemed to hang heavy with the weight of Sonia's manipulation, her constant undermining of those around her. Barry's resentment was clear, and Gus could feel the anger building inside him as he listened to the story unfold. It wasn't just the cruelty of the rumours, it was the way Sonia seemed to twist everything to suit her own needs, regardless of who she hurt in the process.

Barry took a deep breath, his tone softening a little. "I don't know what it is about her, Gus. She's just toxic. Ever since she came out here, everything's been different. It feels like we can't escape her."

Gus, for his part, was quietly processing everything Barry had shared. He could tell that Barry had been trying to protect his family and his father, but the poison Sonia had spread had clearly left deep scars. The rumours, the lies, it wasn't just the weight of the past that hung over them, but the ongoing damage she caused in their lives.

Lynette had left her mobile phone on the bar counter when Gus walked in after returning from Richmond. The phone was ringing, its unique and obscure ringtone blaring through the quiet house. Gus hesitated for a moment, wishing he had grabbed a beer first, but then answered the call.

"Lynette's phone," he said, his voice slightly distracted as he picked up the phone.

"Gus, Graham here, how's it all going, mate?"

"Mate, it's all good. Got all the cattle on, just got back from town with some more grog, and I've employed another guy to start tomorrow. Just about to crack a beer and... that's about me."

Graham chuckled on the other end. "Well, I've got a bit of news for you. Actually, quite a bit, and I need to get a couple of photos from your place that the boffins took, though it seems they've somehow erased themselves. Would you mind having a couple of guests? Stefanie said she'd love to come out, but she doesn't want to impose. She's thinking of staying at the pub in Richmond."

"Bullshit! You'll be staying here," Gus said, his voice firm. "In fact, Barry had the Mobile Butcher out here, and we've got some nice beef just about ready for tomorrow. Lynette'll be over the moon, she loves having visitors. So, don't worry about the pub. You'll be staying here." Gus paused. "What time are you thinking of arriving?"

Graham responded, "We should be there around four."

"Sounds good. I'll make sure we're ready. See you then."

Gus then went out to his ute, continuing the task of putting the slabs of beer into the cool room. He also grabbed a carton of Oyster Bay Sauvignon Blanc, as well as two fairly heavy boxes that he'd picked up from the post office. The boxes were addressed to Lynette, so he placed them neatly by the entryway.

As Gus was making his way back into the bar, he found Lynette already there, having heard her phone ringing. He explained that he had taken the call and passed on the details about the visitors.

"I just wish all this drama would end," Lynette said, a touch of frustration in her voice. "Don't get me wrong, I'm looking forward to seeing Stefanie and of course Graham, but I've had enough of all the chaos. I just want things to settle down here, everything is going so well with the cattle, the house is looking perfect, and we've started the veggie garden. We're even planning to fix up the Manager's House for Janice, Hailee, and Willem. I just want things to stay peaceful, with no more drama. Let's leave the past behind and focus on building something good here. I just want to forget everything else."

Gus nodded in agreement. He, too, was done with the past. His focus was squarely on the cattle and ensuring everything went smoothly for the next six months. He was looking forward to managing the property without any more distractions or complications. "I'm with you, Lynette. Let's just get on with life and leave all that other stuff behind."

"Cheers," Lynette said, raising her stubbie with a smile.

"Double cheers," Gus responded, holding up two fresh stubbies from the bar fridge, the cool bottles a welcome relief from the heat of the day.

The next day arrived, and it was one of those perfect days typical of this time of year. The temperature hit a scorching 38°C, but the night had been cool, around 19°C, and no rain was forecast for at least another week. All in all, it was a beautiful day.

Gus made his way to the meat room at the cattle yards. The room was just a large mobile cool room that had been set up on blocks after its wheels were removed. It was connected to the property's power supply, which also ran the water pumps and various equipment needed at the yards. Inside, the temperature was a steady 12°C, which was a welcome relief after being out in the heat.

The room, measuring 2.4 meters by 6 meters, was fully equipped with three stainless steel benches, a band saw, a tool rack with bone cutters and hand saws, and knives securely fastened in scabbards attached to the benches. At one end of the room was a large wash tub with hot and cold water taps, along with a standard double kitchen sink. Along the opposite wall were two long rails for hanging hooks, where beef was suspended.

Gus took one of the midsections of beef that had been hanging, and with the precision of a seasoned butcher, used the bandsaw to cut four tomahawk steaks, each weighing around 500 grams.

Around 4 PM, just as Graham had promised, he and Stefanie arrived. Both Gus and Lynette greeted them warmly at the porte-cochère, exchanging air kisses and hugs before leading them to the cool verandah, where drinks were served. Graham excused himself, asking if he could take a few photos for the forensics team.

"Go for it," Lynette said with a wave, clearly more focused on the social aspect of their visit.

Gus raised an eyebrow, curious. "Where do you need to take these photos?"

"Three angles of the ceiling framing around the access door," Graham explained. "Once that's out of the way, I can relax. Let me fill you in on the latest in the saga of Woolgar River Park."

But before he could continue, Lynette interrupted with a wry smile. "I'm sure it's not just the saga of Woolgar River Park you're here for, Graham."

"Well, you're right," Graham said with a chuckle. "But before we dive into that, I need to take care of business. Then, we'll get to the juicy stuff."

Lynette rolled her eyes but was clearly glad to see them. Gus, too, was looking forward to a break from the constant drama, even if it was just for an evening.

"Graham, don't take offence, but we've had a gut full of the so-called saga. We've just about lost interest," Lynette said, her tone firm but calm. "We think it's causing a huge disruption to our lives, to the extent that it might be detrimental to us continuing to live here. We've made a decision to forget all about the past issues with this place. The bottom line is, we just want to get on with a new chapter in our lives."

The verandah fell silent for a moment. Stefanie, standing beside Graham, didn't know where to look. She had been telling him for ages not to bring his work home with him, hearing about police matters day in and day out really got under her skin. And now, it seemed, he was causing tension with friends over the same issues. She could see that Lynette was clearly fed up, but what could she say? She just stood there, silently hoping Graham would take the hint.

Lynette went inside to fetch a round of drinks, giving everyone a moment to breathe.

When she returned with the drinks, Graham, seemingly unperturbed and as thick-skinned as ever, continued, "Well, that's good to hear, because what I have to tell you will bring all the events at this property to a conclusion." He paused, took a long sip of his drink, and then leaned back in his chair, clearly relishing the dramatic effect. "Of course, that is, if you'd like to hear it."

Graham pulled out his laptop from his bag and opened it. He began reading aloud from a 'Confidential' police report that, he explained, was related to charges pending against Richard Kemp.

The report revealed that Richard Kemp was a solicitor based in Horsham, specializing in property conveyancing. However, Kemp's career had been somewhat lacklustre, marred by his laziness and a number of personal issues, including drinking and gambling. Conveyancing, it seemed, was one of those tasks that required minimal effort, so Kemp managed to keep his business running with the help of two female clerks who had solid experience in the field. They had moved from Melbourne, eager to escape the hustle and bustle of city life.

It was noted that Kemp was rarely in the office after eleven in the morning, preferring to spend his time at local race meetings or at the Horsham Sporties Club. Though his business appeared to be thriving, Kemp had been known to extend his services in less-than-legal ways to help out friends in sticky situations.

When Jason Strange, a known figure in local real estate, presented Kemp with an opportunity involving a substantial profit, around the two million dollar mark, Kemp was all in.

The first red flag appeared when one of the clerks noticed a discrepancy during a property search. The sale price of a property didn't match its approximate valuation. Furthermore, the buyer was a newly registered company, with one of its directors listed as Susan Little, Kemp's wife, using her maiden name. Even more troubling was the fact that there was no proof of the seller's identity, a key legal requirement. To top it off, the settlement funds were to be paid into an account in the name of Sonia Teague, rather than a joint account of the vendors.

When the clerk raised these concerns with Kemp, he simply shrugged them off, explaining that while there was indeed a conflict of interest, he could easily fix it by using his name in one instance and his company name in the other. The clerk, though doubtful, ultimately deferred to Kemp, who was, after all, the legal expert.

In short, Kemp and Strange had registered a company called Queensland Associated Pastoral Pty Ltd, with each of their wives as directors under their maiden names. The company signed a deal to purchase Woolgar River Park for 2.1 million dollars, paying a deposit of 210,000 dollars. However, despite being receipted, this deposit had not been paid into any bank account associated with the real estate office handling the transaction.

The plan was for the company to hold onto the property for a short period, about two years, during which they would show consecutive financial losses. Afterward, the plan was to sell the property at an inflated market valuation of around seven million dollars, resulting in a profit of about 2.5 million dollars each for the directors, after avoiding taxes like capital gains.

Graham closed his laptop and finished his drink.

"Wow," Lynette said, her voice mixed with disbelief and intrigue. Gus, equally stunned, nodded in agreement. "That's... really something. We didn't expect that."

Graham, sensing they were hooked, added, "The best part is yet to come. Let me grab the drinks this time, I've got a load of them in the boot, and they're probably getting a bit too warm for my liking."

Gus helped Graham carry the drinks into the cool room and then placed a few cold ones in the fridge at the bar. When they returned to the verandah, Graham took a seat, his expression serious.

"Well," Graham began, "Owen Harrigan walked into the Townsville police station yesterday morning. He handed himself in, and later that morning, he was charged with the murder of Lachlan Teague."

The words hung in the air like a thick cloud. Lynette and Gus exchanged a look of stunned disbelief. The world around them seemed to stop for a moment as they processed what Graham had just said. It was as if all the chaos that had been brewing for so long was finally coming to a head, and the truth was more twisted than they had ever imagined.

The air on the verandah felt suddenly heavy, the weight of the news sinking in as everyone waited for the next words to fall.

Graham took a slow, deliberate sip from his drink, savouring the silence that had fallen over the group. He revelled in the astonished expressions on their faces, knowing that he had just delivered something truly shocking. After a moment, he leaned forward, his voice steady as he resumed his account.

"When Owen entered the police station that morning, he asked to see me," Graham began, his eyes flickering with the memory of the events. "I had just arrived myself, and the Desk Sergeant called to inform me who was asking to see me. He asked if he should escort Owen up to my office, and of course, I agreed."

Graham took another long drink, letting the suspense build before continuing. "Owen walked into my office and greeted me like an old friend, as if nothing was out of the ordinary. He said, 'I believe you've been looking for me.' I corrected him, telling him that the police were actually looking for him. He chuckled and said, 'Well, they can't be looking too hard, because I've been sitting in reception waiting to see you for the last ten minutes.' We both had a laugh over that."

He paused briefly, reflecting on the moment. "Then, Owen's demeanour shifted. He became serious and told me he needed to talk to me about something important. I asked him if it was about the real estate contracts, but he assured me it had nothing to do with that. Instead, he said it was about Lachlan Teague."

Graham's voice softened as he continued. "Owen told me that he hadn't seen Lachlan in a while. Sonia had been fending him off, claiming that Lachlan was either asleep, in the shower, or too ill to talk. Eventually, Owen grew frustrated with being pushed away and decided to take matters into his own hands. He said he didn't want to hurt Sonia, but he needed to see Lachlan, and if Sonia was the only thing standing in his way, he was willing to push past her. After all, if she left, there would be no one left to care for Lachlan."

Graham paused, letting the gravity of Owen's words sink in before continuing. "Owen approached the house that day, knocking loudly on the door. Normally, Sonia would shout out, asking who it was and what he wanted. But this time, there was no answer. He couldn't tell if she was home because the garages were always shut and locked, almost like the place was a fortress. But Owen remembered seeing her retrieve a key from a large concrete bowl near the laundry door. So he went over to see if it was there. He found the key easily, opened the laundry door, and replaced it when he was done."

Graham took a deep breath. "Owen then went upstairs to find Lachlan in his bed. The sight of him shocked Owen. Lachlan was a complete wreck. He was awake, but barely. When he saw Owen, he muttered the word 'pain.' Owen wasn't sure if that's what he said at first, but Lachlan repeated it, 'pain.' Then, with what little strength he had left, Lachlan begged Owen, 'Get ma gun from the wee desk and shoot me. Ah canna handle this no more, you must get ma gun noo, ah tell yer.'"

The group remained frozen, listening intently as Graham's voice grew more pained. "Owen told him no, he wouldn't do it, but Lachlan kept begging. He was crying, pleading for the end. Owen, torn, went to the desk where he knew the gun was kept. He had taken it out for shooting on occasion. He opened the polished wooden case, removed the pistol, and loaded it, knowing full well that what he was doing was wrong. But Lachlan's suffering was too much for him to ignore."

Graham's eyes clouded as he recalled the next moments. "He brought the loaded pistol to Lachlan, who took it from him with difficulty. Lachlan placed the barrel in his left ear, and without hesitation, he pulled the trigger. There was little noise, a soft FSSST sound, like popping the cap off a bottle of beer, and that was it. Lachlan was dead."

The room was deathly silent, the weight of Graham's words settling in. Graham paused, looking at the three faces before him. "Owen couldn't believe it. He couldn't believe he had handed Lachlan the gun. He knew it was wrong, but Lachlan had been in such pain, and Owen felt powerless to do anything else. Lachlan had taken the gun from him so quickly that Owen didn't even think he could have stopped him in time. There was no blood, none. No blood from the wound, not even a drop. Owen checked, he looked into Lachlan's ear, expecting to see blood pouring out, but there was nothing."

He took another sip of his drink, his voice lowering. "Owen lifted Lachlan's head to check for the exit wound, where the blood should have been. But there was no blood, no sign of injury. Lachlan's face looked peaceful, no longer contorted in pain. It was like all the suffering had vanished in an instant. Owen put Lachlan's head back on the pillow, then took the pistol and went into the bathroom. He wiped it down carefully with a towel, making sure it was clean, and placed the magazine back into the pistol case."

Graham's face grew more somber. "Owen was about to return the gun to the desk drawer, but then he remembered the hidden compartment that Curtis had installed when building the house. Owen thought it would be a good place to stash the gun, so Sonia wouldn't find it. He also remembered Lachlan's rifle and shotgun, and decided to put those in the compartment too. He didn't really know why, but something told him it was better to hide them."

Graham took a breath, steadying himself. "Afterward, Owen left the house and waited for Sonia's call, which came the next morning."

The three friends sat in stunned silence, unable to fully process what they had just heard. Graham, unfazed, rose from his chair. "I'll grab the drinks this time," he said, his voice steady. He walked into the kitchen, leaving the others to reflect on the devastating events he had just recounted.

"What will happen to him now?" Gus asked, his voice tinged with concern.

Graham leaned back in his chair, looking out at the quiet night as he answered. "I went down with him to Homicide and told the Sergeant to take his statement, charge him with murder, but to look after him. The most likely scenario at this point is Manslaughter, and under the circumstances, with a good lawyer, he probably won't serve time in prison. As for the whole real estate contract matter, Owen didn't profit from it. He signed his own name; he didn't try to forge Lachlan's. The real crook in this whole thing is Sonia."

Lynette leaned forward, her curiosity piqued. "What's the word on Sonia?"

Graham sighed, shaking his head. "We've learned a lot. Her real name isn't Sonia Teague, it's Sonia Herin. She's Italian, from a town called Villaciambra near Palermo in the south of Italy. That's where we found her. Initially, we thought there might be grounds for murder charges, and we even considered seeking extradition. But with the charges now focusing on fraud and a few other offences, it's probably not worth the international hassle. If she ever returns to Australia, though, we'll have her the moment she touches down."

Gus, who had been quiet for a moment, nodded thoughtfully as he got up to pour more drinks. "I'm so glad you came here tonight," he said, his tone lighter. "I'm sure Lynette and I will both sleep much better now."

Graham smiled wryly, taking a sip of his own drink. "It's been a hell of a ride," he said. "This whole saga is unbelievable. It all started with Sonia selling a property she didn't even own, using a crooked real estate agent who, with a shady solicitor, set up a company to buy it for far less than its actual value. The solicitor pushed through the conveyancing without verifying the legal ownership of the vendors. He even approved the settlement funds to be paid into an account with a name that wasn't tied to the property title at all."

He paused, letting the weight of the situation settle in before continuing. "Everything was approved, and the settlement was about to go through. But within seven days of that settlement, a new owner pops up, because Lachlan made a will with Malcolm. Malcolm found out about Lachlan's death and contacted Angus. If that hadn't happened, the settlement would have been finalised, the money would have gone into Sonia's account, and she would've been on a plane to Italy, rich and untouchable. No one would have been any wiser."

Graham's voice softened, almost to a whisper, as he reflected on the twists of fate that had led them to this point. "And had anyone other than Lynette found that spent .22 casing in the garden, it would have been discarded with the trash, and Lachlan's death would've been just another mystery. There would've been no suspicion. No investigation. Just a quiet, inconspicuous death."

The group sat in silence for a moment, each person grappling with the enormity of the events that had unfolded. Then Graham, always the storyteller, broke the silence with a thought that had been lingering in his mind.

"You know," he said, his voice taking on a more reflective tone, "there's always been talk about a curse on this property. Some Aboriginals claim Kurrie placed a curse on the land. People say it was responsible for the downfall of the Southwell family. The death of Owen's wife, Jenny, maybe it was all just tragic coincidence. But who knows?"

He paused again, and when he spoke next, his voice lowered, as though revealing something secret. "Did you know that there was a massacre on, or near this property, in 1881? It happened after the murder of a police sub-inspector, Henry Kaye. He had taken an Aboriginal man prisoner along with a group of others. It's rumoured that Kaye's men, deeply distressed over his death, retaliated by massacring the entire group of prisoners."

Graham's eyes darkened as he looked out into the distance. "You can read into things however you want. Who knows? History, like that of this property, is bound to scare some people away. Others, though, will shrug their shoulders, move on, and enjoy life. In the end, we all make our own peace with things, don't we?"

He stood up, brushing off the heavy air in the room with a wry grin. "Anyway, enough of all that," he said, raising his glass. "It's your shout."

End........

TASK

The Task

My name is, Jack Holden. I am a building and construction project manager.

Now!… How's this for a yarn? It happened to me a while ago, when I was waiting for my next job to start. Sit back and have a listen………

At the time, I had no projects lined up for at least seven months. In other words, I was effectively unemployed, with very little money in the bank to fall back on, so I was, quite literally, broke. Thankfully, I did own my home and car, which meant my monthly expenses were relatively low.

One afternoon, while chatting with someone at the local RSL, they mentioned a platform called "AirTask" as a good option for casual, on-demand work that lets you set your own terms of employment. Intrigued, I decided to check it out later that evening.

After a bit of research, I quickly grasped how the platform worked. The concept was simple: browse tasks posted by others, find one you're interested in, submit a price you're happy with, and wait to see if you're chosen for the job. Scrolling through the options, I noticed there weren't many tasks available in the Cairns area. However, one listing did catch my attention.

The task was titled: "Wanted: car and driver for a one-way trip from Cairns suburb to Darwin City." The ad had been posted four days earlier, so I assumed it might already have been taken. Still, after scanning all the local listings and finding nothing else of interest, I circled back to the Darwin trip. It intrigued me. The post was sparse on details, there was no mention of timing or specifics, but I figured, "What the hell?" and decided to submit a quote anyway.

Using Google Maps, I calculated the distance from Cairns to Darwin to be roughly 2,700 kilometres. In theory, I could cover that in three days of driving, but realistically, I doubted many people would want to endure 900 kilometres a day with early starts and minimal stops. So, I adjusted my estimate to a more reasonable six days of driving, with five overnight stays along the way.

Breaking it down, I worked out my costs:

Fuel: Approximately $600 for the entire trip.

Accommodation and meals: Around $200 per day, totaling $1,000 for five nights.

Unforeseen expenses: I added $400 as a buffer for anything unexpected.

That brought the total for the trip to $2,000. Of course, I'd also have to make the return journey, doubling the total to $4,000.

Satisfied with my calculations, I submitted my quote and crossed my fingers. This wasn't just about making money, it was also a chance for a bit of adventure.

I was about to submit my offer of $4,000 for the task when it struck me: $4,000 barely covered my costs to drive to Darwin and back. It didn't account for wear and tear on my car or any other incidental expenses. After some quick thinking, I decided to double the price to $8,000 to leave a margin for profit.

Then, another thought hit me, this job had likely been snapped up already. The ad was four days old, after all. So, as a final touch, I added another $2,000 to the price. Why not? It was a long shot anyway. With that, I submitted an offer of $10,000 to drive one person from Cairns to Darwin.

As I clicked "Confirm Price" on the website, I chuckled to myself. "What a waste of time," I thought. "Who in their right mind would pay ten grand for a lift to Darwin?" I shook my head, got up, and headed to the fridge for a beer.

I had barely settled into my chair, drink in hand, when my laptop emitted its signature "blahblimpbip" notification sound. I glanced over, and to my surprise, it was a message from AirTask. I opened it, and there it was: a congratulations message, complete with a contact phone number for the task.

At first, I was convinced I'd made a mistake. I immediately checked the price, certain I must have accidentally submitted $1,000 instead of $10,000. But no, the price was correct. My heart raced. "There has to be a catch," I thought. "Who's going to pay ten grand for a ride to Darwin?"

Still in disbelief, I dialled the phone number provided. After a couple of rings, a polished and professional voice answered, "Hello, Thomas speaking."

I hesitated for a moment before nervously replying, "Hi, this is Jack Holden. I submitted a price on AirTask, and I…"

Before I could finish, Thomas cut me off. "Excellent!" he said enthusiastically. "Thank you for your interest. I presume you've read and agreed to the conditions?"

"Uh, yes," I replied, still trying to process the situation.

"Fantastic," Thomas continued. "I've already submitted payment to AirTask. They'll forward fifty percent of the rate to you upfront, and you'll receive the balance once I confirm the job is complete. Today is Tuesday. I'll be ready to travel by Thursday, does that work for you?"

I paused for a moment, stunned by how quickly everything was happening. "Uh, yes, Thursday works," I finally managed to say, my mind still racing.

As I hung up the phone, a wave of disbelief washed over me. Somehow, I had just secured a $10,000 job driving someone from Cairns to Darwin.

After confirming the task, Thomas asked for my email address so he could send over the details of his collection point and the date he needed to be in Darwin. He also asked which route I planned to take, though he quickly added that it didn't matter much to him. What did matter, he noted, was comfortable accommodation and a good selection of evening meals.

That evening, I sat in a kind of stunned disbelief over what had just transpired. It seemed too good to be true, and I couldn't shake the feeling that I might have made some sort of mistake. How had I managed to secure a $10,000 job to drive someone across the country?

The amazement only deepened the next morning when I checked my bank account. There it was, a deposit of $4,750. This was fifty percent of my submitted task price, minus AirTask's 5% commission. Seeing the money in my account made everything feel much more real, though it still seemed almost surreal that someone was willing to pay that kind of money for a road trip.

Later that day, I received an email from Thomas Reginald Dobson, detailing the arrangements. He instructed me to pick him up from the Cairns Hilton Hotel at 9:00 a.m. on Thursday morning. The email noted that he would have two pieces of luggage: one large bag weighing approximately 25 kilograms and a smaller one of around 12 kilograms.

Thomas also included a request for an itinerary, suggesting around 500 kilometres of driving per day with a lunch stop. He expressed a preference for hot meals during these breaks and stated that hotels would be suitable for overnight stays.

It was all so specific yet perfectly reasonable, and the formal tone of his email only added to my impression that this was indeed a serious arrangement. I began sketching out the route, carefully factoring in his requests and preferences. This was shaping up to be more than just a job, it felt like the beginning of an adventure.

I had about five hours to prepare an itinerary, so I grabbed a stubbie from the fridge and got to work. Using Google Maps, I plotted a route that would satisfy Thomas's preferences for comfortable travel, meal stops, and manageable distances.

We would depart Cairns at 9:00 a.m. on Thursday, heading west toward Croydon, a journey of about 525 kilometres. I planned a lunch stop at the Mount Garnett Hotel, roughly 160 kilometres into the drive. Given the road conditions, this leg would take around three hours. From Mount Garnett, we'd continue to Croydon, aiming to arrive by 5:00 p.m.

For Friday, the plan was to travel from Croydon to the "Four Ways" roadhouse for lunch, then press on to Mount Isa for the evening. This leg would be longer than Thomas's requested 500 kilometres, closer to 640, but suitable accommodation options made it the most practical choice.

Saturday's leg would take us from Mount Isa to the Barkly Homestead, about 450 kilometres away, with a lunch stop in Camooweal. From there, I tentatively planned two solid days of driving to reach Darwin, but I decided to leave the finer details of the latter half of the trip open, depending on how things went.

Satisfied with the plan, I faxed the itinerary to Thomas Reginald Dobson. By the time I'd packed my own bag, loaded my Engel 45-litre fridge into the back, and fuelled up my 2019 Subaru Outback, the perfect choice for a road trip like this, I still hadn't heard anything back from him. Taking his silence as a sign that everything was in order, I went to bed feeling prepared for the journey ahead.

The next morning, I drove into the porte-cochère of the Cairns Hilton just before 9:00 a.m. Standing at the curb was a portly man with thinning grey hair and a balding crown. He looked to be in his early sixties, wearing a blue blazer and khaki pants. Beside him were two pieces of luggage: a large bag and a smaller one.

I pulled up in front of him, popped the rear door open, and stepped out of the car to introduce myself.

"Pleased to meet you, Jack," he said, extending his right hand with a warm smile.

"You too, Mr. Dobson," I replied, shaking his hand.

"Call me Tom," he said, before walking to the passenger side of the car. He opened the door, adjusted the electric seat to move it back, and settled in, all while leaving his bags at the curb.

For a brief, mischievous moment, I considered driving off without the luggage. But I thought better of it, walked over to the passenger side door, and asked, "Do you have any bags you'd like me to load into the back?"

He grinned. "Just the two you see there," he said, nodding toward the luggage.

I stifled a sigh, picked up the bags, and stowed them in the back. Clearly, this was going to be an interesting trip.

Thomas said very little as we set off, and I wasn't sure how to break the silence. After a few moments, I decided to comment on the weather. "It's a great-looking day," I said, hoping to spark a conversation.

He nodded in agreement, then replied with a question. "Lunch at Mount Garnett, you said?"

"That's right," I confirmed. "I've never been to the pub myself, but I've heard the meals there are quite good."

He gave a noncommittal "Hmm," and the conversation stalled again.

As I drove along Sheridan Street toward Smithfield, preparing for the turnoff to the Kuranda Range, I couldn't help but notice how quiet Thomas was. It wasn't an uncomfortable silence exactly, but it was clear he wasn't inclined to chat much.

The climb up the winding Kuranda Range Road began, and still, he said nothing. About halfway up, I had a thought. I eased off the accelerator and slowed down considerably.

It wasn't long before Thomas broke his silence. "This road is shocking," he said, his voice tinged with indignation. "It's an absolute disgrace. Imagine the poor people who have to navigate this nightmare every single day!" He continued on for a bit, detailing his thoughts about the inadequacies of the road and the hardships of the locals who relied on it.

I nodded along, making sympathetic sounds as he spoke, but inwardly, I smiled. I had just discovered the key to drawing him out: the speed of the car. I realised that if I drove slowly enough, he'd feel compelled to comment, and once he started, he seemed more comfortable continuing.

With this newfound knowledge, I made a mental note to adjust my driving accordingly for the rest of the trip. Sometimes, it's the little things that make all the difference.

It was a pretty uneventful trip between Kuranda, which is bypassed and Mareeba, which is also bypassed. It was just pass the Mareeba air field that we became stuck behind a Toyota Yaris which appeared to be carrying two Nuns. I had a couple of opportunities to get around them but I thought it may be too nerve racking on my passenger so I chose to wait until the overtaking lane just before Walkamin, then I overtook them and Thomas gave them a long look as we went past them.

"Strange people", Thomas went on, "you know they have it all wrong, don't you". I told him that I didn't know what he mean't as I am not really into religion and he went into a great explanation about Jesus being crucified on the cross and how that killed him. I was just thinking to myself, oh no, not a religious nut, when he went on saying that religious people wear miniature crucifix's around their necks, but if Jesus had been stabbed by a sword, then would they all be wearing miniature swords around their necks?

We both had a bit of a chuckle, I must admit that I had never heard anything like that before. He didn't stop there though, "Don't get me wrong Jack, I am not knocking religion and I have the upmost respect for other peoples beliefs, but in my profession I have to analyse everything".

Of course that left it to me to ask Thomas what profession is he referring to? "Aircraft Engineer", Thomas said without looking at me, then continued, "most churches have a large crucifix on or around the church, if you consider that Jesus was killed by a crucifix, then viewing the crucifix logically, it should be a warning to stay away. The same as the symbol of a lighting bolt on an electricity cabinet, it is warning of a hazard to life".

As we continued up the highway, Thomas turned to me and asked, "Have you read the Bible? What are your thoughts on it?"

Caught off guard, I paused before replying, "I've read parts of it when I was much younger, but honestly, I don't remember much of it."

Thomas nodded knowingly. "Most likely because you couldn't understand it, most people can't. It's only a couple of thousand years old, after all. And if you go back just another thousand years, as Erich Von Däniken will tell you, alien spaceships and astronauts were visiting Egypt. The people back then thought they were gods. Sorry, but there are just too many inconsistencies and incredibilities in those stories for me."

His response surprised me, blending skepticism, ancient astronaut theory, and a touch of humour. I chuckled politely, unsure how to follow up, and the conversation lapsed into silence again.

We were approaching Atherton and heading onto the Kennedy Highway toward Ravenshoe when Thomas spoke up once more. "Atherton. That's near where the two girls were murdered back in 1991, Julie Anne Leahy and Vicki Arnold. More specifically, it happened at Cherry Tree Creek, between Herberton and Atherton."

He continued, "The police called it a murder-suicide, and the coronial inquest came to the same conclusion. But there's been endless debate. Two coronial inquests, three police investigations, two Criminal Justice Commission inquiries, and even a state government review. And in the end, no one was ever charged."

Thomas glanced over at me. "If you're interested, Robert Reid wrote two excellent books about the case. You should read them sometime."

I murmured something neutral in response, unsure how to process the sheer amount of detail he'd just shared.

The Subaru's dashboard showed an outside temperature of 29°C, but the climate control kept the interior at a comfortable 22°C. Thomas hadn't mentioned the temperature, so I assumed he was content. We bypassed Ravenshoe, and I figured we'd settle back into quiet, but Thomas had more to share.

"Years ago, something interesting happened in Ravenshoe," he began. "The local volunteer fire service was doing some back-burning exercises around the area when they came across a suspicious pit in the ground. They started digging and found it was full of firearms. Rifles, shotguns, quite a collection."

He leaned forward slightly, clearly relishing the story. "One of the volunteer firefighters recognised one of the guns. He said it had been surrendered to the local police station by his father just a few months earlier during the firearms amnesty. Imagine that!"

I raised my eyebrows, intrigued.

"That left the volunteer captain in a real bind," Thomas continued. "He knew he had to report the discovery to the police. But if what the firefighter said was true, it meant the local police station, the very place he'd have to report it to, might have been responsible for hiding the firearms in the first place."

He chuckled darkly. "That's the kind of moral dilemma you don't learn about in training."

I shook my head in disbelief. "What happened next?"

Thomas continued that he volunteer fire service captain acted quickly and contacted a senior police officer in Brisbane. Police were dispatched from Cairns to collect the firearms, and they conducted checks against serial numbers and the surrendered firearm lists. This resulted in the local police officer being detained for questioning, and a replacement officer was promptly installed at the local police station.

I couldn't help but marvel at the whole situation. What an act of audacity! The amount of money that could be made selling firearms like that… it was staggering to think about. But what intrigued me even more was the question that had been lurking in my mind since the start of the trip: who exactly was Thomas? For an aircraft engineer, he seemed to know an awful lot about what had happened around the area.

It was just past 12:40 p.m. when we pulled up in front of the Mount Garnett Hotel. We both got out of the car and walked into the bar. Thomas, leading the way, reached the bar first and turned to me. "Would you like a beer?" he asked.

I paused for a moment, wondering if this was some kind of test. "I'd love a beer," I said, "but I'd better stick to a coke since I'm driving."

Thomas raised an eyebrow. "A couple of beers wouldn't hurt, especially with a meal. But it's up to you!"

"Alright, I'll have a XXXX Gold stubbie, thanks," I said.

To my surprise, Thomas was also a fan of XXXX Gold, and we cracked open the first beers while we looked at the menu. As a steak lover, I went with the rump steak, no gravy. I pulled a $50 note from my wallet, ready to pay for my meal.

But before I could do anything, Thomas immediately said, "I'll have the same," and pulled out a $50 note. "Replace yours back in your wallet," he added with a smile, "I'm covering all meals and accommodation for the trip to Darwin." Then, he added, "I thought you said you read and agreed to the conditions of the task."

I feigned a look of confusion. "Oh, I forgot that part," I said with a chuckle, "I didn't think it included drinks."

Thomas shook his head and grinned. "Of course it includes drinks."

Well, that was a win-win, I thought, as I relaxed into the meal and the second beer. Thomas asked how far it was to Croydon while ordering our third beer. I estimated it was about a four-hour drive. Then he asked if I had an esky in the car.

"I've got a car fridge I can turn on," I told him.

"Perfect," Thomas said, "I'll grab an additional six-pack of Goldies for the fridge."

I was starting to think that Thomas, the aircraft engineer, might be alright after all. This trip was shaping up to be better than I expected.

We drove through Georgetown without stopping, and Thomas made only one brief comment, noting that it was a major goldfield area. He mentioned that during the wet season, from late October to April, the bridge over the Etheridge River would typically be closed for three to four months, effectively cutting off the Gulf Development Road to Georgetown.

Around 5:30 p.m., we arrived at the Club Hotel in Croydon. We checked in through the bar and enjoyed two drinks before heading out to collect our bags from the car and check out the rooms. I threw my bag onto the bed in the old, but tidy and sparse room, and then headed back downstairs to the bar.

When I got there, Thomas was already at the bar, having just ordered a beer. As soon as he saw me coming, he waved to the lady behind the bar and said, "Make that two!"

Thursday night at the Croydon Club Hotel was quiet, but the pub was filled with people from the cattle and horse industries, real down-to-earth folks who were great to talk to. It was clearly cattle country, and you could tell by the conversations that this was their world. The steak was excellent, and both Thomas and I thoroughly enjoyed our 400-gram rump steaks, cooked medium-rare. After the meal, we decided on an early night and were in bed by around 10 p.m., discussing the plan for the next day. We agreed on a 9 a.m. start, which would get us to the Four Ways Roadhouse around 12:30 for lunch.

The next morning, we left the pub at ten minutes to nine and drove over to the Gulf Gate BP Roadhouse to fuel up. As I was finishing putting about $76 worth of petrol in the tank, Thomas leaned over and handed me a $100 note. "Here, Jack, use this," he said. I was a bit taken aback, first, he was covering food and accommodation, and now he was paying for fuel too.

We settled into the 370-kilometre, three-and-a-half-hour journey, and I remarked on how dry everything was. There were fire bans in place across the region, and fires had already destroyed over forty houses around Tara. More fires were threatening homes near the Sunshine Coast and on the Tablelands. Thomas nodded gravely and added, "The volunteers in the fire service are the real heroes. They save lives and properties, and the government does next to nothing for them. They've introduced a system where they pay volunteers after a ten-day period of fighting fires, but it's a joke. It's a variable day rate based on their regular salary. For example, if a guy earns $200 a day in his regular job, after fighting fires for ten days, they'll pay him $200 a day, but it's capped at $6,000 per year. But if another volunteer, who's a pensioner, fights fires alongside him, they pay him next to nothing."

I was taken aback by the harshness of his words.

Thomas shook his head in frustration. "You know, Jack, there are 28,000 volunteer firefighters in Queensland and 1,400 rural fire brigades. They received just a little over one billion dollars in the last Queensland budget. It's nothing for such a huge task over such a vast area. Meanwhile, the government thinks $7 billion is fine to spend on the Olympic Games. I'd much rather see that money go toward better firefighting equipment and more fully-paid rural firefighting staff."

I nodded, realising how deeply passionate he was about the issue.

We arrived at the roadhouse, and Thomas told me to go in ahead of him while he made a phone call. I went into the bar, ordered two stubbies of Gold, and grabbed two menus. Finding an empty table, I sat down and began scanning the menu while I waited for him. I was nearly done with my first beer when Thomas came in, grabbed his stubbie, and almost downed half of it in one go. Glancing at the menu, he turned to me and said, "Could you get me a rump steak, medium-rare?" He handed me a $100 note. "I'll be right back."

The steaks arrived, and I grabbed two more Gold stubbies. Thomas walked back inside just in time. The steak itself had a really good flavour but was tough. The chips, however, were another story. Thomas said they should be "shoved up the arse of the prick that cooked them" – they were disgusting, in his words.

Thomas then told me we had to make a little detour into Cloncurry on the way to Mount Isa, adding that we'd need to plan for an extra day in Mount Isa. He mentioned he'd pay me for the additional day, which was perfectly fine with me.

Once back in the car, Thomas said we had to go to Daintree Street in Cloncurry, to the Council Chambers. I agreed, and we set off for Cloncurry, just 190 kilometres away.

Thomas mentioned that we were booked into the Ibis Hotel for both Friday and Saturday nights. He added that he had some business calls to make on Saturday morning but wouldn't need me, as he'd be picked up from the hotel and dropped back later that morning. He most likely wouldn't want to travel a long distance that afternoon, so I would be free to amuse myself for the day. Then, he handed me a roll of hundred-dollar bills and said, "That's for the extra day!"

We didn't spend much time at the Council Chambers in Cloncurry. Thomas went inside while I parked the car, and he was back just after I parked. I barely had enough time to count the money he had given me, ten one-hundred-dollar notes, before Thomas returned carrying a laptop bag. He asked me to open the back of the Subaru, which I did by remote. As I went to the back to assist, I noticed Thomas opening his large suitcase to place the laptop bag inside. I happened to glance inside the suitcase and saw that it was almost empty, with only a black coat or cloak in it.

After placing the bag inside, Thomas got into the car, and we headed toward Mount Isa.

I asked Thomas why he preferred driving to flying, especially when it involved such long distances. He replied that he was never in a hurry and liked to make a bit of a holiday out of traveling. Plus, he said, if he had flown to Mount Isa, he would have had to hire a car to get to Cloncurry, then fly on to Darwin. After that, he'd either have to fly back to Brisbane or Cairns and then hire a car to get to Palmerston and other areas around Darwin.

"Ah, so you're on business then. I thought you might be retired and just tripping around," I commented.

"Semi-retired would be more accurate," he responded, "but I do love tripping around, especially like this, with someone to drive me and company along the way. Not to mention, I drink too much to drive."

"You said you are an Aircraft Engineer. Is that the business you're conducting on this trip?" I asked.

"Jack," Thomas said, "I think you're a decent sort of chap, very respectful for your age, which I'd guess is around the forty mark. But Jack, if we're going to get along, and if you're interested in more work with me, maybe much more, actually, you need to learn to stop asking too many questions."

I felt a bit like an idiot. I had probably been a little too inquisitive. So, I told him I'd stop with the questions, and he nodded.

"That's good," he said, "but don't worry, we'll get along just fine. You'll learn more about me as we go along." He paused, then added, "I don't want you just to drop me off in Darwin. If it's agreeable with you, I'd like you to ferry me around Darwin for a few days. I'll pay for the fuel and pay you $1,000 per day."

I nearly choked trying to get a "yes" out of my throat.

We arrived at Mount Isa, and Thomas told me to head straight to the hotel on the corner of Camooweal Street and Rodeo Drive. There was underground parking, but you couldn't get in until you'd checked in. "Wait here near the entrance," he said. "I'll check us in." He was back in a few minutes with a card to open the car park entry.

After getting our bags from the car, Thomas handed me my keycard to my room and said he would meet me at the 'Buffs' Club, just up the street, in about an hour. I thought my room was pretty impressive, so I decided to have a shower and get changed before heading to the club.

I found the club at the top of the street from the hotel, though I had to walk around to the main entrance on Simpson Street. It was quite an impressive club for being out in the bush, I thought. I was running a bit early, so I started looking around when I heard, "Jack, over here!"

Thomas was at the bar and had already ordered a couple of beers. He handed me one, along with a hundred-dollar note, and said, "Go and play the pokies, and meet me at the Frog and Toad Bistro, the club's restaurant, at seven o'clock. I have a meeting with someone at six, and it should only take about an hour." Before I had a chance to respond, he was gone, but the plan sounded good to me.

It wasn't hard to find the gaming lounge. The first thing that struck me was the number of Aboriginal people in there playing the poker machines and drinking coffee. I found out later that as long as they were members of the club, membership costs just two dollars for the year, and they were playing a poker machine, which cost one cent per play, they could push a button on the machine to order a drink and receive free coffee or water right at the machine.

I found a 'Queen of the Nile' machine and invested Thomas's one hundred dollars in five-dollar bets, which quickly dwindled to almost nothing within about twenty minutes. I decided to add another one hundred dollars of my own money. Within half a dozen presses of the button, I landed the free spins and turned it into eight hundred dollars. Suddenly, I seemed to have made a lot of new friends around me. Deciding it was a good time to quit, I grabbed the cash and headed to the Bistro.

As I approached the Bistro, Thomas, in the company of another well-aged gentleman, was just about to enter the dining room. He had just told the receptionist that they would need a table for three. "Good timing," I said with a smile, catching up with them just as they were about to step inside. Thomas turned towards me and, with a friendly nod, introduced me to Robert Fruehauf, an old business acquaintance of his. He then introduced me to Robert as his new PA. I was momentarily taken aback; I had no idea what Thomas meant by PA, but I took Robert's hand, offered the usual pleasantries, and asked after his health.

The receptionist led us to our table, placing menus at each seat. With a warm smile, she assured us that someone would be with us shortly to take our orders.

The menu, I quickly noticed, was quite extensive, with a particularly mouthwatering selection from the grill, which all three of us commented on approvingly. Robert, speaking from experience, remarked that most restaurants in Mount Isa prided themselves on offering great steaks, a reflection of the town's strong connection to the beef industry. Contrary to the popular belief that Mount Isa is solely a mining town, Robert explained that it was just as much a heartland of Australian beef production. In fact, he himself had been involved in the industry for many years, though these days he wasn't as hands-on. Still, he maintained a refined appreciation for good beef, which was clearly evident as he discussed the subject.

Most of the beef produced in the area, he continued, came from the Drought-master breed. A true product of North Queensland, Drought-master cattle were first developed around 1915 by crossing zebuine cattle with British breeds, particularly the Beef Shorthorn. The Drought-master was the first Australian Taurindicine hybrid breed, a cross of Brahman and Shorthorn. This breed was well-suited to the harsh conditions of the region, making it a popular choice among cattle producers in the area.

The waitress arrived promptly, but we weren't quite ready to place our meal orders yet. Thomas, ever the enthusiast for fine wine, wasted no time in ordering a bottle of Paringa Estate Pinot Noir. I had been about to order a beer, but Thomas, with a knowing smile, suggested I hold off on that and try the wine first. Robert, ever the connoisseur, congratulated Thomas on his excellent choice and added, "As usual," with a touch of admiration.

The wine arrived swiftly, and I took a cautious sip. Now, I'm not much of a wine drinker, but I couldn't help but be struck by how brilliant this particular wine was. It had a depth and richness that was unlike anything I'd tasted before. In fact, it reminded me of a German Burgundy I had tried many years ago, smooth, well-balanced, and deeply satisfying. As I savored the flavour, I glanced up, and Thomas nodded toward me knowingly, as if he had anticipated my reaction.

With the wine setting the tone, we proceeded to place our meal orders. Robert, in his usual style, opted for the 300g Black King Sirloin, cooked medium-rare, served with vegetables and a baked potato. Thomas, always one to indulge in the finer cuts of meat, ordered the 350g Wagyu steak, cooked medium-rare, with chips and a fresh salad. I decided to go with the 300g Angus Rump, medium-rare, accompanied by chips and salad.

As the waitress took our orders, there was a comfortable silence for a moment, as we all took another sip of the wine, appreciating its complexity and smooth finish. The evening was shaping up to be quite enjoyable.

Dinner was relatively quiet, with very little conversation beyond the usual small talk about the weather and compliments about the excellent atmosphere at the 'Buffs' Club. The evening had a laid-back vibe, but when I casually mentioned the presence of Aboriginal patrons in the Gaming Rooms, Robert's expression darkened. His voice grew more animated as he spoke.

"These people come in every morning as soon as the Club opens," he said, his tone laced with frustration. "They head straight for the Gaming Room, play one-cent pokies, and drink beers and free coffee in the air-conditioned comfort all day long. It's pathetic. And what's worse, the Government actually pays them to do it. The Club can't stop them either, or they'd be in all sorts of trouble. It's just sad, really. The Government keeps throwing more and more money at the problem, hoping it'll fix itself or just disappear. But it's not going anywhere. It's just a bunch of idiots making bad decisions."

I nodded, taken aback by Robert's vehemence. It was clear this issue was something that really bothered him, and his words hung in the air for a moment before we moved on to lighter topics.

After dinner, Robert bid us farewell with a firm handshake, expressing how nice it had been to meet me. He mentioned he'd most likely see me again on his next visit to the 'Isa'. As he left, Thomas and I headed to the bar for another round of beers before sitting down at a table to chat.

Curious about the "PA" comment earlier, I turned to Thomas. "So, what exactly is a PA?" I asked.

Thomas grinned, clearly enjoying the moment. "Personal Assistant," he said, his voice light. "I figured it sounded better than just 'contract driver.'" His smile faded slightly as he continued in a more serious tone. "But, there might actually be a full-time position coming up. Things are picking up now, and I could use some help." He noticed the surprise and eagerness on my face and quickly raised both hands in a stop gesture. "Don't ask me any questions yet, alright? It's early days. You'll get the details when we hit the road on Sunday."

He paused, took a swig of his beer, and added, "Besides, I don't even know who you are or what you do yet. You can give me your history on the trip. We've got plenty of time for that."

I was still processing the possibility of a full-time role when I offered Thomas $450, half of my pokies winnings, as a gesture of gratitude. To my surprise, he actually accepted it, nodding approvingly. "Good on you, mate. I think things will go well for us." He leaned back in his chair, then stood up. "I'm heading off now, but meet me at the 'Isa Hotel' tomorrow at twelve for lunch. It's on the corner of Miles Street and Rodeo Drive. When you get there, grab a table for six and wait for me."

With the night winding down, I decided I had enough for the evening too. I joined Thomas for the short walk back to the Ibis Hotel where we were staying, reflecting on the unexpected turn of events and wondering what tomorrow would bring.

That night, lying in my hotel room, my mind was racing. I couldn't stop wondering about Thomas. What exactly was he involved in? What kind of business did he run? What had been in that bag he picked up in Cloncurry at the Council Chambers? And who was Robert Fruehauf, an old business acquaintance, as Thomas had said? Robert had mentioned seeing me on his next trip, but I couldn't quite shake the feeling that there was something more going on here than met the eye.

I tossed and turned, my thoughts swirling. But then, as the night wore on, I began to dismiss these questions. So what if I didn't have all the answers? In the grand scheme of things, who cared? This guy, Thomas, seemed to be loaded, he was practically swimming in one hundred-dollar notes, and he wasn't shy about handing them out. And honestly, the money he was offering me was looking pretty good.

A full-time job with him seemed promising. The pay could be lucrative, very lucrative, if things kept going the way they were. I could almost taste the potential. But then, an unsettling thought crept into my mind. What if whatever Thomas was involved in wasn't on the up-and-up? What if I was getting involved in something illegal and didn't even know it? The thought was like a cold chill running down my spine.

I quickly shook off the thought, telling myself I was just being paranoid. There was no reason to jump to conclusions. I had no real proof of anything, just some lingering questions. This could be a great opportunity for me. No need to overthink it.

With that in mind, I rolled over, pulled the covers up, and pushed all those silly doubts to the back of my mind. I had a job to do. Time to focus on the here and now. I would meet Thomas at the 'Isa Hotel' at noon, like he said. Whatever lay ahead, I was going to take it one step at a time.

It only took a few minutes to walk to the Isa Hotel from the Ibis, and as I entered the bustling dining room, I noticed it was quite busy, both in the bar and the bistro. I quickly spotted a waitress and asked for a table for six. She told me there were only two left, so I picked the one overlooking Miles Street. I had just settled into my seat when Thomas walked in, accompanied by two well-dressed men. Both were in suits, one of them with a tie, exuding an air of professionalism.

I raised my arm to signal Thomas as he scanned the now-crowded room. He made his way over, introducing me to his guests. "Jack," he said, "I'd like you to meet a couple of colleagues of mine, John Snape and Bill Collins." I stood and shook both of their hands, offering the usual pleasantries as Thomas continued. "Jack is my new PA, and he'll be coming with us to the races today."

With a nod, Thomas handed me a laptop bag he had been carrying. "Jack, could you take this up to my room at the Ibis and place it in my large suitcase?" he asked. "Don't linger too long; we need to get to the races before two o'clock." He handed me a key card and told me his room number was 302.

I made my way back to the Ibis with the laptop bag in hand. It wasn't particularly heavy, but as I held it, I noticed something unusual: a small zip tie was attached between the two zips, securing the bag and preventing it from being opened. Curiosity piqued, I arrived at Thomas's room and found his large suitcase on wheels tucked in the corner. I laid the suitcase on the bed and opened the front zip.

Inside, I saw the other laptop bag that Thomas had placed there back in Cloncurry. It was the same one, but there was something else that caught my eye. What I had initially thought was a black coat was, in fact, a black drawstring bag. Unable to resist, I gently opened the draw bag and was taken aback by what I found. Inside were several Australia Post prepaid padded envelopes, all empty but addressed to different people. Alongside these were a number of unassembled Australia Post flat-pack boxes, which also bore names and addresses, presumably for delivery.

One particular box stood out. The return name and address on it read "Saibin" and a PO Box number: 932C, Cairns City, Qld 4870. My heart skipped a beat. Something about this felt off, but I couldn't put my finger on it.

I quickly closed the drawstring bag, placed the new laptop bag on top of the other one, and hurriedly zipped the suitcase shut. With a final glance around the room, I left and returned to the Isa Hotel as quickly as I could, my mind racing with questions about what I had just discovered. What was Thomas involved in? And what was all this mail for?

As I approached the table, I noticed that Thomas and his colleagues were already holding drinks. Thomas had placed a cold beer at my seat, and with a grin, he said, "Good, you're back. Let's order."

The steak selection at the Isa Hotel is widely regarded as one of the best in the area. The unique part of the experience is that you get to select your steak cut directly from a chilled display case, and then tell the chef exactly how you want it cooked. For someone like me who appreciates a good steak, this was heaven. After a moment of deliberation, I chose an Angus rib on the bone. Everyone at the table quickly followed suit, agreeing that the rib on the bone was the way to go, with each of us ordering it medium rare, accompanied by chips and salad.

We ordered three more beers each and chatted casually while the meals were being prepared. After a while, we all finished our drinks and decided it was time to head to the races. A short four-minute drive by taxi took us to the Mount Isa Racecourse, the excitement of the day building as we approached the entrance.

I had learnt in the taxi that that both John and Bill both owned race horses together so it was no real surprise when we got to the course that we were able to use the Members Facilities. Chatting to John I discovered that he actually owned a blue metal quarry just out of Mount Isa and that Bill was a transport operator, in both livestock and he had tippers for blue metal products. Very impressive I thought, Thomas certainly seems to have friends in the right circles.

I was quite surprised when I saw John placing bets on the TAB rather than the 'Bookies' on track. He told me that betting with the TAB didn't stuff up the prices so he could put bigger bets on. I said I might put $10 each way on a horse called 'Thespigott' and he said that would be a wast of time and money and said to put $100 each way on his stable mate 'Whattsupp Kid', it was paying $60 for a win and I would most likely win a couple of grand. I thought wow, this is the way to go with these blokes so I did put $200 on the horse and I can't begin to explain how sad I was when the thing came 7th and 'Thespigott' came 2nd. It didn't seem to worry the boys though and they just kept on backing horses and drinking beers like they were going out of fashion.

I had no idea what time it was when we finally made our way back to the Buffs Club for dinner and drinks. By then, it seemed like no one was interested in a big meal; instead, everyone settled on chicken schnitzels and salads, with more beers flowing freely. It wasn't long before we headed into the poker machine room, but by that point, I had had enough. After a long day at the races, I had a 450km drive ahead of me in the morning. I said my goodbyes to the group and made my way out.

As I stepped outside the Club, a few people approached me, wanting to befriend me, asking for cigarettes and money for a taxi. When I told them I didn't smoke and was broke, their friendly demeanour turned to hostility. I was quickly labeled a "fucking cunt" and told I should get out of their country because I was "white shit" and needed a good bashing. I was beginning to feel uneasy when one of the bouncers from the Club stepped in and yelled at them to leave. He threatened to call the police, but before I could even process it, the group turned their anger on me, blaming me for the whole situation because, of course, I was a "white cunt."

I made my way back to the Ibis Hotel, a bit rattled, though relieved to escape without any further confrontation. Still, I couldn't shake the feeling of unease as more people along the way made similar demands for money or cigarettes, hurling insults and telling me to leave their country.

Once I got back to my room, I started thinking about Thomas. I realised that he, being older than me, might not be as lucky in getting past the same crowd. The thought of him getting hassled by the group of Aborigines outside the Club had me worried. I figured I'd better go back to the Buffs and wait for him, so I grabbed my jacket and headed out again.

As I walked back toward the Club, I noticed there were fewer Aborigines on the street, but a couple of bouncers were stationed outside the entrance, which made me feel safer. I went inside and quickly found Thomas, who seemed to be three sheets to the wind at that point. He was genuinely surprised and thankful when I explained why I had returned to wait for him.

"I would've been fine," he assured me, slurring a bit, but his gratitude was clear. To show his appreciation, he bought me another beer, though, honestly, I didn't need it.

It was clear that no matter how much money Thomas had or how well-connected he seemed, there was a different side to the town I hadn't seen before. And though my concern for his safety had been a bit exaggerated, I was glad I'd come back to make sure he got home in one piece.

We were driving towards the Queensland-Northern Territory border, and the quietness in the car was a bit unusual for Thomas. He had been a little subdued this morning, but I wasn't surprised. After all, it had been quite a full day yesterday. He broke the silence, commenting that it had been a great day and then asked if I had enjoyed it. I told him I certainly had, and then I asked him what had happened to the other people he mentioned who were supposed to join us for lunch.

Thomas thought for a moment before responding, "What two other people? There was never going to be any more than the four of us." I was a little confused, but I explained that he had told me to get a table for six. He raised an eyebrow and said, "Yes, because if you get a table for four, it's too squashy. You don't even have room for your drinks, let alone your food."

I chuckled and nodded, thinking that actually made a lot of sense. It was a good idea, and I'd remember it for the future.

We arrived at the Barkley Homestead Roadhouse around two in the afternoon. Thomas, as usual, took care of the room arrangements while I used the $100 note he'd handed me earlier to fill the car. As I was still at the pump, he returned with a key and told me the rooms were far out the back, but that I could park right in front of them. He added that he was in desperate need of a beer and would meet me in the bar shortly. I finished fuelling up, paid the attendant, and asked where the rooms were. She gave me clear directions, and I drove around to the back of the building.

The rooms were simple but neat, nothing too fancy, but clean and cool, with the air conditioning running. It was a bit of a quiet afternoon, and I figured I'd probably spend most of it just relaxing. Thomas had mentioned that he didn't like to travel more than about 500 kilometres in a day whenever possible, and today seemed like one of those days.

I left the room and headed toward the bar to find Thomas. When I walked in, I spotted him immediately, he was standing at the bar with a large fellow who looked like he hadn't seen a razor in a while. His attire consisted of a bright green shirt, khaki shorts, and elastic-sided boots that had clearly seen better days. From his appearance, I figured he must be a truck driver or perhaps a station worker, and it seemed like Thomas had made some casual small talk with him while waiting for me.

What caught me off guard, though, was that Thomas had a drink in hand but hadn't ordered one for me. I was a little put out, but I didn't want to interrupt him, so I moved closer, positioning myself so he could easily spot me.

"Oh Jack!" Thomas said as he turned toward the truckie-looking fellow, "This is my new PA, Jack. Jack, meet Rex Grogan."

I stretched out my hand and shook his. "Dropper, mate. Everyone calls me Dropper. But don't ask why," Rex said with a grin. "I'm buying, what are you drinking?"

I appreciated the offer, but it was still a bit of an awkward moment, Thomas had clearly been comfortable with Rex, and I was just trying to figure out where I fit into the whole scene. It seemed like Thomas and his circle were always full of surprises, and I had a feeling this was just the beginning of many more to come.

We left the bar and settled down at a table with our drinks. As I sat there, I couldn't help but wonder how Thomas knew Rex, as he didn't exactly seem like the type of person you'd associate with someone like Thomas. But I didn't have to wait long for an answer. Thomas explained, "Rex was once a partner with Bill Collins in the stock transport business, but now he runs his own company out of Camooweal."

I felt pretty spot on with my initial assessment of Rex, as he certainly fit the profile of someone who might be involved in the heavy transport business. Rex added with a grunt, "Yeah, I was with the old Bill for a long time until he teamed up with that prick Snape. Couldn't stand him, fucking poufter. Now I run my own show, got a couple dozen road trains. Just making ends meet, but it's a great life." He paused and looked at us both. "Youse blokes gonna have a feed?"

At that, Thomas stood up with a laptop bag in his hand. He said he'd take it to his room and be back shortly. I turned to Rex and asked if he wanted another beer. He gave me a look that I can only describe as amused and asked, "Is the fuckin' Pope a fuckin' Catholic?"

I made my way to the bar, and as I stood waiting to order, I realised something, these were the first beers I'd bought with my own money since the start of the trip. A strange thought to have, but it hit me nonetheless. I returned to the table with the three beers, and Thomas still wasn't back from his room. I couldn't help but wonder about the other laptop bag Thomas had, was it the one I had put in his suitcase earlier, or was there another one?

Rex broke my train of thought, asking, "So, what were you doing before working with this bloke?" I told him I had been a Construction Project Manager in Cairns and was currently in between jobs, just helping Thomas out for the time being. Rex raised an eyebrow and asked, "How well do you know Thomas?"

I replied honestly, "I don't know him very well, but he seems like a nice enough guy." Rex then asked, "What do you think of his business?" Before I could answer, he waved a hand and said, "Shhhhhh, don't worry about it," as Thomas returned to the table.

Rex winked at me and said, "So, I got the name 'Dropper' because I couldn't catch the fuckin' balls when I was fielding in cricket." His smile was wide, and there was a certain rugged charm to him.

As Thomas went to get another round of drinks, Rex passed me a business card with a serious look in his eyes. He said quietly, "Put this away from Thomas's eyes, mate. If you find out anything, give me a call."

Thomas came back just then, and I must have looked a little confused because he asked me if I was alright. I quickly reassured him that I was fine, just starting to get a bit hungry. I began scanning the menu. Rex did the same, and Thomas followed suit. He went to the bar to grab the next round of beers.

I assumed Rex was staying at the roadhouse for the night, so I asked, "What time are you leaving tomorrow morning, and where are you heading?"

Rex took a long pull from his beer before responding, "I'm not staying here tonight. I'll sleep in my sleeper cab for a couple of hours until all the fucking caravans get off the road at about eight pm, then I'll drive through the night to pick up a hundred head near Mataranka in the morning."

I froze for a moment, my mouth hanging open. I was going to say something about drinking and driving, but then I thought better of it. Instead, I stayed silent, my mind racing. The roads here were sparsely patrolled, and I imagined that the few police officers out this way would probably be asleep during the night. It was a more relaxed atmosphere for law enforcement out here, or at least it seemed that way.

Thomas came back with another round of beers just as Rex finished speaking. I realised this trip was shaping up to be even more unpredictable than I'd anticipated.

We all three had T-bones for dinner, as that was pretty much the only option on the menu, and I honestly have no idea how many beers we had that evening. By around seven o'clock, Rex stood up and said he'd better get an hour's sleep before heading off to Mataranka for his early morning cattle pickup. As he left the table, he added he'd better get a nightcap. He returned from the bar with another round of beers.

Thomas turned to me and asked how I felt about going through to Katherine the next day. He explained that it was about 850 kilometres away, but there weren't many places to stop along the way, mostly cabins in caravan parks. I was fine with that; I didn't mind the drive, and I appreciated the creature comforts along the way. We agreed that we would try lunch at Daly Waters, at Rex's suggestion.

Rex finished his drink, placed the empty stubbie on the table, and got up. He shook hands with Thomas, saying he'd look forward to seeing him in about six months, and then shook my hand before heading out of the tavern toward his truck. As he walked away, Thomas and I just shook our heads. "Much better to drive in daylight," Thomas suggested. I agreed. It made sense, given the long stretch of road ahead.

On the way back to my room, I considered checking out the card Rex had given me, but by the time I reached my room, I was completely exhausted. I lay on the bed, still dressed, and within moments I passed out. I must've been out cold, because the next thing I knew, it was seven o'clock in the morning, and a knock at my door woke me from my luxurious sleep.

I opened the door, and there was Thomas, standing with a knowing look as he took in my disheveled appearance. He glanced at my clothes and said, "Good, you're ready to go. Do you want breakfast, or are we getting some down the track?"

I didn't reveal to Thomas how I was feeling, completely drained and still a little drunk, but I simply nodded and grabbed my untouched bag from the other bed. I'd left it there the day before. Without saying much, I followed him out to the car.

We didn't stop for long that day, but around one o'clock, we pulled into the Daly Waters pub. By this point, I was definitely not in the mood for another beer. I just needed a coke and something light to eat. As Thomas went inside the pub, I stayed behind to fill up the car with petrol, once again paid for by one of Thomas's $100 notes. As I pumped the fuel, I found myself looking at the note, wondering if it might be a forgery. The thought brought back the strange memory of Rex's questions from the night before. There was something about that whole situation that didn't quite sit right with me, but I couldn't quite place what it was. Something felt off.

I finished filling up the car and, without a second thought, pocketed the change. Why not? The guy never took it when I offered it to him anyway. I made my way into the pub, dodging the brassieres hanging from the ceiling, and glancing at all the money pinned to the walls, notes from places far and wide, a testament to the many patrons who'd passed through. It struck me that, in another time, this could be a great spot for an evening out. If only I was feeling about 600% better than I did at that moment.

I found Thomas at the bar, and, as expected, he had a **XXXX** Gold stubbie waiting for me. After knocking back two of them, I started feeling significantly better. We each had a sausage roll and began our three-hour journey to Katherine.

Thomas directed me to take the Gorge Road towards the Cicada Lodge, and I followed without question. About 20 minutes later, we arrived at the Lodge.

Thomas had heard good things about the food, so we walked into reception. He told the receptionist he had a booking for two rooms, two nights, under the name "Jack Thomas." She handed him a form to sign, the total amount: $2,200.

"Is that on a credit card?" she asked, a hint of expectation in her voice.

"No," Thomas replied, placing the full amount in cash on the counter.

The receptionist raised an eyebrow. "I'll need an imprint of your credit card for incidentals."

Thomas shook his head. "I don't have a credit card."

Without another word, he scooped the cash off the counter and turned towards the door. "Cancel the rooms," he said flatly. "Come on, Jack."

As we began to leave, the receptionist called after us. "I can talk to the manager."

Thomas didn't even break stride. "Don't bother," he called back. "There'll be a cancellation fee of one night for each room. That's $1,100."

"Good afternoon," he said, and with a casual smile, "Good luck."

The drive back into town was quiet, save for the occasional muttering from Thomas. His frustration with the system was palpable. "Fucking credit cards," he spat. "It's as if the whole world revolves around banks and their exorbitant interest rates. The Reserve Bank hikes the rates, and who benefits? The banks. They've made record profits this year, and the government keeps funnelling more money to them. Why? It's obvious. Someone's getting a fat backhander or, at the very least, extremely low-interest loans. And this cashless society the government's pushing? They want the banks to run everything so they can charge whatever they want. No competition. They're all in on it together."

He took a sharp left turn. "Turn left here, Jack. We'll head to Knotts Crossing Resort. At least it's got a bar and a restaurant."

At the Knotts Crossing Resort, there was no mention of credit cards. They gladly accepted cash. The bill for the two rooms for two nights came to a much more reasonable $1,160. Thomas grinned. "That leaves us with more to spend at the bar. Speaking of which, I'll meet you there in twenty minutes."

We found our rooms, and I parked the car close to mine. Tossing my bag onto the bed, I headed out to find the bar and restaurant. When I walked in, I was the only one there, the bar didn't open until four o'clock. I had about ten minutes to kill, and frankly, I was hanging out. Just then, Thomas stuck his head through the door.

"Come on, Jack," he said. "I've got a taxi waiting outside."

I slid into the back of the cab, with Thomas already settled up front, his mind already on the night ahead. "Katherine Club, mate," he instructed the driver, before turning to me with a wry smile. "A man's not a fucking camel, Jack," he added, as we started our journey into town. His remark, though cryptic, was delivered in his usual dry tone, a reminder of the way he saw the world, always a little rough around the edges but full of meaning, if you cared to look.

There was no more signing in to clubs now, not since the whole Covid situation turned everything upside down. These days, you just walk in. No fuss, no questions asked. We made our way to the bar, where the usual hum of conversation and clinking glasses filled the air. It had that comforting buzz that made a night out feel like it had potential. We grabbed a spot, got our beers, and settled in.

I couldn't resist asking Thomas, "So, are you entertaining clients tonight?"

"No, tomorrow night," he replied casually, his eyes scanning the room as he took a swig from his beer. "Tomorrow, I've got some business to attend to, but you can take it easy around the resort if you want. I won't need you. But feel free to join me and one of my cronies for dinner at the restaurant. It's bloody great food, especially the steaks."

I was curious, of course. Curious about Thomas's business, what it really was, and how he operated. But the opportunity to ask never seemed to come. Instead, we spent the evening enjoying a few more beers, playing the pokies, and then heading to the Club for a solid dinner. Afterward, we caught a cab back to the resort, the night still young but winding down.

We got dropped off at the main entrance, and Thomas turned to me with a grin. "Enjoy your day off tomorrow," he said. "I'll see you at the restaurant around six."

That night, I slept like a log, completely wiped out. I didn't stir until well after nine-thirty, which meant I'd missed breakfast. No worries, though. I figured I could sort myself out. I drove into Katherine, grabbed a Quarter Pounder at Maccas, and then swung by the bottle shop for a carton of XXXX Gold stubbies and a couple of bags of ice. I stashed them all in my big esky and headed back to the resort for a slow, easy day. I spent a few hours by the pool, enjoying the solitude. There wasn't a soul in sight, and it felt like my own private retreat. I cracked open a cold one, let the warmth of the sun soak in, and felt the day stretch out in front of me.

When six o'clock rolled around, I was showered and changed, ready to meet Thomas at the restaurant.

Thomas was already there when I arrived. He introduced me as "Jack, his PA" to Paul Jensen, the man sitting across from him. I shook Paul's hand, noting his grip was weak, but he gave me a smile that felt almost too rehearsed. I sat down at the table for six, which made me chuckle inside, remembering Thomas's reasoning for needing such a big table. It was one of his quirks, always preparing for the unexpected, even if the only people there were the ones he invited. The waitress came by, delivering drinks to the table. All of us ordered the same thing: XXXX Gold stubbies. It seemed like a safe bet.

She then asked if we wanted the menus now or if we'd wait for the others to arrive. Thomas, as always, was dismissive. "Bring out the menus," he said. "The others are unreliable."

The waitress gave Thomas a skeptical look. The restaurant was beginning to fill up, and I could see her weighing the pros and cons of using these extra seats. But Thomas seemed oblivious to it, completely unfazed by the growing tension. It wasn't that he didn't care, it was more that he didn't see any reason why he should.

Paul, on the other hand, seemed like an amiable sort, at first glance. Thomas had introduced him as a poultry farmer, someone who worked with eggs and poultry. "Mainly chooks and some turkeys, anything for a quid really," Paul added with a laugh that didn't quite reach his eyes.

I couldn't help but study Paul more closely. He was thin, too thin, in fact, and looked like he was running on fumes. I'd guess he was around sixty, maybe a little more, and there was something about him that screamed exhaustion. The kind of weariness that goes beyond just hard work, it felt deeper, like a man worn down by years of stress. To top it off, his hairstyle, a comb-over that looked like it hadn't seen a good barber in years, was almost enough to make me cringe. It was the kind of look that made you feel embarrassed for him, sitting across from me like that. Yet Thomas seemed completely at ease, as if this was just another night with another acquaintance.

Paul didn't seem to notice my discomfort, though. He kept chatting about his poultry business, his voice picking up speed as he spoke about the intricacies of farming, the challenges, and the occasional windfall. Still, I couldn't shake the feeling that there was something off about him. Something hidden beneath that thin exterior, and it wasn't just his failing health.

As the night wore on, the conversation shifted, becoming more about business and less about small talk. But I found myself distracted, wondering just how much of what Paul said was true, and how much of it was a mask to hide the cracks in his life. What was really going on in his world? I had no answers, but I couldn't help but feel that I was getting a glimpse of something far more complicated than what Paul was letting on.

The waitress brought out six menus, casting a quick, knowing look in our direction. I had to fight to keep a straight face, my eyes darting toward the ground to suppress the laughter bubbling up inside. It was as if she'd seen this all before. The table, despite being large enough for six, felt oddly small for just the three of us.

Thomas and I both ordered the 400-gram Ribeye with chips and salad, and Paul, ever the poultry advocate, opted for the Special Chicken with chats and broccolini. He looked at us both with a sort of smugness and said, "I have to be seen supporting my industry. These people buy a fair bit of food from me." I raised an eyebrow but said nothing.

Once the orders were in, Thomas stood up from the table, excusing himself with a casual, "I'll be back in a minute or two. Gonna grab some more beers." He threw a glance over at Paul, adding, "I'll get you a Great Northern Light this time," before he walked off, carrying his laptop bag as he went.

A few minutes later, Thomas returned, the laptop bag gone, replaced with two gold stubbies and one Great Northern Light. The meals arrived almost immediately after, and I dug in. The ribeye was nothing short of excellent, perfectly cooked, juicy, and tender, the way a good steak should be.

Paul, on the other hand, seemed to settle back in his chair, eyeing our meals with a look of mild regret. "I would've rather had the steak," he admitted, but then he took a bite of his chicken and seemed to come to a reluctant conclusion. "But this chicken's superb," he said, pushing his comb-over back into place with one hand as he chewed, his hair looking a little worse for wear with each movement.

Dinner was, for the most part, quiet. The conversation was sparse, almost nonexistent at times. Paul was one of those people who answered every question with either a "yes," "no," or the ever-popular "I don't really know."

It was a little like pulling teeth, trying to get anything remotely engaging out of him. To make matters more mundane, Paul cut himself off after two beers. "I've got to drive," he said, as if that somehow made him an upstanding citizen in a sea of bad habits.

By the time we finished our meals, it was around seven-thirty. Paul announced that he'd better be on his way. "I'll see you in six months," he said, his voice carrying an odd finality.

Thomas didn't miss a beat. "About six months, Paul. I'll let you know when it's getting close, alright?" he replied, a polite but dismissive tone in his voice. And just like that, Paul was gone, leaving the two of us at the table.

Once Paul had left, Thomas turned to me with a glint in his eye. "You wanna go back to the Club? Have a few more drinks, maybe play some pokies?" He was already pulling out his phone to call for a taxi, clearly set on going whether I tagged along or not.

"Why not?" I shrugged, not having anything else pressing on my mind. Besides, a few more beers seemed like a good way to cap off the night. So, with that, we headed out, leaving the restaurant behind in favour of another round at the Club. The night was still young, after all.

We were on our third beer, or maybe it was our fourth by then, as we wandered around the pokies. Thomas was keeping a steady $5 bet, having a bit of luck on his side. He passed me on his way to grab two more stubbies and, without skipping a beat, handed one to me as he returned. We clinked our bottles, and he went right back to his machine, focusing intently on his next spin.

Suddenly, a scream pierced the air, a blood-curdling, full-throated scream that sent a shiver down my spine. It was coming from the direction of where Thomas had been playing, and I could hear the rising buzz of people gathering. Intrigued and a bit concerned, I walked over, making my way toward the scene.

There, in the centre of the crowd, was a young man, maybe in his late twenties, holding his hand in a way that immediately told me something was terribly wrong. His hand was crushed, blood pooling around it, and there was beer splattered across the poker machine. The man was screaming "Sorry! Sorry!" over and over, his face twisted in pain.

Then I saw Thomas, who was standing just outside the circle of onlookers, watching the whole spectacle unfold with an almost detached interest. "You are so lucky," he said coldly, eyeing the young man, "The last man who stole from me is dead."

Without missing a beat, Thomas bent down and ripped the poker machine playing card from the man's mangled hand. "Thieving prick," he muttered under his breath, holding the card up as if it was the most natural thing in the world.

The Duty Manager from the Club arrived quickly, assessing the situation with a glance. He didn't need much time to figure out what had happened: the young man had clearly tried to cash in on Thomas's machine using his playing card. And in the worst timing possible, Thomas had just returned in time to catch him mid-swipe. The result? The young man's hand had taken the brunt of Thomas's full beer bottle, which Thomas had apparently smashed down in the heat of the moment.

"Are you okay, Thomas?" the Duty Manager asked, looking at him with concern.

"Not really," Thomas replied with a smirk. "I just lost a full beer."

The Duty Manager, clearly trying to maintain a professional demeanour despite the chaos, promised, "I'll replace it for you once I get this fella out of here."

Thomas didn't seem to care at all about the young man's condition. In fact, he laughed and added, "I hope he wasn't the Club's pianist." His tone was casual, almost flippant, and I couldn't help but feel a slight unease. The coldness in Thomas's voice, the sheer lack of empathy, was unsettling.

I stood there, processing the bizarre scene, thinking that maybe I should be a little more cautious around Thomas. He seemed like the kind of guy who could be a great ally, but I couldn't help but wonder what would happen if you ended up on his bad side. Better as a friend than an enemy, I thought.

As for Thomas, he was unfazed. He walked back to the bar, collected his replacement beer, compliments of the Duty Manager, and returned to his poker machine, as if nothing had happened. The whole incident seemed to roll off him like water off a duck's back. It was a surreal moment, one that made me realise just how much of a character Thomas really was.

We were leaving the Club about half an hour after the incident, the air still thick with tension, though Thomas seemed completely unbothered. He'd called for a cab, and we made our way outside to wait under the Club's porte-cochère, the covered area where people waited for rides. It was quieter now, and there were a few benches scattered around. But sitting there, I couldn't shake the feeling that something wasn't quite right.

Then I saw him.

The young man with the crushed hand was sitting there, flanked by two friends. As soon as he spotted Thomas, his face twisted with a mix of anger and desperation. Without a word, he and his two companions stood up and began walking toward Thomas. It was like a switch had been flipped, the tension in the air thickened instantly.

The Club's white Toyota courtesy bus was parked just to the right of the entrance, and the three men skirted around it, approaching Thomas from his right. Everything happened in a blur, but I had a clear view, maybe two meters behind Thomas, as we walked toward the exit.

The first man, a stocky figure with a thick beard, lunged at Thomas. Without a word, Thomas lowered his arms to his sides, leaned forward, and delivered a headbutt with surprising force. The impact was immediate, the man dropped to the ground, out cold, before anyone could react. But Thomas didn't stop there. In one smooth motion, he raised his right fist high above his head, like a hammer, and brought it crashing down on the second guy's skull. This man went down just as fast, collapsing to the ground with a sickening thud.

By this point, the friend with the crushed hand had already bolted, running out of the porte-cochère and into the carpark, just as a police paddy wagon appeared at the exit-only drive.

The police car stopped, and the officers quickly got out. By then, the man with the crushed hand had vanished, and the second man was struggling to his feet, helped up by the stocky guy, who was now groaning on the ground.

The officers turned to me, their attention now on me as I stood there, stunned. One of them asked if I was okay. I nodded, still processing what I had just witnessed, and looked around for Thomas. But he was already gone. It was like he had melted into thin air.

The officers watched as the two remaining men stumbled out of the Club's entrance, out onto the street. They climbed into the back of the paddy wagon and followed them down the road. Just as the police car drove off, a taxi pulled into the parking lot and drove up to the entry.

I didn't have time to think before Thomas appeared from behind the courtesy bus, as if he'd been there the whole time, invisible. Without a word, he opened the taxi door, and we both climbed in. "Knotts Crossing, thanks, mate," Thomas told the driver, who nodded and turned the cab to the right.

The drive was silent, just the sound of the tires humming on the road. As we pulled into Knotts Crossing, Thomas spoke up, breaking the silence. "Darwin tomorrow, Jack. Meet you for breakfast about eight. We'll head out after that. Goodnight, Jack."

I wasn't sure what to make of it all. The whole night felt like something out of a bad dream, but it was real, too real. As I sat in the back of the cab, I couldn't stop thinking about Thomas, about his calm demeanour in the face of violence, the strange way he seemed to glide in and out of situations without leaving a trace. Something about him didn't sit right, and I was more determined than ever to learn more about his background.

In the car, as we started the drive to Palmerston, Thomas mentioned that we'd be stopping for lunch at the Palmerston Tavern in Chung Wah Terrace. He had to meet someone there at one o'clock. The drive was smooth and uneventful, with very little traffic on the road. I had been trying to find the right moment to bring up last night's events at the Katherine Club without causing any tension, but before I could figure out how to broach the subject, Thomas beat me to it.

"Those fucking dickheads last night," he said, shaking his head as he glanced out the window. "What's wrong with people? That silly prick trying to cash out my money on that machine, and then those other dicks with him outside the Club."

I nodded in agreement, feeling a mix of sympathy and concern. The recent spate of violence in Katherine and Alice Springs had been hard to ignore, and I knew Thomas's experience fit right into the broader narrative. I hesitated for a moment, trying to find the right words, but Thomas saved me the trouble.

"Those types shouldn't mess with a taekwondo sensei, even if he's sixty-three years old," he added, a hint of seriousness slipping into his voice. We both shared a quick laugh, but I could tell that he wasn't entirely joking. The way he'd dispatched those guys last night had left an impression, one I knew I'd have to keep in mind.

We were about an hour out of Palmerston when I finally decided to ask. "Thomas, I know I shouldn't ask too many questions, but these clients you meet up with...?" I trailed off, unsure of how to phrase it. Before I could finish, Thomas cut me off with a grin.

"And all these laptop-type bags too, were you going to say? I've been expecting you to ask much sooner than this, Jack," he said, his tone light and almost teasing. "I know it might look a bit sus. Is that what you wanted to ask me?"

I was a little taken aback by his quick response. I had half-expected him to scowl or get defensive, but instead, he seemed entirely relaxed, even jovial. I looked at his face for a moment, trying to gauge if he was joking, but he just gave me a small smile and a shrug.

Thomas continued, reading the unspoken question in my eyes. "I understand it looks funny, but it's all above board, I promise. Let me explain how it works."

With that, he launched into a detailed explanation of his business, clearing up my confusion.

"I'm an Aircraft Engineer, just like I told you on the first day," Thomas began. "All the people I meet on these trips are aircraft owners, either fixed-wing pilots or helicopter operators. My company provides a one-of-a-kind, computer-aided maintenance program for their aircraft."

He went on to explain how his company uses a sophisticated system involving a data collection unit installed in the aircraft. This machine sends data directly to his company, which allows them to remotely adjust and calibrate various aspects of the aircraft without having to send out a licensed maintenance engineer each time. The system is designed to save both time and money for the aircraft owners.

"The data box itself needs to be reset and recalibrated every six months or so," Thomas continued. "When it's time for a reset, new units are sent out by Australia Post to the aircraft owner. They simply replace the old unit with the new one, then put the old one in the bag that's provided and hand it over to me when I visit. The thing is, Australia Post won't accept the old units back for shipping because when they scan them for security and border control, it corrupts the data stored on them. And that data is crucial for maintaining the aircraft's maintenance schedule."

I was beginning to understand, but Thomas noticed my lingering skepticism.

"Did you think I was dealing in some illicit products, like drugs or something, Jack?" he asked with a laugh, as if the thought had never crossed his mind. "I suppose it does look a bit shady, doesn't it? But no, I promise you, all these people I've met so far are legitimate aircraft operators. Sorry to spoil your suspicious imagination, old chap," he added with a wink.

I chuckled, feeling a little embarrassed for having jumped to conclusions. The explanation made sense now, and I could see how the whole setup could easily raise some eyebrows, especially with all the travel and the bags that seemed to hold more than just technical equipment. But it was clear to me now that Thomas's business was legitimate, even if it did have a bit of an unusual vibe.

Let me tell you, I was immensely relieved. It had been playing on my mind for days, and now, looking back at the people Thomas had met with and the bags they had handed over, it all made sense. I realised that I had let my imagination run wild for no reason. When Thomas had first told me he was an aircraft engineer, I had subconsciously examined his hands, expecting them to be the rough, calloused hands of a mechanic. But instead, his hands were clean, smooth, and well cared for, a stark contrast to what I had expected.

The dinner meetings had also seemed odd to me at first, no business discussions, just brief exchanges and handing over of those mysterious bags. But now I understood. There wasn't really any business to discuss. It was all about exchanging the data units, a task that happened twice a year, and there wasn't much more to say about it.

As we pulled up to the Palmerston Tavern, Thomas casually mentioned that the man we were meeting, Grant Pollock, owned a car wash business. He added, "If you want to engage in conversation, that's the topic to go with. Don't bring up his helicopter unless he does. It's like asking someone about their car when you first meet them, just don't." I nodded, grateful for the advice, and promised to mind my own business. "No worries," Thomas said with a grin, "Let's go grab a beer."

I was introduced to Grant Pollock at the Palmerston Tavern, and we sat down at a table. Grant seemed like a likeable guy, probably in his early fifties, though he came across as a bit full of himself. As he placed his laptop bag on the table, I immediately recognised it for what it was, a data unit, just like Thomas had explained. Grant handed it over to Thomas, who then passed it to me, asking me to take it out to the car and place it in his suitcase. I did as asked, and within half a minute, I was back at the table.

We all ordered the daily special, T-bone with chips and salad. I stuck with just one more beer, knowing I still had to drive another twenty-odd kilometres into Darwin. I asked Grant how the car wash business was going, and he gave me a smug grin. "Which one?" he replied. Turns out, he owned five car washes in and around Palmerston and Darwin.

We didn't linger in Palmerston for long. After lunch, we set off for the Skycity Casino in Darwin, where we were staying. This was going to be my second-last day with Thomas, and while I was ready for the trip to be over, I had genuinely enjoyed the journey from Cairns to Darwin. It had been an experience.

As we pulled up to the drop-off zone in front of the casino, Thomas suggested that I park the car while he checked us in. I parked in a well-lit area under a floodlight, feeling secure, and then headed back to the reception. Just as I walked in, I caught sight of Thomas paying the receptionist in crisp one-hundred-dollar bills. I couldn't help but chuckle to myself, thinking, I hope he's got plenty left for tonight.

The rooms at Skycity Casino were impressive, and Thomas had certainly booked us the best available. Our rear balcony opened directly into the swimming pool, offering a perfect escape. I grabbed a cold Heineken from the mini bar, which was nice enough, but I knew there was something better waiting for me. The pool was enormous, stretching out across the entire lower level of the complex and connecting all the rooms. After a quick swim, I found the lagoon bar and decided a XXXX Gold stubbie was the way to go. I charged it to Thomas's room, after all, it was his treat. The heat outside was brutal, around 38 degrees Celsius, but in the pool, it felt absolutely magical.

Thomas had mentioned that he had some phone calls to make, so we were meeting at the IL Piatto Restaurant inside the casino at 6 PM. It was only 5 PM, so I decided to stay in the pool a little longer and enjoy another two cold Goldies before swimming back to my room to get ready. It was such a relaxing experience that I almost didn't want to leave, but I knew dinner was waiting.

At exactly 6 PM, I found IL Piatto Restaurant and was greeted by the steward at the door. He asked if I had a reservation, and I wasn't sure under what name Thomas had booked. As I glanced around, I spotted Thomas waving from across the room and pointed in his direction. The steward, without a moment's hesitation, led me over to his table, ignoring my attempt to tell him I was fine on my own.

Sitting across from Thomas was a woman I hadn't expected, this time, his client was a lady. Or perhaps "woman" is the better term. They were both seated as I approached, and Thomas introduced us. "Jack, this is Clare. Clare, meet my new PA, Jack."

I greeted her, "How do you do, Clare?" and she shot back, "I'm doin' ok, mate. How 'bout you?" Her casual, no-nonsense manner instantly put me at ease, though I wasn't sure what to make of her straightforward demeanour.

Just as I sat down, the waitress brought a tray with three XXXX Gold stubbies and glasses. As she began to pour one into the glass, Clare shot her a look and said, "Don't pour the bastards out, mate. You'll fuck 'em." Both Thomas and I burst into laughter, and I quickly agreed, "They're already in the glass, that's fine." The waitress, clearly disapproving of Clare's bluntness, simply left the three opened stubbies on the table and walked away.

Soon, she returned with three menus. As I glanced at them, I noticed there was no table for six this time, just the three of us. I figured that was probably a good sign.

Clare had a data unit bag with her, one of those familiar bags I now knew all too well. After some small talk, Thomas turned to me and asked if I could take the bag to his room. He handed me his key card and said I knew exactly where to place it. I assured him it was no problem and that I'd be right back. As I stood up to leave, I could tell this dinner would be just as interesting as the last, but the focus would shift, at least for now, from any more violent incidents to the more mundane details of the job.

On my way to Thomas's room, I realised it was only two doors down from mine. As I approached, I couldn't shake the curiosity about the laptop bag. It wasn't secured with cable ties like usual, which seemed a little odd. I entered Thomas's room and immediately noticed the large suitcase lying on the spare single bed. I opened it to place the laptop bag inside, along with the others. But curiosity got the better of me, and I just had to take a quick peek at what was inside the bag.

When I opened it just enough to catch a glimpse, I was struck speechless. The bag wasn't filled with data units like I had expected, it was packed with bundles of one hundred dollar bills, each held together with a rubber band. My heart skipped a beat. I couldn't process what I was seeing at first; it didn't make any sense. I panicked, fumbling to zip the bag up as quickly as I could, but my hands were shaking, and I struggled to close it. Every second felt like an eternity, and I kept telling myself, "Hurry, hurry," but it was as if time had slowed down. The suitcase suddenly wouldn't close properly, and I had to open it again and try to force it shut, only for it to resist, making the situation feel even worse. I was certain that Thomas would walk in at any moment and catch me, and the thought terrified me.

Once I finally managed to close the suitcase, I quickly left the room, trying to collect myself. At the entrance to the restaurant, I stopped to steady my breathing, feeling the heat in my face from the shock. I knew I must have been blushing, and I was embarrassed by the rush of emotions I felt. I couldn't believe what I had just discovered.

Back at the table, I couldn't shake the thought of the money I had seen. I automatically drained my beer, hoping to calm myself down. Luckily, Thomas and Clare had finished their drinks, and they didn't notice. I offered to go grab more, but when I went to the bar, the waitress refused to let me take the drinks and insisted on delivering them herself.

I returned to the table with nothing but a mental buzz, still trying to process what I had seen. Both Thomas and Clare were engrossed in their menus, barely glancing up as I sat down. I was still distracted, my mind racing. The situation with the money felt so surreal that it was hard to focus on anything else.

Trying to pull myself together, I glanced at the menu. Thomas commented, "Looking at this, it seems that the only steak they have here is Scotch Fillet for $62. That's ridiculous. I do not eat Scotch Fillet steak."

Clare, who seemed a bit less experienced with fine dining, responded, "I don't eat out much, but I thought Scotch Fillet was one of the best cuts. I usually buy either Rump or Porterhouse from the butcher."

Thomas shook his head and replied, "Indeed not. It's actually rated number four in terms of flavour by the Australian Beef Board." He continued, "Rump is number one, followed by Sirloin, which is also known as Porterhouse or New York cut. Fillet, either Eye or Tenderloin, comes in third. Scotch Fillet, also called Rib Fillet or Rib Eye, is fourth, and funny enough, the last on the list is the old 'T' Bone."

I was still digesting the information Thomas had casually shared about steak cuts, but the image of the money-filled laptop bag kept coming back to haunt me. The conversation around me seemed to blur, and my mind kept returning to the strange discovery in Thomas's suitcase. What did it all mean? And what was really going on with Thomas?

Thomas continued with his explanation about steak preferences, making it clear that while it was all a personal matter of taste, Scotch Fillet was, to him, a cut of meat that was tender but tasteless, inferior in comparison to other cuts. For that reason, he wasn't going to waste his time eating at the Casino's restaurant when the menu didn't appeal to him. He announced that we'd be dining at the Casino's other restaurant, "The Vue," and made his decision clear.

As we stood up to leave, the waitress arrived to take our orders. Thomas, with his usual directness, simply told her, "The menu doesn't suit us this evening, so we'll be dining elsewhere." The waitress asked if there was something in particular that didn't meet his expectations, and Thomas replied with a smile, "If the chef doesn't know what the local and visiting members of the Australian community prefer to eat, he's either in the wrong business or the wrong country." He handed her his room number, asked her to charge the drinks to his account, and finished with a polite "Good evening, madam."

With that, we left the restaurant and made our way downstairs to The Vue. Once seated at a table for six, we each ordered a beer and placed our orders for dinner: two 350g rump steaks, medium rare, with chips and salad, and one 200g sirloin steak, medium rare, with potatoes and red wine jus. Thomas couldn't help but point out that, in The Vue, the three meals cost $110, whereas in the previous restaurant, they would have cost $186 for steaks that weren't even his first choice. We all agreed with him, and I went ahead and ordered more beers, settling in for what promised to be a much more enjoyable meal.

With the change of dining venue, I momentarily forgot about the bag. We had a fantastic evening, filled with delicious food, plenty of beer, and great conversation. As we ate, Clare began sharing details about her life, which I found fascinating. She owned a small tourist business that she ran from her property on Victoria River, near Timber Creek, about 600 kilometres west of Darwin. The property had once belonged to her father, and it was a vast expanse of around 300,000 acres that featured some of the most stunning gorges and waterways.

Clare explained how she had started her tourist business, which had initially been inspired by her friends from her nursing days in Adelaide. During one Christmas holiday, she had invited a group of them up to her father's property. While there, she showed them some of the secret Aboriginal caves nestled in one of the many picturesque valleys on the land. These caves were so secret that even the local Aboriginal communities didn't know about them, thanks to her father's strict policies on restricting access to his land.

It was fascinating to hear Clare talk about her business, her father's land, and the rich history behind the property. The conversation flowed easily, and the evening was truly enjoyable, though in the back of my mind, the image of the money-filled laptop bag still lingered, adding a strange undercurrent to what had otherwise been a pleasant night.

It was common knowledge that Clare's father, Colin McIntyre, had always been a very secretive and somewhat intimidating figure in the region. He had hired people to patrol his vast property, ensuring that no one stayed longer than necessary. Anyone found trespassing, even if they had a lawful excuse, was quickly ejected from the property. It was also widely known that several people, up to six, had mysteriously disappeared near or around his property, including Telstra workers and even one police officer. The only time anyone else had been allowed on the property was to search for these missing people, though they were never found. Clare's voice took on a dark tone as she recalled her father's words: "Missing people that nobody really missed at all."

Now, with the cattle gone, the property was used for a very different purpose, tourism. Clare had turned the land into a tourist destination, complete with an airstrip to fly visitors in from Kununurra for day trips to explore the surrounding area. "It's money for old rope, mate," Clare said, taking a swig of her beer. "Suits me to me cotton socks because I don't have to do a thing or see any prick. The tourist company does it all and just sends me the money."

As the evening progressed, Clare seemed to be on a mission to drink the Casino out of its XXXX Gold stubbies. Thomas and I, naturally, assisted her in this endeavour. Clare, it turned out, was a VIP member of the Casino, and she invited us to the exclusive Arafura Room. We were quickly introduced to an atmosphere of plush carpet and luxurious furnishings, but as we made our way in, I couldn't help but feel like I was contributing to the Casino's upgrade in a way I didn't quite understand.

I decided to leave Thomas and Clare to their VIP room activities and retreated to the general Casino area, where I spent the rest of the night trying to win back the money I had lost in the exclusive room. I had a great time, but something kept nagging at the back of my mind.

When I finally returned to my room and laid down in bed, my thoughts kept drifting back to that laptop bag, and the money I had seen inside. How much money was there, really? Were all the bills $100 notes? Had the bundles been laid in the bag lengthwise or sideways? I ran the questions through my head again and again, desperately trying to recall the details.

Yes, they had been longways. There were two bundles, I was sure of it, but how deep were they? I remembered the thickness of my own $100 bills and pulled up the details in my mind, 158mm by 65mm each. I couldn't measure the thickness of the bundle itself, but I had my own money to compare it to. I had $5,000 on me, and that was about 7mm thick. I guessed that each bundle in the bag would be about 30mm thick, which meant each bundle contained around $20,000.

At this point, I couldn't take it anymore. The curiosity was driving me crazy. I jumped out of bed, dressed quickly, and grabbed the keys to my car. My Subaru was parked under a floodlight in the carpark, and I could see it clearly. I unlocked the car, opened the console between the front seats, and pulled out my small Promat tape measure, something I had gotten years ago from a passive fire protection representative.

With tape measure in hand, I went back to my room. I wasn't about to take a wild guess anymore, I had my own $5,000 to measure, as well as my own laptop bag, which I used to carry my MacBook Air. After measuring a $100 note, I found that it measured about 158mm x 65mm. I couldn't measure the thickness of the notes in the bag directly, but my $5,000 stacked up to about 7mm in thickness. Given that the bundles in Thomas's suitcase seemed to be about 30mm thick, I estimated that each bundle contained around $20,000.

As I sat there, running the numbers through my head, I couldn't help but think about how much money was actually in that bag. Would there be $40,000 or more? How many bundles had been in the suitcase? The answers seemed just out of reach, but the fact that I had seen so much money left me feeling uneasy. I tried to shake the thoughts from my mind, but the image of those bundles stayed with me long after I put the tape measure down.

The realisation of the money in Thomas's bags was consuming me. As I lay there in bed, wide awake, the numbers kept running through my mind. My laptop bag, which measured 350mm long and 250mm high, easily accommodated six bundles of $20,000, with two bundles across and three deep. That meant $120,000 in each bag. However, looking at my laptop bag and comparing its thickness with Thomas's bags, his laptops definitely looked at least twice as thick as mine, I started to realise that each of Thomas's bags could easily hold up to three times that amount. If that was the case, then each bag could hold anywhere from $120,000 to $360,000.

Now the scale of it all began to sink in. I had counted six bags Thomas had collected: one from the unknown person at Cloncurry, one from Robert Fruehauf at Mount Isa, one from either John Snape or Bill Collins at Mount Isa, one from Rex Grogan at the Barkley, one from Paul Jensen at Katherine, one from Grant Pollack at Palmerston, and the last from Clare last night. Seven bags. But what about any others? How many more bags had he collected that I didn't know about? The possibilities seemed endless.

My mind raced, calculating the total amount of money Thomas could be carrying. If each bag held just under $120,000, that was already nearly $1 million. But if each bag held closer to $360,000, that would put the total at over $2.5 million. The thought made my head spin. I tried to push it aside, but it kept coming back.

After two more Heineken beers, I finally went back to bed around 3:30 AM, exhausted but still unable to quiet my mind. I managed to fall into a restless sleep and awoke around 7:30 AM feeling dreadful. My head ached, and my thoughts were sluggish, weighed down by the money I had discovered.

Despite feeling awful, I forced myself to get up, get dressed, and head down for breakfast.

The room felt suffocating, and as I sat at breakfast, the weight of what I had learned kept pressing on me. How deep was Thomas's involvement in all of this? How much of it was just business, and how much of it was something else entirely?

I didn't see Thomas or Clare at breakfast, and for a moment, I enjoyed the solitude as I dug into my rissoles with bacon, hot chips, orange juice, and a cappuccino. The meal was comforting, and it helped ground me after the restless night I'd had. I was just about to head back to my room when it hit me again, the thought that had kept me awake most of the night. What was the deal with all the money? What had I gotten myself tangled in? I couldn't shake the feeling that something was off, and I started to wonder if Thomas had noticed my unease, if he somehow suspected that I had figured things out.

Then, the real question hit me: where the hell was all this money coming from, and what the hell was it for? I didn't have answers, and it only made my stomach churn. All of a sudden, I didn't want to be here. I didn't want to be anywhere near Thomas. My thoughts flashed back to Katherine, to the way Thomas had handled those young men. He was in his sixties, not exactly what you'd call in peak physical condition, but the way he moved that night, quick, precise, almost frightening, left me shaken. How could someone that age move with such speed and confidence? It had been startling. And depending on which side of the equation you were on, it was downright scary.

That realisation hit me like a ton of bricks: I was starting to become afraid of Thomas. Very afraid. The way he had dealt with those men, and the way he handled situations, calm, collected, but with an undercurrent of something far more dangerous, was making me question everything. Why hadn't he shown up for breakfast? Why was he being so distant?

Just as I was spiralling, my phone rang, snapping me out of my thoughts.

"Jack, where are you, old son?" Thomas's cheerful voice came through the phone, sounding completely normal, "Are you coming down for breakfast? We've got to get going by 9:30, Clare's organised a cruise on the harbor for lunch."

I felt an overwhelming wave of relief wash over me. Thomas sounded like himself, nothing was wrong. I'd worked myself into a frenzy over nothing. Maybe the money in that last bag from Clare was just to cover some expenses for whatever they had going on. After all, Thomas had always told me that the bags contained aircraft computer units. There was no reason to think otherwise, right?

I told Thomas I'd finished breakfast but was ready to meet him at the car when he was ready. He told me not to worry about the car, "We'll cab it," he said. "That way, we can enjoy drinks with lunch. But if you'd rather drive, it's up to you."

I agreed to the plan, feeling much lighter now that the storm in my mind had passed. Despite my earlier fears, things were starting to feel more like the relaxed trip I had originally thought it would be. But as we got closer to the day's activities, I couldn't help but wonder just how much I was really understanding about Thomas, and about where this trip was taking us.

It was decided that we would take a taxi, and I met Thomas in the reception area, where we both waited for Clare. She arrived shortly after, and we left for Tipperary Waters Marina, where one of Clare's tourist operators had arranged a luncheon cruise around Darwin Harbour on a twenty-metre catamaran.

The cruise was nothing short of wonderful. The boat was spacious, with only the catamaran staff and the tourism agent, Adrian Fox, joining the three of us on board. The top aft deck was beautifully set up with a large dining table for four, which struck me as typical of Thomas's style, nothing ever seemed to be done in small doses. A table for eight made up for just the four of us; it was extravagant, yet somehow fitting.

Adrian, who appeared to be in his early thirties, was impeccably dressed, far more so than I was in my Columbia shirt and shorts. He introduced himself and explained that if anyone didn't like prawns, they would likely go hungry, as that was the main feature of the lunch. It struck me as unusual but fitting for such a luxury setting. As the boat sailed, we relaxed and enjoyed the cold beers and an endless supply of prawns, and I found myself more at ease as the scenery passed by.

However, my jaw nearly dropped when Adrian casually mentioned that it was, in fact, his boat. I was stunned. How did someone so young, and so seemingly well-off, come to own such a luxurious vessel? It made me wonder about the world these people lived in. Later, I learned that Adrian was also one of Thomas's clients, which only deepened my realisation that all of Thomas's clients were incredibly wealthy, involved in diverse and high-stakes industries. It was a world that felt so foreign to me, and I suddenly felt like I didn't belong at all.

But as I sat there, sipping my beer and chatting with Thomas and Clare, I began to appreciate the generosity Thomas had shown me. It was easy to forget my earlier suspicions about the money and the bags, especially as I continued to drink. The thoughts that had plagued me the night before seemed almost laughable now, and I found myself blaming the beers for my overactive imagination. I told myself it was all forgiven and pushed aside the doubts. This was a day of relaxation, and I decided to enjoy it for what it was, a gift.

Adrian's background story, shared with us over beers and prawns on the catamaran, was both fascinating and unexpected. When Clare asked if he was born in Darwin, we were all surprised when he revealed that he was, in fact, born in Vanuatu. His family's origins were British, though, which made his connection to the island even more interesting.

Adrian explained that his grandfather had moved to Vanuatu, then known as the New Hebrides, during World War II. He was stationed on the island of Espiritu Santo with the Royal Australian Navy. After the war, Adrian's grandfather saw an opportunity to capitalise on the vast amount of military surplus left behind by the U.S. military. The U.S. Navy, having no use for much of the equipment and supplies, decided to abandon a massive stockpile of vehicles, machinery, and goods at various Pacific bases, including Espiritu Santo.

In 1946, the U.S. Navy had deemed much of the gear unnecessary and too expensive to ship back to the States, and they were eager to offload it. Attempts to sell the surplus to the French for a fraction of its value failed when the French hoped the U.S. would simply leave it behind. In response, the U.S. Navy's Seabees constructed a ramp into the sea near Luganville Airfield, and the surplus was dumped into the ocean. The base was officially abandoned in February 1946, and the site, now known as Million Dollar Point, is a popular tourist attraction.

Adrian's grandfather, with his sharp business sense, recognised the value in salvaging this abandoned military equipment and turned it into a fortune. He established a marine salvage business on the island, recovering some of the gear dumped in the sea, and from there expanded into a range of businesses, including a tavern that eventually grew into a well-known hotel and tourist resort.

Adrian's father followed in his grandfather's footsteps, moving to Iririki Island near Port Vila, where he also established a successful tourist resort. Adrian spoke with a sense of pride about his family's legacy, especially how they had capitalised on the unique opportunities that arose from the aftermath of the war. It was a piece of history that tied them to Vanuatu in a way that was both remarkable and uniquely tied to the island's development as a tourist destination.

I was captivated by Adrian's story, realising that his background, much like the people he worked with, was tied to an extraordinary world of wealth, legacy, and ambition. It gave me a new perspective on the people Thomas surrounded himself with and, for a brief moment, I felt both awed and out of place.

Adrian shared more about his background, revealing that he was born in 1979, just a year before Vanuatu became an independent republic. His parents had brought him back to Australia in 1989, where they settled in Darwin, and he had embraced life there ever since. He seamlessly continued in the family tradition of tourism, building on their legacy with a quiet confidence and flair. So much for my guess at his age, I had him pegged as much younger. It was a testament to his polished demeanour and youthful energy.

After our leisurely cruise, we returned to the marina, where Adrian offered to drive us over to the Dinah Beach Yacht Club. It was a short trip, and we were soon seated in the open bar, enjoying cold beers and a laid-back atmosphere. From our vantage point, we could see a couple of yachts careened on the beach. Their owners and crews were hard at work, scrambling to complete their repairs before the tide returned to reclaim them. It was a fascinating, almost theatrical scene, a mix of urgency and the peculiar calm that seems to hover over the Darwin waterfront.

Adrian, always the epitome of efficiency, had to leave us not long after arriving. Before departing, he handed Thomas a laptop bag with a casual air that belied its potential significance. "I've arranged an Uber for you," he said, brushing off any fuss. "It's booked and paid for, and it'll be here at three o'clock. Have a great rest of your day." With that, he bid us farewell and left, disappearing into the mid-afternoon like a man with a dozen more things to accomplish.

We found ourselves with about forty minutes to kill before the Uber arrived, so we ordered another round of beers and settled into the ambiance of the Yacht Club. The gentle murmur of conversations mixed with the clinking of glasses and the occasional shout from the yacht crews. It was one of those moments where time seemed to stretch in a pleasant haze. I was beginning to feel a bit more like myself, the earlier beers wearing off just enough for clarity to return.

By the time the Uber pulled up, I was teetering on the edge of exhaustion. The ride back to the Casino was uneventful, but I caught myself nodding off a couple of times, lulled by the soft hum of the car and the afternoon heat.

When we arrived, I told Thomas and Clare I'd see them later, and we parted ways in the lobby. My room felt like a sanctuary as I closed the door behind me. The bed was calling, and I knew a quick nap would be essential if I was to keep up with whatever the evening might hold.

The Uber came to a smooth stop at the main entrance of the Casino, and the three of us strolled into the cool, air-conditioned foyer. We were making our way toward the bar when I decided to call it a day, at least for a little while. "I'll catch up with you guys later," I said. "I need a nanna nap." I veered toward the hallway that led to my room, already picturing the relief of lying down.

As I turned, Thomas stopped me with a quick request. "Jack, drop this in my room on your way past, will you?" he said, handing me the laptop bag. He gestured casually with his hand. "Just slide the key card under the mat, mate. We'll catch up for dinner about seven, same place as last night."

"No worries," I replied, taking the bag from him. It felt heavier than I remembered the others being. Shrugging it off as nothing, I walked briskly toward Thomas's room, the slight weight of the bag a nagging presence.

On the way, I noticed something unusual: this bag didn't have zip ties on the zippers like the others had. I tried to push the thought away. Maybe I'd let my imagination get the better of me last night. I resolved to convince myself there was nothing out of the ordinary about these bags, or the money I suspected was inside.

When I entered Thomas's room, the large suitcase was still sitting where I'd seen it last, on the spare single bed. I walked over to place the laptop bag on top of it. But something made me pause. Before I realised what I was doing, my hands were unzipping the bag just enough to sneak another peek inside.

And there it was.

Fuck me.

The bag was packed full of $100 notes, their distinct green edges peeking out from neatly stacked bundles. My heart was pounding, but this time I didn't rush. I leaned in closer, taking a good look at the arrangement. The bundles were arranged in two neat layers. There seemed to be two stacks of two bundles laid longways across the bag, each about four bundles deep.

I couldn't help it; my mind started calculating. Four stacks, each four bundles deep. That was sixteen bundles in this one bag alone. If each bundle held $20,000, that meant this single laptop bag contained $320,000. And this was just one bag.

The weight of what I'd seen hit me like a brick. My chest felt tight, and I suddenly became acutely aware of my surroundings, as though Thomas could walk in at any moment. My nerves got the better of me, and I quickly zipped the bag shut and placed it on top of the others in the suitcase.

I locked the room and hurried to my own, clutching my key card tightly as if it were the only thing tethering me to reality. Once inside, I threw myself onto the bed, trying to shake off the adrenaline coursing through my veins.

I'd planned to nap, but I knew it was a lost cause. My mind was spinning with questions, scenarios, and anxieties. I lay there staring at the ceiling, replaying the scene over and over, the image of those stacks of cash etched into my brain. Sleep was out of the question. All I could do was think, and the more I thought, the more uneasy I felt.

I slipped into my togs, walked out onto the deck, and dived straight off into the pool. The cool water was a welcome relief, washing away some of the tension that had built up over the past couple of days. I swam a few lazy strokes to the swim-up bar and rested my elbows on the edge. "XXXX Gold, thanks," I said to the bartender, who handed me a cold stubbie.

As I took a long sip, my thoughts turned back to Thomas's suitcase. By my calculations, it must hold around two and a half million dollars, if all the laptop bags were stuffed with money. It seemed a fair estimate, given what I'd seen. But I told myself again, firmly this time, that it was none of my business. Whether it was legal or illegal, it had nothing to do with me. That was Thomas's world, not mine, and I wanted to keep it that way.

"Great day," came a voice beside me.

I turned to see a dark-skinned man with unmistakable Aboriginal features swimming up to the bar.

"Sure is," I replied. "Doesn't get much better than this."

He smiled as he ordered a beer. I took another sip of my XXXX Gold, then asked, "You a local?"

"Nah, mate. Just 'cause I'm black doesn't mean I live in the NT," he replied with a laugh. Then, with a cheeky grin, he added, "You gonna have another bottle of that cat's piss, or what?"

Before I could respond, he ordered me another XXXX Gold along with his stubbie of One Fifty Lashes. I drained the rest of my first beer as he slid the fresh one across the bar to me.

"Cheers," I said, lifting my bottle in a toast.

"No worries, mate," he replied as he charged the drinks to his room.

I held out my hand. "Jack Holden."

He put down his beer and gave me a firm handshake. "Jamdamarra Gurumarra. Nice to meet you."

"That's a bit of a mouthful," I said, grinning. "Where are you from, India, I suppose?"

He threw back his head and laughed. "Nah, mate! Not a bloody curry muncher. My mum's an Abo, well, her mum was, and her dad was white. My dad's a white bloke too. He's alright, though, for a whitey. Just call me Tim. I only told you the full name to shit-stir you. I don't use it, and neither do my mum and dad. Just the grandparents, to keep the old traditions alive."

"Well, Tim," I said, raising my bottle again, "cheers to that."

"Cheers, Jack," he said, clinking his stubbie against mine.

We both leaned against the bar, sipping our beers, and the conversation began to flow easily. Tim had an irreverent sense of humour, and his sharp wit made it clear he wasn't one to take himself, or anyone else, too seriously. For the first time in days, I felt myself truly relax.

Tim leaned casually against the bar, sipping his beer, and asked, "So, you on holidays, mate?"

I shook my head. "Not quite yet. As of tomorrow, though, I will be. My task contract expires today."

He raised an eyebrow. "Task contract? What's that supposed to mean?"

I explained the nature of task-based work, detailing how I'd been brought on for specific projects and assignments. Tim listened intently, clearly intrigued.

"Never heard it called that before," he admitted. "I've heard of 'Air Task' and 'Tasker,' but never thought it involved this kind of work. What exactly do you do?"

"Only a fill-in job," I replied with a shrug. "My real gig is as a project manager in the building construction industry."

Tim gave an impressed nod as I signalled the bartender for another round. "Your shout?" he asked with a grin.

"Yeah, mate," I said. "Want another two Indians making love on the riverbank?"

Tim chuckled and held up his bottle. "It's called James Squire One Fifty Lashes, thank you very much. And yeah, I'll take another."

"James Squire, eh?" I smirked. "Might as well be water. You sure you don't want a real beer?"

We both laughed as the bartender handed over our drinks.

As we settled back into conversation, I learned more about Tim. Despite his youthful appearance, he was actually a barrister. He had recently left a position as a prosecutor with the Northern Territory and was on his way to Brisbane to take up a similar role in about three months.

"I'd never have guessed," I said. "You look way too relaxed for a prosecutor."

Tim laughed. "Yeah, mate, I get that a lot. Born and raised in Longreach, Queensland. My dad was a police sergeant, worked his way up to Inspector. Mum was in the force too, as a liaison officer. That's how they met."

"No kidding," I said, genuinely impressed.

"Yeah. After finishing school in Longreach, I headed to the University of Queensland to study law. Worked my way through Brisbane, Sydney, Canberra… eventually landed in New South Wales with the Department of Prosecutions, then transferred over to the Director of Public Prosecutions in the NT."

"Quite the journey," I said.

"Yeah, but now it's time for a change of scenery."

Tim leaned back and asked, "So, when are you heading back to Queensland?"

I hesitated. "Honestly, I'm not sure yet. I was thinking of leaving tomorrow, but I haven't made up my mind."

Tim's face lit up. "If you can wait until Saturday, I'll ride with you. Split the fuel costs, of course. That's if you don't mind?" He paused and added with a grin, "I promise I'm not a serial psychopath."

I grinned back. "I know that."

Tim leaned in, his expression turning mock-serious. "But how do you know I'm not a serial psychopath?"

I raised an eyebrow and shot back, "Do you have any idea what the odds are of two serial psychopaths being in the same car, driving from the NT to Queensland?"

Tim burst out laughing, nearly doubling over as heads around the pool turned to look at us. His laughter was infectious, and soon I was chuckling along with him.

As we recovered, Tim slapped the bar. "Alright, mate, we need another round after that one."

I nodded. "You're on."

Tim looked momentarily sheepish and apologized for inviting himself along on my trip back to Cairns. "Sorry, mate, I was out of line," he said.

I waved it off. "Not at all. Actually, I think it's a great idea. Sounds like it'll be a lot of fun, and I can certainly handle another night here at the casino."

Relieved, Tim smiled. "Thanks, Jack. I appreciate it. I've just got to finish up at my old office on Friday, tie up some loose ends, and then I'm free. I've already moved out of my rental, so that's why I'm staying here, a bit of a treat for myself before the move."

"Fair enough," I said. "I've got plans this evening, but how about we meet for breakfast tomorrow around eight?"

"Sounds good," Tim replied. "We can plan the trip then. See you tomorrow."

I headed back to my room to freshen up and decided to sort out my accommodation for the extra night. At reception, I was told my current room was fully booked for Saturday night, but they could offer me a room in the older part of the casino. I quickly agreed, paid for it to secure the booking, and then wandered into the bar for a cold beer.

Feeling lucky, I decided to try my hand at the poker machines. To my surprise, I hit a small jackpot and walked away with a tidy win of $5,000.

By the time seven o'clock rolled around, I made my way to the Vue restaurant. Thomas and Clare were already there, each with drinks in hand, and to my delight, they had thoughtfully ordered one for me as well.

Thomas raised his glass. "Cheers, Jack. Thanks for the great ride over. It's been an excellent trip, and you've done a stellar job behind the wheel."

Clare followed suit, raising her beer. "Cheers, Jack!"

I lifted my glass with a grin. "Cheers, you two. It's been a great little adventure, and excellent company to boot."

As we settled in, Thomas leaned over. "I cleared it with the 'Task' people earlier today. They've transferred your remaining balance this afternoon. Hopefully, it'll hit your account tonight. If not, it should be there by Monday morning at the latest."

"Appreciate it, Thomas. Thanks again," I said.

Thomas smiled and reached into his pocket, pulling out a wad of cash. He handed me $2,000. "Here, this should cover fuel and accommodation on your way back."

"Another bonus?" I said, laughing in disbelief. "You're unreal, Thomas. Thanks!"

He winked. "You earned it, mate. Now let's enjoy dinner."

Dinner was excellent, a near-repeat of the previous night, as all of us ended up ordering the same meals again. The conversation was lighthearted and relaxed, with the warmth of familiarity settling over the table. At one point, I casually mentioned to Thomas that I could be available if he needed a driver in the future. He nodded thoughtfully and replied, "I'm not planning on going anywhere for a while, but keep an eye on the 'Task' site, that's where I find all my drivers. And don't worry, mate, I've got your number. I'll keep in touch."

It felt reassuring to know I might hear from Thomas again, and I thanked him for everything he'd done for me over the past week. The evening continued on a high note, and after dinner, we drifted into the casino for one last attempt at improving our financial fortunes.

By eleven-thirty, fatigue was setting in. I shook hands with Thomas and gave Clare a warm goodbye, thanking them both for an incredible experience. "Safe travels, Jack," Thomas said, raising his glass. I waved them off and headed to bed, content and ready to move on to the next chapter of my journey.

Saturday morning, I packed my bag and dropped it off at reception, asking them to transfer it to my new room when it became available. With that sorted, I made my way to the Vue for breakfast, eager to find Tim. He wasn't there yet, so I helped myself to the buffet, piling my plate with bacon, eggs, and fruit. I had just settled down at a table when Tim wandered in, greeting me with a cheerful "Morning, mate." He headed straight for the buffet line to get his breakfast.

While waiting for him to return, I checked my bank account on my phone. To my delight, the $4,750 from the 'Task' company had already been deposited. I couldn't help but smile, nine days of work had netted me $9,500, including the $2,000 Thomas had handed me last night for the trip home. With Tim chipping in for half the fuel costs, it was shaping up to be a win-win situation all around.

As Tim returned with his plate, I couldn't resist sharing the good news. "The 'Task' payment hit my account already," I said with a grin.

"Nice one, Jack," Tim replied. "Looks like you've had a pretty good run this week!"

I nodded. "It's been a solid stretch, good work, good people, and now, a good road trip ahead. Let's enjoy breakfast and make a plan for the drive."

Tim raised his coffee cup in a mock toast, and I couldn't help but feel a sense of optimism for the journey that lay ahead.

"What's the plan for this arvo, Jack?" Tim asked as we finished breakfast. "I'll be done at work around one o'clock. If you want to pick me up, I'll be waiting at the Public Prosecutor's Office on The Esplanade."

"No worries," I replied.

He smiled. "Great. After that, I'll give you a tour of the city." With that, Tim finished his coffee, waved me off, and hopped into a taxi to head to work.

I decided to make the most of the morning by relaxing at the pool, letting the warm sun and cool water melt away any lingering thoughts about the trip ahead. By twelve-thirty, I had moved into my new room, tossed my bag inside, and hopped into the car to head downtown.

Tim was waiting outside the Public Prosecutor's Office as promised, perched on a bench across the street with a laptop bag slung over his shoulder. The sight of the bag made me grin as I was reminded of Thomas's infamous laptop bags filled with cash.

"What's so funny?" Tim asked, catching my amused expression.

"It's a long story," I said with a chuckle. "I'll fill you in tomorrow on the road to Queensland."

I handed him the keys and said, "If we're doing a city tour, you should drive. I'd get us lost in five minutes."

Tim didn't need convincing. He slid into the driver's seat, and off we went, winding through Darwin's highlights. Over the next couple of hours, Tim showed me everything from Lee Point and Tiwi to the bustling Casuarina area. We crossed over to East Point, with its serene coastal views, before looping back into the heart of the city and finally returning to the casino.

By mid-afternoon, we were comfortably settled into the casino's beer garden, sinking into lounge chairs with cold beers in hand. The warm breeze carried the faint hum of conversation and clinking glasses from the other tables, setting the perfect backdrop for a lazy afternoon.

"So," Tim said, leaning back and taking a sip of his beer, "you're officially unemployed now. What exactly did your job entail anyway?"

I laughed, thinking about the simplicity of it all. "It wasn't much, honestly. This guy, Thomas, just wanted someone to drive him from Cairns to Darwin, but with a cap of about five hundred k's a day. I saw the ad on the 'Task' site and thought, why not? When I did the math for fuel, food, accommodation, and added a decent profit margin, it came to ten grand. I submitted the quote thinking I had no chance, like, who'd pay ten grand to get from Cairns to Darwin by car? But somehow, I got the job."

Tim raised an eyebrow. "Seriously? Ten grand for that?"

I nodded, grinning. "It gets better. Thomas covered all the fuel, food, accommodation, and drinks on top of that. It was the easiest money I've ever made."

Tim let out a low whistle. "You really struck gold there, mate."

"Yeah," I said, clinking my bottle against his. "It's not every day you get paid to enjoy a road trip."

Tim leaned forward, his expression a mix of curiosity and amusement. "Alright, so what's the catch? There's always a catch."

I smirked, swirling my beer. "Let's just say the guy wasn't exactly your average traveler. But that's another story, for the road tomorrow."

Tim laughed, shaking his head. "You've got me intrigued now. Guess I'll have to wait for the Queensland leg to hear the rest."

"Trust me," I said, "it's worth the wait."

Tim leaned back in his chair and nodded. "Sounds like a definite winner of a gig. What sort of business was this guy in?"

"He's an aircraft engineer," I replied, leaning in as I explained. "His company deals with clients who have these computer modules installed in their planes. Apparently, they need regular swapping out or maintenance. Thomas mentioned meeting with a few of these clients along the way. He'd have dinner meetings with them at some of the stops. Sounded legit enough, but the whole setup still had a bit of a strange vibe to it."

Tim raised an eyebrow. "Weird, but plausible," he said thoughtfully. Then he got up to grab another round of drinks.

I was about to mention the stacks of money I'd found in Thomas's laptop bags, but before I could, Tim's phone rang. He stepped away to take the call, and by the time he returned, the moment had passed, and the topic slipped my mind entirely.

We spent the rest of the evening chatting over beers, enjoying dinner, and playing a few rounds on the pokies. I decided to call it an early night to ensure we'd get a good start on the drive the next day.

The next morning, Sunday, I was loading my bag into the back of the car when something caught my eye, a glint of sunlight reflecting off something tucked behind the wheel well. I reached in and pulled out a pair of sunglasses, sleek and unmistakably Bolle. A pricey pair, to say the least.

"Must be Thomas's," I muttered to myself. Dialling his number, I was surprised when the automated message told me the number wasn't connected. Thinking I might have dialled it wrong, I tried again with the same result.

Just as Tim walked up with his bag, I waved him off. "Give me a minute. I need to sort something out at reception."

At the front desk, I handed the sunglasses to the receptionist. "Hi, could you please return these to Mr. Thomas Dobson? He was staying in room 173."

The woman behind the desk checked her computer, her brow furrowing slightly. "I'm sorry, but there's no one by that name registered here."

"He was in room 173," I insisted.

She double-checked and then said, "Room 173 was registered to a Mr. Jackson. He checked out yesterday morning."

I blinked in surprise. "Mr. Jackson? Are you sure?"

"Yes, quite sure," she said with a polite but firm smile.

"Thanks," I said, slipping the sunglasses into my pocket as I walked back to the car.

As I climbed into the driver's seat, I turned to Tim with a grin and put on the Bolle's. "Another win," I said, adjusting them on my face.

Tim chuckled, shaking his head as he slid into the passenger seat. "Looking sharp, mate."

With that, we pulled out of the casino's car park and onto Route 1, the Stuart Highway, ready to begin our journey south.

We decided to break the trip into manageable legs: first, a three-hour drive to Katherine for lunch, then another three hours to Daly Waters for an overnight stop. A solid plan.

"Do you know a good place for lunch in Katherine?" Tim asked as we cruised down the Stuart Highway.

"I don't know Katherine very well," I admitted, "but the Katherine Club has decent food and cold beer, so why not give it a shot?"

Tim agreed, and the mention of the club reminded me of a story about Thomas. "Funny thing," I began, "Thomas once clocked a pair of 'Brothers' right outside the Katherine Club door. You wouldn't think it, but the old guy moved like lightning."

Tim raised an eyebrow. "Seriously?"

"Yeah. He said he used to be a Tae Kwon Do teacher. Guess that explains it," I replied, laughing. The memory made me think of something else. "Speaking of Thomas, there's something else I didn't tell you."

"Oh?"

"Well, the bags. You know, the laptop bags. They were full of cash."

Tim stared at me, wide-eyed, his jaw dropping slightly. "You're joking."

"Nope. At least two of them were. That's all I checked."

"Two? But were the others the same?"

"They looked identical. Same brand, Xenon by Samsonite, and they all seemed full but not bulky. I mean, the last bag I looked into, I saw two stacks thick, two wide, and four deep. If each bundle was $25,000, that's $400,000 per bag."

Tim whistled low, processing the numbers. "How many bags were there?"

"I think seven," I said, running the math in my head. "That's... two and a half million dollars. Can't be legal. Can it?"

Tim shook his head, still skeptical. "It all sounds like bullshit. Whatever you're on, Jack, I'd like some of it."

I laughed, agreeing it sounded surreal when laid out like that. "The whole trip seems delusional. I mean, the price he paid me to drive him to Darwin, plus covering fuel, accommodation, meals, drinks, even money for pokies, it's like money was no object. And don't forget your Bolle sunnies," I added, grinning.

Tim chuckled but grew serious. "Maybe we should analyze the whole thing. It'll help pass the time on the road."

"Fair enough," I said. "Could be interesting."

Tim leaned back in his seat, thinking aloud. "Alright, for starters: why did he hire you to drive him to Darwin? He had stops along the way, right?"

"Yeah, Cloncurry, Mount Isa, Barkly Station, and Palmerston. All on the way," I confirmed.

"But why drive? He could've flown and hired cars for the remote locations. Flying would've been faster." Tim paused, pulling out his phone. "No signal. I'll check regional flight options when we get to Katherine."

"Here's another thing," I added. "Thomas didn't use a credit card the entire trip. Not once. Every payment, hotels, meals, drinks, was in cash. At the Katherine lodge, he paid cash for the room, but when the receptionist asked for a credit card for incidentals, he withdrew the payment and canceled the booking."

Tim frowned, clearly intrigued. "That's... odd. Maybe he didn't want to leave a paper trail. Credit card transactions are easy to trace. If he avoided flying, that could explain a lot. You need ID to get on a plane, right?"

"Exactly," I said.

Tim nodded thoughtfully. "And where's this 'Tasker' service based?"

"Cairns. Just a small local setup," I replied.

"So," Tim speculated, "Thomas could've gone to them in person and paid in cash there, too. It's all adding up to someone who's very cautious about being traced."

We sat in silence for a moment, the hum of the road the only sound. "Maybe we're onto something," Tim finally said.

"Maybe," I agreed. "Or maybe this is just one hell of a strange adventure."

Tim laughed. "Either way, mate, it's making for a good story."

We kept driving, the vast Northern Territory landscape stretching endlessly ahead, the mystery of Thomas and his money giving us plenty to talk about along the way.

We also concluded that flying would have required Thomas to provide official identification, while renting cars would have necessitated presenting his driver's license, which also serves as photo ID. By hiring me and my vehicle, however, Thomas avoided the need for any such documentation. It was clear he had gone out of his way to travel incognito.

"Alright," I said, summing up, "we've figured out his desire to remain anonymous. Now we just need to figure out why."

Tim nodded, his expression pensive. "What exactly was he up to?"

We arrived at the Katherine Club and made our way to the bar. I ordered one James Squire and one XXXX Gold stubbie, but they didn't have James Squire stubbies, just Forty Lashes on tap. Tim decided he'd have an XXXX Gold stubbie instead. Drinks in hand, we wandered into the bistro and ordered the "Today's Special," a T-bone steak with chips and salad for $17 each. After collecting our order numbers, we found a table amidst the busy Sunday crowd.

As we waited for our meals, our conversation naturally circled back to Thomas. More specifically, to the enigma of what he might have been doing.

"I just remembered," I said suddenly. "One of his clients gave me a business card. He didn't seem too fond of Thomas. I might've left it in the car… or maybe it's in the pocket of the shirt I wore that day, which should be in my dirty clothes bag."

Tim leaned forward, intrigued. "Who was it?"

"It was a truckie we met at the Barkly Station roadhouse. His name escapes me at the moment, though," I replied, racking my brain.

Our steaks arrived, and we were pleasantly surprised by their quality, far better than expected. Over another round of beers, Tim offered to take over the driving to keep things fair, and I agreed.

Before we left, I popped open the car's back hatch and rummaged through my travel bag. Digging through my dirty clothes, I found the shirt and, tucked into its pocket, the business card. "Here it is," I said, holding it up. "Rex Grogan, Livestock Transport, with his mobile number."

"Think we should give him a call?" Tim asked.

I nodded. "Might as well try while we've got good reception."

Dialling the number, I was met with Rex's voicemail: "You've reached Rex Grogan, Livestock Transport…" and so on. I hung up, deciding to try again later.

As we pulled out of Katherine, my phone rang. The caller ID showed a number I didn't recognise. Answering it, I heard a gruff but familiar voice.

"This is Rex Grogan. I had a missed call from this number," he said.

"Hi Rex, it's Jack. We met at the Barkly Station roadhouse last week. Do you remember?"

There was a pause before Rex replied. "I do. Did Thomas put you up to calling me?"

"No, not at all," I assured him. "I'm not working for Thomas anymore. I just thought I'd see if we could catch up for a chat."

Rex seemed to consider this for a moment. "A chat's fine. I'll be at Renner Springs tonight if you're around that way."

I glanced at Tim, who was nodding in agreement. "We've just left Katherine, so we should be at Renner Springs by six, no problem," I told Rex.

"Alright then," Rex said. "I'll see you in the bar."

"Sounds good. See you there," I replied before hanging up.

I slipped the phone back into my pocket, feeling a renewed sense of curiosity. Whatever Thomas had been up to, maybe Rex could help shed some light on it. The road ahead suddenly seemed a lot more interesting.

I turned to Tim and said, "I should've checked with you first, but I think it'll be fine." Tim waved it off, saying, "It's just a couple more hours down the road, and it can't be worse than Daly Waters." We both laughed, knowing how long that drive had felt. We were making good time, cruising at 130 kilometres per hour, so we still decided to stop at Daly Waters for a beer, a quick pit stop, and a change of drivers. We finally arrived at Renner Springs at 5:50 PM, just ten minutes before six.

We checked in at reception and were lucky enough to get the last two available dongas. After dropping off our bags, we headed straight to the bar. The moment we walked in, it was impossible not to spot 'Dropper', Rex Grogan. Most of the other patrons were wearing casual, brightly-coloured clothes, but Rex stood out, his presence unmistakable. Tim looked at me and said, "I'll bet you anything that's our guy." As we approached, I greeted Rex, "Hey Rex, how's it going, mate? This is my mate Tim."

"Tim, eh? As long as it's not that bloody Tom, the arsehole," Rex chuckled, shaking Tim's hand. "What are you drinking, boys?"

We ordered XXXX Gold stubbies, and after a moment, I asked Rex if he wanted to sit at a table. He agreed, and we found a spot where we could all settle down with our beers.

"Did that prick send you two down to talk me into it?" Rex asked, getting straight to the point once we were seated. I assured him again that I no longer worked for Thomas, and that Tim had never even met the guy. I explained that I was traveling back to Cairns with Tim and had simply wanted to catch up with Rex if he was around.

Rex seemed to relax a bit, nodding. "Alright, that's fine. But I want nothing to do with Thomas." I couldn't resist asking, "Why's that?"

His answer caught me completely off guard. "Well, I thought you might have known, but that bastard John Snape, you know, Bill Collins' new partner, talked me into getting this 'good deal' from Thomas, just like Bill and John had. He was paying twenty percent on cash investments, in cash, no questions asked. Twenty percent tax-free, as long as the tax people didn't find out. It sounded too good to be true, so I jumped in."

I was stunned. Rex continued, "Both John and Bill had put in five hundred thousand each, and were getting a hundred grand a year, paid half-yearly, all in cold hard cash, and no tax. So I thought, what the hell, I'll do the same. I handed that prick the money last week, right when you were here. But after he took it, I started to get worried. I didn't know the bastard from Adam, it was only because of Bill and John's recommendation that I even considered it. But then I found out Bill had only just got in on it last week, the same as me. That's when I started to panic. I can't afford to lose five grand, let alone five hundred thousand."

Rex drained his stubbie in one go, giving me a look that was part frustration, part resignation. "It's your shout, Jack," he said, the mood now a little heavier.

I took it all in, the weight of the situation dawning on me. Thomas had always seemed a little off, but I had no idea he was involved in anything like this. What the hell had I gotten myself tangled in?

I stood at the bar, still trying to process what Rex had just revealed. My mind was spinning, trying to make sense of the bizarre situation we'd gotten ourselves into. As I waited for our drinks, I glanced back at the table and saw that Tim was deep in conversation with Rex. I could tell that something more was being discussed, but I couldn't quite focus on it yet. When I returned with the drinks, I caught the tail end of Rex's words: "... anyway, it's all fixed now, no damage done."

I sat down and immediately asked, "Did you get your money back, Rex?"

"Sure did," Rex replied confidently. "Thomas called me up and asked where I was, where I'd be that night. A bloke showed up where I was supposed to meet him and handed me a bag with all the cash intact. Said it was from Thomas."

"Wait, Thomas's bag?" I asked, confused.

Rex nodded, a grin spreading across his face. "Yeah, the little briefcase thing. When you decide to sign up with him, he sends out this bag through Australia Post. It's got instructions on how to pack the money into it, everything. What a load of shit, right?"

I sat there, processing his words. I couldn't believe what I was hearing. A briefcase for cash, instructions on how to pack it? This all seemed so absurd, yet here we were.

Dinner that night at Renner Springs was surprisingly good, the best steak I'd had in a while, to be honest. We ended up drinking more beers than we'd planned, and around 10:30, Rex stood up, saying he needed to get some rest in his truck. He had to be in Cloncurry early tomorrow to collect 300 head of cattle for Charters Towers. But before heading off, he said, "I'll have one more nightcap."

As we finished our last round of beers, Tim casually remarked, "Bit of a gamble, leaving that kind of money in your truck, Rex."

Rex looked down at his feet, and for the first time that evening, we noticed a small laptop bag at his side. Rex grinned at Tim, his expression shifting to something a little more serious. "If any bastard can take that bag from me," he said, his voice low and steady, "they'll have fucking earned it."

Tim and I exchanged glances, the weight of Rex's words sinking in. Whatever was in that bag, it was clearly something Rex valued, something he wasn't about to let go easily.

We were back in the car at eight o'clock on Monday morning, making good time as we headed toward Mount Isa. With not much of note between us and our destination, we planned a brief stop at Barkley Homestead for brunch.

As we drove, Tim broke the silence. "I reckon your old mate Thomas has got a Ponzi scheme going," he said, his voice casual but with an undercurrent of suspicion.

"What's that? What's a 'Ponzi' scheme?" I asked, only vaguely familiar with the term but not entirely sure what it entailed. I had heard of it before but couldn't put the pieces together.

Tim turned to me, shaking his head. "It's a scam, Jack. It's a high-interest investment scheme that doesn't really exist." He paused, making sure I was paying attention. "The definition of a Ponzi scheme is a swindling investment operation that attracts new investors by promising them high returns with little or no risk. The money the new investors put in doesn't get invested like they think; instead, it's used to pay off earlier investors."

I frowned, trying to wrap my head around it. "Sorry, mate, I might be a bit slow when it comes to finance, but it sounds like good odds to me."

Tim chuckled, but there was no humour in his eyes. "Here's how a Ponzi scheme works, Jack." He settled into his explanation, clearly wanting to make sure I understood.

"Step one: Thomas convinces an initial group of investors to back an imaginary company, one that doesn't actually exist."

"Right, so it's all made up," I said, beginning to follow along.

"Exactly. Step two: The investors, lured by the promise of big returns, give Thomas their money. But instead of investing it, Thomas keeps it for himself."

"Okay, I'm with you so far."

"Step three: To make it look like their money is actually paying dividends, Thomas then goes out and finds more people to invest in this fake venture, often, the people who've already been scammed bring in their friends and family, thinking it's a legit deal."

"Sounds like a pretty good scam," I muttered, already thinking of how easy it might be to fall into that trap.

Tim nodded. "It's effective, all right. But step four is where the real deception happens. New investors, drawn in by the promises of easy profits, hand over their money, which Thomas then uses to pay dividends to the original investors. He might also pocket some of it for himself. And then steps three and four repeat until there are no more new investors, and the whole thing collapses."

"So, it's not illegal, then?" I asked, still not fully grasping the seriousness of what Tim was saying. "It seems like it's all above board."

Tim looked at me sharply. "No, Jack. A Ponzi scheme is very illegal for two big reasons. First, the person running it is deceiving everyone into backing a venture that doesn't even exist. There's no product, no service, just the promise of more money coming in. That's fraud right there."

I nodded, beginning to understand.

"And second," Tim continued, "the criminal has to make the fake business seem legitimate. That usually involves forging documents and falsifying information that they submit to government agencies to make it all look real. That's a serious crime, Jack. You can't just make up a company and expect to get away with it."

"Wow," I said, my mind racing with everything Tim had explained. "So if Thomas is running a Ponzi scheme, he's in serious trouble."

Tim nodded, looking out the window as we sped down the highway. "Exactly. It's only a matter of time before it all comes crashing down. But the real question is, how deep is Thomas involved in all of this, and what's he planning to do next?"

We drove on in silence, both of us lost in thought, each of us wondering how much further down the rabbit hole we were about to go.

I was beginning to piece everything together, the whole scope of the situation starting to make sense in my mind. I suggested to Tim that all those bags

Thomas had collected on this trip were likely from new investors. Tim paused before replying, confirming my suspicion.

"Yeah, you're right," Tim said. "Either new investors or existing ones increasing their investments. It's pretty good money, too. Twenty percent on five hundred thousand will double your money in five years."

I nodded but added, "Except they don't get their initial investment back."

Tim glanced at me, his expression thoughtful. "Exactly. Some of them might get their money back, and some may even reinvest. It's the early investors, those who got in early, that are the ones who end up looking like they're making a fortune. They become the best advertisement for the whole scam. Ponzi schemes rely on that, make a few people look successful and the rest will come flocking in. Plus, these schemes are always hush-hush, by invitation only. They're not something you talk about to outsiders."

"So, it's all secretive," I muttered, processing the information. "And in this case, cash is king. No records, no tax."

Tim grinned. "Right. It's all about keeping things under the radar. It's why no one notices anything for a while." He paused before adding, "So, what does Thomas do with the money? He wouldn't just deposit it, right? How does he avoid suspicion?"

I was starting to catch on, the pieces falling into place.

"Simple," Tim replied. "He could call himself a professional gambler. In Australia, a gambler's winnings are generally tax-free. He only has to deposit one of those laptop bags full of cash into his bank, call it a 'good day at the races' or some bullshit like that, and then he can withdraw money for whatever reason he wants, buy houses, cars, whatever. It all looks legitimate."

I sat back, my mind racing with the implications. The scheme was more elaborate than I had initially thought. But the thought that kept running through my head was what I should do about it.

"Do you think I should dob Thomas into the police, Tim?" I asked hesitantly. The idea of a reward was starting to creep into my thoughts, and the desire for justice was beginning to take over.

Tim looked at me seriously, but his face was unreadable. "Could be the way to go, Jack. But you've got to remember something, you're involved in it. In fact, you're probably more involved than you realise."

I furrowed my brow, confused. "What do you mean?"

"Well," Tim continued slowly, "you're complicit in it. You've got a share of the money, remember the ten grand you got and all the accommodation, meals, and drinks? That's money that came from the scam, Jack. You're deep in it."

I felt my stomach drop as his words sank in. "Tell me that you're fucking kidding me, Tim," I said, my voice rising in panic. "Don't mess with me like that. You're scaring the shit out of me now."

Tim raised his hands in mock surrender. "I'm just saying, Jack. You're more involved than you think. You need to think about what that means before you make any decisions."

The weight of his words hung in the air, heavier than I had expected. A cold realisation crept over me, and I suddenly felt like I was in way deeper than I ever intended.

Tim's words hit me like a ton of bricks. I could feel my heart racing as the realisation of what Thomas had just said sank in. The call had been brief, cryptic, and, frankly, chilling. "I'm sending you a little message to help you remember", those words echoed in my head, sending a wave of anxiety through me. What did he mean by that? What message was he talking about?

I took a few deep breaths, trying to steady myself, but I couldn't shake the unease that had crept into my gut. I looked over at Tim, who was now staring at me with a mixture of concern and disbelief.

"You're not making this easy, are you?" Tim said, his voice half-amused but mostly serious. "You really know how to pick friends. Sounds like you've got him worried, or you've got him pissed off, at the very least."

I wasn't sure whether I should laugh or panic. The tension in the air was palpable. "What the hell does that mean, Tim?" I asked, my voice shaky. "What the hell is he going to do?"

Tim rubbed his chin, clearly processing the situation. "I think Thomas is just trying to intimidate you, Jack. He knows you've got the goods on him, and now he's trying to put a little fear in you, make you think twice about going to the cops." He paused for a moment, glancing at the phone before continuing, "But whatever it is, I don't think you should be scared of him. He's bluffing. He's trying to scare you off, maybe even threaten you with some kind of retribution."

"But what if he's not bluffing?" I asked, my voice barely above a whisper. "What if something happens? What if he really does send me that 'message'?" My mind was racing, images of some kind of revenge playing out in my head.

Tim was quiet for a moment, his eyes narrowing as he considered my words. "You know, I've heard stories of guys like him," he said slowly. "People who try to control others through fear. They get away with it for a while because they know how to manipulate situations, but in the end, they're just cowards. They're all bark and no bite."

I wasn't so sure. Thomas's tone had been too calm, too controlled. He knew exactly what buttons to push, and for a brief moment, I felt like a pawn in some twisted game I didn't fully understand.

"Look," Tim said, shaking his head as though trying to snap me out of my thoughts, "we'll deal with it. You're not alone in this. You've got me. We'll get through it, but first, we need to keep our heads cool. No point in panicking."

I took a deep breath, trying to steady my nerves. "You're right. We can't do anything until we get back to Cairns anyway. I'll figure it out then."

Tim gave me a reassuring smile, though I could see the concern in his eyes. "That's the spirit. And like I said earlier, I'll go with you when you report it. No one's going to make this harder than it already is."

We parked the car outside the Ibis and grabbed our things. My phone sat in my pocket, silent now, but I couldn't shake the sense of foreboding. I glanced at Tim as we walked into the lobby. "Do you think he's really capable of something… worse?" I asked, half to myself.

Tim didn't answer right away. He seemed to weigh my words before finally saying, "I think he's a lot of talk, Jack. But maybe it's better to play it safe for now. The Australian Federal Police will know what to do if things get bad. You'll be fine."

But I wasn't so sure. As I stepped into the lobby of the Ibis, I couldn't shake the feeling that the worst was yet to come.

We checked into the Ibis and agreed to meet in the foyer before heading to the Buffs Club for dinner. It had been a long, exhausting day, and the weight of everything was starting to catch up with me. Tim's talk about Thomas and his 'Ponzi' scheme had stirred up doubts and fears I hadn't fully acknowledged until then. And just when I thought it couldn't get any worse, Thomas had called. The direct threat he had made on the phone was enough to send my mind racing. I was genuinely scared. My stomach was a tight knot, and I couldn't shake the feeling that something terrible was just around the corner. But as I stood there with Tim, I found some comfort in his steady presence. He had a way of remaining calm in the face of uncertainty, offering practical advice and reassurance that made the situation feel a little less overwhelming. Tim's encouragement had carried me through the day, and now, after that unnerving call, his support felt more important than ever.

We found ourselves at The Frog and Toad Bar and Grill, trying to shake off the day's events. The warm, relaxed atmosphere of the place was a welcome change, but I still couldn't fully relax. I had ordered the Black King Sirloin steak, something to ground me in normalcy, while Tim had chosen the Herb-Crusted Rack of Lamb. As usual, he had a XXXX Gold with his meal, warming to it more with each passing day. But despite the good food and the familiar comfort of Tim's company, my mind kept circling back to Thomas and the looming threat. The atmosphere of the restaurant couldn't quite drown out the storm cloud that hung over me.

Tim had mentioned earlier how unfortunate it was that we hadn't recorded the phone call. If things escalated, having that recording could've been crucial. But, as he pointed out, there wasn't much point in reporting the threat to the local Mount Isa police. They wouldn't be equipped to handle it, and I didn't even know where to begin with something this complicated. Instead, Tim advised me to report everything to the Australian Federal Police once we made it back to Cairns. "The threat is concerning, Jack," he explained in his usual calm manner, between bites of his lamb, "but the police can't do much with just threats. They'll need more to take action."

I wasn't so sure, though. "Mate, I can't stop looking around," I admitted, my voice tight with anxiety. "I keep thinking Thomas might be sitting in here somewhere, watching me." The thought of him lurking nearby made my skin crawl. The feeling of being watched was unsettling, and the more I looked around the room, the more paranoid I became.

Tim paused, setting his glass down with a soft clink. His expression softened as he met my eyes. "Well, brother, we'll get a good night's sleep tonight. It'll help clear your head. And tomorrow, we'll head off early. Don't worry about it too much tonight. We'll figure things out when we get back to Cairns." He thought for a moment before continuing, "Do you want to go through Townsville or cut through Ravenshoe? There's about an hour's difference."

I mulled it over, weighing my options. "Ravenshoe's a bit of a detour, right? Townsville's closer and on the main highway, which feels safer to me. Plus, I'll feel more comfortable on the better roads, and we'll have more choices for hotels when we get there."

Tim nodded, looking relieved. "Yeah, you're right. Better roads through Townsville, and it's closer. We'll be in Cairns by mid-afternoon the next day. Sounds like the right call."

The conversation helped distract me from the constant worry gnawing at my insides. Still, the unease didn't fully fade. My thoughts kept returning to the phone call, to Thomas's chilling words: "I'm sending you a little message to help you remember...you'll find it in tomorrow's news." What did he mean by that? Was I truly in danger, or was he just trying to intimidate me? The uncertainty was maddening. But I couldn't afford to dwell on it for too long. We had a plan, and we'd figure it all out when we reached Cairns.

We finished our meals, and despite the lingering anxiety, I felt somewhat better knowing Tim had my back. His ability to stay calm and focus on the solution made me feel less alone in all this. After dinner, we walked back to the Ibis, the cool night air doing little to settle my nerves. The streets were quiet, our footsteps echoing as we made our way back. Tim gave me a reassuring pat on the back. "We'll be fine, Jack. Just keep your head on straight. We'll sort this out, one step at a time."

As we turned in for the night, I tried to push the worry from my mind. Tomorrow was another day, and there was still a long drive ahead. But even as I lay in bed, trying to rest, I knew that things were far from over. In fact, deep down, I had a sinking feeling that things were about to get even more complicated.

We were well on our way the next day, Tuesday, and had a great run to Cloncurry, where we decided to stop for breakfast at the Red Door Café. The morning was clear, and we had a long stretch ahead of us, almost nine hours and 800 kilometres to Townsville. As we pulled out of Cloncurry and hit the open road, everything seemed to be going smoothly. That is, until we heard the news.

It came through on the radio just after we left town, a report about a road train accident near the Mount Lindsay turnoff, right back where we'd just passed through. The radio broadcasted that a road train carrying three hundred head of cattle had left the road, killing the driver and many of the cattle. The details were sparse, and the driver's name wasn't mentioned, but I could feel the blood drain from my face.

The cabin fell silent. I could feel Tim's eyes flicking to me as he instinctively reached for the radio dial and turned down the volume. He was the first to speak, his voice quieter than usual. "That couldn't have been Rex Grogan, could it? We should keep an ear on this, Jack."

"I just fucking hope it wasn't," was all I could manage to say. My voice shook, and I could feel a cold sweat breaking out across my back. My stomach twisted in a knot, and I tried to focus on the road ahead, but my mind kept racing.

Tim glanced over at me again, his expression unreadable. I could tell we were both thinking the same thing but neither of us was willing to say it out loud: Could that accident be the message Thomas had warned me about? Had it been a twisted way of getting back at me?

We didn't talk much for the next stretch of the journey. The weight of the situation hung heavy between us, the silence punctuated only by the hum of the engine and the occasional passing truck. It was hard to shake off the thought that Rex's death, and the terrible accident, could somehow be connected to Thomas's threat.

When we stopped for lunch at the Royal Hotel in Hughenden, we ordered beers to settle our nerves. As we sat down to eat, the TV screen in the corner of the pub flickered on, broadcasting the latest news update. Tim and I both looked up as the anchor read out the details of the accident from earlier that morning.

"Rex Grogan from Katherine died at the scene of a road train accident this morning on the Barkley Highway, just west of Cloncurry," the newsreader reported. "Also killed in the crash were fifty-three head of cattle out of the three hundred being transported. Authorities believe the road train lost control on a corner sometime before 2 a.m. and veered off the road, going down a steep embankment. Police are taking the prime mover to Mount Isa for further investigation into what caused the accident."

My stomach dropped. I felt the weight of the news sink in as the details hit me like a punch to the gut. Rex Grogan. The name sounded so final now. Tim looked at me, his face pale as he processed the information.

"Jesus, Jack," Tim said quietly. "Do you think that was... I mean, it's too much of a coincidence, isn't it? After everything that's happened?"

I didn't answer at first. I couldn't. My mind was spinning, the thoughts swirling too fast for me to catch. Was this the message Thomas had been talking about? The one he promised would be in the news the next day? Was Rex's death some kind of twisted warning, or was it just a tragic coincidence?

The silence between us grew heavy, and I could tell Tim was thinking the same thing I was: How deeply were we involved in all of this? Was this road train accident just the beginning of something much bigger than we could have ever imagined? And if so, what did Thomas want from me?

We finished our lunch in a haze, neither of us in the mood to enjoy the rest of the meal. The thought of what had happened to Rex, the cattle, and the possible link to Thomas's scheme hung over us, casting a shadow on the rest of the day. And as we got back on the road toward Townsville, I couldn't shake the feeling that the world was closing in on me, and I was caught in the middle of something far darker than I ever could have anticipated.

I suddenly felt a wave of nausea hit me, my body went shaky, really shaky. The kind of tremors you get when your mind and body can't catch up with the gravity of a situation. Tim immediately noticed and told me to calm down.

"How the fuck can I calm down, Tim? This prick is a fucking murderer!" I could hear the panic in my own voice, but it was impossible to suppress. The news about Rex's death felt like a punch to the gut, and now my brain was scrambling to process everything. The idea that this could be linked to Thomas, that it might be his way of sending me a warning... it was too much to handle.

"You can't say that, Jack. It's not conclusive," Tim replied, his tone firm but trying to be calming. "It could just be a fluke. Just settle down before you have a stroke. Look at all the piss that bloke drank the other night. He definitely wouldn't have been legal to drive, let alone capable. He could've been, probably was, in the same condition last night at some pub. That's what might have caused it. Relax, mate. Just... fucking relax."

Tim was right, of course. Rex had been a notorious heavy drinker, and if he'd been anywhere near as intoxicated as he had been the other night, there was no doubt he wouldn't have been fit to drive. The idea of Thomas orchestrating something so specific, a road train accident, seemed a bit far-fetched when I really thought about it. It wasn't like Thomas had the power to make a truck driver crash. I had to pull myself together. Tim was right again; if I didn't, I was going to end up in a mental spiral, and that wouldn't do anyone any good.

"You're right," I muttered, trying to steady my breathing. "I need to calm the fuck down."

I shifted my focus, thinking about our next steps. I turned to Tim, who was still looking out the window, his expression thoughtful. "Hey, what do you think about staying at the Casino in Townsville tonight?" I suggested. "We could have a night out, you know, just relax a bit. We only have a four-hour drive to Cairns tomorrow."

Tim seemed to like the idea. "Yeah, sounds good. But I've got to make a call first. Do you mind if I drive for a bit while I look up a mate on my phone?"

"Not at all," I replied, my voice steadier now. "Go ahead."

As we rolled out of Hughenden, Tim pulled out his phone and started dialling. He was speaking to someone in Brisbane, and from the snippets I overheard, it sounded like he was telling them about the road train accident. My ears perked up when I caught the words "information" and "items found in the truck." Tim hung up after a few moments.

"That's a new workmate of mine," Tim explained casually, almost as if he wasn't talking about a potentially dangerous situation. "He's my assistant in my new job in Brisbane. Even though I don't start for another three months, I thought I'd give him a task, check out that prang and see if there's anything suspicious. I also asked him to look into the contents of the prime mover's cabin. You know, like if there's a laptop bag full of cash lying around in it somewhere. It doesn't hurt to find out what we can."

I blinked in surprise, realising just how much Tim had already planned without me even knowing. I had forgotten that Tim was soon to be appointed to the Queensland Director of Public Prosecutions Office as a Crown Prosecutor. With that kind of position, he would have quite a bit of pull with the Queensland police. No wonder he was so calm about all of this, he could handle things on a much bigger scale than I ever could.

We continued driving, but as we approached Charters Towers, Tim's phone rang again. He answered it, and I could tell from his tone that it was important. "Send the information to the Townsville police," he instructed. "Mark it confidential, attention Tim Roberts. Have them deliver it to the Townsville Casino. I'll be there later tonight."

After hanging up, he looked at me with a hint of satisfaction. "Well, Jack, maybe there's something fishy about the prang. I'm getting a progress report on the investigation into the accident. We should know more tonight."

His words did little to settle my nerves, but they did give me a sense of purpose. Maybe, just maybe, we were getting closer to the truth. If there was anything off about Rex's accident, we'd find out soon enough. But with each passing mile, I couldn't shake the nagging feeling that this was only the beginning of something much bigger, and far more dangerous, than we had bargained for.

We checked into the Casino in Townsville around 5:30 PM, the bustling atmosphere of the place already starting to settle in. At the front desk, there was an envelope waiting for Tim. After securing two rooms on the same floor, we had our bags sent up and made our way to the bar to unwind with a cold beer. Tim sat down at a table while I went to grab the drinks, trying to shake off the unease of the last few days.

When I returned, Tim had already opened the envelope and was reading through a report. "It seems a witness saw Rex's truck pulled over on the left-hand side of the road, just opposite the embankment where it eventually went down," Tim said, reading aloud from the document. His voice was steady, but I could see the wheels turning in his mind as he processed the information. "It was in a dangerous spot, and there was another car, a Landcruiser, stopped in front of it, with two people standing by the truck. The witness thought the truck had broken down, so he didn't stop, assuming the people in the Landcruiser were offering assistance. This was around 1:30 AM."

I leaned in, my interest piqued as Tim continued, "Police later found the spot described by the witness and parked near it. They observed tyre tracks in the soft ground, suggesting that a heavy vehicle had started from that point, there were deep imprints that gradually became shallower as the truck gained traction. They made a cast of the marks, and it was a match with Rex's truck tyres."

I felt a chill run down my spine as Tim read on. "Further investigation revealed that the truck was stationary just before crossing the road from the left-hand side to the right, then plunging down the embankment. The driver's head injuries were inconsistent with someone being inside the truck when it rolled, and it was discovered that Rex wasn't wearing a seatbelt at the time of the crash. They also found no unusual contents in the truck's cabin. The truck has been taken to Mount Isa for further examination."

Tim finished reading the report, and we sat there in silence, both of us trying to digest the implications of the findings. We were in the lounge, overlooking the hotel's swimming pool. The cool, inviting water looked tempting, but neither of us was in the mood to relax. We were too absorbed in the tragic circumstances of Rex Grogan's death.

"It seems your friend got the five hundred thousand back, or the first responders had a big win," Tim remarked with a wry smile, still absorbed in the report. "The accident was reported by another truck driver at 2:30 AM, who saw a headlight beam coming from down the embankment and called 000. Other motorists reported cattle on the road. When police arrived, they didn't try to climb down to the wreck. Instead, they called fire and rescue from Cloncurry, who arrived within fifty minutes. Looks like the laptop bag may have gone before the services even got there."

I felt a knot tighten in my stomach as I processed this. The thought of the bag, and possibly the money, vanishing before authorities could even investigate made it feel like Thomas might be one step ahead of everyone. I couldn't shake the question that had been gnawing at me. "Do you think Thomas may have intercepted Rex, taken the money, then attacked him and drove the truck to the embankment before sending it over?"

Tim looked at me for a moment, his expression serious. "I think you might be pretty spot on with that scenario, old chap," he said quietly. "It might be time to get in touch with the local cops."

The weight of what we were discussing hung in the air, but we didn't have time to dwell on it. Despite the tension, we decided to enjoy the evening. A few more beers helped loosen the knots in my stomach, and by the time we headed to bed, the events of the day didn't feel as suffocating as they had earlier.

The next morning, as we set out for Cairns, we made the decision to report what we knew to the Townsville police. It was a strikingly modern police headquarters on Sturt Street, and when we approached the reception desk, we told the constable on duty that we had information about the truck accident west of Cloncurry. The constable made a quick call and then hung up before dialling again. He spoke for a few moments, then turned to us. "Someone will be with you shortly. Please take a seat."

We didn't have to wait long. A senior constable emerged from a door to the left of the reception area and asked us to follow him. Tim and I exchanged a glance before we complied, the seriousness of the situation settling over us once again. What we knew was troubling enough, but what the police would make of it was the next step in this increasingly tangled web.

As we entered the Senior Constable's office, we were greeted by a man with a calm, professional demeanour who introduced himself as Senior Constable Darren Metcalf. I extended my hand and introduced myself. "Jack Holden," I said, shaking his hand firmly. Tim followed suit, offering his own handshake, and then added, "Constable, I'm the new Crown Prosecutor, set to take up my position in about ten weeks. I've already obtained a full police report regarding this accident, but both Jack and I have additional information that may be of assistance to you."

The constable's eyes widened in surprise at Tim's statement. He quickly looked at both of us, his expression betraying his uncertainty, before suggesting, "I think it would be best if I get my superior to speak with you in this instance." He stood up from his desk and told us to wait. "I won't be long," he said, leaving the door slightly ajar as he exited.

Just a few minutes later, the door opened again, and Senior Constable Metcalf returned, accompanied by a man who appeared younger, with a shaved head and a neatly trimmed beard. He wasn't in uniform, but rather dressed casually in an open-necked white shirt and light grey cargo pants. He looked sharp and composed as he entered the room.

"Good morning, gentlemen," he said, his voice authoritative yet polite. "I'm Senior Inspector Jeff Carghill. Which one of you is the CP?"

Tim extended his hand with confidence. "That's me," he said, shaking the inspector's hand. "This is my friend, Jack Holden."

"Good morning," I said, nodding as the inspector acknowledged us both. He then motioned for us to follow him to his office, asking Senior Constable Metcalf to join us. We ascended the stairs to a spacious office, where we were seated around a large conference table. The inspector took a moment to size up the situation before asking Tim, "Are you officially engaged with this accident, sir?"

Tim paused for a moment, then answered, "Officially, no. But personally, I'm in a position to offer information that could assist the investigation. Jack and I both have details that might be valuable. Also, this incident may be connected to an alleged crime that has not yet been reported to the Federal Police."

The inspector processed this for a moment, his brow furrowing in thought. After a few seconds, he nodded and lifted the phone receiver. "I'll need a stenographer to take down everything," he said, his voice calm but firm. "And please send up some fresh cold water bottles." He hung up the phone, then turned back to us with a serious expression. "Looks like this is going to be a long morning, gentlemen."

As we settled in, I began recounting the details of my "task" engagement with Thomas Dobson, explaining how it all tied into the events surrounding Rex Grogan. Tim confirmed our meeting with Rex at the Renner Springs Roadhouse and the telephone call we had received the night before the accident, with Rex speaking loudly enough for us to hear his plans via hands-free speaker in my car.

We went over the key details: Rex had been carrying a laptop bag, supposedly containing five hundred thousand dollars, when we met him in the bar. He had told us he was heading to Camooweal the next morning to collect three hundred cattle, which would be transported to Charters Towers. Based on what we knew, that laptop bag should have been with him in the truck when it went off the road and plunged down the embankment.

The inspector listened intently, his expression thoughtful. He made no attempt to interrupt as I detailed the connection between Rex's movements and the money. Once I had finished, he took a moment to absorb the information before speaking again.

"Based on what you're telling me," he began, "it seems there's more to this than just an accident. We're going to have to investigate further, and we'll certainly need to contact the Federal Police. But for now, this new angle might help us piece together what actually happened."

We all sat back in our chairs, the gravity of the situation sinking in. Tim and I had hoped the information we provided might give the police a clearer picture of the events, and it seemed that we had succeeded. The inspector was already making plans for the next steps, and I could tell that the wheels were now in motion.

As the stenographer arrived and began setting up, we were offered cold water and encouraged to relax as much as possible. Despite the ongoing tension, I couldn't help but feel a sense of relief. The investigation was no longer just a vague series of events; it was becoming something much more substantial. And perhaps, just perhaps, the truth was closer than we had thought.

Inspector Carghill had been diligently making notes in his folder as he listened to our account. After a moment, he looked up at Senior Constable Metcalf and instructed him to gather a complete report on every Tomas Reginald Dobson in Australia. Then, he turned to me with a focused gaze and asked, "Can you recall the names of everyone you've met while in the company of Thomas Dobson? Every detail, every interaction you can remember, no matter how small, could be vital." He continued, "Take your time, accuracy is key here. The Federal Police will need that list, along with any information you can provide."

I nodded, feeling the weight of the task. It wasn't just a matter of remembering names, it was about piecing together a puzzle that could lead to something far larger than I had originally anticipated. Inspector Carghill was right to ask for as much detail as possible.

He then asked for a list of places where I had dined with Thomas, the times and dates of those meals, so that video footage could potentially be used to identify him and any associates he might have had. I began to mentally retrace my steps. "I know I ate at the Buffs Club in Mount Isa," I said, trying to recall exact details. "And the Isa Hotel, too. Dates and times aren't completely clear, but I can estimate when they happened." I also mentioned the Darwin Casino, where Thomas and I had frequented the restaurants, as well as the Dinah Beach Yacht Club.

After I provided the necessary information, the inspector nodded thoughtfully. "Good. These are critical details," he said, jotting them down. He then added that copies of the security tapes from the restaurants I had mentioned would be at the police station by two o'clock that afternoon. I would need to identify Thomas Dobson from these tapes by the end of the day. The implication was clear: the urgency of the situation meant that our plans to head to Cairns would be delayed by at least a day.

I called the Casino to extend our booking, securing rooms for the night without any trouble. The slight inconvenience of the delay was nothing compared to the task at hand. I was thankful that Tim was with me, offering both moral support and invaluable legal insight. His presence made the entire process far more manageable, especially considering how the Townsville Police treated him with such deference. I knew that if I had been on my own, I wouldn't have been sitting across from a Senior Police Inspector, and the process would likely have been far more drawn out and less efficient.

After lunch, we returned to the Police HQ. I was shown a series of security footage from the clubs and restaurants I had mentioned. As the clips played, I had little trouble picking out Thomas from the crowd. There he was, standing next to me at the bar at the Buffs Club, sitting across from me at the Isa Hotel, and mingling with others at the Darwin Casino and the Dinah Beach Yacht Club. I recognised nearly every face in those tapes, Thomas's clients, the people I had met in his company. The constable who was showing me the footage carefully made stills from the film clips, ensuring that each person I could identify was captured clearly.

With each still, I could feel the gravity of the situation settling in. I wasn't just recalling people I had met; I was identifying potential connections to Thomas's larger operation. The information I was providing had real-world implications, and the more I thought about it, the more I realised how far-reaching this investigation might become.

The photographs were compiled and sent out to police stations across the country, with a request for the detainment of Tomas Reginald Dobson for questioning in connection with the ongoing police inquiries. As I sat there, absorbing the magnitude of the task ahead, I couldn't shake the feeling that things were only going to escalate from here. But for the first time in a while,

I felt like we were on the right track, like the pieces of the puzzle were finally falling into place.

Tim had suggested we invite Inspector Jeff Carghill for dinner that evening at the Townsville Casino, and I thought it was an excellent idea. After all, this man had been incredibly helpful throughout the day, coordinating reports and gathering information that was critical to the investigation. His professionalism and respect for Tim had made the entire process go much more smoothly than I had expected, and it felt right to show some gratitude for all his efforts.

As we settled into a quiet corner of the casino restaurant, enjoying a cold drink while we waited for our meals, I couldn't help but notice how comfortable the atmosphere felt. Despite the tension of the day, there was a sense of camaraderie between us, perhaps it was the shared understanding of the seriousness of the situation, or maybe it was just the fact that we were able to take a moment to breathe and reflect.

To my surprise, as we began talking more casually, Inspector Carghill mentioned that he and I had gone to the same high school in Canberra, and roughly around the same time. The revelation caught me off guard. I had no idea that our paths had crossed before, but the more we talked about it, the more I realised how many similarities our pasts shared.

I explained to the Inspector that I had grown up living with my parents on a property on the outskirts of the Australian Capital Territory (ACT). Each day, I would take the school bus into Lyneham High School. I completed my Year Twelve there before deciding to pursue further education at the Canberra College of Advanced Education, where I earned a diploma in advanced science for building and construction. It was a time of change and opportunity for me, and I was eager to start my career.

After finishing my studies, I secured employment with the Department of Housing and Construction. At the same time, I bought a home at Isabella Plains, a quiet, suburban neighbourhood that felt like a fresh start. However, the cold Canberra winters soon began to wear on me, and after several years, I decided to make a move to Cairns in Queensland to escape the harsh, chilly climate of the south. I had always wanted to live in the tropics, and it seemed like the perfect time to take the plunge. The warm, sunny weather and laid-back lifestyle of Cairns were a welcome change from the colder, more regimented lifestyle I had left behind.

Inspector Carghill listened intently, nodding as he shared his own experience. It turns out, he had grown up in a similar part of Canberra and had followed a somewhat parallel path, working his way through various roles before making his way into the police force. We spent a few more moments reminiscing about our school days, though the conversation quickly shifted back to the matter at hand.

The bond that was forming between us seemed to go beyond our shared history. Despite the gravity of the situation, there was a sense of ease in our conversations, and the shared respect for each other's backgrounds made the whole evening feel unexpectedly comfortable. It wasn't just about the investigation; it was about the unspoken understanding that, at the core, we were all just people trying to do our best in difficult circumstances.

As the evening went on, we enjoyed a good meal and some much-needed lighthearted conversation. For a moment, the weight of the investigation seemed to lift, and we were able to appreciate the unexpected connections we'd made, both in our shared past and in the work we were doing now.

Jeff, on the other hand, had taken a different path after finishing Year Twelve at Lyneham High. Instead of heading into the building and construction field like me, he had enrolled in the Australian Federal Police and attended the Police Academy at Barton. He had lived in a unit in Barton during his training and soon after obtaining the rank of sergeant in ACT Policing, he made the move to Townsville, where he joined the Queensland Police. His career had clearly progressed with dedication and focus, and as he spoke about his experiences, I couldn't help but admire his drive.

The evening had been flowing smoothly, and I was beginning to feel more at ease, but that sense of relaxation evaporated when Jeff casually suggested that I keep on my toes and stay vigilant for a while. He leaned forward slightly, his tone turning serious.

"Why is that?" I asked, alarmed by his sudden shift in demeanour.

"Well, Jack," Jeff began, his gaze steady, "the latest news indicates that Thomas Reginald Dobson doesn't actually exist, nor does his company 'Saibin'. It seems he's been operating under an assumed name for quite some time now. And once he finds out the police are looking for him, he might just make a connection between that search and you. It didn't take him long to reach out when he learned you were talking to Rex Grogan, he warned you off. Now, if he finds out we're after him, who knows what he'll do. Does he know where you live? I mean, your address, not just Cairns."

I froze, the weight of his words sinking in. "No," I replied, my voice tightening, "I don't think so. I don't think I ever mentioned where I actually live."

Jeff's eyes were sharp. "Well, think about it, Jack. Was he ever left alone in your car when you weren't around? Do you have your car logbooks or other information in the vehicle that might reveal your address? This guy isn't stupid. If he doesn't already know where you live, it wouldn't take much for him to find out. So... just be careful."

I felt a wave of unease wash over me. I'd always thought I'd been cautious, but now, in the context of what Jeff was saying, I realised how easily things could have slipped under my radar. Thomas had already shown that he was calculating, and the thought that he might know more than I'd originally assumed was unsettling.

Tim, who had been listening intently, seemed to sense my unease and quickly tried to ease the tension. "Jeff, I'll be staying with Jack at his unit in Cairns for the next few weeks," he said, trying to lighten the situation. "We'll keep an eye out, make sure everything's good, and hopefully, by the time we leave, Thomas will be behind bars."

I could see Tim's attempt to comfort me, but his words didn't offer the reassurance I had hoped for. "I very much doubt that," Tim replied, his tone more somber. "It's going to be incredibly difficult to place Thomas at the scene of the accident, let alone tie him to Rex's death. Look at how he's covered his tracks with you, the only evidence that you even know him is the security footage from various establishments, and that doesn't prove much. There's no direct evidence that he's associated with you, or that you brought him to Darwin. There's nothing concrete that links him to the hotels or motels you stayed at, and there are no complaints from his so-called 'clients' involved in the alleged Ponzi scheme, except maybe Rex."

Tim's analysis struck home. Despite all the suspicion, despite the strange coincidences and the growing evidence that something was wrong, the case against Thomas seemed to hinge on so many unanswered questions. I wasn't naïve, I knew that for all the police work, all the theories, and all the speculation, they still lacked the hard evidence to definitively tie him to the crime. And that reality made my stomach churn.

But Jeff's warning still echoed in my mind. Thomas was a ghost, moving through the shadows, and I wasn't sure I wanted to stick around long enough to see if he would find me.

"I hear you, Tim," I said, my voice low. "But something about this whole thing feels off. We've only scratched the surface. If he's really as elusive as you say, it's just a matter of time before he slips up. He can't hide forever."

Tim nodded, though his expression remained serious. "Maybe. But until we have something solid, we have to be careful. You've got more on your plate than just a potential run-in with him, Jack. Let's not lose sight of what we know for sure."

The weight of the conversation lingered in the air as we continued our meal, each of us lost in thought. Despite the momentary sense of normalcy, I knew that the storm was far from over.

Jeff agreed with Tim's assessment, and in a low, confidential tone, he shared the first steps of the police investigation with us. "The first move is to talk to Bill Collins," Jeff said, his voice serious. "It seems that Bill was once in a partnership with Rex Grogan. We're hoping to plant a suggestion in Bill's mind that Thomas Dobson might have had something to do with Rex's death. To be honest, Jack, it's our only shot. We're really hoping that Bill will have some empathy for Rex and be willing to cooperate."

Tim, ever the realist, chimed in with a dry remark. "It's not the end, though, Jack. The Federal Police will be going after the Ponzi side of things. They're going to interrogate all the known associates and find a weak link. Once they get a confession, or at least evidence, that the scheme exists, Thomas is done for."

Jeff nodded solemnly. "If they can find him," he added, a grim expression crossing his face. "And I don't think this Thomas Dobson is going to be easy to find. He's slippery, no doubt about it. Just be cautious, Jack. I'm telling you, we don't know who this guy is or what he's capable of. You need to be prepared for the worst. It's no use pretending everything will be fine because we don't know if it will be. You need to understand what I'm saying, and honestly, it might be a good idea for you to lay low somewhere else for a while."

Tim, ever the strategist, offered a suggestion. "What about putting a watch on Jack?"

Jeff shook his head, a wry smile playing at the corners of his lips. "Mate, you're in the better position to do that. You know how difficult it is for me to get something like that organised. I've got to jump through more hoops than you can imagine. Why don't you nominate Jack as a prime witness for the Feds?"

Tim hesitated, his brow furrowing slightly. "The Feds don't even know about it yet. We were planning on reporting it tomorrow."

"Well, they know now," Jeff interjected. "I sent the file to the Federal Police this afternoon. You should have a file reference and a contact name for who will be handling their side of the investigation by tomorrow morning. I'll pass that information on to you. But the thing is, you need to get to the AFP in Cairns as soon as possible. They're at 110 McLeod Street, easy to find."

The conversation drifted to lighter topics as the meal continued, but the weight of what Jeff had shared lingered in my mind. By the time dinner was over, we had all enjoyed several beers, and despite the gravity of the situation, the night had provided a much-needed distraction. When I finally stumbled back to my room, exhaustion overtook me, and I fell into a deep, untroubled sleep. But as morning broke, so did the realisation that the nightmare was only beginning.

I awoke with a jolt, my mind racing with the thoughts of yesterday's events. The weight of the conversation with Jeff, the looming uncertainty about Thomas, and the unsettling feeling that I was now entangled in something much larger than I had ever anticipated, pressed heavily on me. "Fuck no," I muttered, frustration bubbling up inside. "Aagh, fuck it, this is going to be a nightmare."

I shook off the lingering dread, showered, and dressed quickly, determined to face the day. Heading downstairs, I found the breakfast buffet by the pool, and there was Tim, looking just as rough as I felt. I couldn't help but think to myself, I hope I don't look as bad as he does. Tim had stayed up with Jeff the night before, discussing the finer details of the investigation. I had left them just before midnight, and judging by the state Tim was in, it seemed like he hadn't fared much better.

"Suffer, Tim," I thought with a smirk, though I wasn't sure if it was sympathy or just the sheer frustration of the situation that made me feel that way.

Despite the hangover and the gnawing anxiety about the situation, I knew that the day ahead would be crucial. There were steps to take, calls to make, and, most importantly, a dangerous man to track down. With the looming threat of Thomas Dobson and the increasing pressure of the investigation, I had to brace myself.

By the time we were back on the road to Cairns, a normally easy four-and-a-bit-hour drive, Tim still didn't look any better. I had completely forgotten about Thomas for the moment; my primary concern was whether Tim was going to lose his breakfast in my car. His face was pale, his expression strained, and I could tell the hangover was still gripping him tightly.

It was still early, about 8:45 a.m., when my mobile rang through the hands-free speaker. We both assumed it was Jeff, likely calling with the AFP contact name and the next steps for the investigation. Tim groaned and muttered, "He's fucking early, fucking legend," clearly irritated by the timing, but when I saw the name pop up on the screen, I realised it wasn't Jeff. It was Steve, the manager of the complex where my unit is on the Esplanade in Cairns.

"Jack, can you talk, mate? Steve here at Palisade's," Steve's voice came through the speaker, sounding unusually serious.

"Yeah, Steve, I can talk. How's everything?" I replied, puzzled as to why he would be calling me so early.

"Mate," Steve's voice dropped a notch, "your unit burnt out last night…"

I froze. "What?" I cut him off. "What… are you saying? You're fucking kidding me, Steve. No… way."

"I wish I was kidding, mate, but it's all gone. There's fuck all left inside. Happened around midnight, when the smoke alarms went off in your unit, and the neighbours woke me up. By the time the fire department arrived, it was too late. It's all gone, mate. Sorry… really am, mate."

I felt the air leave my lungs, my chest tightening as I processed the words. It couldn't be true. My mind refused to accept it, my thoughts blurring together in disbelief. This wasn't happening. It couldn't be. I pinched myself, trying to wake up from some kind of nightmare. This wasn't real.

"Are you still there, Jack?" Steve's voice cut through the fog. "Jack…?"

"Yeah… I, fuck me… I… fuck, Steve, let me have ten minutes, and I'll call you back. This can't be right, Steve. Must be a fucking mistake…" I quickly hung up, unable to process any more. My hands were shaking as I gripped the steering wheel, trying to regain some semblance of control.

Tim, who had been dozing off in the passenger seat, was suddenly wide awake. He sat bolt upright, his hangover momentarily forgotten, his face now grave. His voice was low but filled with disbelief. "Not… not a fucking coincidence," he repeated, shaking his head slowly, disbelief mixing with concern. "This is not a coincidence, Jack. This is very serious shit. We need to get onto Jeff… and now."

I could barely think straight, my mind still trying to make sense of the phone call. My unit? Burnt to the ground? The implications were too overwhelming. But Tim's words broke through the fog of confusion. I pulled the car over onto the verge of the road and stopped, my hands still trembling.

Tim was already pulling out his phone, dialling Jeff. He spoke with urgency as he relayed the news, his voice sharp. "It's gone, Jeff. The unit's gone. The place burnt down last night, everything's gone. We need to act fast."

Jeff's voice came through the speaker a moment later. "No worries, be there soon," he replied, his tone calm but filled with a sense of purpose.

Tim turned to me, his expression hardening. "What's happening?" I asked, still struggling to keep up with the situation, my emotions running high.

"Move over, brother. I'll drive from here on," Tim said, his voice steady despite the urgency of the situation. Before I could protest, he was already out of the passenger seat and taking control of the wheel. He did a sharp U-turn, the tires screeching slightly as he turned the car around. "No Cairns today, my friend," he muttered, his gaze fixed ahead as he sped back toward Townsville Police HQ.

I didn't say anything. My thoughts were still scattered, trying to process everything. The fire, the loss of my home, the escalating danger of our situation, it was all spinning out of control. But one thing was clear: the stakes had just gotten much higher.

Jeff had called Tim back, and as Tim continued to drive, I took the call. Jeff's voice was calm but urgent, as he instructed, "Head to the lower car park ramp. When you get there, call me back, and someone will open the door and show you where to park."

It didn't take us long to get back to the station, and we followed his instructions precisely. As we reached the ramp, the roller shutter began to rise, and a Police Constable approached the driver's side window. Without a word, he gestured for Tim to follow him. We did as instructed, and moments later, we found ourselves heading toward Jeff's office.

Upon arrival, we were greeted by two other men, both casually dressed. They stood up as we entered, and Jeff introduced them.

"Matt Doheny and Brett Manning," Jeff said, his gaze shifting between us. "Matt and Brett are taking you guys, " he looked at Tim, ", to the Gold Coast for a while until we get a better grip on what's going on. We're putting you into protective custody, Jack. Sorry, you don't get a say in it. Tim, looks like you're starting work early, as the Commissioner wants you on this case. But you do get a say."

Tim, ever the professional, nodded without hesitation. "Fine with me," he said. "Happy to do it. Don't look too sad, Jack. This won't be too bad. You'll see."

I could hear the sincerity in his voice, though a small part of me bristled at the thought of being thrust into protective custody. It felt surreal, the rapid turn of events. But I had no choice in the matter, and as much as I wanted to protest, there was an unspoken understanding that this was for my own safety. As unsettling as it was, the gravity of the situation made it clear, this wasn't going to be a temporary inconvenience. This was a serious move, and the implications of Thomas Dobson's actions had just gone from bad to worse.

Matt and Brett led us to a secure section of the station, where we were given a few minutes to gather our thoughts. The ride to the Gold Coast, still a bit of a blur, seemed like a long road ahead, but one thing was certain: my life, as I had known it, was about to change.

Jeff continued, his tone steady yet urgent. "The plane will be in Townsville at one-thirty this afternoon, so you've got some time to prepare. Get your bags from the car, and make sure you're ready. I'll take your mobile phone, Jack, sorry, mate, but it's a security thing. Don't worry, though. You've got a couple of hours before the flight. Matt and Brett will help you with your bags, put them in the car that will take you to the airport, and then escort you to our lounge while you wait."

I nodded, still processing the sudden shift in circumstances, but trying to keep my composure.

"Tim, I'll be in touch with you through the Police network, or by phone if necessary," Jeff continued, looking directly at Tim. "Stay alert, and stay safe. I'll make sure we keep the lines open for any updates. You're both in good hands here."

He gave us both a firm handshake, his eyes full of resolve. "See you soon, I'm sure. Just take it easy for now. Everything's in motion, and we'll handle the rest."

With that, Jeff stepped away, his business-like demeanour unwavering, leaving Tim and me to absorb the situation. The weight of everything that had happened in the past twenty-four hours was beginning to sink in, and as much as I appreciated Jeff's support, the reality of it all was almost overwhelming.

Matt and Brett, who had been standing by quietly, offered small smiles of reassurance as they motioned for us to follow them. As they led us down the hall, my mind was still racing. Protective custody? A flight to the Gold Coast? My life had been turned upside down in a matter of hours.

Despite the anxiety swirling inside me, I tried to focus on what Jeff had said. We had a few hours to prepare, a bit of time to breathe before the next chapter of this strange, dangerous ordeal unfolded. If anything, I was grateful that, at least for the time being, I wasn't facing it alone. Tim, ever the professional, was by my side, and Matt and Brett seemed more than capable of handling the logistics.

"Come on, let's get our bags," Tim said, giving me a nudge as he glanced at me. "It's a weird ride ahead, but we'll get through it. Just take it one step at a time."

Matt and Brett, both Queensland Police Sergeants, immediately put us at ease with their easygoing demeanour. Despite the serious nature of the situation, they seemed like genuinely nice guys. Both were clearly looking forward to the short holiday at the Gold Coast, and their jubilant and friendly personalities made the tense atmosphere feel a little lighter. Tim, ever the pragmatist, chuckled and told them, "The sooner you stop calling us 'Sir,' the better we'll all get along." I agreed wholeheartedly, and the guys quickly dropped the formalities, which seemed to make everyone feel more relaxed.

As Matt went out to grab some pizzas and cokes, Brett and I settled in the secure Police lounge area. The space was simple but comfortable, with a few worn couches and a table scattered with police reports and miscellaneous papers. We had a chance to chat more about what was going on, and Brett, in his calm, methodical manner, gave us an update on the truck accident.

"The witness who saw the truck stopped on the side of the road was interviewed by the police at Charters Towers," Brett began. "He couldn't really give much of a description at first, but then he remembered something important. He'd completely forgotten that he had a dash cam in his car. When the police asked him about it, he had no idea it could have been helpful."

Brett paused, letting the information sink in before continuing. "The SD card from the witness's car was taken, and it revealed a clear recording of the event. The truck was well over the road, and the witness had to cross the unbroken lines to pass it. It was a pretty tight squeeze. But the most telling part of the footage was when it showed two male figures standing near the front of the truck, one of whom seemed to move towards the rear of a white Landcruiser. The strange thing is, he appeared to be blocking the number plate of the Landcruiser, or at least trying to obscure it."

He leaned forward, his expression more serious. "The number plate of the Landcruiser, though, was clearly visible in the footage, and that's something we can follow up on. We'll be running that through the system as soon as we can."

Tim, who had been quietly listening, raised an eyebrow. "That could be important. If there's something more to this than just a truck accident, it's starting to look like we've got a connection to something bigger."

I nodded in agreement, the weight of the situation beginning to feel more tangible. Brett's update added another layer of complexity to the case, and it was clear that the more we learned, the more the story started to unravel. Thomas Dobson was no longer just a mysterious figure, his connection to Rex Grogan's death was becoming harder to ignore.

When Matt returned with the pizzas and cokes, we took a break from the conversation to eat, but the looming sense of uncertainty hung over us. No one knew where this was going, but it was becoming clear that we were all in it together, and the stakes were rising with every new piece of information.

The vision from the dash cam had provided a critical breakthrough in the investigation. One of the males captured on the footage had been identified from an image I had previously shown to the police, and it was confirmed to be Thomas Dobson. The other man in the footage was recognised by a car dealer from Stuart Park, Northern Territory, as Jason Reynolds from Millner, also in the Northern Territory. Reynolds had just purchased the white Landcruiser for cash the previous day, and the license plate had not yet been transferred from the dealership to the individual. The police were now actively searching for both of these individuals.

Brett leaned forward in his seat and relayed the update. "We believe both Thomas Dobson and Jason Reynolds may be somewhere in the North or Far North Queensland region. We need to exercise caution, though. They may be dangerous if approached."

The revelation made everything feel more real. We were no longer chasing a vague suspect; now, we were dealing with two individuals who could pose a real threat. The weight of the situation was starting to settle in.

The Gold Coast

The ride to the airport was anything but comfortable. The back of the unmarked Toyota Camry police car was cramped with Brett on one side of me and Matt on the other. Tim, in the front, looked much more at ease, talking to the driver. As we made our way toward the Garbutt RAAF base entry on Ingham Road, it became clear that our departure from Townsville was going to be anything but routine.

When we arrived at the base, we were stopped by the sentry guards. The driver spoke to one of the guards, who made a quick phone call, then instructed us to drive directly onto the tarmac at the air movement wing. The urgency of the situation seemed to escalate with each passing moment.

An RAAF officer was waiting for us at the air movement wing and directed the driver to stop just meters from a Gulfstream G280 jet aircraft. Brett motioned for us to remain still, and Matt got out of the car to speak with the officer. After a brief exchange, Matt nodded and returned to the car, signalling us to follow him.

"Here we go," Brett said firmly, his tone leaving no room for hesitation. "You two go directly to the aircraft, just follow Matt. I'll handle the baggage. Now... GO."

With those words, everything shifted into high gear. We quickly exited the car and followed Matt as he made his way toward the waiting jet. The sounds of the tarmac beneath our feet and the distant hum of aircraft engines heightened the surreal nature of the moment. This wasn't just an ordinary flight, it felt like we were stepping into the unknown, into something far bigger than what we had initially imagined. The stakes were rising, and with each passing second, the mystery surrounding Thomas Dobson seemed closer to unraveling.

Matt was already waiting at the foot of the stairs when we arrived, and he led us directly to the front boarding stairs. As we quickly ascended, the pilot was waiting at the top and greeted us with a friendly nod. "Sit wherever you like," he said casually, gesturing to the ten luxurious-looking seats inside the cabin. Matt added that there were no other passengers today, so we had our pick of the seats.

After taking a moment to settle in, we all made ourselves comfortable. Brett had already taken care of our luggage, stowing our bags in the aircraft's storage compartments before joining us in the cabin. As the main door was securely closed, the engines roared to life, and we began our ascent, leaving the ground behind.

The flight itself was smooth and incredibly fast. Just one hour and fifteen minutes later, we touched down at the Gold Coast airport, Coolangatta, marking the quickest and most comfortable flight I'd ever experienced. As we taxied to the opposite side of the terminal, I struck up a conversation with Brian, one of the pilots. He told me that Queensland Police now had two Gulfstream G280 Jets in their fleet, each costing around thirty million dollars. He was clearly enthusiastic about their capabilities, explaining how the planes were perfect for the vast distances between towns in Queensland. With a cruising speed of 850 kilometres per hour, they were around 250 kilometres per hour faster than a commercial jetliner, making them a great asset for the police force.

We made our way to the maintenance area of the airport, where we disembarked and climbed into an unmarked police car waiting for us. The driver navigated through the busy Gold Coast streets, and before long, we were in the heart of Surfers Paradise. We turned off the main road into Hanlan Street and then veered into a private car park ramp. The ramp led us down to a double roller shutter, which the driver had already activated. The large door slowly began to rise, and we waited for it to open enough for the car to pass through.

Once the door was high enough, we proceeded into a poorly illuminated parking garage. The sparse lighting cast shadows over the concrete walls, and we slowly drove along what seemed like a long concrete masonry wall that met an intersecting wall on the left. This new section had another roller shutter, though smaller than the first one, and it was closed. The driver called a number on his mobile phone, and after a moment, the second door started to rise. As it did, I noticed two security cameras mounted near the top of the wall where it met the next level of the building.

We drove through the second roller shutter into a small, secure compound. The area, about thirty meters wide and fifty meters long, was entirely empty except for our car. The roller door behind us had already closed by the time we stopped. We got out, leaving the driver inside the car, and Matt retrieved our bags from the boot.

Following Brett, we moved to what appeared to be a stainless steel elevator door. There were no up buttons or keypad, just the door itself. Next to it was another door with a sign that read, "Fire Door, Do Not Block." The space was eerily quiet, and other than the elevator and the fire door, there was nothing else in sight.

As we stood there, Matt rejoined us with the bags, and the elevator door suddenly opened. I noticed more security cameras mounted high on the walls of the compound, and another was positioned inside the elevator. The four of us stepped into the elevator, and as the door closed behind us, it became clear there were no floor indicators or buttons. The doors shut automatically, and with a soft whir, the elevator began to rise.

The movement of the elevator was smooth and almost imperceptible, but the silence within made it feel like we were being transported deeper into some unknown, highly secure location. We had no idea where we were heading or what awaited us, but the sense of uncertainty was palpable. It felt as though we were on the verge of uncovering something much larger than we could have anticipated.

The elevator ride seemed to last longer than expected, and as it came to a smooth stop, both Tim and I were caught off guard when the rear wall of the elevator suddenly slid open. We turned around in unison, and following Matt and Brett, we stepped out into what appeared to be a luxurious rooftop penthouse. As soon as we exited the elevator, the breathtaking view of the ocean immediately captivated us, the blue expanse stretching far beyond the horizon, calming yet surreal in its beauty.

"Follow me, please, gentlemen," said a voice behind us. We turned to find a slim, somewhat older man, balding and dressed in a dark blue suit, beckoning us to follow him. We obediently followed him to the left of the elevator, where he led us into a small but well-appointed conference room. The space had a large, polished table with ten chairs neatly arranged around it, and the minimalist design created an air of quiet authority.

We stopped at the table, and Matt, with a practiced ease, handed a plastic clipboard to the man in the suit. "This is Inspector Ian Gregory," Matt said, "He'll be looking after you both from here on." With that, we shook hands with Inspector Gregory, and he invited us to sit. As we did, Matt and Brett exchanged their goodbyes, wishing us good luck. Matt briefly mentioned that he and Brett needed to head to Brisbane to catch the last flight back to Townsville at 7:30 PM.

Tim and I exchanged glances, still processing the fact that Matt and Brett were not going to be staying with us as we had initially assumed. It was another surprise in what was already becoming a series of unexpected twists, and we couldn't help but feel that many more surprises were still to come.

As the door closed behind Matt and Brett, leaving us alone with Inspector Gregory, he smiled and said, "Please, call me Ian. No need for the formalities." We both nodded and assured him that we preferred to use first names as well. The stiffness of "Sir" was unnecessary now, and we were eager to relax and begin understanding what was to come next in this strange and uncertain chapter of our lives.

Ian gestured for us to make ourselves comfortable and took a seat at the head of the table, his posture relaxed yet authoritative. The atmosphere in the room was markedly different from the cold, impersonal nature of the police station. Here, there was a quiet professionalism mixed with a touch of personal warmth, and it felt like the first real opportunity to breathe since all of this had begun.

We were still digesting the fast pace of everything when Ian began to speak again, this time, with a slight shift in tone, as though he were about to provide us with some much-needed answers.

Ian sat at the head of the large table, his posture commanding yet relaxed. Tim and I took our seats on either side of him, the polished spotted gum tabletop gleaming under the soft lighting, its rich wood grain almost gleaming with its own silent authority. Matt had placed our bags at the end of the table, and I couldn't help but notice the faint shift in Ian's expression as his gaze flicked over the bags. I had the distinct feeling that the impeccable, somewhat sterile nature of the place didn't quite mesh with the casualness of our arrival, though he said nothing about it.

"We don't know how long you fellows will be our guests here, but we think you'll find it comfortable," Ian began, his voice smooth and measured. He paused for a moment, giving us a chance to adjust to the sudden formality of the situation. "Now, let me explain the house rules," he continued, leaning forward slightly as he spoke, his tone suggesting he'd done this many times before.

First, Ian made it clear that we had our own private rooms, each fully equipped with a shower, toilet, and a television that offered a seemingly endless array of entertainment options: Netflix, Prime, and likely more. It was almost too luxurious to fully grasp in the moment. "For your own safety," Ian added, "each room will be automatically locked from 10 PM to 7 AM every night. It's a precaution, and we ask that you respect it."

He paused for a moment, allowing that information to settle in, then continued, outlining the rest of the rules. There was no standard exit from the building other than the fire escape, which was, naturally, locked during regular conditions. This wasn't a place where we could simply come and go as we pleased, and it was clear that security was top priority.

However, Ian quickly assured us that we were free to use the facilities inside and outside the unit. "The lounge area is yours to enjoy," he said. "There's a pool table, a fully stocked bar, which is restocked every day, and an outdoor swimming pool on the deck. We also have an external lounge area." It sounded almost like a vacation getaway, but the underlying tension of our situation lingered in the air.

As for meals, Ian informed us that they would be served in the dining room. "The meals aren't prepared here," he explained, "but are reheated on-site. You'll need to choose all your meals and snacks the day before, and there's a full-time steward who will coordinate everything for you. They'll also keep the entire area tidy, so don't hesitate to reach out to them if you have any specific dietary requirements or other needs."

The list of rules was detailed, and though the luxury was undeniable, it was clear that we were still very much under the watchful eye of the authorities. The words "guests" and "comfort" seemed almost out of place given the context, yet they gave us a strange sense of reassurance.

After a few moments, Ian smiled slightly, as though he could sense the weight of what he had just shared. "It's a secure environment," he said, "and we'll make sure everything is handled so you can focus on getting through this. If there's anything you need, just ask. The steward will see to it." His tone softened a bit, and I could almost feel the protective nature of the place surrounding us, a barrier that would shield us from whatever dangers still loomed beyond these walls.

Tim and I exchanged a glance, still processing the situation. We had no choice but to follow these rules, and yet, there was something oddly reassuring about the structured environment Ian had outlined for us. It was a strange kind of security, but it was the best we could hope for, at least for now.

Ian continued to explain the house rules in his calm, methodical way, outlining that we needed to be out of our rooms each day between ten and eleven o'clock for the housekeeping staff to perform their duties. "Other than the rooms you've been assigned, the entire area is under constant surveillance," he added, his tone more matter-of-fact than comforting. He went on to explain that there was a security guard stationed in a room next to the meeting area, providing round-the-clock vigilance.

"There's also a monitored telephone available in this room for your use," Ian continued. "However, be aware that the system will automatically delete any words that could compromise security. This phone does not take incoming calls, only outgoing ones."

Tim and I exchanged a look at the mention of the monitored phone, security was clearly airtight here. We were guests in a very controlled environment, a far cry from any normal vacation retreat.

Ian's voice softened a little. "Other than that, gentlemen, you are free to do as you wish. Tim, you'll have access to updates through your laptop on the police web, so you'll be kept up to date on your situation. Jack, the AFP will be here to interview you at nine o'clock tomorrow. I imagine that might be a lengthy process, and I assume Tim will be sitting in on it…"

Before Ian could finish, the telephone on the desk buzzed, cutting him off.

"Yes?" Ian answered, his expression momentarily shifting to focus on the call.

"Your car is waiting downstairs, sir," the voice on the intercom announced.

"I'm on my way," Ian replied, then looked at us. "Grab your bags, and I'll find the steward. I'll be gone after that."

We collected our bags, still processing everything, and Ian led us to the steward. She was a pleasant woman in her mid-fifties with an air of professional warmth. She introduced herself and assured us that we would find our way around the penthouse. "I'll be here until eight o'clock this evening, so don't hesitate to ask for anything you need," she said with a smile.

She guided us to our rooms, which were as luxurious as one might expect from such a high-security facility. Our rooms were large and well-appointed, with plush bedding and modern furnishings that exuded a sense of comfort, despite the tense nature of our circumstances.

Before she left, the steward handed us a meal request form for the following day. Tim and I both filled it out, somewhat amazed by the wide variety of options. It certainly seemed like a five-star experience. She mentioned that tonight's dinner would be chicken parmy, as a convenient choice given our late arrival. We assured her it wasn't an issue, and before she left us to settle in, we asked her about the location of the bar.

"The bar is just around the corner," she replied with a smile. "Help yourselves, and if you need anything else, just let me know."

Once she had left, Tim and I stood there for a moment, taking in the luxurious surroundings. The whole place felt like a high-end hotel, but there was an undeniable air of caution. We were safe here, for the moment, but the sense of unease still lingered, as did the knowledge that we were far from out of the woods. But for now, we'd make the best of it.

Under different circumstances, this place would have been paradise. A luxurious penthouse with every amenity at your fingertips, the soothing sounds of the ocean in the distance, and all the time in the world to relax and unwind. But of course, if the circumstances were different, I wouldn't be here at all. Instead of feeling like a retreat, this penthouse felt more like a gilded cage. Safe, yes, but with a constant reminder that the storm was still brewing on the horizon.

Tim and I sat in the outdoor lounge, enjoying a cold stubbie of Great Northern, the only small solace I could find in the haze of my thoughts. Tim had his MacBook Air open, scanning the police web for updates. As usual, there was nothing of significance, no new developments that could offer any comfort or clarity. The atmosphere was heavy, and it was clear we were both carrying a lot of weight on our shoulders, even though we tried to keep the mood light.

We didn't talk much. I wasn't sure what to say. How could you fill the silence when your mind is occupied with the weight of a burned-out unit, a long list of unanswered questions, and the lingering fear of a person named Thomas, someone who had already demonstrated that he could be far more dangerous than I had originally thought? The fact that Thomas had said he was a Sensei in Taekwondo suddenly struck me as important. I hadn't mentioned it to the police, hadn't connected the dots between his possible martial arts background and the brutal nature of Rex's injuries. I knew then it was something I needed to pass along.

Our dinner arrived, and Alice, the steward, called us in to eat. She had been kind and accommodating, though I couldn't shake the feeling that she was just another part of the system keeping us under constant watch. The meal was perfectly prepared, chicken parmy, just as she'd promised. Tim and I ate in silence, each lost in our own thoughts, before I finally decided I needed to rest.

By eight o'clock, I was in my room, completely drained. It had been a monstrous day, emotionally and physically. The shock of my unit burning down had hit me harder than I expected. I couldn't escape the nagging thought that it was no accident, that it was a signal, a warning that things were escalating beyond my control. The police had moved quickly after the fire, pushing me further into a corner, and suddenly, I found myself fearing for my life again. Thomas, or whoever he was, had become my primary concern.

The next morning, as I sipped my coffee and tried to shake off the haze of a restless night, I mentioned the Taekwondo detail to Tim. "I didn't tell the police about it last night," I said, feeling the weight of the omission. "Thomas said he was a Sensei. It might help with identifying the injuries Rex sustained."

Tim immediately pulled up the case notes on the police web. "I'll add it now," he said, typing away quickly. "We can't afford to leave anything out."

His fingers moved swiftly across the keyboard as he added the detail to the case notes, ensuring that the police would have all the information they needed. I watched him work, feeling a strange mix of gratitude and unease. The sense that we were doing everything we could to piece together the puzzle was comforting, but I couldn't shake the feeling that the pieces were slipping through our fingers, just out of reach.

We were still in the dark, and it was becoming increasingly clear that our only hope was to outsmart the very people who were after us.

The Federal Police arrived almost exactly at nine o'clock. We had just finished breakfast in the dining room, and had been getting ready for their arrival. As the clock ticked toward the hour, we settled into the meeting room, adjusting our chairs and getting ourselves mentally prepared for what was about to unfold. Janice, the morning steward, came in and introduced the officers.

"Inspector Gerald James and Senior Sergeant David Caruthers," she announced as they entered the room.

Tim and I stood, shaking hands with both officers. "Jack Holden," I said, introducing myself, and Tim followed suit.

Inspector James and Sergeant Caruthers looked around the room, clearly impressed by the luxury of the penthouse. They exchanged brief glances before turning their attention back to us. We couldn't help but exchange smirks, but we quickly shifted our focus. It was time for business. We had to get down to the details, and I had a feeling this conversation wasn't going to be as straightforward as we'd hoped.

I retold the entire story as best I could, starting from the beginning, recounting everything I remembered, from meeting Rex to the days leading up to his death and everything in between. Tim was quick to jump in and fill in a couple of blanks that I had missed. We both knew that the more detailed and precise we could be, the better chance we had at getting to the bottom of this. The last thing we wanted was for the authorities to think we were leaving out crucial information.

But Inspector James and Senior Sergeant Caruthers didn't look shocked or surprised by anything I told them. They were calm, professional, but not particularly alarmed by the gravity of the situation. Instead, they seemed almost matter-of-fact about it.

"It's a pretty frequent occurrence, Jack," Inspector James said, leaning back in his chair. "Ponzi schemes like this are a dime a dozen. They're everywhere.

What makes it so difficult to crack is that, while the scheme is running smoothly and victims, or rather, the recipients, are getting their promised returns, no one's going to report it. The victims don't even realise they're part of a scheme. Until it unravels, that is."

I nodded, processing what he said. It made sense in a twisted way. For the people involved in these schemes, everything seemed to be going as planned until the money stopped flowing, and by then, it was often too late.

"Exactly," I replied. "But it wasn't just the money. There's something else going on here. Something about Rex's death, and the connection to Thomas, just doesn't add up."

Senior Sergeant Caruthers chimed in, his tone thoughtful. "We're well aware that these schemes tend to attract more than just the typical financial crooks. Sometimes, they can lead to much darker activities, violence, threats, even murder. If this Thomas guy is involved, it's important to understand what role he plays in all of this, beyond the money."

I agreed, but it wasn't easy to shake the unease that had been building in me ever since Rex's death. I knew we were getting closer to the truth, but every step forward seemed to pull us further into murky waters. The more we learned, the more dangerous it all felt.

"We're going to need everything you've got, Jack," Inspector James said, cutting through my thoughts. "Any bit of information, no matter how small. These cases are like a spider's web, pull one thread, and the whole thing can unravel, but it can also snap back and tangle you up in ways you didn't see coming. We need to be careful."

Tim and I exchanged a glance. It was clear we were in over our heads, but there was no turning back now. We had a choice: keep moving forward and risk everything, or go back to the shadows and let the truth remain buried. We couldn't, in good conscience, do the latter.

"We'll cooperate fully," Tim said, his voice steady but with an underlying urgency. "We don't know everything, but we know enough to know that this is bigger than just a financial scam. People are getting hurt. And we need to find out why."

"If a recipient does, however, discover that they've unwittingly invested in a Ponzi scheme, they face a difficult dilemma," Gerald continued. "The decision becomes whether or not to report it. If they do, they risk causing the scheme to collapse immediately, resulting in a total loss of all the money they've invested."

David nodded grimly before adding, "We've seen cases where victims, once they realise what's happening, have attempted to withdraw from the scheme.

They quickly find themselves either threatened with violence or, in some cases, have completely disappeared. The stakes are high for these people, and they often find themselves trapped, caught between the fear of losing everything and the risk of retaliation."

Gerald leaned forward, his expression serious. "You see, the people who get involved in these schemes really believe they're onto something great. We've just had a bad case up in Townsville. It involved a lot of pensioners and retirees, people who, for all intents and purposes, should be enjoying the last years of their lives in peace. Some of them took out a mortgage on their homes to borrow a significant portion of the home's equity, typically around seven to eight percent, then invested it in what they thought was a legitimate investment consortium. They were promised returns of around twenty percent, sometimes as high as twenty-five percent. To them, it appeared like they were making a safe profit each year, around twelve percent after they paid off the interest on their bank mortgage."

Tim and I exchanged uneasy glances. The math was simple enough, and it made perfect sense from the victims' perspective. But the harsh reality behind those numbers was beginning to sink in.

"They can't lose, they think," Gerald continued, his tone almost sympathetic, "until the scheme begins to collapse, either due to no new investors coming in, or exiting investors pulling their funds out. Or worse, the operator siphons off the money, scoops up the haul, and bolts to another country. By then, it's always too late. The damage is done, and millions, sometimes tens of millions, are lost."

David added with a resigned sigh, "The problem is that the AFP doesn't discover these schemes until it's already too late. By the time we're aware of them, they've already caused significant harm to a lot of people. The perpetrators are long gone, and we're left trying to pick up the pieces and track them down."

The weight of their words hung in the air, and I felt the full gravity of what they were telling us. Ponzi schemes weren't just financial frauds; they were traps that ruined lives. The people who got involved, victims in every sense of the word, were often left with nothing but broken dreams and shattered trust.

Tim, ever the optimist, broke the silence. "So, what can we do about it? Is there any way to stop this before it goes any further?"

Gerald exchanged a look with David before answering. "The best thing you can do, Tim, is to stay involved and keep feeding us any information you have. We're going to do everything we can to track down the people behind this, but you need to be prepared that this is a long game. We may not see results right away, but if we keep at it, we'll get somewhere."

David nodded in agreement. "The key is to keep digging, keep your eyes open. These schemes usually leave a trail, and if we can follow it, we'll catch up with the people responsible. But, for now, we need you both to stay safe. The more you know, the more danger you're in."

The conversation turned somber as we discussed the next steps. There were still so many unanswered questions, so much we didn't know about Thomas, about Rex, and the network behind the scheme. But one thing was clear: we were now fully enmeshed in something far bigger and more dangerous than we had originally thought.

Gerald nodded grimly before continuing, "The victims of these schemes often end up becoming the villains themselves, unwittingly perpetuating the fraud by helping to keep it afloat. Many of them don't realise they're trapped in a cycle they can't escape. When they start to understand that it's a scam, they can't back out without risking losing everything. So, to protect themselves, they do everything they can to recruit others, family members, close friends, into the scheme, often with the false promise of a 'secret investment opportunity.' The victims become recruiters, hoping to delay the inevitable collapse long enough for them to bail out."

I could now fully appreciate the vicious cycle these people were stuck in. The investors weren't just naïve; they were complicit in a system that preyed on their greed, fear, and desperation. Even if they knew, deep down, that they were involved in something illegal, the thought of losing everything would drive them to keep quiet and keep the scheme running as long as possible. They weren't going to talk to us. They weren't going to rat out the very thing that was keeping them from total ruin.

"It's a damn tight spot," Tim muttered under his breath, clearly feeling the weight of what we were up against. He was right. How could we expect anyone to come forward when their own survival depended on the secrecy of the scheme?

Gerald continued, pulling our attention back to the more immediate dangers at hand. "As I'm sure you're aware, this Thomas Dobson alias is classified as a very dangerous individual. That's part of the reason you're in protective custody right now, Jack, not just on a simple protection plan. The AFP believes we may actually have a real shot at dismantling this scheme, but only if you're alive to testify. If you're dead, we lose everything, and the chances of getting the people behind it only grow slimmer."

I felt a chill run through me. It wasn't just about the money or the scam anymore; my life was at stake. The fact that I was a target, and not just some collateral damage in a bigger game, began to feel very real.

"Fortunately," Gerald added, "we've got some unexpected help on this case. The Crown Prosecutor, of all people, got involved by pure coincidence. The fact that she crossed paths with you and, by extension, with Rex Grogan, has proven to be a stroke of luck. We might have the key to breaking this wide open if we play our cards right."

The mention of Rex's name sent a shiver down my spine. If we were really on the verge of cracking this thing, it was more dangerous than I'd ever realised. And Rex, the so-called 'murder victim,' might not have been the only casualty in this game.

Gerald stood, signalling the end of the conversation. "Alright, gentlemen. You're going to be briefed further when we have more updates. But for now, stay vigilant. Don't trust anyone. Keep your heads down. We'll be in touch as soon as we have more information. You're not alone in this."

Tim and I exchanged a silent glance as we watched the two officers leave. The weight of our situation settled heavily on our shoulders. We weren't just pawns in a game anymore. We were the keys to breaking open a criminal enterprise, and the stakes had never been higher.

Gerald nodded solemnly and continued, "The plan is to get Dobson into custody." He paused, allowing the words to settle. It was clear that this was the key to everything , capturing him meant unraveling the entire scheme. However, David's sharp tone cut through the moment as he interjected, his frustration evident.

"We know that's bloody obvious, Jack," David said curtly, his words laced with impatience. "But this bloke is fucking smart. It's a damn fluke that the Queensland cops even identified him from the dash-cam footage. He was clever enough to notice when the witness drove past and tried to get in the way of the number plate, just in case the car had a dash-cam. Think about it, Jack. How clever was he to even think that way? Even the bloody witness didn't remember he had a dash-cam in his car. This guy's a step ahead, always. He's smart, Jack. He's very smart."

David's words hit me with a force I wasn't expecting. I had already known that Dobson was dangerous, but hearing it put so bluntly, realising just how much effort he'd put into covering his tracks, made me more uneasy than I had been before. The way he operated was meticulous, almost surgical in its precision. He hadn't just been a criminal; he was playing a long game, anticipating every move. His ability to think ahead of everyone else, to predict even the smallest detail, made him a formidable opponent.

I nodded slowly, processing the gravity of what David was saying. Dobson was no ordinary criminal. He wasn't someone who made mistakes. He had been one step ahead of the authorities every time they had tried to catch him. If we were going to take him down, we'd have to be smarter than him , or at least find a way to outmanoeuvre him in his own game.

"Alright," I said, my voice steady but with a hint of resolve, "so what's the next step?"

Gerald exchanged a glance with David before responding. "The next step is to keep our cards close to the chest. We can't let Dobson realise we're onto him. We have to wait for the right moment, and we have to use everything we have. His arrogance will be his downfall, but we need to be patient. One wrong move, and he could slip away again."

David sighed, his gaze intense. "That's the hard part, Jack. You're right. We've got one shot at this, and we can't afford to screw it up. He's been laying low for a reason. He's biding his time, waiting for someone to slip. The moment we make a mistake, he'll be gone."

I understood the weight of what they were saying. This wasn't just about catching a criminal; it was about dismantling a carefully constructed empire. And if we were going to do that, every move had to be calculated, precise, and executed with perfect timing.

"We'll get him," I said firmly, though I knew it wasn't going to be easy. "But we'll need all the help we can get."

David looked at me with a small, grim smile. "Don't worry, Jack. We've got resources. We've just got to make sure we use them the right way."

The conversation shifted after that, but the reality of what we were up against hung in the air. This wasn't just a case anymore. It was a battle of wits, and Dobson was playing to win. The question was, were we clever enough to beat him at his own game?

"This is where Tim comes in," Gerald explained patiently, his voice steady as he outlined the plan. "We don't know who this bloke is, and we don't know where he is. Even if we did, we have nothing concrete on him to warrant an arrest , nor do the state police. But…" Gerald paused, ensuring the weight of his words was felt. "As soon as we do catch sight of him, we'll be arresting him , or rather…" he added quickly, seeing the sharp look on Tim's face, "we'll detain him for an indefinite period, simply to ensure he misses making those crucial interest payments to his victims."

I was stunned by the brilliance of the plan. "How smart is that?" I said, genuinely impressed by the strategy. "But… how does Tim help? I don't get it."

Gerald's eyes flickered to Tim, who had been listening attentively, his expression unreadable. Gerald continued, explaining how Tim would play a critical role. "Tim will be the key player when it comes to the legal side of things. He'll be working behind the scenes with the respective magistrates each time the Queensland police apply for an extension of detention time for Dobson. In essence, he'll be playing chess with the legal system, ensuring that every time they need more time to keep him detained, Tim will be right there, supporting the request."

I still didn't entirely understand how this would work, but it was starting to make sense. "And when the extensions run out?" I asked, trying to piece it together.

Gerald gave a nod of approval. "That's when Tim's role really kicks in. When we can no longer extend his detention, Tim will make formal charges against Dobson. The moment those charges are filed, he'll set a hearing date, and we'll play the waiting game. The hope is that we can drag the proceedings out, extend the hearings as much as possible, and buy us the time we need."

I felt a sense of growing clarity. "So, we're not just trying to arrest him, we're trying to keep him in the system as long as possible, preventing him from making payments or fleeing."

"Exactly," David chimed in, his tone resolute. "The longer we can keep him tied up in court proceedings, the more time we have to track down the rest of his operation. It's a strategy designed to disrupt his ability to pay back his victims , and if we're lucky, it'll start unraveling his entire scheme."

I could see how Tim's role would be crucial in executing this. It was a waiting game, but one that required finesse and legal manoeuvring. The pressure would be immense, but Tim seemed unfazed by the responsibility. It was a tactic designed to buy us time, to cripple Dobson's operations bit by bit, all while we made strategic moves to take him down.

I turned to Tim, who had been quiet up until this point. "You okay with that?" I asked.

Tim gave a small, determined nod. "We're in this together, Jack. It's not going to be easy, but it's the best chance we've got. And I've got your back."

Gerald's voice broke in, and I could see the weight of the operation bearing down on him as well. "We're all in this, Jack. And if anyone can outsmart

Dobson, it's going to be us. But it's going to take patience, precision, and trust. We just need to make sure we're always one step ahead."

The plan had started to take shape, but I could already feel the gravity of the situation. This wasn't just a case anymore , it was a chess match with a dangerous man, one who wouldn't hesitate to make a move if we showed any weakness. And if we were going to win, we had to play the game better than him.

The ultimate goal for the AFP, as Gerald laid out, was the collapse of the "Ponzi" scheme and the subsequent charging of the elusive Thomas Reginald Dobson. That's where I, Jack Holden, came into play as a witness. The scheme's downfall would trigger the legal process, and in the aftermath, tax evasion charges could be brought against the participants. But in the meantime, there was a glimmer of hope that the Queensland police might have enough evidence to tie Dobson to complications surrounding the death of Rex Grogan.

"In reality," Tim added, his voice steady but with an edge of irony, "we're going to detain an 'innocent' man, in the eyes of the law, for anywhere between six to twelve months on bogus charges, all while we work to gather genuine evidence for real charges."

I furrowed my brow, still trying to wrap my head around the plan. "But isn't that illegal?" I asked, the words feeling heavier as I spoke them.

Tim gave a short, humourless laugh. "Not if you're the Queensland Crown Prosecutor," he quipped. "But that's not something anyone needs to know. It's a very privileged position , more like bending the law a little to make it work the way it's supposed to, especially when it comes to assholes like Dobson."

Gerald, who had been listening intently, nodded in agreement and elaborated further on the plan. He explained that, based on what I had told them, it seemed Dobson was continuing to recruit more investors, evidenced by the collection of laptop bags that appeared to contain significant sums of money. If what both Tim and I had gathered was true , that Rex Grogan had claimed the interest rate on the investment was twenty percent, paid twice yearly in cash with no mention of a fiscal year cutoff , it was likely that interest had been accruing the moment the money was handed over to Dobson.

This would mean that the scheme was growing, continuously attracting new victims while simultaneously bleeding the ones who had already invested. It was becoming increasingly apparent that Dobson had been clever enough to design a system that kept people quiet, even when they suspected they were being scammed. And the longer it went on, the more dangerous he became.

Gerald's tone shifted slightly as he elaborated on the legal strategy. "Dobson's ability to avoid detection up until now has been largely due to his careful avoidance of leaving any direct trails, but once we lock him down, we can apply pressure. The longer we can keep him detained, the more time we have to unravel the full scope of his operation."

I could feel the weight of what they were saying, the gravity of the case and the risks involved. This wasn't just about arresting a man; it was about dismantling a complex criminal operation that had ensnared dozens, if not hundreds, of people. And the way they were going to do it , bending the rules, playing the system to their advantage , was unsettling, but it was also a necessary evil.

I looked at Tim, whose calm demeanour had never wavered, and realised that the legal system was going to have to stretch in ways I hadn't anticipated. I wasn't sure how I felt about that, but there was no denying that the stakes were incredibly high. If this worked, it would be a major blow to Dobson and his network, but if it failed, the consequences could be disastrous for everyone involved.

The plan was set in motion, but the road ahead was uncertain. The more I learned, the clearer it became: this was no ordinary case. This was a high-stakes game with a dangerous man at the centre of it all. And it was going to take everything we had to outsmart him.

Based on everything I had shared, Gerald and Tim seemed to be piecing together a clearer picture of Dobson's operation. It was now apparent that Dobson wasn't just collecting money from new investors , he was also distributing funds to keep the existing ones satisfied. The pre-addressed, unassembled Australia Post boxes and other packages he was traveling with were a clear indication that he was sending cash directly to investors, trying to maintain the illusion that the scheme was still profitable.

However, this raised an important question: how was Dobson managing to keep track of all the transactions and the numerous investors he had? With so many people involved, it would be nearly impossible for him to handle all the paperwork and ensure that dividends were paid out on time without help. From what we could infer, it seemed that he was working on a three-month cutoff cycle for paying dividends. This made sense , without a system in place to track everyone individually, the three-month period would allow him to somewhat streamline the payments and keep things under control for a while.

"He may already have engaged help," Tim suggested, his voice thoughtful as he typed rapidly on his laptop.

Gerald nodded, considering the possibility. "True. We just don't know the scale of his operation yet. But the fact remains, we won't find out the full extent until someone starts to raise a red flag, and that's likely to happen only when the dividends stop coming. Right now, the key is to get ahead of that."

Gerald's gaze shifted to me. "Jack, we need to start compiling a list of the known contributors to the scheme. You'll have the most insight into that, so we'll rely on you to get this together. Once we have the list, we'll get our financial experts to analyse each investor, piece together the connections, and dig into how Dobson is managing the operation."

I nodded, immediately getting to work. It wasn't easy to recall every name, but with Tim's help, I began running through the people I remembered being involved, from those who had invested directly with Dobson to the ones I had heard about secondhand. Tim dutifully recorded the names on his laptop, tapping away with quick, methodical precision. Each name added weight to the growing list, a list that would eventually allow the authorities to trace the reach of Dobson's scheme and hopefully track down more of his victims, if not potential accomplices.

As I continued, I couldn't help but wonder how many others were out there, quietly losing everything, completely unaware of the dangers they were involved in. Some had probably been investing in the scheme for years, and they would only realise the truth when it was too late. The more we dug, the more complicated this whole thing became. But the only way to bring Dobson down was to keep going, to keep connecting the dots, and to expose the operation before it could claim any more victims.

I began recounting the details as best I could remember, piecing together the moments when I had met Thomas, or whoever he truly was, during the past few days. It was strange, almost surreal, but I knew I had to get it all down if we were to make any headway with the investigation.

"Number one was at the Council Chambers in Cloncurry," I started, my voice steady but with an underlying sense of frustration. "I didn't see anyone there, Thomas had left me in the car while he went inside. He wasn't gone long, but when he returned, he had a bag with him."

Gerald, sitting across from me, nodded, his attention sharp. "We think there may be some corruption within the local council here," he replied, his tone reflecting both curiosity and caution. "We have a small team investigating it. Could be very interesting. Please, go on."

I continued, focusing on each encounter. "The second one was in Mount Isa. Robert Fruehauf, a cattle breeder, I think. He handed over a bag to Thomas."

"Okay," Gerald murmured, jotting down notes. "Go ahead."

"Number three was John Snape, the quarry owner. No bag there, though. Number four was Bill Collins, a transport operator. He gave Thomas a bag."

I paused for a moment to gather my thoughts, remembering the details clearly but struggling to process them all. "Then, we went to Barkley Homestead. Poor old Rex Grogan was there, and he handed over a bag to Thomas."

Gerald's face tightened at the mention of Rex's name, and I could sense the weight of the investigation bearing down on us all. "Go on, Jack," he urged.

"The next stop was Katherine. Paul Jensen, the chicken farmer, gave Thomas a bag as well. Then to Palmerston, where Grant Pollock, who owns a few car wash businesses, also handed over a bag to Thomas." I remembered each of these encounters in vivid detail, how each person seemed so normal, unsuspecting of the bigger picture.

"We then traveled to Darwin, where we met Clare McIntyre," I continued, my mind shifting back to the chaotic days. "She gave Thomas a bag too. And finally, on the Harbour cruise, it was Adrian Fox, who also handed over a bag."

I exhaled, the recounting of the names and details making everything feel even more real, like the pieces of a puzzle slowly starting to fit together.

"That's all the people I met with Thomas," I concluded, the weight of the list sinking in. "Or whoever he is," I added, the doubt in my voice reflecting my growing suspicion that the man I had been dealing with might be a much larger figure than I'd initially thought.

Just as I finished, the intercom buzzed, announcing that lunch was being served in the dining room. It was a welcome interruption, as my mind felt heavy with all the details I had just shared.

Gerald glanced at his watch and then at me, his expression thoughtful. "Good work, Jack. This is a good start. Let's take a break, but when we get back, we need to start piecing all this together."

Tim, who had been typing furiously on his laptop, looked up at me, his face a mix of concern and focus. "It's getting bigger, isn't it?" he asked, almost to himself.

I nodded slowly. "Yeah, but we're getting closer. We just need to keep pushing."

As we stood up and made our way to the dining room, the weight of the investigation hung in the air. It wasn't just about Thomas Dobson anymore, it was about the many lives he had touched, and the lives he was about to ruin if we didn't act fast.

Alice, the steward, escorted us to the dining table and served the pre-ordered meals. Tim and I were each given a plate of chicken parmigiana, while the AFP officers had the same. It struck me then that they must keep a stockpile of this dish frozen for occasions like these. I hadn't considered having a beer with my lunch, but Alice, ever attentive, asked both Tim and me if we'd like one. It seemed like a good idea, so we agreed, while the other two opted for a coke.

As we sat down to eat, the atmosphere shifted from tense to relaxed, the earlier weight of the conversation lightening, if only briefly. It felt almost normal, despite the strange circumstances we were all in. The chicken was surprisingly good, comforting in a way, as if offering a brief moment of normalcy amidst the chaos.

After finishing our meals, the AFP officers thanked me and assured me that it would only be a matter of days until Thomas Dobson, or whoever he really was, was locked up in the watch house. I would be free to return to my life, they said. It was a comforting thought, but I couldn't ignore the fact that things would never be the same.

I reminded them quietly, "I no longer have a home to go to," and the words seemed to hang in the air between us. There was a moment of awkward silence, and I could see the flicker of guilt pass between them, though neither said anything. In the end, all they offered was a polite "goodbye" before they made their way to the elevator.

Tim and I lingered for a moment, the heaviness of the conversation settling in. We decided to spend the afternoon by the pool, enjoying the sun and sipping on beers. It was the first time in days that I felt like I could breathe a little easier. We didn't talk much, both of us lost in our thoughts, though every so often one of us would remark on something trivial, small things that felt significant in their own right.

While lounging by the pool, I received a call from Steve, the manager of my unit complex. He was checking in about the fire and the insurance process. The unit insurance covered accommodation until my place was habitable again, and Steve had already arranged another fully furnished unit for me to move into. His professionalism was a small comfort in all the chaos.

As we talked, I became acutely aware of the heightened security, and I'd forgotten the protocols in place. When Steve asked me where I was staying, I was about to say "Gold Coast," but before I could finish, the phone emitted a sharp beep, cutting my words off mid-sentence. It was the security system, kicking in as soon as it sensed something potentially compromising. I quickly corrected myself and told Steve that I would keep in touch, careful not to say anything more. It was a reminder that everything I said was being monitored.

On the same call, I also got an update from my contents insurance company, which assured me that a cheque for the full insured amount would arrive within two weeks. The financial reassurance was welcome, but it didn't fully alleviate the unease I felt about everything that had happened.

Later, Janice, the afternoon steward, came by to check if we had any laundry. She handed us bags to place our clothes in, asking us to mark our names on the bags. The simple task of sorting laundry felt almost grounding, something small to focus on in a world that felt completely out of control. I felt the weight of my situation in every little action, but for the first time in days, I allowed myself to feel a semblance of peace, even if it was fleeting.

The walls of this place felt like they were closing in on me, and I was becoming more and more fed up with being stuck in this confined, monitored environment. The sense of being constantly watched, unable to go anywhere or do anything normal, was starting to wear thin. I mentioned my frustration to Tim, hoping for some sympathy, but his response was typical.

"You're a fucking idiot," he said with a sharp laugh, rolling his eyes as he grabbed another beer. "Go grab a cold one and stop whining. Dinner's coming soon, and I'm looking forward to my Sydney Rock Oysters and my Tomahawk Rib Steak."

His words gave me pause. I'd completely forgotten about the menu we'd filled out yesterday for tonight's dinner. I had ordered the oysters too, along with a massive 500-gram King Island steak. The realisation lifted my spirits instantly. The thought of a good meal made the whole situation feel a little less bleak. I grabbed the fresh stubbie Tim handed me and took a long, satisfying sip. Maybe being stuck here wasn't so bad after all, not with a meal like that to look forward to.

It was Friday, and even though it had only been five days since we left Darwin, it felt like weeks. The days had been such a blur, so much had happened in such a short time. I couldn't help but hope for some resolution. The uncertainty gnawed at me, and all I wanted was to return to a normal life, whatever that was now.

Tim broke my thoughts as he glanced up from his laptop, the glow of the screen lighting up his face in the otherwise dim room. "Got news," he said, tapping the keys. "Northern Territory Police have taken Jason Reynolds into custody. No charges against him there, so he'll be extradited to Townsville over the weekend." He looked up at me with a grin, his tone light. "Looks like it's getting closer. Mr. Big will be next, right?" He laughed, but it didn't quite reach his eyes. I could tell he was as eager as I was for things to wrap up, but we both knew there was still so much that could go wrong.

Despite his attempt to ease the tension, the anxiety lingered. Sure, things were moving forward, but it felt like we were stuck in a waiting game. What would happen once they finally cornered Thomas Dobson? Would they have enough evidence to bring him down? Would it all come together, or would he slip away yet again? The uncertainty of it all was maddening.

But for now, I pushed those thoughts to the back of my mind and focused on the small comforts around me. A cold beer, a fantastic meal on the way, and the company of a good friend. Those little things were enough to keep me grounded in the moment. I could at least enjoy a few hours of peace before everything exploded again. Hopefully, it wouldn't be long before this nightmare was over, and I could return to some semblance of my old life.

I had expected a dull, uneventful weekend, but that assumption quickly proved wrong. I had always thought that the police only worked Monday to Friday, so I was caught off guard when Tim brought forth more intriguing updates from the police web.

Apparently, Jason Reynolds hadn't been wasting any time. As soon as he arrived in Townsville, Queensland police had him in for questioning. According to the report, they informed him that he had been identified as being present when the road train, driven by Rex Grogan, was stopped near Cloncurry between one and three in the morning on Tuesday. Reynolds was told that it was alleged he had assaulted Grogan, causing injuries that led to Grogan's death. He was also informed that he would be charged with manslaughter or murder in connection with the death of Mr. Grogan.

But that wasn't all. The police also alleged that Reynolds had been responsible for causing the road train, which Grogan had been operating, to plunge down an embankment near Cloncurry on that same morning. The report indicated that Grogan's body had been placed in the truck, an attempt to cover up the crime and obstruct justice. Reynolds was facing charges for both the attempted cover-up and for the damage caused to the truck, its contents, and the livestock that had been aboard.

As if that wasn't enough, the police had further allegations against Reynolds. It was said that he had entered the Palisade Apartments on the Esplanade in

Cairns on the night of Wednesday, where he allegedly committed arson. According to the report, Reynolds had forced an accelerant under the front entry fire door of unit 435, then ignited it, setting the place ablaze.

The sheer scale of the accusations was staggering, and it seemed the police were finally piecing together the puzzle. My mind was racing with questions, but I knew it was just a matter of time before everything started to come to light. For now, all I could do was wait and watch as the investigation unfolded. It appeared that the walls were closing in on Reynolds, and I couldn't help but wonder what would happen next.

Jason Reynolds was quick to shift the blame onto the person he claimed had been with him during the events surrounding Rex Grogan's death and the fire at the Palisade Apartments. According to Reynolds, the person responsible for both was Thomas Brent, the man who had hired him as a personal assistant the previous Sunday in Darwin. When the police pressed him for details about this individual, Reynolds provided a description and mentioned that Brent had engaged him for several tasks.

The first task Reynolds recalled was picking up a car on Brent's behalf. According to Reynolds, Brent had shown him an advertisement for a used Toyota 2000 series at a dealership in Stuart Park, Northern Territory. Brent had handed him $150,000, asking him to negotiate a lower price for the car, which was listed for $149,000. "Get it for less and keep the change," Reynolds said Brent had instructed. He also explained that Brent asked him to register the car in Reynolds' name, as Brent didn't have a Northern Territory driver's license, promising to change the registration later.

The second task that Reynolds had performed for Brent was a more dubious one: tracking down a man who had purchased a truck from Brent but had stopped making payments. Brent, according to Reynolds, had asked him to locate this individual and, if necessary, repossess the truck. This was the point where things began to take a more sinister turn. Reynolds described how, on the night of Tuesday, after leaving Mount Isa at midnight and heading toward Cloncurry, the pair encountered a truck on the road that Brent believed was the one owned by the delinquent buyer.

Reynolds explained that as they approached the truck, Brent had seemed unusually tense. "As I was overtaking it," Reynolds said, "Brent had his head down as if he was trying to hide. Then, after I passed, he looked back and said, 'That's my truck. Keep going, and we'll find a place to stop him.'" At that point, the two of them continued on their way for another ten minutes, before they reached a particularly steep and winding section of the road. Reynolds said Brent instructed him to pull over at a small lay-by on the left side near a cutout.

Reynolds admitted that he thought the location was dangerous and voiced his concerns to Brent, but the older man insisted. "This will do," Brent had replied. Even though Reynolds felt uneasy, he followed Brent's instructions. The scene was set for the tragic events that followed, an ill-advised stop that would lead to the death of Grogan and a trail of destruction.

The story Reynolds was telling to the police painted a picture of a man who had found himself caught up in something far more dangerous and complex than he had anticipated. But in the eyes of the law, his actions, and his connection to Thomas Brent, would soon be under intense scrutiny.

We waited in tense silence, the only sound the faint hum of the truck's engine as it slowly descended the hill, its exhaust brakes hissing intermittently. As the truck grew closer, I could make out its massive frame in the dim light, and Brent, ever the strategist, calmly instructed me to get out and stop the truck. He made it clear that if the driver recognised him, there would be no chance of stopping. So, the task fell on me.

When the truck finally pulled up, I was shocked by how close it came to the cruiser, it was as if the driver had aimed straight for us. I thought for sure it was going to hit us. The last half of the trailer was still hanging out into the road, and the driver was absolutely yelling abuse at me, swearing and shouting like I had never heard before. I was still trying to process what was happening when, in an instant, Brent was out of the cruiser and up to the driver's side door. He moved so fast I could barely believe it. Within a couple of seconds, he had the door open, and I was left stunned by the speed of his actions.

The truck driver stopped his barrage of insults immediately as soon as Brent swung the door open. I was still standing in front of the truck, trying to make sense of what was going on, but the truck's glaring headlights made it hard to see much. Then, just as quickly as he'd rushed to the truck, Brent was back beside me, his voice low and almost dispassionate. "Looks like the poor old bastard had a heart attack," he said, glancing back toward the driver, now slumped in his seat. "I thought he was dead."

At that exact moment, a car appeared from behind the truck, struggling to navigate around it. The driver swerved into the opposite lane, clearly trying to avoid the scene. I figured they might stop, but Brent was already back toward our car, waving them on urgently. "Keep moving," he called out, as if it was all just part of the routine.

Then, with a calmness that sent a chill down my spine, Brent muttered something about the dead driver: "Now that the bastard's dead, I'm never going to see that money he owes me." In the blink of an eye, he had already decided what to do next. "I'll put the truck down the bank, claim the insurance. That's the only way to recover anything from this mess."

I stood there in disbelief. The plan, if you could even call it that, was as ruthless as it was wild. Brent wasn't just a man who acted fast; he was a man who saw opportunity in chaos, a man who made decisions in an instant, regardless of the consequences. And in that moment, I realised just how dangerous he truly was. The cold pragmatism of it all left me wondering what else he was capable of. But as wild as the idea was, it didn't seem far-fetched coming from him. Brent had already crossed lines that most people wouldn't even dream of, and now he was prepared to go even further.

Reynolds continued with his statement, his words leaving me utterly speechless. I couldn't believe what I was hearing, as the events unfolded like something straight out of a movie. Brent, without a second thought, climbed into the truck's cab, moved the elderly driver over with a quick, almost nonchalant shove, and began rifling through the cab. Within moments, he grabbed what looked like a bag, jumped out, and ordered me to put it into the cruiser. While I was busy loading the bag into the vehicle, Brent didn't waste a second. He hopped back into the truck, turned the wheel, and steered the massive vehicle straight across the road, heading for the drop-off. As if it was the most natural thing in the world, he jumped out of the moving truck, letting it roll to a stop by the embankment. The whole scene was surreal, like something from an action movie, but real. It was unsettling, to say the least. My heart was pounding in my chest.

Once the truck had been abandoned in its precarious position, Brent calmly ordered me to head toward Cairns, suggesting we take the back way through Ravenshoe. I did as he asked, my mind still reeling from the craziness of the moment. The drive was long and tense, spanning over eight hours. We stopped briefly around 10 o'clock at a place called Greenvale to grab a bite to eat and use the bathroom. After that, Brent took over the driving, and we pushed on, finally reaching Cairns at around 3 a.m. When we got there, Brent wasted no time. We went to Bunnings, where he bought a 20-litre fuel drum, before heading to a shopping mall in Earlville. We both grabbed a hamburger and a Coke, a strange moment of normalcy in the midst of everything else. But Brent wasn't done. He went into Big W and bought a backpack and a bicycle pump. Then, as if it were an ordinary trip to the store, he grabbed a small stay-sharp knife on the way out.

By the time we finished all our errands, it was nearly six in the evening. We found a service station, where Brent filled up the Land Cruiser and topped off the 20-litre fuel drum with a mix of half petrol and half diesel.

We made our way slowly down the Esplanade and parked near Muddy's Fish and Chip Café. Brent told me to get into the driver's seat and wait while he worked. He opened the back hatch, took the flexible connection from the fuel pump, and attached it to the pump's end. With the same cold efficiency, he used the stay-sharp knife to cut off the valve connector from the flexible coupling. Brent then carefully placed the fuel pump and the bag into the backpack, slung it over his shoulder, and headed off toward a Woolworths grocery delivery truck that was parked nearby.

The clock on the dashboard read around 6:20 when Brent set off. He was gone for what felt like ages, and I began to wonder what he was up to. It must have been nearly seven when he returned, but he acted as though nothing unusual had happened. "Head to the airport," he told me, as though it were a perfectly normal instruction. I had no idea where I was going, so he had to guide me step-by-step. The airport was surprisingly close, and within just a few minutes, we arrived. Brent gave me specific directions on where to park the Cruiser, and I followed them without question. The whole situation was beginning to feel even more disjointed and strange. The more I tried to make sense of it, the less it all added up. I was starting to realise just how deep Brent's plans went, and how far he was willing to go to make them a reality.

Brent had been toying with the bag he'd taken from the truck while I was driving toward the airport, his hands fidgeting with it in a way that made me uneasy. I had no idea what was inside, but the way he handled it, so casually yet deliberately, added another layer of tension to the already strange day. We finally arrived at the airport and parked the Land Cruiser. As I was about to get out, Brent set the bag down on the seat and handed me ten thousand dollars in cash. My heart skipped a beat, and I stood there for a moment, utterly shocked.

He told me to grab my bag and catch a flight back to Darwin, as if it was the simplest request in the world. I stared at the cash in my hand, still trying to process what was happening. I had been through so much already, but this felt like a whole new level of absurdity. He asked if there was a problem, and I shook my head quickly, not wanting to give him any reason to think I was questioning him. I was genuinely afraid of what might happen if I got on the wrong side of this man. He was too calm, too collected, there was something about him that felt off, something dangerous. It wasn't just the way he handled situations, but the way he exuded a quiet menace that made you think twice before crossing him.

"Ten grand's good chaff for a couple of days' work," he said with a smirk, as though this was all just business to him. "See you around."

I nodded quickly, not wanting to argue or ask any more questions. The last thing I needed was to make him angry. With that, I grabbed my bag and stepped out of the car, watching as Brent turned and walked away, disappearing into the night. He moved with such ease, like everything was going exactly as he had planned. The money in my hand felt heavy, but it was nothing compared to the weight of the situation.

I stood there for a moment, the surreal nature of it all hitting me. How had things escalated so quickly? What was in that bag, and what was he planning to do next? I wasn't sure, but for now, all I could do was follow his orders. I made my way inside the airport, still reeling from everything that had just happened.

"Fark..." was all I could manage in response to the statement from Jason Reynolds that Tim had just read aloud to me. My mind was reeling as I processed the depth of what Reynolds had admitted to, and all I could think was that this was far beyond any fiction I had ever read. It was like something straight out of a thriller, but this was real life.

"It has the makings of a great movie," Tim said with a wry grin, as though the absurdity of it all hadn't sunk in for him yet. "Dobson, or Brent, whoever he is, driving that car. He won't last long. Surely the cops should get onto him now if he's still driving that thing."

I shook my head, trying to wrap my brain around everything. I could barely process it. How could someone be so cold, so calculating? And how was he getting away with it all?

Just then, Tim's phone rang, cutting through my thoughts. He gave me a quick look before wandering off toward the bar to take the call. I tried to focus, but the events from the past few days kept swirling in my mind. It was as if everything was moving too fast, and I was struggling to catch up.

Tim returned a few minutes later, his expression serious. "That was Jeff Carghill from Townsville Police," he said, his tone clipped. "He wants to know what to charge Reynolds with. I didn't hesitate, told him murder and arson should do for now."

I nodded, the weight of those words settling heavily on my chest. Murder and arson, it was hard to fathom, but I knew it was all true. The things Reynolds had described, the brutality, the lies, it was beyond anything I could have imagined.

"I'll come up there next week if you can organise it," I said, feeling a new sense of resolve. "I can make some deals with Reynolds. He might crack if we apply enough pressure." I wasn't sure what kind of leverage we could use on him, but I knew we had to try.

Tim gave me a sharp nod. "Jeff said Tuesday should be good. He'll organise everything. You'll get your chance to talk to Reynolds then."

It was strange. Despite everything that had happened, despite the danger, there was a sense of inevitability in the air. We were getting closer to the endgame. But what would happen when we finally caught up with Dobson? Would we be able to get him to crack? And more importantly, would we finally uncover the full scope of his operation?

I could only hope.

"So you're leaving me here on my own, you prick?" I exclaimed, the shock clear in my voice as Tim dropped the bombshell.

Tim just shrugged with a grin. "Yeah, fuck slumming it here. Life's too short for this treatment," he laughed, clearly unfazed. "I have to do my job, and I can't do it from here. Sadly... but I reckon you'll be out of here by Tuesday anyway."

I raised an eyebrow. "Do you really think so?"

"If not sooner, old son," Tim replied with a wink, a tone of certainty in his voice. "Once they get that Dobson prick locked up, you'll be good to go. He won't be getting out real quick, and I'm going to make sure of that." His confidence was reassuring, but I still couldn't shake the lingering tension. "Are you going to head back to Cairns, or do you want to hang around Brissy for a while? I've got a unit near South Bank, big place, four bedrooms, three bathrooms, lock-up parking. All the bells and whatevers. You're welcome to crash there for a bit if you want."

I couldn't help but be impressed by the offer. A place like that, in the heart of Brisbane, would be a good spot to lay low for a while. "Wow, thanks, Tim. That's really generous, and I do appreciate it," I said, genuinely touched. "But I think I'll head back to Cairns. It's been a hell of a ride, but I think I need a bit of a break... somewhere familiar."

Tim nodded, understanding. "Fair enough. Cairns it is, then. Just make sure you keep your head down for a while. Things are getting messy, and you don't want to get caught in the crossfire."

"Yeah, I'll keep that in mind," I said, grateful for the support. "I'll be in touch, though. And thanks again, Tim. Really."

"No problem," he said, slapping me on the back. "Take care of yourself. Once this all blows over, you'll be able to breathe again."

As he walked off, I couldn't help but feel a little more optimistic. Things were moving fast, and while it wasn't over yet, there was light at the end of the tunnel. All I had to do was get through the next few days, and then I'd be free, hopefully.

It wasn't long before Tim's mobile rang again, and this time it was Jeff Carghill from Townsville Police. He wasted no time with pleasantries, diving straight into business. "Tim, I've got news. If you and Jack want to travel to Townsville today, I can organise a flight for you both. What do you think?"

Tim looked at me, his face unreadable for a moment. He paused the call and turned to me. "So, what's the verdict? Do you want to go to Townsville today?"

Without hesitation, I shot him a grin and responded with a fire in my voice, "Fucking oath."

Tim laughed, clearly relieved that I wasn't hesitating. "Alright, I'll let Jeff know. We'll be there, soon enough."

He unpaused the call, relaying my response to Jeff, who was on the other end of the line, no doubt ready to spring into action. Within minutes, the arrangements were in motion. The excitement was palpable; the feeling of anticipation buzzing in the air. This was it, the next step in a whirlwind that had taken me far beyond what I ever imagined.

As Tim ended the call, he gave me a nod. "We're on our way. Pack your shit, Jack. We're going to Townsville today."

I could hardly contain the sense of urgency building inside me. It wasn't just the promise of action or the potential end to this drawn-out situation. It was the knowledge that whatever was coming next, it was about to change everything. I grabbed my things quickly, feeling a mix of adrenaline and anxiety surge through me. This was happening.

Within the hour, we were ready, heading to the airport, my mind racing. I had no idea what was waiting for us in Townsville.

About an hour later, Jeff called back with an update. "No go for today, fellows," he said, his voice calm but direct. "Unless you want to catch a domestic flight out of Brisbane at 9:56 tonight. But if you prefer, we can push it to tomorrow morning."

Tim and I exchanged glances, and without hesitation, we both responded in unison, "No way. Tomorrow's fine."

Jeff chuckled, clearly relieved. "Tomorrow it is, then. I'll have a car pick you up at 8:30 AM, and we'll get lunch together when you arrive in Townsville. See you then."

It was a strange sense of calm that settled over me after that call. A whole day without the urgency of the situation hanging over me felt like a gift. It was like the pressure had been lifted, and the danger had momentarily faded into the background. For the first time in what felt like weeks, I allowed myself to breathe. Maybe Thomas wasn't a threat anymore, at least for the moment. I had to believe that.

Tim and I spent the rest of the day playing pool, getting more than a little tipsy in the process. The atmosphere felt relaxed, and we even convinced the building's security guard to stay after his shift, join us for a couple of beers, and have a few rounds of pool. The camaraderie was unexpected, but it was a welcome distraction.

"Strange," Tim muttered as we were getting ready to head to our rooms later that evening. "I'm just starting to enjoy the place, and now it's time to leave."

I nodded in agreement, a quiet sadness settling in. We'd only just begun to unwind, and now we were already preparing to leave.

The next morning, at exactly 8:30 AM, the elevator doors opened. But to my surprise, there was only one police officer waiting for us, and he was wearing plain clothes. He introduced himself as Constable Roger Zammit and had a slight Indian accent that piqued my curiosity. As we descended in the elevator, I couldn't help but wonder what had changed. The previous few days had been a mix of tension and moments of relief, but now, the air was charged again with uncertainty.

We climbed into the parked police car, and from the moment the doors shut, I knew we were in for a wild ride. Constable Zammit's driving was fast, aggressive, and reckless. Every turn felt like we were on the edge of losing control, and the intensity of the ride made me feel like I was in a chase scene from a movie. The harsh screech of tires as we skidded around corners and the adrenaline pumping through me only made it worse. I could see Tim's knuckles turning white as he gripped the seat, and I tried not to show my own anxiety. We arrived at the airport maintenance buildings with our hearts racing.

When we finally got out of the car, the sight of the King Air 360 aircraft waiting for us only added to the surreal feeling of the whole situation. It wasn't exactly the type of plane you usually take on a regular flight, and the setting felt out of place.

Tim muttered under his breath as he climbed aboard the aircraft, his voice tinged with a mix of sarcasm and disbelief, "Hmmmmm. We're definitely no longer the flavour of the month."

I didn't know whether to laugh or feel more uneasy. The whole thing felt like a dramatic shift, and the realisation hit me: this was no longer a casual trip, and we were far from the comfortable civilian life we once knew. What awaited us in Townsville? Was it just a simple meeting or something more significant? The weight of it all hung in the air, but all we could do was sit back and brace ourselves for whatever came next.

The flight on the King Air 360 was a solid three hours, and I was thankful for the small luxuries onboard, particularly the loo. It made the time pass more comfortably. By the time we landed at Townsville RAAF base Garbutt just before midday, I was eager to stretch my legs and get out of the cramped cabin. We made our way from the plane to the waiting area at the "Air Movements" section, which was located a bit of a walk away. The hot midday sun hit us as we carried our bags, and I could already feel the difference in the humidity compared to what we had left behind in Brisbane.

It didn't take long for Jeff to arrive, his familiar face breaking through the bustle of the airport.

"I wasn't sure what you blokes wanted to do," Jeff began, his voice casual, "so I booked you both into the Casino for tonight. You can sort yourselves out from there. I also booked lunch at the casino for you. And Jack, if you want, I can have your car dropped off at the Casino so you don't have to worry about driving and can have a drink."

His offer was practical, considering the situation. It was better to keep things simple and safe, especially with the constant risk of being targeted. "You don't have to come into the station tomorrow," Jeff continued, "which might actually be a good idea. We're not sure if your friend has any connections in Townsville. He knows what your car looks like, so it's better to be cautious." I nodded in agreement, not wanting to take any chances.

"Typical copper," Tim grinned as he elbowed me lightly. "Why don't you drop your car off at the cop shop, Jeff? We'll grab a cab to the casino, and you can have a few beers too. Seems fair, right?"

Jeff raised an eyebrow at Tim's suggestion but was quick to agree. "It's organised," he said with a shrug, pulling into the police pick-up area. As the car came to a stop, a constable climbed into the back with me, and we were off to the casino.

The drive was relatively uneventful, and we arrived at the casino shortly after. The constable took my car back to the police station as we stepped out, our bags in hand. The sun beat down, but the cool, air-conditioned interior of the casino was a welcome relief. I could tell that Tim was already looking forward to the night ahead, and I was equally ready to unwind.

It felt odd being in this unfamiliar city, but with things cooling down on the work front, I could finally allow myself to relax, at least for the time being. As we entered the casino, I couldn't help but feel that we were being watched. Maybe it was just my imagination, but in this line of work, you learn to trust your gut. Whatever came next, I was ready to face it.

We checked in and made our way to the bar to join Jeff, who had already gotten drinks for us. He greeted us with a smile and a nod as we settled around a table. The ice-cold stubbies were a welcome relief after the long journey, and we raised our bottles in a toast. "Here's to a job well done," I said, appreciating Jeff's role in the recent developments.

Jeff shook his head, dismissing our praise. "Don't congratulate me, fellas. It was the team in Rocky who found him. All I did was follow the lead from the car we tracked, which, as we know, had the registration."

"For a smart guy, Dobson is getting very dumb," Jeff continued, his voice taking on a more serious tone. "He's slipping up in ways that aren't usual for someone like him."

"Maybe it's just a mistake," Tim suggested, tapping his beer. "It's not uncommon for really clever people to forget simple things. He wouldn't have known that the Landcruiser's description hadn't been made public. He wouldn't know that the car that passed by that night reported seeing them near the truck. And he wouldn't know we've got dash cam footage with the registration number either. He probably assumed we didn't have anything on him."

I nodded, following Tim's reasoning. It made sense. "So what's he been charged with?"

Jeff leaned back in his chair, taking a sip of his drink. "He hasn't been arrested yet, Jack. He's only been detained. It's up to Tim to decide what to charge him with. We've got about twenty hours before we have to formally charge him."

Tim glanced at me, then at Jeff. "Right now, we don't have enough on him to go strong with murder and arson. Charges like those draw a lot of media attention, and magistrates take notice of that too. We don't want to fuel the press more than necessary."

Jeff nodded in agreement, understanding the delicate balance we had to strike. "So, what do you suggest?" he asked.

Tim took a thoughtful pause before speaking. "We need a charge that's serious enough for us to oppose bail, but not one that will bring the media storm. So, I think we go with theft of a motor vehicle. It's a pretty standard charge, and no magistrate is going to give it too much thought, just a quick glance and maybe a decision on bail. But we'll oppose bail and show the magistrate how flighty Dobson is. We've got the stolen vehicle in Darwin, seen in Cairns, and then caught in Rockhampton. That's enough to make it clear he's a flight risk. It'll be tough for them to even think about granting him bail."

I was impressed with Tim's approach. It seemed like a clever way to handle the situation without overloading it too soon. "And if that doesn't work?" I asked, still not fully understanding the legal complexities.

"If it somehow falls through, we've still got the big charge in the back pocket," Tim replied, his voice steady and calm. "Murder. But we're not ready to throw that card yet."

I could tell Tim was already thinking several steps ahead, which was reassuring. It wasn't just about getting Dobson locked up, it was about making sure the case held up, without risking things falling apart due to hasty decisions. We all sat in silence for a moment, each of us processing what needed to be done. The plan was in motion, and now it was just a matter of waiting for the right moment to act.

"Let's get this done," Jeff said finally, breaking the silence. "We'll keep our heads down, work our angles, and make sure this bastard doesn't get out."

I couldn't agree more. I felt the weight of the situation, but with Tim's strategy in place, I was more confident than before. Whatever happened next, we were ready.

Tim leaned back in his chair, looking thoughtful as he turned to Jeff. "I hope we can strike a solid deal with Reynolds tomorrow," he said, his voice low. "At least enough to sink Dobson for good." Jeff nodded, his expression grim but hopeful.

"Reynolds went to water as soon as he found out murder and arson charges were on the table," Jeff replied. "He's already starting to crack. He's ripe for making a deal, especially if it means taking Dobson down."

Jeff went on to brief us on how Dobson's mugshots, fingerprints, and DNA had been circulated across Australia and sent to Interpol. Authorities were hoping that Dobson had a prior record, which could help tie him to other crimes or even provide a clearer picture of his background.

The conversation shifted toward Dobson's origins, and Jeff mentioned something that piqued my interest. According to Reynolds, when he had been with Dobson in Cairns, Dobson seemed to know the area well, navigating without the help of the car's GPS. It was a detail that suggested Dobson wasn't just passing through; he knew Cairns like a local.

"The police in Cairns checked the security footage from the Hilton Hotel that Thursday morning," Jeff continued. "Reynolds said he picked Dobson up there, but there were no signs of Dobson staying at the hotel. The footage showed him walking up to the porte-cochere, which indicates he wasn't a guest. And when the staff from all shifts were shown pictures of Dobson, they didn't recognise him. He wasn't a guest, and no one remembers seeing him inside."

Tim rubbed his chin thoughtfully. "So he wasn't staying at the Hilton. He was just there to make it look like he was, right?"

Jeff nodded, his brow furrowed. "Exactly. He wanted Jack to believe that the person he was picking up didn't live in Cairns but had come from somewhere else, likely interstate."

Tim raised an eyebrow, the pieces clicking into place. "Which means…" He trailed off, looking at me for confirmation.

I answered along with Tim, "He lives in Cairns."

Jeff looked at us with a nod of approval. "Well done. You might make good coppers after all. Yes, that's what we believe. Dobson is from Cairns. We're focusing our efforts on ID-ing him in that area. Cairns isn't a huge city, only around 160,000 people. You'd think someone would recognise him or know who he really is."

It made sense. If Dobson was a local, it was only a matter of time before someone would have seen him, or someone in Cairns would know more about his past. The key now was to find the right person who could put a name to his face. Dobson had been careful, but his cover was beginning to crack, and we were getting closer to learning the truth.

"Right, we also had a conversation with Bill Collins in Mount Isa," Jeff continued, his voice steady but filled with subtle tension. "We approached him under the guise that the truck and trailers involved in the fatality might still have financial ties to him. He denied it, claiming they were most likely fully owned by Rex himself. But we didn't stop there. We casually mentioned that a witness at Renner Springs had overheard Rex the night before the crash, speaking about some major financial investment deal that had gone wrong and that he was planning to speak with Bill Collins about it. When we dropped that bomb, Bill's face went pale. He struggled to form words and finally, barely above a whisper, said he didn't know anything about it. It was so obvious he was lying."

Tim nodded, his expression thoughtful. "Yeah, he reacted like a deer caught in headlights. The moment we mentioned Rex, he cracked."

"It seems Bill Collins is definitely a lead worth pursuing," Jeff added, his voice dropping as he exchanged a knowing look with Tim. "We've passed along our report to the Feds. They'll take it from here."

Tim raised an eyebrow, looking at Jeff. "And on that note, what's the next step?"

Jeff grinned. "Well, Tim, we've made all our information available to the AFP. If you keep going down this path, who knows, the Attorney General might even get you on his team to handle the prosecution."

Tim chuckled at the thought, his usual nonchalance momentarily replaced with a glimmer of pride. "I can't even imagine that. Prosecuting a case like this? Sounds like a dream, but also a nightmare."

I blinked in disbelief, still processing the whirlwind of events that seemed to be happening faster than I could keep up. "I can't believe how quickly everything is moving. This is all happening so fast."

Jeff smiled, a little amused. "You'd be surprised, Jack. When you have people from all over the country in law enforcement pulling in the same direction, it becomes a well-oiled machine. It's incredibly effective. But, I'll be honest with you," he added with a wry grin, "sometimes it all goes to shit too, and that's when you see the chaos. But most of the time, it works."

Tim chimed in, chuckling. "Yeah, the speed and precision you see in movies? That's the result of a lot of years of hard work, and a hell of a lot of screw-ups along the way."

I couldn't help but laugh. Despite the gravity of the situation, the banter between them lightened the mood. It was a reminder that even in the face of something as serious as murder and financial deceit, humour and camaraderie could still be found.

Just as we were getting comfortable, Jeff suddenly reached into his pocket and pulled out my mobile phone, handing it to me with a grin. "Almost forgot, Jack. Here's your phone. Make sure you keep in touch, alright? I'll be in Cairns next week, so I'll look you up."

I took the phone from him, still somewhat in awe of how quickly everything was unfolding. "Thanks, Jeff. I'll be sure to keep you updated."

As we sat there, waiting for the next phase of the investigation to unfold, I couldn't help but feel a sense of purpose. The pieces were slowly coming together, and while I still had questions and doubts, there was a glimmer of hope that justice might be served soon. The future was uncertain, but for the first time in a long while, I felt like we were on the right path.

The next morning, my car was delivered to the casino as promised, and after a brief exchange of goodbyes, I was on my way. Tim and Jeff had both reassured me that they would keep me updated on both the Dobson and Reynolds cases. They mentioned they'd have some useful information by the afternoon, and I made a mental note to check my emails as soon as I got to my temporary accommodation.

The drive back to Cairns was pleasant, a calm respite after everything that had transpired. By one o'clock that afternoon, I found myself at the unit, staring at the mess that awaited me. Steve, the complex manager, greeted me with some news. He told me that the clean-up was just starting, as the Queensland Fire and Emergency Services investigators had only recently cleared the scene. They had been preventing anyone from entering the unit while they conducted their investigation. Steve also mentioned that the police had seized all the security camera footage and were in the process of taking fingerprints around the complex.

Steve led me to my new temporary unit on level six. "What do you think?" he asked, showing me around. "It's a nice place, isn't it?"

I nodded, impressed. "Yeah, this is great, but I'll be glad when I can move back into my own unit."

He smiled. "Well, we'll get it cleaned up soon. I expect I'll have a restoration timeline by next week. We've got a builder lined up."

The unit was fully equipped and self-contained, though it was missing a few essentials, like a coffee machine and internet access. I decided to tackle those problems first. My unit complex was in a 5G coverage zone, so I popped over to the Telstra store at Cairns Central, where I was able to pick up a 5G modem. Afterward, I swung by Harvey Norman's and picked up the DeLonghi coffee machine I'd been eyeing, along with a couple of bags of coffee beans. A quick stop at Coles for some groceries and then I made a final stop at the bottle shop for a few cartons of my "medicinal compound", XXXX Gold Stubbies.

By the time I returned to the unit, it had been a productive afternoon. I was feeling pretty good about getting everything in place, though I still needed to buy some new clothes. But that could wait until tomorrow. As soon as I had the 5G modem set up, I started checking my emails and messages. I had just cracked open one of the stubbies I'd put in the freezer, despite already having cold ones in the fridge, when I received a flood of messages from Tim.

I cracked a smile, knowing that whatever news was coming, it was bound to be significant. With a beer in hand and the quiet hum of the city outside, I settled in to catch up on the latest updates.

The search for information on the alias "Dobson" in the Cairns area has yielded promising results. The Cairns Casino's security system played a pivotal role in uncovering crucial details. The casino's facial recognition system identified Dobson under the name Malcolm Stevens, a member of the "Reef Rewards" program. Stevens was listed in one of the casino's highest reward categories, which included perks such as complimentary stays at the casino's hotel and access to VIP parking in the basement. The Casino's security operations manager confirmed that Stevens' car, a black BMW X5, was currently parked in the VIP parking area.

Further investigation revealed that the car's entry had been logged by the automatic number plate recognition (ANPR) system. The vehicle had entered the casino's parking lot at 8:48 PM last Thursday and had been there since. The security manager provided the vehicle's description and registration number, giving the police a concrete lead to follow.

The police traced the vehicle's registration details back to Malcolm Stevens, revealing his listed address on Clarke Street in Manunda. However, when officers visited the property last night, they discovered that it was being rented through a local real estate agency. The estate agent's records only indicated the owner's details as a post office box located in Port Douglas. A subsequent visit to the post office led investigators back to the Clarke Street address, suggesting that the information was deliberately obscured, a deliberate smokescreen, it seemed.

Undeterred, the police expanded their investigation by reviewing traffic camera footage from the roundabout at Port Douglas Road and the Captain Cook Highway. The footage, taken between 6:00 AM and 8:00 AM that morning, showed a black BMW X5 with the same registration number as Stevens' vehicle passing through at 6:40 AM.

Further inquiries with Ergon Energy revealed an electricity account under the name Malcolm Stevens at a property on Wharf Street in Port Douglas. This led investigators to visit the location, where they discovered that the property had been transferred into Stevens' name just 18 months ago. Property sales records indicated that Stevens had purchased the property for a substantial 4.2 million dollars.

The pieces were falling into place, Stevens, or Dobson, had clearly been operating under an elaborate cover, shifting between multiple addresses and using various aliases to conceal his true identity and activities. With this new information, the investigation was gaining momentum, and the focus was now squarely on Stevens' ties to the property in Port Douglas.

Later that evening, Tim called me to check if I had received his email. I thanked him and told him I had received it. I also mentioned that I thought the police's work was absolutely brilliant. Tim, in his typical modest way, downplayed it, calling it just another day of normal police work. He explained that these kinds of operations happen all the time, but the public has no idea how much effort goes into them. I, however, found it nothing short of remarkable.

Tim then shared some more updates. He informed me that the Australian Federal Police (AFP) were applying for a search warrant at the Wharf Street address in Port Douglas the following morning. He said it would be interesting to see how things unfolded. The Queensland police would be accompanying them, and Tim promised he'd let me know as soon as he got the full report.

Tim also revealed that he had successfully gotten what he wanted from Reynolds. Reynolds had agreed to testify against Stevens, who was now the prime suspect in the murder of Rex Grogan. The charge of arson would soon follow once the fire services investigators submitted their report. Reynolds had also sworn to testify against Stevens for that charge as well. It was a significant breakthrough.

"To round it off," Tim added, "You should be pretty safe up there now. This guy Stevens won't be getting out of jail for quite a while. The police, by the way, have decided to keep a watch on you for a little longer, just for your own safety."

I was startled by this news. "I had no idea they were watching me," I admitted.

Tim replied casually, "They were with you all the way to Cairns today, and even followed you around the shops this afternoon."

"Wow, they must be really good at their job," I said, still processing the information. "I didn't notice a thing."

Changing the subject, I mentioned, "Well, while I've got you, I was wondering... I still need to do some more shopping tomorrow. My insurance money hasn't come through yet, and the only real cash I have left is from Stevens. I mean... Thomas. And I was thinking maybe..."

Tim's tone shifted abruptly. "You didn't ask me that," he interjected firmly. "There's nothing in any of your statements to the police about payment from Stevens, alias Thomas. I've checked, and there's no need to add that to your statements. The magnitude of this case would render any minor payments irrelevant, and no one will ever look into it, I assure you. So, just let it go."

I nodded, understanding his point. "Thanks, Tim. I'll be looking forward to hearing the news from Port Douglas tomorrow," I said, then we ended the call.

As I set my phone down, I couldn't help but feel a sense of relief. The pieces were finally falling into place, and Stevens, the elusive figure I had been unknowingly connected to, was starting to crack under the pressure. I could only hope that tomorrow's developments would bring us even closer to closing this chapter for good.

The next day passed in stark contrast to the chaos of the past three weeks. It was surprisingly quiet. I spent most of the day trying, and failing, to identify the 'minders' Tim had told me were keeping an eye on me. Although I thought I had spotted one of them at a café, he turned out to be a tourist from Sydney.

By mid-afternoon, I was feeling restless, waiting anxiously for Tim's daily report, particularly on the search in Port Douglas. My nerves were heightened as I cracked open another beer, already downing several by the time the report finally came in at around 3:30.

The report was worth the wait. Police had gained access to the Wharf Street property in Port Douglas under a search warrant issued earlier that morning at the Cairns Law Court. What they discovered inside was staggering. A comprehensive search revealed a significant cache of items, including seven million dollars in cash, which was promptly seized. Additionally, sixteen Rolex watches, valued at an estimated $1.4 million, were found, along with a Mercedes Maybach, a luxury car worth about $600,000.

But it wasn't just physical assets that had been uncovered. Among the items seized was a Mac Desktop PC. On this device, police found an Excel spreadsheet that detailed the collection and distribution of large sums of cash, listing various names, contact numbers, and locations stretching from Townsville in the south, all the way up to Darwin in the north, covering key areas like Cairns and the Gulf country. This spreadsheet appeared to be part of a larger operation, designed to track and manage these illicit transactions. Further investigation revealed that the data was being sent in real time from a linked MacBook Air, which had been found on Stevens when he was arrested.

The news came thick and fast. Malcolm Douglas Stevens, the man who had been at the centre of this entire operation, was officially charged by the Queensland Police with the murder of Rex Grogan, as well as for the wilful damage to property belonging to Grogan. He was also charged for the wilful damage and death caused to livestock belonging to others, and for the arson of a home unit in Cairns. Stevens pleaded guilty to all of the charges.

Later that afternoon, the Australian Federal Police (AFP) added their own charges. Stevens was charged with running a fraudulent enterprise with the intent to withhold tax payments from the Australian Federal Government. He was also charged with non-registration of investments, fraudulent investments, and accepting cash funding under fraudulent investment schemes. As with the state charges, Stevens pleaded guilty to all the federal charges as well.

The developments were significant, but I knew there was still much to come. The case was far from over, and the web of deceit Stevens had spun was only beginning to unravel. As I processed the news, I couldn't help but feel a sense of relief, knowing that Stevens was finally facing the consequences of his actions. Yet, I knew that the real work was just starting, and there were still many pieces left to put together.

The day Stevens was charged marked exactly three weeks since I'd picked up Thomas, or whatever the hell his name was, from the Hilton in Cairns. Three weeks, what a rollercoaster it's been! Honestly, I was just looking forward to everything finally winding down, to getting my unit back, and to moving on from what I'd once thought would be a profitable venture. The whole ordeal has left me questioning whether it was worth it in the first place. If it hadn't been for Tim, I might've ended up losing everything I made from "whomever", the police would have seized it all.

Looking back now, it feels like I didn't gain much. I lost my unit for nearly three months, and in the grand scheme of things, the whole adventure probably wasn't worth the trouble. You might think it was some grand tale, an exciting adventure, but believe me, it wasn't one I was eager to have. There were moments that were downright terrifying. I didn't know who I could trust or if I'd even make it out unscathed. The tension was palpable.

Now, I'm not expecting any kind of reward for my involvement, nor do I think I'll ever be recognised for my efforts. Instead, I'll likely be called as a witness in both state and federal cases against Stevens. Once convicted, he'll likely spend the rest of his life in prison, serving concurrent sentences for at least forty-five years. That means I'm safe here in Cairns for a long time to come, but I'm not sure I'll ever feel truly at ease again.

One thing that has come from all this, however, is two solid friendships: Tim Roberts and Jeff Cargill. I'm sure we'll remain friends long after the case is closed. They've been unwavering throughout the chaos, and I'll always be grateful for their support.

Others I've shared this story with have expressed doubt about the whole ordeal, skeptical of the twists and turns it's taken. But, a few have suggested that it could make a compelling read, maybe even worth turning into a book. So, who knows? Maybe this crazy "TASK" will become a story worth telling, in more ways than one.

End.........

DYING TO FIND GOLD

The morning sun had already begun its relentless climb over the eastern horizon, casting a golden glow over the tropical expanse of Cairns. The humidity clung to the air like a damp blanket, thick with the scent of earth and salt carried in on the coastal breeze. It was barely past seven o'clock, yet the mercury had already surged to twenty-eight degrees Celsius. The promise of another sweltering December day hung heavy in the atmosphere.

Sam Young, his calloused hands gripping the wheel of his battered 1973 Toyota FJ50 Land Cruiser, swung the vehicle into Batway Place, the engine growling like some great beast stirring from slumber. He rolled to a halt outside number seventeen, the home of Mick West, his wife Emily, and their three children.

At the top of the driveway, beneath the shelter of the carport, a well-worn swag lay unrolled beside a rugged seventy-litre esky, its smaller companion nestled against it. A minelab metal detector stood propped against the wall, flanked by two sturdy backpacks, their straps taut and ready for the journey ahead.

The screen door banged open, and Mick strode out, his easy confidence as tangible as the rising heat. Behind him, two of his children followed, his nine-year-old son leading his three-year-old brother by the hand. The younger boy's face was a mask of distress, streaked with the drying remnants of fresh tears. His wails punctured the humid morning air.

"Dad, you promised!" the child sobbed, his small hands clutching at his father's leg, his pleas desperate and raw.

Emily stepped forward, her voice soothing yet firm as she bent to console him. "Next time, love. I promise." She smoothed his hair before rising to help Mick lift the larger esky, her toned arms flexing against the weight of it.

Mick caught sight of Sam and grinned, his sun-creased face breaking into a knowing smile.

"On time! Well done, mate," he called, his voice rich with approval.

Emily, always the gracious hostess despite the early hour, offered Sam a warm smile as they heaved the esky onto the back of the FJ50's tray. "Good morning, Sam," she greeted, brushing an errant strand of hair from her face as she stepped back.

Sam returned the smile, wiping a bead of sweat from his brow as he surveyed the gear. The day stretched ahead of them, filled with the promise of adventure, the thrill of the unknown waiting just beyond the confines of the suburban street.

The morning air was thick with the scent of sun-warmed bitumen and the distant tang of salt drifting in from the Coral Sea. Sam was already out of the cab, his boots crunching against the gravel as he strode toward the top of the driveway. His shirt clung to his back, already damp with sweat, and he wiped a forearm across his brow before reaching for the rest of the gear.

"Good morning! Bloody hot already, eh? And it's going to be even worse up on the Marian," he said, his voice carrying the easy drawl of a man accustomed to the harsh Queensland heat.

Emily shot him a knowing look, hands planted firmly on her hips. "Yeah, well, don't you go stopping at the Marianvale Pub to cool down, will you? I know you two buggers, metal detecting my arse. You're only going up there to get on the piss."

Mick let out a deep chuckle, the kind that spoke of years of friendship and well-worn habits. Sam grinned, flipping open the lid of his esky and fishing out a cold xxxx Gold. With a practiced flick of the wrist, he tossed it to Mick.

"You're wrong, Em," he said, the mischief plain in his eyes. "We're looking for gold this weekend. Here, Mick, first gold for the trip."

Mick caught the can effortlessly, the condensation already pooling against his fingers. He rolled it between his palms before shaking his head with a smirk. "Too early for me, mate."

Emily snorted, crossing her arms as she eyed them both. "Yeah, until you get around the corner."

The laughter that followed was rich and full, blending with the calls of lorikeets in the trees. The weekend stretched ahead, ripe with promise, adventure, and, if Emily was right, a fair bit of beer as well.

The morning heat was rising steadily as Mick crouched to say goodbye to his children, ruffling the hair of his eldest before scooping the youngest into a brief embrace. Emily stood by, her arms crossed but her eyes soft with the quiet understanding of a wife who had seen this ritual countless times before.

Mick turned to her, pressing a kiss to her lips, too short, too fleeting, but filled with meaning. "See you Sunday arvo," he murmured, his voice low.

Sam, already climbing back into the Land Cruiser, gave a lazy wave. "See you all," he called as Mick slid into the passenger seat beside him.

Emily stepped back, hands on her hips, watching them with an amused shake of her head. "Be careful, you two," she said, knowing full well that her words would be met with grins and good intentions rather than strict adherence. The kids waved enthusiastically as Sam swung the Land Cruiser into a tight three-point turn, the tires kicking up a puff of dust. Mick leaned out the window, giving one last wave as they rumbled down Batway Place, the roar of the old FJ50 breaking the quiet hum of the neighbourhood.

As they rounded the corner, the suburban world fell away behind them, replaced by the vast sprawl of the north. The Kuranda Range loomed ahead, the dense green of the rainforest rising in jagged peaks against the clear blue sky. The road stretched before them, twisting and climbing into the wild.

Sam reached down, his fingers closing around the beer he had stashed out of sight when he arrived at Mick's place. With a grin, he held it up in salute. "Are you having one, Mick?"

Mick let out a bark of laughter, already reaching for the smaller esky by his feet. His fingers found the familiar chill of an ice-cold can, and he cracked it open with a practiced flick of the tab.

"Is the Pope a Catholic, Sam?" he replied, raising his own can in a toast as the Land Cruiser roared up the highway, carrying them toward the untamed promise of the north.

Sam grinned, shaking his head slightly as he took a pull from his beer. He had known Mick for the better part of a decade now, their friendship forged under the unrelenting sun of the Cairns construction scene.

They had first crossed paths on a job site, building a series of cottages for a local builder. Mick had just finished his apprenticeship, fresh-faced and full of piss and vinegar, carrying himself like a man who had single-handedly invented the trade. For Mick, everything was a competition, every frame stood, every board nailed, every truss secured had to be done at breakneck speed.

Sam could still remember the morning the builder had rocked up on site, Mick trailing behind him like a young bull champing at the bit.

"This is Greg's replacement," the boss had said. "Mick, meet Sam. Catch you later."

And just like that, the kid was in his charge.

At first, Mick's overconfidence had grated, but there was no denying the bloke had talent, and soon enough, their working relationship had morphed into an easy camaraderie. By the time the cottages were finished, they were more than just site mates, they were proper mates.

Mick's passion was fishing; it consumed him. He could talk endlessly about tides, tackle, and the best bait for barramundi. Sam, on the other hand, had little patience for sitting around, waiting for a fish to bite. His heart lay in the land itself, in the thrill of discovery, the gleam of something ancient buried beneath the earth. He was a seasoned fossicker, his weekends spent scouring dry creek beds and forgotten gullies in search of gold. When he had finally taken up metal detecting, it seemed only natural to invite Mick along for a weekend trip.

Mick had been skeptical at first, more interested in knocking the top off a few beers than swinging a coil over the dirt. But all it had taken was one small, sun-warmed nugget glinting in his palm, and he was hooked. From that moment on, they were partners in the hunt, bound by dust, sweat, and the unspoken promise of fortune hidden beneath the rugged northern soil.

As they tore up the road toward the Marian, Sam cast a sidelong glance at his mate and smirked. Funny how life worked. A decade ago, they were just two blokes on a building site. Now, they were chasing gold together, the lure of the wild country calling them once again.

The old FJ50 was no thoroughbred, built more for rugged endurance than speed. It guzzled fuel with the same relentless enthusiasm that Sam downed his beers, fast and without apology. The petrol engine roared as they pushed on through the open roads of the north, the heat rising in shimmering waves off the bitumen.

By the time they rolled into Marianvale, it was just after ten o'clock. The dust from the road clung to the Cruiser's battered panels, giving it a sunbaked, well-travelled look. They pulled into the service station, the pump clanking as Sam filled the tank, watching the numbers climb higher with a wry shake of his head.

"Thirsty old bastard," he muttered, patting the side of the Land Cruiser as the fuel glugged into its greedy belly.

Mick stretched his legs, hands on his lower back. "Since we're here, might as well grab a couple of cold ones."

Sam didn't need convincing. Minutes later, they were seated in the bar of the Junction Hotel, the air thick with the smell of spilled beer and sun-warmed timber. A couple of old-timers sat in the corner, their conversation as slow and measured as the country itself.

By the time they'd finished their drinks and swapped stories with the fossickers Sam knew from past trips, the day had edged forward faster than planned. It would be a long haul yet, pushing past Thornborough, skirting Glen Russell, and finally winding their way into the Mount Marian ranges.

The terrain ahead was treacherous, deep ruts, loose gravel, and climbs that would test both man and machine. If they were lucky, they'd make camp by four o'clock, but Sam knew better than to put faith in schedules out here. The land dictated the pace, not the other way around.

As expected, it was well past that when they finally reached their chosen campsite, the long shadows of the range stretching across the valley. The sun dipped low, bleeding gold and crimson across the sky as they scrambled to set up camp before darkness swallowed them whole.

Sam worked quickly, pitching his large marquee tent while Mick gathered firewood. The familiar rituals of camp life took over, gear unpacked, the fire coaxed to life, and the crisp evening air carrying the promise of a hard-earned meal.

Sam hauled the whole rump of beef onto the tailgate of the Cruiser, the thick slab of meat rich and red beneath his knife. He steadied it with his left hand and began slicing two thick steaks, the blade gliding through the flesh. The steel of the tailgate was firm, but the plastic chopping board beneath the meat was slick with juices. It shifted unexpectedly.

A sharp sting tore through his hand as the blade bit deep below his thumb, carving through flesh and unleashing a bright crimson flow.

"Bloody hell!" Sam jerked back, watching in stunned silence as blood splattered onto the tailgate, mingling with the dark juices of the beef.

Mick, crouched by the fire, looked up sharply. "Christ, Sam! What have you done?"

Sam pressed his free hand against the wound, feeling the warm pulse of his own lifeblood seeping through his fingers. He gritted his teeth, shaking his head.

"Just gave the Cruiser a fresh paint job, that's all," he muttered through clenched teeth, his usual bravado straining under the pain.

The wilderness was indifferent to injuries, and out here, a mistake could mean more than just a scar. Mick was already on his feet, heading towards the first-aid kit. The night had settled in, but the adventure was far from over.

Mick was on his feet in an instant, yanking a crumpled handkerchief from his pocket and pressing it against Sam's bleeding hand.

"Hold that there, mate," he said, already moving toward the Land Cruiser where the first aid kit was stashed. He pulled it open, rummaging through its contents before finding an Elastoplast large enough to do the job.

Sam gritted his teeth, watching as Mick unwrapped the bandage. "This is why I drink, you know. Stops the hands from shaking."

"Yeah, well, maybe you should drink less when you've got a bloody knife in your hand," Mick shot back, smirking as he wrapped the wound tight.

With the crisis over, they cracked open another beer, the fire flickering against their faces as they laughed at Sam's 'near-death experience.'

"Could've gone to the bone, you know," Sam said, flexing his fingers theatrically. "Might never have been able to hold a beer again."

"Now that," Mick said, taking a swig from his can, "would've been a real tragedy."

With the laughter still lingering between them, Sam turned his attention back to the meal. He retrieved his homemade contraption, a beast of a thing he had cobbled together from two wire oven trays, held together at one end by links of chain and welded handles at the other, giving it the appearance of a giant waffle iron.

He laid the contraption open, placed two thick steaks on the bottom tray, then clamped the top tray over them, securing it with the heavyset handles. With a practiced hand, he placed the whole rig over the hot coals, counting down the seconds in his head. One minute per side, no more, no less.

As the meat sizzled and the aroma of seared beef filled the night air, Mick leaned back on his elbows, taking in the vast stretch of stars overhead. This was what it was all about, the open sky, the crackle of the fire, the smell of charred meat, and the promise of gold lying somewhere beneath the earth, waiting to be found.

With their hunger satisfied and the fire burning low, they settled into their swags, the world shrinking to the quiet sounds of the bush. Sam shifted his arm beneath his head, staring up at the night sky.

"You reckon we'll find anything this time?" Mick murmured, his voice thick with beer and sleep.

Sam exhaled slowly, a grin tugging at the corner of his mouth. "Only one way to find out, mate."

The fire popped, the embers glowing like molten gold, as the two men drifted into the kind of sleep that only comes after a hard day's journey into the wilderness.

The next morning, with the sun already pushing the temperature up, Sam and Mick finished their breakfast and set about assembling their metal detectors. They worked methodically, each lost in thought, before finally discussing where they might focus their efforts for the day.

Mick, eager to test out his brand-new top-of-the-line Minelab detector, had his sights set on following the river. With the wet season making an early start, the water was running strong, cutting fresh channels through the earth. He figured the force of the water might have unearthed something worth finding. Sam, on the other hand, remained loyal to his older, well-worn Minelab, a machine he trusted like an old warhorse. He decided to work the ridgeline where he had struck gold on past trips, betting that the land would still have more to offer.

By ten o'clock, they were ready. Each man shouldered his gear, exchanging a nod before setting off in opposite directions. The plan was simple, work their chosen ground for a couple of hours and meet back at camp around midday.

The sun was high by the time they returned, both covered in sweat and dust. Sam arrived first, grinning as he rattled the small vial in his hand.

"Twenty-five grams," he said, tipping the gold onto his palm so Mick could see. The small nuggets and flakes gleamed in the light.

Mick, however, had considerably less to brag about. He sighed, dropping his own find onto the table. "One-point-seven grams." He shook his head. "This new bloody detector should come with a refund policy."

After a quick snack and a couple of cold beers, they set out again, returning to their morning's hunting grounds with renewed determination.

By late afternoon, Mick was growing frustrated. His detector beeped and whined over false signals, leading him to nothing but rusted scraps and bits of worthless metal. He had chosen a section of the river where the water cascaded down a washout of large rocks, figuring that heavier gold might have settled in the crevices. But despite the promising terrain, his haul remained pitiful. The sinking sun painted the sky in shades of amber and rose, and by five-thirty, Mick had had enough.

He trudged back to camp, kicking at the dirt as he walked. Arriving at the campsite, he saw no sign of Sam yet. With a sigh, he grabbed a cold beer from the esky, popped the top, and took a long, satisfying swig before wiping down his detector and hooking it up to the booster pack he had brought along for charging.

Finally, he pulled out his gold scales, setting them up on the table. He tipped his entire day's haul onto the scale, 1.7 grams from the morning, a measly 0.8 grams from the afternoon. He let out a dry chuckle, shaking his head.

"At this rate," he muttered to himself, taking another sip of beer, "I'd better hold on to my bloody day job."

He leaned back in his chair, listening to the crackling fire and waiting for Sam's return, wondering if his mate's luck had held out or if the ridge had betrayed him as the river had betrayed Mick.

After Mick's third beer, he began to feel the first prickle of unease. Sam should have been back by now. He reached for the handheld UHF radio clipped to his belt and pressed the call button. "Sam, you there, mate?"

Silence.

He waited a moment and tried again. The radio crackled, but no response came. That wasn't unusual in this rugged country, where massive boulders and thick stands of scrub could block a signal, but still, something gnawed at Mick's gut.

An hour passed. The sun had dipped below the horizon, the sky a deepening indigo, and still no sign of Sam. Mick tried the handheld again, his voice sharper now. "Sam, come in."

Nothing.

His gaze drifted to the LandCruiser. The vehicle's UHF had a stronger signal. He climbed into the driver's seat, flicked the switch, dead. The damn thing wouldn't work without the ignition on, and Sam had the keys. Mick rummaged through the usual hiding spots, the glovebox, the visor, under the seat, but they weren't there. He exhaled sharply, glancing toward the darkening bush.

No point panicking. Not yet.

He busied himself gathering more firewood, the darkness pressing in fast. Soon, he had a roaring blaze, its flames licking high into the night. If Sam was lost or disoriented, the fire would serve as a beacon, guiding him home. As an extra measure, he dug out Sam's old metho-fuelled pressure hurricane lamp, pumped it to a steady glow, and hoisted it onto the roof rack of the LandCruiser. It cast an eerie circle of light around the vehicle, shadows dancing in the flickering glow.

One last time, Mick raised the handheld radio. "Sam, you better not be off drinking with a bloody gold rush ghost. Get your arse back to camp."

Silence.

He settled into his chair, eyes locked on the surrounding darkness. His instincts told him that heading out now, with only his torch and the fickle light of the fire, would be madness. The high tussocks of grass and scattered boulders would twist and shift under the beam, playing tricks on the eyes. Even a man who knew this country well could find himself turned around in the dark.

No, if Sam was lost, he'd likely stay put until first light and then make his way back.

Mick stared into the fire, sipping another beer, forcing himself to stay calm.

Nothing to worry about. Not yet.

Mick had managed to snatch a few restless hours of sleep, but when he jolted awake, it was with a start. His eyes darted to his watch, almost seven o'clock. A cold weight settled in his gut as he turned his head toward Sam's swag, expecting to see his mate's broad frame sprawled out beneath the canvas. But it was empty, untouched.

Mick was on his feet in an instant, grabbing the handheld radio and thumbing the call button. "Sam, come in. Where the hell are you?"

Only static replied.

He tried again, his voice sharper now. "Sam, answer me, mate."

Nothing.

Mick exhaled through his nose, pushing down the worry creeping into his chest. He strode toward the direction Sam had set off the afternoon before, his boots crunching on the dry earth. "Sam!" he called out, his voice cutting through the morning silence.

Nothing but the rustle of the breeze through the scrub.

Calling was pointless, he realised. If Sam was close enough to hear, he would have responded. If he wasn't, Mick was just wasting breath. He pressed his lips together, scanning the land before him, then started moving again, slower this time, following the rough trail leading up toward the ridge where Sam had been searching for gold.

A thousand possibilities churned in Mick's mind. Had Sam taken a bad fall? Was he lying somewhere with a broken leg, unable to move? Or worse, had he been bitten? The thought sent a shiver down Mick's spine. It was unlikely, both men were seasoned in the bush and wore thick gaiters around their boots, well aware of the deadly King Browns and Taipans that thrived in this land. But unlikely didn't mean impossible.

The sun was already climbing, the air thickening with heat. Mick clenched his jaw and kept walking, his eyes sweeping the ground for any sign of his friend.

Mick stood at the edge of the camp, hands on his hips, heart hammering against his ribs. He didn't know what to do. It was nearly ten o'clock on Sunday morning. By now, they should have been packing up, loading the Landcruiser, and heading home with a few stories and a bit of gold to show for it. But Sam wasn't here. Sam wasn't anywhere.

Should he wait longer? Should he go looking? Looking... where?

His gaze drifted toward the ridge where Sam had headed the day before. That was the only lead he had. Tightening the straps of his backpack, he set off, climbing steadily, the heat pressing down on him like a lead weight. The climb was slow and punishing, the scrub clawing at his legs, the sun relentless overhead. It took him an hour and a half to reach the top, his shirt soaked in sweat. From up here, all he could see was an endless sprawl of bushland, dense, unyielding, and empty.

Mick pulled the handheld radio from his belt, pressed the button. "Sam, come in. Where the hell are you?"

Only static answered him.

He cursed under his breath, scanning the terrain, searching for something, anything, that might tell him where Sam had gone. Nothing. No footprints, no broken branches, no sign of his mate at all.

Gritting his teeth, he started moving along the ridge, heading north toward the higher ground and the massive boulders that jutted from the earth like ancient sentinels. If Sam had been up here, he might have climbed to get a better view, might have,

Mick stopped himself. He was guessing. That's all he was doing. And he was guessing blind. Another hour and a half passed, his legs burning, his water running low. There was nothing. No clue, no sign. Just bush and rock and silence.

A heavy knot formed in his gut. Sam was lost. Or injured. Or both.

There was only one thing left to do.

Mick turned back the way he'd come, following his own tracks carefully. He wasn't about to get lost out here as well. He needed to get back to camp. He needed to get help.

It was nearly two o'clock when Mick returned to the camp, the midday sun beating down like a relentless hammer, burning the earth and everything it touched. The weight of each footstep felt heavier as he made his way toward the familiar sight of their campsite, hoping, no, praying, that Sam would be there, waiting, perhaps lounging under the shade of the canvas tent with his broad grin, ready to laugh off the previous day's mishaps.

But there was no Sam.

Mick's chest tightened. A cold knot formed in the pit of his stomach, and the quiet stillness of the empty camp filled his ears like a deafening roar. His mind spun with thoughts he couldn't grasp, and for a moment, panic began to claw at him like a wild beast. He stood there, frozen, staring at the empty ground, his heartbeat thundering in his chest. What now? Where was Sam?

The reality began to settle like the suffocating heat, dragging him down. Mick's first instinct was to start packing up. Throw everything in the back of the Landcruiser, make the drive back into town, get help. But then, like a sudden slap to the face, another thought hit him with brutal force. What if Sam came back while he was gone? What if Sam returned to an empty campsite, the gear packed away as though they'd never been there, and thought Mick had abandoned him?

No, better to leave it all. Better to leave the camp as it was. At least that way, if Sam came back, there would be some semblance of a plan, a sign that Mick hadn't given up. He couldn't leave, not yet. But something else was gnawing at him now.

Mick looked around, his mind racing. The keys. He needed the keys. The Landcruiser keys. They had to be here. Somewhere.

He couldn't help but feel that sense of dread creeping up his spine. What if Sam had taken them? Could he have taken them with him into the bush? No, Mick told himself. Sam wouldn't have done that. Not when the very thought of losing the keys in this godforsaken scrub would drive him mad. No, the keys had to be here, somewhere, hidden, tucked away safely. Sam would never leave them to chance.

Mick's heart pounded as his eyes scanned the camp, desperately searching for the familiar jangle of metal. His hands started to shake as he sifted through the gear, moving things around with increasing urgency. The air felt thick with the oppressive heat and the growing realisation that time was slipping away faster than he could grasp it. He had to find those keys. Without them, he couldn't get the car started, couldn't get to help. And without help, Sam,

Where would Sam leave the keys? A safe place, somewhere he knew they wouldn't get lost. Mick's mind raced through the options. The glovebox? No. In the ignition? No, he would never leave them in there. Where else?

Each passing second felt like an eternity as Mick turned over every corner of the camp, his breath coming faster, more shallow. Focus, he told himself. He couldn't let the panic take over. Sam was depending on him. He had to find those keys. They had to be here.

Mick tore through the camp like a man possessed, his hands trembling as he ripped through every corner, every bag, and every piece of gear, desperate to find the keys. His eyes were wild, darting from one place to the next, as his mind raced. The keys had to be here. They had to be. But as he scoured every inch of the ground, the air around him growing thick with the weight of his mounting anxiety, Mick found nothing. No keys. Not under the tarp, not in the cooler, not hidden in the folds of their blankets. Not a trace.

His breath came in short bursts as he moved toward the Landcruiser, his heart pounding against his ribs like a war drum. They must be in there, surely, hidden somewhere in the truck. Mick slid onto the driver's seat and began methodically searching the vehicle, hands shaking with urgency. He checked under the mat, rifled through the ashtray, and lifted the seat cushions, all the while hoping against reason that the keys would just magically appear. But there was nothing. His pulse quickened. His eyes burned with the sting of sweat as he began pulling at the door panel, trying to pry it loose, searching for some hidden compartment or anything that could possibly contain the damn keys.

They have to be here, he thought, his mind spiralling into frustration. With a savage growl, Mick slid out of the truck and knelt beside the wheels. He lifted the first tire, peering underneath, then the next, checking every possible hiding place. He even looked behind the spare wheel, convinced that Sam, in some twisted act of foresight, had left them there. But there was nothing. No sign of them anywhere.

He stood up abruptly, fists clenched, the heat pressing in from all sides, stifling and suffocating. Think, Mick, he forced himself to calm down, though every muscle in his body screamed for action. You'll have to hotwire it.

He didn't even pause to think about the impossibility of the task. Desperation was his only guide now. He fumbled inside the glovebox, hoping to find something that would help, any tools, any wires, any way to get the truck moving. But there was nothing. Not a damn thing. Not even a pair of pliers.

Then, he remembered. Tools. Sam's toolbox. It had to be somewhere. Maybe Sam had left something in the car, a wrench, a screwdriver, anything. He tore through the contents of the Landcruiser once more, but again, there was nothing but the barest of essentials, some rope, a first-aid kit, a few cans of beans, and an old pair of gloves.

His frustration was mounting. Sweat dripped into his eyes, blurring his vision as he reached under the dashboard and started pulling at wires, trying to manipulate them with his hands, even though he knew it was futile. He had to get the ignition lock off, he had no choice.

Mick's fingers found something, a bolt. No, four bolts. Four thick, stubborn bolts. His heart sank as he realised what they were. Shear bolts. The ones that were used to secure the ignition lock. Designed to be tightened with a socket until the head sheared off, intended to prevent car thieves from easily dismantling the ignition system. But there was no socket. No tools. Nothing. His stomach twisted into a knot as the realisation hit him with the weight of a thousand tons.

It's impossible.

His chest tightened, the room closing in around him as the suffocating heat mixed with his sense of impending doom. He tried to hold it together, to think clearly, but his mind was clouded with rage and helplessness. Without warning, Mick snapped.

"Fuck!" His voice split the air as he hurled the handful of tools in his grip into the dirt, the sound of metal crashing to the ground almost drowning out the roar of his own frustration.

His hands shook violently as he stood there, staring at the Landcruiser, as if willing it to answer back, to give him the solution he so desperately needed. But it remained silent, indifferent to his plight, just like the wilderness around him. He was alone in this godforsaken place, with no way out, and no way to find Sam.

Mick's breath came in shallow gasps as he turned his back on the truck. His mind was a storm of panic and disbelief. Sam was still out there. Alone. Injured, or worse. And Mick? He was stuck. No truck, no keys, and no way to get help.

The firelight from the campsite flickered in the distance, casting long shadows across the landscape. The night was coming, and Mick knew that every second spent in this helpless state was another second lost. He had to find Sam. He had to act.

As the last rays of sunlight bled from the sky, casting a fiery orange glow over the scrubland, Mick stood at the edge of the camp, his gaze drifting over the rugged wilderness stretching out before him. The sun had dipped beneath the horizon, and the cold breath of night was already creeping in. It was only a matter of hours before the darkness would be all-encompassing. He had a decision to make, a grim, daunting decision. The truck was useless without the keys, the ignition locked tight, and the tools useless against the shear bolts. There was no other choice but to walk.

He gathered another pile of firewood, each branch snapping under his grip like the last brittle threads of hope. His head was spinning, his legs felt unsteady, and a cold sweat was starting to bead on his forehead. Nausea churned in his gut, but there was no time to sit back and let the fear consume him. Sam was out there, somewhere, and Mick had to get help, fast. Marianvale was the nearest town, a good day's walk. He had to make it there, somehow, and pray that someone could help him find Sam.

As Mick turned to prepare for the long night ahead, his eyes landed on the esky, the one Sam had packed with supplies. His stomach growled, reminding him how little he had eaten since the previous night. He opened it with trembling hands and pulled out the rump steak. The thick, red slices seemed to mock him, but it was the only thing he had to eat. The fire crackled as he threw a slab of the meat onto the makeshift grill Sam had used so many times before. The aroma of the steak cooking on the flames seemed to ground him for a moment, a simple, comforting reminder of better times.

As the meat cooked, Mick's thoughts wandered. He should cook more to take with him, enough for the walk to Marianvale, and more than enough to keep his energy up as he fought his way through the bush. He needed to leave at first light, to find the quickest path to town before the heat of the day wore him down.

But then, as the steak sizzled on the fire, another thought struck him, and for a moment, he stopped in his tracks, staring at the meat as it seared. Emily. She would have been worried by now, he realised. Of course, she would have called the police. She must have, she must have. She'd be frantic by now.

For the first time since the worry had set in, Mick felt a fleeting glimmer of relief. If Emily had contacted the authorities, it was possible that help would be on its way soon. But as he chewed the tough meat, savouring the smoky flavour, the fleeting moment of relief was shattered, replaced by a cold, creeping dread.

Emily knew where they were going, sort of. She knew they'd passed Marianvale and were heading toward Mount Marian, but beyond that, she had no idea. She didn't know the terrain, the vast, unforgiving wilderness that surrounded them. This was no easy place to search, and the area was far too vast. It was remote, an expanse of jagged mountains and dense brush. If Emily had called the police, they'd have no idea where to start looking.

Mick's stomach churned again, not from hunger but from the crushing weight of the realisation that they were lost in a land that could swallow them whole. Even if Emily had alerted the authorities, how would they find them? This was a vast wilderness. A single wrong turn and they could be swallowed by it for days.

He shoved the remaining steak into his mouth and washed it down with a mouthful of beer, the cold liquid doing nothing to quench the heat of his frustration. It didn't help to think of it, but Mick couldn't stop himself. He ran through the worst-case scenarios over and over in his head, each one darker than the last. What if Sam was injured? Or worse, what if he was dead? Mick's throat tightened as he pushed the thought away, willing himself to think logically. Sam was tough, he'd survive. But the hours that had passed were gnawing at Mick's mind. Every moment he spent sitting here, every moment he waited for Sam to return, meant another minute lost in the wild, another moment further from salvation.

With the last of his meal gone and his mind filled with dread, Mick rose from his seat, a sense of determination settling over him like a thick blanket. There was no time left to waste. He could not wait any longer. He had to make the walk to Marianvale, alone, with only the night to guide him. The terrain was harsh, and it would be a gruelling march, but it was the only choice he had. Sam was still out there, and Mick would do whatever it took to find him.

With the last embers of the fire crackling in the distance, Mick gathered his gear, he would cut some meat to take in the morning and some water for the journey. He checked his radio one final time, but there was no response. He had no choice. He couldn't stay here any longer, at first light he would head out.

Mick lay in the darkness of his swag, staring at the faint outline of the ridge above him, his mind tossing and turning like a storm-tossed sea. It was a restless night, but despite the gnawing worry and the biting cold that crept into his bones, sleep had come to him in short, unexpected bursts. He had slept, but only in fits and starts, and when the first sliver of pale light touched the horizon, Mick was already wide awake.

His heart thudded in his chest as he scanned the camp, his eyes wild with a desperate hope that maybe, just maybe, Sam had returned in the dark. But the camp was empty. The silence was deafening. No Sam. Just the wind whispering through the trees and the faint crackling of the dying fire. Panic surged through Mick's veins, a sharp, cold knife in his gut. What had happened to his mate? Had he gotten lost? Injured? Worse?

He scrambled from his swag, the rough fabric brushing against his skin as he rushed to the fire. The coals still smouldered, but Sam's presence was missing, completely gone, as though the earth had swallowed him whole. Mick's breath quickened as the reality of their situation began to sink in.

He had to act. And he had to act quickly.

Mick moved in a blur of motion, tearing into Sam's esky for the remaining slabs of meat. His hands were unsteady as he sliced off another thick piece of rump, cursing under his breath. Every movement felt rushed, as though time itself was working against him. He didn't have time to think, he had to move.

With the meat packed and tucked into his backpack, he grabbed the small water container, Sam's trusty two-litre bottle, and slung it over his shoulder. Mick's eyes darted around the camp, desperate for something, anything, that could help him. He rifled through the rest of the gear, searching for another water container. The only other option was a heavy ten-litre jug, but Mick knew it would be a burden, especially with the long journey ahead. He tossed it aside, cursed, and made the decision to leave it behind.

As the early morning light spread across the land, Mick steeled himself. He had no idea where Sam was, or if he was even still alive. But he couldn't sit here any longer. The only chance he had was to walk out of this hellhole and find help. Marianvale was the nearest town. If he could just make it there, if he could just get to that town, then maybe someone could help. But even as the thought crossed his mind, Mick realised the enormity of the task ahead.

The Landcruiser's tracks were still fresh on the ground, and Mick's eyes instinctively followed them. The track leading away from the camp was rough, jagged, and barely passable, but it was the only way out. He knew the terrain, Sam's Landcruiser had covered it more than once, and Mick's mind calculated the distance to the main road. It was about eight kilometres, if you could even call it a road. The track was nothing more than a scar through the bush, a narrow strip that had been trampled by countless tires over the years. Mick pushed forward, his boots crunching in the dry earth, the sun beginning to climb higher in the sky as the heat of the day set in.

But as he walked, something began to nag at him. His mind, always sharp and calculating, noticed something odd. The tracks in the dirt, the ones that had followed, Sam's Landcruiser, were starting to thin out. There were no other recent marks, no sign of other vehicles, no fresh impressions of tires.

Just the faint remnants of Sam's cruiser's arrival tracks. Mick's heart sank. He had no way of knowing what had happened to Sam, but now he realised the grim truth: there would be no help, no safety until he reached town, and that meant walking alone through forty-five kilometres of unforgiving wilderness.

Mick didn't stop to second-guess himself. There was no time for doubt. He needed to focus, to keep moving. The distance between him and Marianvale now felt like an insurmountable chasm. But he calculated as he walked, measuring out the journey in his mind. At a steady pace of four kilometres per hour, it would take him around fourteen hours to make it to town, if he didn't stop and if no one came down the track.

The weight of the backpack felt heavier with every step, but Mick didn't slow. His mind was too focused on the task ahead. Every step, every mile, brought him closer to the help he so desperately needed. He didn't dare think of the worst, didn't dare entertain the thought that Sam might not make it, that he might be lost or worse. Not yet.

Mick's eyes burned with exhaustion as he trudged forward, his thoughts drifting from one grim scenario to another. But his legs kept moving, the steady rhythm of his steps the only thing that anchored him to the world as the harsh sun bore down on him. One foot in front of the other. That's all he had. That's all he could do. The track was long, but he would walk it, no matter what. For Sam. For his mate.

Mick halted in the middle of the track, sweat trickling down his brow and his breath coming in shallow gasps. The harsh reality hit him like a physical blow, the distance, the weight of the water, the relentless sun on his back. It wasn't going to work. He had to admit it. He needed more water. The small two-litre container he carried was bone dry. He could feel the dryness creeping into his throat, and his body was beginning to feel the strain.

His head pounded as, in his mind, he looked down at the ten-litre water jug, left behind in his haste, mocking him from where he'd abandoned it. A sinking feeling gnawed at his gut. He had been so desperate to keep moving, to get to town, but now the hard truth settled over him like a heavy cloak, he couldn't keep going without more water.

With a weary sigh, Mick turned back. Every step felt like it required twice the effort, but there was no other choice. He had to get the water. He couldn't risk dehydration. He couldn't risk running out of the one thing that might keep him alive long enough to make it out of this hellhole.

The sun was climbing higher in the sky as Mick trudged back towards the camp, every muscle aching from the earlier trek. By the time he reached the site, it was just after ten in the morning. His eyes immediately scanned the camp in a silent, desperate hope, maybe, just maybe, Sam had come back in the night. But there was no sign of him. The camp was empty, just as it had been before.

Mick's stomach twisted with a familiar knot of dread. He swallowed hard, shaking off the thought, and grabbed the heavy ten-litre water jug by its handle. His legs trembled under the added weight as he turned around, setting his sights on the track to Marianvale for the second time. He was moving slower now, the additional water a constant reminder of how treacherous this journey had become.

The track stretched out before him like a ribbon of dust and earth, winding through the bush in a way that seemed endless. With every step, Mick could feel the weight of the heat pressing down on him, as if the sun itself had turned against him. His mind raced as he walked, trying to calculate how far he had gone and how much further he had to go. He reckoned he had covered about thirty kilometres by now, maybe a little more, the sweat stinging his eyes as he pushed forward. Eight hours of walking had brought him this far, and still, Marianvale felt as distant as it had the first time he'd set foot on the track.

The sun beat relentlessly, casting long shadows as the day wore on, but as Mick trudged along, it wasn't the heat that worried him anymore. It was the encroaching darkness. He had been moving steadily, taking short, irregular rests to sip from his smaller, two litre water bottle, but he was growing weary. Every breath felt laboured, and each footstep seemed to come with increasing effort. The remaining six litres of water in the ten-litre jug were a bit easier to carry now, but the weight was starting to take its toll.

Mick paused again, resting his hands on his knees, feeling the ground beneath him, trying to stay grounded. He took another swig from the two-litre container, the water sliding coolly down his throat, but it wasn't enough to revive him. He needed more. The dry heat had drained him in ways he couldn't fully comprehend, and it was clear now that he would have to keep moving, no matter the cost.

It wasn't long before the first signs of dusk began creeping across the land. The sky, once so brilliant and bright, began to darken as heavy clouds rolled in from the distance, heralding the start of the wet season. Mick glanced up at the sky with a mixture of dread and resignation. The storm clouds were gathering quickly, and as the light started to fade, the track in front of him grew indistinct. The trees, the underbrush, the very earth beneath his feet seemed to swallow up what little daylight remained.

As the night descended, the darkness thickened, so absolute that it felt like the world itself had vanished. The road ahead was swallowed by the blackness, and Mick found himself stumbling, unsure of where the path even lay. He stopped for a moment, trying to steady himself, but the night held no mercy. Without any light, it was impossible to see where the track veered or where he might have gone wrong. The heavy clouds overhead blocked out the stars, leaving him with no point of reference.

He knew he couldn't keep walking in this, he wasn't sure where the road even led in the blackness, let alone which direction he was supposed to go. Mick's survival instincts kicked in. He couldn't risk getting lost in the night, not with the weather closing in and the uncertainty of what lay ahead. He had no choice but to stop.

With a frustrated grunt, Mick set his heavy load down at the side of the track, his body sagging with exhaustion. He looked at the sky, willing the storm to hold off just a little longer. But the thick, oppressive clouds made it clear that the rain was coming. He needed to find shelter, even if just for a few hours. Walking through the night wasn't an option anymore.

Mick crouched down by the track, the weight of the day finally crashing over him. His thoughts turned to Sam, where was he? What had happened to him? And why hadn't he returned? Mick had no answers, but as the night air grew cooler and the distant rumble of thunder began to echo through the sky, Mick knew that no matter what happened, he had to survive. He had to keep going, for both their sakes.

For the first time since setting off, Mick felt an unsettling chill run down his spine. He had been so focused on putting one foot in front of the other, on the sheer will to survive, that he had failed to consider the essentials. There was no thought given to finding a place to sleep, no planning for the cold night air, no fire to stave off the coming dark. It was absurd, really. How had he not brought anything to sleep on or in? And the thought of starting a fire seemed laughable now, he had no lighter, no matches, nothing to ignite the kindling with. His only light was the waning glow of the moon somewhere above, which was now quickly fading into an oppressive, lightless night.

He cursed himself under his breath, feeling the weight of his unpreparedness pressing down on him like the oppressive heat of the day. He should have planned better. Should have packed smarter. Should have known. But he hadn't. And now, he was alone, in the wilderness, with nothing but the harsh earth beneath him and the seemingly endless road ahead.

But just as the reality of his predicament was about to crush him, a strange sound cut through the night.

At first, it was faint, just a whisper on the wind, barely perceptible above the constant hum of his own tired breathing. It sounded odd, like the distant crash of a tree being felled, but broken, as if the air itself were twisting around the noise. The faint, crashing sound would come and go, echoing through the dark, its rhythm erratic and unsettling. Mick's senses, already on edge from the exhaustion and isolation, flared to life as the noise grew louder, then quieter, only to build again. It was unnerving. It sounded almost like an animal in distress, or perhaps something much more sinister. The hairs on the back of Mick's neck stood on end. Was it a thunderstorm? A creature? The wind itself?

His tired, clouded mind tried to make sense of it, but it was all too much. His thoughts swirled and tangled, and fear, sharp and insistent, gnawed at him. The noise grew more consistent, louder, its vibrations now rattling the ground beneath his boots. Mick's pulse quickened. Panic threatened to take hold. Was it a storm? Was it something else?

Then, a realisation pierced through his confusion.

It was a vehicle. A car, perhaps. Or something even worse.

His eyes, straining against the darkness, began to pick out the flickering glow of lights through the haze of the night. The sound that had seemed so alien and foreign now seemed to make more sense. A car, but not just any car. The lights were wide and blinding, like twin suns cutting through the dust-choked air. They were the high beams, piercing, unforgiving, and something more: spotlights. The kind of light you'd see on the front of a military vehicle or a hunting rig. The noise, the thundering roar of the engine, was unmistakable now. A diesel. Not just any vehicle, but one built for rough terrain. A beast of a machine.

Mick's heart pounded in his chest. His mind went wild with the implications. Was it a rescue team? Or was it someone far worse? His thoughts raced in the dark, but they couldn't keep up with the growing terror as the sound of the vehicle approached.

As the lights grew nearer, it was as if the very road before him became a tunnel of blinding light. The lights shone straight at him, throwing harsh shadows that danced across the ground. The beam was so bright, so blinding, it seemed like the very sun had come down to consume him. The ground trembled beneath his feet, and Mick, in a frenzy of confusion and terror, staggered to his left. His foot caught on the raised edge of the road, and in an instant, he was tumbling sideways, landing heavily on his left side with a grunt of pain.

His mind screamed to get up, to move, to do something, but his body, exhausted and weak from the journey, betrayed him. He pushed himself to his knees, still dizzy from the fall, and tried to rise, but the blinding light from the vehicle was upon him now, flooding his senses with its intensity.

The diesel engine growled to a halt, the sound of it fading, replaced by the more familiar thrum of an idling engine. Mick's heart thudded in his chest as he heard the door open with a loud creak, the sound reverberating over the distant thrum of the diesel. It was the only sound in the world now. The door opened wider, the heavy scent of diesel and dust filling the air.

Mick's heart stopped for a moment as he turned toward the source of the noise, his eyes squinting against the blinding light. Who was it? And what did they want?

The question hung in the air like the electric tension before a storm.

The harsh voice sliced through the silence of the night, making Mick's blood run cold. "Sam Young or Mick West by any chance?"

Mick blinked, his heart hammering in his chest as he struggled to focus on the figure in the headlights. It was the voice of authority, gravelly, unyielding. The sudden recognition of the situation slapped him in the face. Police. He was no longer alone in this desolate stretch of wilderness.

"I'm Mick... I can't find Sam, he's lost," Mick stammered, his words ragged, his mind racing.

A large, calloused hand clamped onto Mick's arm like a vice, jerking him forward with no consideration for his physical state. Mick barely had time to steady himself before the officer was guiding him with surprising force toward the passenger side of the Landcruiser. The door was flung open with a loud squeal of protest, and Mick was practically shoved into the seat.

The officer's movements were swift and purposeful, not a word spoken as he slammed the door shut behind Mick. He moved around the vehicle with ease, and Mick could hear the jarring sound of the door opening once more. The engine rumbled to life, and the headlights blazed in the rearview mirror like twin suns as the police cruiser roared down the track.

The officer, a burly man with a voice as rough as the land itself, finally broke the silence. "So, what's the go, mate?" His tone was dismissive, as if Mick's story was just another routine call. "Where do you reckon your mate Sam is?"

Mick's hands gripped the seat, his knuckles white with the tension coursing through his body. "Sam's gone missing. I think he's lost... or hurt. I don't know. I'm just trying to get help, to find him."

The officer grunted, his eyes fixed ahead on the road, his gaze unwavering even as Mick spoke. He'd seen it all before. These things had a way of going sideways, two blokes out in the bush, one with too much to drink, the other too far gone to think straight. And in the end, someone gets hurt, or worse. But Mick wasn't making sense to the officer, not yet. Not until he heard more.

"Where exactly has this mate of yours gone missing, mate?" the officer asked, voice tinged with a growing impatience, already forming his own conclusions.

Mick swallowed, a dry lump lodged in his throat. "It's about thirty klicks from here... just off the main track, and then another eight or so to the camp. I, "

"Is that right now, mate?" The officer cut him off, the words dripping with sarcasm. "Well, sorry to say, it's too fucking dark to be gettin' off this bloody track looking for some lost bloke. We'll come back in the daylight."

Mick's gut twisted. This was real. They were going to leave him out here, leave Sam. He could feel the anger bubbling up, hot and bitter in his chest, but it was quickly drowned by the crushing weight of helplessness.

The officer, whose patience had clearly worn thin, turned the wheel with a sharp, forceful motion, the tires squealing as they swung the Landcruiser around. The headlights cut through the darkness, illuminating the track ahead.

Mick sat in stunned silence, unable to comprehend the dismissal in the officer's words. He had no choice but to endure the jarring rumble of the police cruiser, as it bumped and jostled its way back toward the town. The officer asked him one final question before the weight of silence settled between them like a heavy blanket.

"You need medical attention, mate?" he grunted, the words laced with that same unfeeling indifference.

Mick barely registered the question, his thoughts spinning in a thousand directions at once. He shook his head, the exhaustion in his limbs overwhelming. "No... no... I just need to find Sam." His voice was hoarse, drained from the stress, the fear, the anxiety.

The officer didn't respond. The engine roared on, and Mick, staring out into the night, knew that the time was slipping away. Every minute that passed, the chances of finding Sam, of saving him, slipped further from his grasp. The helplessness settled like a stone in his gut, cold and heavy, and Mick knew it was going to be a long, hard night.

Back at the police station, Mick could feel the oppressive weight of frustration and confusion building with every passing second. The sergeant didn't bother with pleasantries, didn't even offer a handshake. Instead, he barked at Mick in that gruff, no-nonsense voice that had become all too familiar. "Write a statement," he commanded. "Make sure it's legible, so I can fuckin' read it."

The words hung in the air like an insult, but Mick didn't have the energy to argue. He sat down at the grimy desk, the harsh fluorescent lights buzzing above him, and began to write. His hand moved quickly across the paper, but his mind was elsewhere, on Sam, on the long stretch of bush that had swallowed his friend, on the twisted labyrinth of uncertainty that gripped his every thought.

As his pen scratched out the details of the trip, Mick's voice was barely a whisper. "Has my wife Emily been told I'm safe?" He hadn't realized how much that question had been gnawing at him until now.

The sergeant barely looked up from the form he was reading, his bulk shifting in the creaky chair. "I'm about to contact my boss," he muttered, his words thick with indifference. "Then he'll make sure your missus is told where you are. Anyway, you can call her after you finish that statement. Would you like a coffee? I don't have any food."

Mick didn't care about food, didn't care about coffee. He just wanted to know that Emily knew he was still alive. His fingers cramped as he wrote, but he pushed through the pain, finishing the statement with as much detail as he could muster.

When he handed the crumpled paper to the sergeant, he was met with a look of disdain, the man barely lifting an eyebrow as he read over the words. Finally, after what felt like an eternity, the sergeant grunted in what might have been approval, or something else entirely.

"Do you have a fossicker's license?" he asked, his voice flat.

Mick stared at the sergeant, his mind spinning in disbelief. A fossicker's license? Now? The absurdity of it hit him like a slap across the face. He was standing here, in a police station, worried sick about his missing friend, and the only thing this man cared about was a license?

"My friend's missing, up there," Mick said, his voice rising as the anger finally bubbled to the surface. His hands clenched into fists at his sides. "We're talking about a man who could be lying somewhere hurt or worse, and you're asking about a fucking license?"

The sergeant's expression didn't change. He didn't flinch. "For starters," he said, his voice cold and commanding, "don't call me 'mate.' You call me Sergeant. And under these circumstances, we treat everything as suspicious. You're being detained tonight in the cells. You're not under arrest, just detained."

Mick's stomach dropped, a sickening twist of disbelief and fury tightening his chest. "What the hell are you talking about?" he snapped. "My friend's out there, and you're locking me up? I've already told you everything!"

The sergeant wasn't fazed. "We'll visit the site in the morning. It'll be declared a crime scene, keep it clean and undisturbed until we've made our assessment." He paused, his gaze locking with Mick's, and Mick felt the weight of those words like a vice on his chest.

Mick opened his mouth to argue, but the sergeant's next words silenced him. "Now, you can use the landline telephone here to make a call to your wife, but make it brief." He motioned to the corner of the room, where the old-fashioned telephone sat, its receiver dangling like a lifeline.

Mick stood there for a moment, staring at the phone. He couldn't believe what was happening, this wasn't how it was supposed to go. The urgency in his gut told him that every minute that passed without Sam was a minute too long. But here he was, being treated like a criminal in the very place that was supposed to help him.

With a quiet, resentful sigh, Mick moved toward the phone, the weight of the situation pressing down on him with every step. He had to call Emily, had to reassure her. But as he picked up the receiver, a part of him was already dreading what the morning would bring.

Sergeant Tom Kearns had seen it all. An old veteran of the force, his sun-weathered face and grizzled demeanour told the story of a man who had lived through more than his share of the rough edges of the law. He'd been through the grinder before, dragged through the coals after a botched case where the crime scene had been left unsecured, the evidence tainted by incompetence. That mistake had cost him dearly, and ever since, he'd been determined not to make the same error twice. This time, he would be meticulous, he would leave nothing to chance.

As Mick's voice crackled over the phone, trying to explain the grim situation to his wife, Kearns was already at work. His fingers were steady as he typed out an urgent message to the police command centre at Mareeba, requesting a full scientific and forensic team for the following morning. Marianvale was a long way from the nearest city, and with the isolated nature of the area, it could take hours before they had any kind of backup. But Kearns was no stranger to working under pressure, and he wasn't about to take any risks. This situation had the makings of something far bigger than a simple missing person.

He stared at the computer screen for a moment before hitting send, the quiet hum of the police station a stark contrast to the storm raging inside his mind. The crime scene would be locked down, and nothing, not even the most minute detail, would be overlooked. The sooner they had forensic experts on the ground, the better. Tomorrow, he'd see to it that every corner of that camp was examined, from the tracks in the dirt to the smallest scrap of evidence. But for now, he had other matters to attend to.

As Mick hung up the phone, his face pale and his eyes haunted by the dread of the unknown, Kearns stood silently, observing the young man with a mixture of pity and professional detachment. The look in Mick's eyes told him everything he needed to know, this was more than just a search for a missing person. There was something deeper at play here, something darker.

Mick's voice broke through his thoughts. "She's on her way up here, Sergeant. Emily's coming to pick me up."

Kearns' lips twisted into a grim smile. "No, she's not," he replied, his tone flat. "You're being detained here tonight. We'll check out the camp first thing in the morning, and then we'll start the search for your mate. You're staying put, Mick. And I suggest you call her and tell her that. No one's going anywhere tonight."

Mick's face crumpled with frustration, but he knew the sergeant was right. "I'll call her again. I'll tell her I'll be here until tomorrow. I'll explain. Thanks, Sergeant."

The phone call to Emily had been a strained one. As soon as she had heard Mick's voice, the hysteria broke through like a dam crashing under a flood of water. Her voice trembled with fear, her words tumbling out in a rush. "Mick, what's happened to Sam? Where is he? What do you mean he's missing? Are you alright? Oh God, Mick, tell me you're alright..."

And now, as he had called her the second time, Mick's heart clenched as he listened to her frantic voice. It was clear she was struggling to comprehend the enormity of the situation, just as Mick was. "I'm fine, Em, I'm fine," he said, his voice thick with exhaustion. "Sam's gone, though. I don't know where he is, but I'm being detained for the night. They'll send a team up tomorrow to search, and then we'll know more. But for now, I can't leave the station. So don't come up here, I need you to stay put and wait until I call you tomorrow. You don't need to come up here yet." Mick repeated.

Emily's sobs echoed through the phone, and Mick felt a pang of guilt gnawing at him. He wished he could hold her, reassure her, but he had no answers, and the uncertainty hung over them both like a storm cloud. "Mick," Emily gasped, "this doesn't make sense. How could this happen? Why didn't you find him? Why didn't you, "

"Emily, I need you to listen to me," Mick interrupted, his voice rough. "Please, just wait until tomorrow. I promise I'll call you as soon as I know more. You don't need to come up here. Just stay safe, okay? I'll see you tomorrow."

He could hear her struggling to breathe through her sobs, but eventually, she agreed. "Okay," she whispered, her voice barely audible. "I'll wait. Just... just come home safe, Mick. Please."

"I will, Em. I will," Mick replied, the words feeling hollow in his mouth as he hung up the phone. He stared at the receiver for a long moment, his mind racing. Sam was out there somewhere, lost, hurt, or worse, and all Mick could do was wait. Wait for tomorrow. Wait for a search party. Wait for the answers that might never come.

With a weary sigh, Mick settled back into the hard, cold chair. "Goodnight, Emily," he whispered to the silent air, though he knew she couldn't hear him. He looked forward to seeing her tomorrow, but deep down, he knew that the tomorrow that awaited him might bring more questions than answers.

When Mick's voice crackled over the phone, the words tumbling out in a rush, Emily's world seemed to fall apart in a whirlwind of panic. Her heart leaped into her throat, and her breath caught in her chest. "What happened? What do you mean, Sam's missing? What do you mean he's gone?" she demanded, her voice rising with the rising tide of terror flooding her.

Mick's voice, rough and taut with weariness, tried to steady her, but there was no calmness to be found in the words that followed. "Em, I don't know where he is. I've been looking, but he's lost. I'm fine, but we've got to wait until tomorrow. They're sending a team to search the area. I'm being held here for the night. They won't let me leave. You can't come up here now."

The phone line crackled in the silence between them, and Emily's grip tightened on the receiver as if she could somehow hold onto him through the line. "What do you mean detained? Why can't I come get you?" Her voice cracked, the raw emotion breaking through the cracks in her facade of calm. "You can't just stay there. I'll drive up and get you right now."

"Em, listen to me!" Mick's voice broke through, strained with frustration and exhaustion. "I need you to stay put. They won't let me go until tomorrow, and there's nothing you can do tonight. The police are coming to search for

Sam first thing in the morning. I'll be fine. Just wait until I call you tomorrow, okay?"

The words seemed to hang in the air, distant and surreal, as if they came from someone else, someone far removed from the terror Emily was feeling. She struggled to process the words. Sam was lost, Mick was stuck in a cell, and she was powerless, trapped in a sea of fear and helplessness. Her mind raced, trying to make sense of it all, but it was as if the ground had been swept from beneath her.

"You don't understand!" she cried, her voice quivering with the weight of everything she couldn't control. "I can't just sit here while you're out there, while he's out there, somewhere... hurt or lost or, "

"I'll be back tomorrow, Em," Mick interrupted, his voice firmer now. "I promise. You have to trust me. Just take care of yourself, okay? I'll call you as soon as I know more." The words were hollow in his own ears, but he needed her to hear them, to believe them, if only for the night. He needed her to stay calm.

Emily's sobs broke through the phone, and Mick felt every one of them like a blow to the chest. "I can't lose you, Mick. I can't lose him. I can't, "

"I know, Em," Mick murmured, his voice full of helplessness. "I know. Just wait for me. I'll come back to you. I'll find him. I swear to you." He swallowed hard, trying to steady the tremor in his voice. "But for now, just,… just go to sleep, okay? We'll talk tomorrow. I love you."

The words seemed inadequate, but they were all he had. A long pause followed, the sound of Emily's ragged breathing filling the space. Finally, she whispered, a small, broken sound. "I love you, Mick. Please,… please come home."

"I will, Em," Mick said softly, though deep down he wasn't sure if he would. "Goodnight. I'll see you tomorrow."

With the click of the receiver, the silence in the small, cold police station felt deafening. Mick sat there for a long while, staring at the phone, his mind racing. He knew he had no answers. He knew nothing of Sam's fate, nothing of what had happened out there on the tracks. Only one thing was certain, he couldn't leave the station, not yet, and there was nothing Emily could do but wait.

And so, in the quiet of that sterile room, Mick allowed himself a moment to close his eyes, to steel himself for the uncertainty ahead. Tomorrow, they would search for Sam. Tomorrow, they might find answers. But tonight,…

tonight, he had nothing but his own fear and the gnawing feeling of helplessness.

Mick awoke with a jolt, the clang of the cell door scraping open cutting through the haze of sleep. For a moment, his senses were foggy, but the sharpness of the morning light and the steady hum of the police station slowly brought him into full awareness.

A figure stood in the doorway, a tall, athletic-looking young constable, maybe in his late twenties, with a tight, purposeful stance and a face that suggested discipline. "Morning," the constable said, his voice smooth but with a distinctive accent. "Breakfast?" he asked, his hand motioning toward the table beyond the cell.

Mick rubbed his eyes and stretched stiffly, the weight of the previous day's events still heavy on his mind. "I suppose I could eat," he mumbled, getting to his feet. His stomach growled in protest; the events of the past twenty-four hours had left him with little appetite, but now the gnawing hunger was a reminder of just how long it had been since he'd last eaten a decent meal.

The constable led him down a narrow corridor and into what looked like a small lunchroom. On a table, two slices of toasted bread sat on a plate, accompanied by a metal mug filled with black coffee, a tub of margarine, and a plastic knife. The whole spread was simple, utilitarian, no frills, just fuel for the day.

"Help yourself," the constable said, gesturing with his chin. "No milk or sugar for the coffee, unfortunately. But the boffins will be here around nine to take you up to your camp, get the search going. Best eat up while you can."

Mick nodded, trying to shake off the grogginess that still clung to him. He picked up the mug, cradling it in his hands, letting the warmth seep into his cold fingers. The coffee was harsh, black and bitter, but it would do. As he reached for the toast, a thought struck him, and he glanced up at the constable.

"Are you from South Africa?" Mick asked, his curiosity getting the better of him. The constable's accent had nagged at him ever since he'd first heard it, and now that he was more awake, it sounded unmistakably like a South African's.

The constable gave a short nod, his lips twitching into a small smile as though he'd been asked this question a hundred times before. "Yes, I'm from Paarl, just north of Cape Town," he answered, his voice carrying the lilt of his homeland despite the clear effort to flatten it.

Mick found himself intrigued. "Paarl, huh? Still sounds like you've got a bit of the old accent," he said, taking a bite of the toast. It was dry, but it was food, and at that moment, that was enough.

The constable chuckled, the sound rich and warm. "Yeah, well, I've only been here just over two years. I was in the South African Police Service, SAPS, then moved into the STF, Special Task Force. But after a while, it felt like I was working for people who didn't appreciate what I was doing, you know? Unappreciated.

My folks moved to New Zealand, so I thought I'd give Australia a shot. Anyway, name's Jonty Wagner," he said, extending a hand across the table.

Mick shook his hand, the grip firm but friendly. "Mick West," he replied, still trying to wake up fully. "Sounds like you've been through some heavy stuff."

Jonty shrugged, the movement easy, almost casual. "You could say that. But, like I said, it wasn't the same when I came here. Different world, different problems." His eyes darkened briefly, a shadow passing over them before he straightened up, clearing his throat. "Anyway, you'd better hurry. The lab team will be here soon, and you don't want to keep them waiting."

Mick nodded, suddenly aware of the urgency in the air. He took another swallow of the coffee and set the mug down. The search for Sam was about to begin in earnest, and Mick's nerves were already fraying at the edges. He still had no idea what had happened to his friend, but he knew one thing for sure: whatever it was, it was no longer just a case of a missing man, it was something much darker, something far worse. And the clock was ticking.

The sun had already climbed higher in the sky when two detectives walked into the lunchroom, the crisp clatter of their boots on the tiled floor echoing in the otherwise quiet space. The first, a tall, broad-shouldered man with dark, intense eyes, was Damien Crowe. The other, Richard Thomas, was slightly shorter, but his sharp features and methodical gait made it clear that he was just as formidable.

Richard stepped forward first, a white pair of nylon overalls in his hand. He tossed them at Mick without so much as a word of introduction. "Get undressed, place your clothes on the table, and put these on," he ordered, his voice flat, leaving no room for discussion.

Mick felt a cold knot tighten in his stomach as he obeyed, removing his clothes and folding them neatly on the table as instructed. He pulled on the overalls, their fabric stiff and unfamiliar, and felt the chill of the material against his skin. As he did so, Damien Crowe produced a large white plastic evidence bag, its surface gleaming in the harsh fluorescent light of the room.

"Spell your surname, Mick," Crowe's voice was businesslike, but there was an edge to it.

Mick, feeling his pulse quicken, stammered out the spelling of his name as Crowe scribbled it on the bag with a thick black texta. Once the bag was marked, Crowe moved quickly, folding Mick's discarded clothing with precision and dropping them into the bag. The weight of the situation was sinking in now, a gnawing sensation of dread creeping up his spine as he realised just how far this had gone.

Without another word, Mick was escorted outside and shoved into the back of a police Landcruiser wagon, its doors slamming shut with a finality that echoed in Mick's mind. The vehicle rumbled to life, and the two detectives took their places in the front seats. Crowe, silent and unreadable, gripped the wheel, while Thomas's eyes flicked to the rearview mirror, his expression distant.

The drive was a quiet one, the road stretching out before them in long, dusty stretches. It wasn't until they reached the rough, uneven trail leading up to the camp behind Glen Russell that Mick began to feel his nerves truly unravel. It was only the second time he'd been to this place, and despite his best efforts to remember the turns, the landmarks, the exact path to follow, he found himself feeling lost again. The Landcruiser bounced and jolted over the rough terrain, the suspension groaning under the strain. Finally, they came to a halt about thirty metres from the camp, the engine cutting out with a sharp hiss of steam.

"Out," Crowe's voice came from the front, cold and impersonal. "Don't move until I tell you."

Mick climbed out of the vehicle, the air thick with the heat of the day. As he stood there, trying to steady his breathing, he saw two more police vehicles pull in behind them. Officers in dark uniforms emerged, some with equipment bags, others with the grim set of faces that only came with the weight of experience. They moved with practiced efficiency, and Mick felt the weight of their eyes on him, the feeling of being cornered tightening in his chest.

Crowe motioned for Mick to move forward, leading him toward the camp. The officers gathered around, forming a loose circle around Mick. He felt small under their scrutiny, the tension thick in the air.

"Okay, West. Run us through what happened here over the weekend," Crowe's voice was clipped, a sharp edge to it, like he was testing Mick's resolve, pushing for something more. The words stung, as if they carried an accusation beneath them.

Mick's mind raced, trying to find the right words, the right details. His throat was dry, his heart thudding in his chest. He cleared his throat, trying to steady himself, and began to speak, his voice quieter than he intended.

"This is where Sam and I set up camp last Friday afternoon," Mick began, pointing toward the area where the remnants of their campfire still smouldered faintly. "We spent the night here. On Saturday morning, we split up to go metal detecting. He went off in one direction, and I went the other. We agreed to meet back for lunch around midday. After we ate, we went out again to continue the search, each of us with our detectors."

Mick paused, his mind tracing the events with a brutal clarity. He swallowed hard, then continued.

"But when Sam didn't show up by the afternoon, I tried to contact him on the UHF radios we had. No response. I walked up to the ridge, thinking I might spot him from there. But he was gone. I couldn't find him, and when I went back to camp, I realised I'd lost the keys to the Landcruiser. That's when I decided I had to leave the camp and try to get help. Yesterday morning, I set off towards Marianvale."

Crowe's gaze never wavered, his expression unreadable as Mick spoke. The silence that followed felt oppressive, like the weight of the world had settled on Mick's shoulders. He could feel the eyes of the officers on him, but he kept his head down, unwilling to meet their gaze.

"Anything else you think we should know?" Crowe asked, his voice cold but edged with something darker, something Mick couldn't quite place.

Mick shook his head, feeling the fatigue in his bones, his mind spinning with worry for Sam. "No, that's it. That's everything I know."

The detectives exchanged a quick glance, and then Crowe gave a short nod. "Alright. Let's get started," he said, his tone leaving no room for argument.

The interrogation room at the Mareeba police command centre was cold and sterile, the harsh fluorescent lights above flickering intermittently, casting an eerie glow on the bare walls. Mick sat at the small, metal table, his hands resting on the worn surface, his eyes darting to the door every few seconds, waiting for the detectives to return. His thoughts were a tangled mess of fear, confusion, and worry for his friend Sam. The silence in the room stretched on, suffocating him, each passing minute feeling like an eternity.

It had been nearly an hour and a half since Damien Crowe and Richard Thomas had left him alone, and Mick's patience was wearing thin. He tried to focus on the events of the weekend, the walk up the hill, the moments spent with Sam, the discovery that his friend had gone missing. But the more he thought about it, the more the gnawing feeling in his gut grew. Something wasn't right. He was being treated like a criminal, when all he wanted to do was find his friend.

The door finally swung open, and Damien Crowe stepped inside, his cold, calculating eyes locking onto Mick. Richard Thomas followed closely behind, his face impassive as always, his sharp features betraying no emotion.

They sat down across from Mick, and for a moment, the room fell into a tense silence. Then, Damien broke it with a question that hit Mick like a slap in the face.

"What was it that you argued about, Mick?" Crowe's voice was low, almost casual, but the weight of the question hung heavily in the air.

Mick blinked, taken aback. "Sorry, what did you say?" he stammered, his mind racing to process the question. "I don't know what you mean. I never argued with Sam. We always got along really good, that's why I was camping out with him. We get along. He's my best mate."

Richard Thomas leaned forward slightly, his gaze sharp, calculating. "Why were you jealous of Sam, Mick? Because he wasn't tied down with a wife and kids, because he could do what he wanted, when he wanted? Is that it?" His tone was insistent, as if he were prying for something Mick didn't want to admit.

Mick's chest tightened, the frustration bubbling over. "Look," he snapped, his voice rising, "I don't know what you guys are on about. My mate Sam is missing, and I should be out there helping to find him. Why have you got me in here? What's happening?" His voice was raw, laced with a desperation that made his words feel jagged in his mouth.

But the detectives weren't done. Damien Crowe's eyes narrowed, his lips curling into a slight smirk as he leaned in. "Why did you kill Sam?" he asked, his voice a venomous whisper that seemed to send a chill through Mick's veins. "How much did he leave you in his will? Did you know that you're the sole benefactor? Big dollars, Mick. What plans do you have now?"

The accusation hit Mick like a punch to the gut. His blood ran cold, and for a moment, the room seemed to close in around him. His fists clenched involuntarily, the sudden surge of anger making his pulse quicken. "Fuck off!" he shouted, standing up abruptly, the chair scraping loudly against the floor. "Sam was my mate! No way would I harm him! What's with you guys? You're sick. The pair of you!"

But Crowe and Thomas weren't backing down. Crowe's gaze was unwavering, and his voice dropped even lower, almost coaxing. "We know you killed him, Mick. Just tell us where you put his body. Come on, man, get it off your chest. We're here to help you, Mick."

Mick's head spun. His thoughts were a blur of disbelief and rising panic. He could feel the walls closing in around him, the heat in his chest intensifying. The words were too much, too absurd to comprehend. How could they accuse him of something so monstrous? He felt trapped, suffocated by the weight of their questions, their insinuations. He opened his mouth to protest, but no words came out. All he could hear was the pounding of his own heart, the blood rushing in his ears.

The silence stretched on, thick and suffocating. Mick took a deep breath, trying to steady himself, to regain some semblance of control. "You don't know what the hell you're talking about," he muttered, his voice hoarse. "Sam's out there, and I'm going to find him. I'm not the one who did anything to him."

But Damien Crowe's expression remained unyielding. He leaned back in his chair, folding his arms across his chest, the faintest hint of satisfaction playing at the corners of his mouth. "We'll see about that, Mick. We'll see."

Mick felt the room closing in around him. The air had thickened, laced with the scent of sweat and stale coffee, and the relentless scrutiny of the two detectives bore down on him like a vice tightening around his chest. He had come here expecting help, expecting urgency in the search for Sam. Instead, he was caught in a web of insinuations and half-truths, forced into a corner by men who had already decided he was guilty.

A cold realization settled over him like a shroud, this was turning into a nightmare far worse than the one he had already been living. It was bad enough not knowing what had happened to Sam, but now it seemed the police were convinced that he had killed his best mate and hidden the body somewhere in the wild, unforgiving bush.

Mick took a deep breath, forcing himself to stay calm. He needed to regroup, to take control of the situation before they twisted his words further. His voice was steady when he finally spoke.

"I need to talk to a lawyer."

Richard Thomas' lips curled slightly, almost as if he had been expecting this. His eyes gleamed with something unreadable as he leaned forward, his tone dripping with feigned curiosity. "Why would you need to talk to a lawyer if you're as innocent as you say you are?"

Mick didn't blink. "I need to talk to a lawyer," he repeated, this time with more force.

Damien Crowe let out a short, humorless chuckle. "Why?" he demanded. "You say you haven't done anything. You haven't been arrested. So why the sudden need for legal counsel?"

Mick met his gaze head-on. "If I'm not under arrest, then I'm free to leave," he said evenly, watching their reactions closely.

Crowe's smirk didn't falter. "Of course, you're free to leave," he said, pushing his chair back and rising to his feet. "I'll go and get your clothes. Forensics should have finished with them by now." He strode to the door, pausing only briefly before disappearing into the corridor.

Richard Thomas remained seated, his fingers drumming absently on the tabletop. He regarded Mick with an expression that was almost paternal, as though he were dealing with a stubborn child. "You're making this harder on yourself, Mick," he said smoothly. "If you just tell us what really happened, we might be able to work something out. We won't be so nice next time. I can promise you that."

Mick said nothing. He had played their game long enough.

Moments later, Crowe returned, tossing a familiar white plastic bag onto the table with a careless flick of his wrist. "You can get changed in the toilets down the hall to the right," he instructed. "Just leave the overalls on the floor in there. See you around, Mick."

Richard Thomas leaned back in his chair, a smirk playing at the corners of his mouth. "Yeah, look after yourself, Mick."

Mick grabbed the bag and strode out of the room without another word. His muscles were tight with tension, his jaw locked against the anger simmering inside him. The air outside the interrogation room felt marginally less oppressive, but he knew the fight was far from over.

As he walked down the corridor, his eyes lifted to the reception area ahead. And then he saw her.

Emily.

She stood there, shifting anxiously from foot to foot, her arms crossed tightly over her chest. The moment her eyes met his, relief flooded her face, but there was fear there too, uncertainty, confusion.

"I'll be there in a minute," Mick called out as he passed, heading toward the toilets to change.

He could feel her eyes on him, filled with questions.

And Mick knew he didn't have any answers.

The clock on the dashboard glowed a pale green, marking the time as just past ten o'clock in the evening when Mick slid into the passenger seat beside Emily. The police command centre loomed behind them, its harsh fluorescent lights casting long shadows across the near-empty parking lot. Emily's hands were gripping the steering wheel so tightly her knuckles had turned white, her breath coming in short, panicked bursts.

"What the fuck is happening, Mick?" she half-screamed, half-sobbed, her voice raw with fear and frustration.

Mick exhaled slowly, staring straight ahead into the darkness beyond the windscreen. His voice, when he spoke, was unsettlingly calm, too calm, considering what had just transpired. "I think these pricks are convinced I've done something to Sam," he said, his tone almost detached. The shock was fading, replaced by something colder, more methodical. His mind was shifting gears, moving away from disbelief and towards action.

Emily's breath hitched, her eyes wide and glistening with tears. "But why? You told them what happened, didn't you? They know Sam's missing, that he could be hurt out there! What the hell are they doing keeping you locked up instead of looking for him?"

Mick turned to her then, taking in the frantic way her hands trembled on the wheel, the way her chest rose and fell in uneven gulps of air. She was in no state to drive, not like this.

"Pull over," he said firmly.

Emily shook her head, as if refusing to acknowledge what was happening. "Mick, "

"Pull over," he repeated, sharper this time. "I'll drive."

She didn't argue. With a jerky motion, she veered the car onto the gravel shoulder, barely managing to throw it into park before breaking down into muffled sobs. Mick got out, moving around to the driver's side, and gently guided her into the passenger seat. He didn't speak. There was nothing to say that would make this better.

As he pulled back onto the road, the tyres humming against the bitumen, Mick finally started to lay it all out. His voice was measured now, deliberate, as he recounted the events of the weekend. He told her everything, the setup of the camp, the metal detecting, how they'd parted ways to search separate areas, and how Sam had never returned. He spoke of the desperate search, of trying to contact Sam over the UHF, of walking out of the bush alone when all other options had failed.

Emily listened in stunned silence, her breath hitching only when Mick told her about the police interrogation. "Jesus, Mick," she whispered. "They really think you, " She couldn't even finish the sentence.

Mick tightened his grip on the wheel. "I don't know what they think. They sure as hell aren't telling me much. All I know is, they're treating me like the prime suspect instead of the bloke who came looking for help."

"Are they even out there looking for Sam?" she demanded.

Mick sighed. "I don't know. They haven't told me anything."

Emily wiped at her face, her fingers trembling. "This is insane," she muttered. Then, as if remembering, she added, "We need to stop at Mum's. Pick up the kids."

Mick gave a small nod. "Yeah."

As soon as they were back home, Mick wasted no time. He picked up the phone and dialled a number he knew by heart. It barely rang twice before a familiar voice answered.

"Mick?" Dennis Kogan's voice was sharp with concern. "What the hell's going on?"

Mick exhaled and launched into it, recounting the weekend's events once more, this time with less emotion and more detail. Dennis listened in silence, not interrupting until Mick finally reached the part about the interrogation, the accusations, the way the detectives had tried to bait him into a confession for something he hadn't done.

Dennis let out a low whistle. "Yeah. That tracks. It's normal for the cops to suspect the last person who saw a missing bloke alive, especially if that bloke is a mate. Standard operating procedure."

Mick gritted his teeth. "Standard? That didn't feel fucking standard to me."

Dennis sighed. "They're trying to rattle you, see if you crack. Once they're satisfied you're not hiding anything, they'll ease up a bit. Might even start being helpful. But until then…" There was a pause, then Dennis' voice hardened. "Listen to me, Mick. Do not go back in for another interview without me or another legal rep sitting beside you. I don't care how friendly they seem, how much they act like they're on your side. You do not walk into that station alone again. Got it?"

Mick's fingers tightened around the receiver. He had always trusted the law. But now… now, it felt like he was on the wrong side of it.

"Got it," he said grimly.

"Good," Dennis said. "Now, get some sleep. You're going to need it."

Mick hung up, but sleep was the furthest thing from his mind.

By the time the first rays of dawn stretched over the Mareeba ranges, the story had already broken. It was all over the morning news, whispered through the corridors of the town, blasted over the radio, and flashing across television screens in kitchens and cafés.

'Police and State Emergency Services have launched a large-scale search for a missing man believed to have vanished in the rugged ranges around Mount Marian over the weekend. Authorities have not yet released the man's name, but it is understood he was accompanied by another individual on a gold fossicking trip. That man is currently assisting police with their inquiries.'

Mick stood in the kitchen, the half-empty cup of coffee growing cold in his hand as he stared at the television screen. The newsreader's polished voice was calm, detached, devoid of the chaos that had unfolded in his life over the past few days.

"Assisting police with their inquiries." He knew what that meant. They were still treating him as a suspect.

He clenched his jaw, forcing down the surge of anger that threatened to rise. This wasn't about him, it was about Sam. They should be out there looking for him, not sitting around playing detective.

Without hesitation, he picked up the phone and dialed the Mareeba police station. The line rang twice before a clipped voice answered.

"Mareeba Police Station."

Mick didn't bother with pleasantries. "It's Mick West. I want to help with the search for Sam."

There was a brief silence, followed by the officer's carefully measured response. "Search operations are being coordinated by the State Emergency Services. If you'd like to assist, you'll need to contact them directly."

Mick's fingers tightened around the receiver. "You're telling me I can't even go out there and help find my own mate?"

"SES has trained personnel on the ground, and they've got things under control."

That was it. Dismissed. Just like that.

Mick's jaw worked as he hung up and immediately dialed the SES. A woman answered this time, her voice softer but just as firm.

"Look, we appreciate the offer, Mr. West," she said after he explained himself, "but we've got enough volunteers on the ground. If you're interested in helping with future operations, we're always looking for new recruits."

Recruits. The word landed heavily, and Mick forced a bitter smile. Sam's missing now, not in six months when I've been trained to tie a rope properly.

He rubbed a hand over his face, exhaling sharply. There was nothing more he could do.

With no other option, he picked up the phone again and dialed another familiar number. His boss answered on the second ring.

"Mick," Kevin's voice was steady, laced with curiosity. "Bit of a bloody mess, eh?"

"You could say that." Mick sighed. "Look, that bloke they're talking about on the news, that's Sam."

There was a pause. "Jesus," Kevin muttered. "You alright?"

"I'll be back at work tomorrow. There's nothing I can do to help. Cops won't let me near the search." Mick kept his voice flat, but the frustration bled through. "They've turned it into a big deal. Even suspected me at one point."

Kevin made a low sound in his throat. "Not surprising. Cops always suspect the bloke closest to a missing person. It's like a script they follow."

Mick exhaled through his nose. "Yeah, well, it's a pretty shit script."

"They'll find him," Kevin said, with the certainty of someone who had seen these things play out before. "It's just a matter of time."

Mick wasn't so sure.

The search dragged on for eight gruelling days, combing through the unforgiving landscape of the Mount Marian ranges. Teams of SES volunteers, police officers, and even local bushmen scoured the rugged terrain from dawn until dusk, hoping to find some trace of Sam Young. Choppers buzzed low over the ridges, their searchlights slicing through the dense undergrowth, while dogs sniffed tirelessly through the gullies and dry creek beds. But the land held its secrets well.

By the following Sunday, with nothing to show for their relentless efforts, the decision was made to scale back the operation. The search teams dwindled. Hope, once a roaring fire, smouldered to embers.

A week later, on another bleak Sunday morning, the official announcement came. The search for Samual John Young was being called off.

Lost. Presumed dead.

The following Monday, Mick rang the Mareeba police station, his voice steady but laced with frustration. "I need to collect my gear," he said, referring to the equipment he and Sam had taken to the camp, their packs, tools, even Sam's LandCruiser, which had been hauled back to the station.

The officer on the other end hesitated. There was a long silence, followed by a curt reply. "Not at this time."

Click.

The line went dead.

Mick stared at the phone in his hand, a slow burn creeping through his chest.

Five days later, on a bright, scorching Friday afternoon, Mick was at work, going through the motions with the mechanical detachment of a man trying to ignore the weight pressing down on his shoulders.

Then they came for him.

Two police vehicles pulled up outside. Before he could react, the officers were on him, plainclothes detectives, uniforms flanking them, the sun glinting off their badges. The words hit him like a hammer.

"Michael Patrick West, you are under arrest for the murder of Samual John Young."

The world tilted.

Handcuffs snapped around his wrists. Rough hands shoved him towards the waiting police car. A blur of voices, faces, his workmates standing frozen, staring as he was bundled into the back seat.

The ride to Cairns was long and silent.

By Monday morning, Mick was standing before a judge in the Cairns courthouse. The prosecution painted their picture in bold, damning strokes, Mick, the last man to see Sam alive. Mick, the one who stood to inherit everything. Mick, the murderer.

Bail was denied.

The heavy iron doors of Lotus Glen Correctional Centre slammed shut behind him.

Six months. Six months of staring at the same grey walls, of waiting, of silence and whispers and the ever-present weight of accusation pressing against his skull.

And then, at last, the trial began.

Tuesday morning, Cairns courthouse. The gallery was packed, reporters, curious onlookers, and those hungry for blood.

The prosecution's case rested entirely on circumstantial evidence. There was no body, no murder weapon, no witnesses. But they had something else.

Tracker Martin Yawapillga.

A seasoned Northern Territory police tracker, Yawapillga took the stand, his weathered face impassive as he described what he had found in the wild country around Mount Marian.

Photographic evidence was presented to the court, Mick's boot prints, distinctive and unmistakable, leading up to the ridge where Sam had been searching for gold. The tracks vanished in the rocky terrain, wiped clean by the hard, unyielding stone.

But they reappeared.

They were there, clear as day, heading back to camp.

Other tracks, Sam's, presumably, were found heading toward the ridge. But none returning.

Then there were the footprints down by the river, winding through the undergrowth on the far side of the camp.

And that, the prosecution claimed, was the story written in the earth.

Mick had led Sam up to the ridge. Something had happened, an argument, a fight. Sam never came back.

Mick did.

And when the sun went down, he had moved through the bush, covering his tracks, hiding the body where no man would ever find it.

The prosecution's case was as ruthless and unrelenting as the land where Sam Young had vanished.

They laid out their final blow with forensic evidence, cold, clinical, and damning.

Blood.

Traces of it had been discovered on various parts of Michael West's clothing. Not his own. The forensic team had tested it, cross-referenced it with medical records. The results were indisputable.

The blood was Sam Young's.

Then came the knife. A sturdy, well-worn 200mm blade, belonging to Sam, its steel edge now a silent witness to whatever had transpired that fateful weekend. Blood samples had been taken from the blade, and once again, the results confirmed what the prosecution had suspected.

Sam Young's blood.

Mick's defence barrister, Robert Callaghan, fought hard to discredit the forensic evidence. He painted a picture of two mates in the bush, roughing it, cooking over an open fire, one of them, Sam, perhaps cutting himself in a clumsy moment, staining Mick's clothes in the process. He leaned on the claim that an accident had occurred on the Friday evening, a minor culinary mishap.

But there was no proof, no corroborating evidence to support the claim. The argument collapsed beneath the weight of the prosecution's case and was swiftly discarded.

As the trial drew to a close, the judge delivered his summation, his voice heavy with contempt.

The air inside the courtroom was thick with anticipation. The jury had been deliberating for almost two full days, and now, as they filed back into the jury box, every eye in the packed room fixed upon them.

Mick West sat stiffly in the dock, his face an impassive mask, but the slight twitch of his fingers against the wooden railing betrayed the storm raging beneath the surface. His lawyer, Robert Callaghan, leaned in slightly, whispering a last reassurance, but Mick barely heard him. His gaze was locked on the foreman of the jury, a broad-shouldered man in his fifties who cleared his throat and stood, clutching a single sheet of paper.

"Members of the jury, have you reached a verdict?" the judge, a stern-faced Justice Malcolm Grey, asked, his deep voice echoing across the silent chamber.

The foreman gave a curt nod. "We have, Your Honour."

The courtroom held its collective breath as the clerk approached and accepted the paper. He adjusted his glasses, glanced briefly at the words, then looked towards Mick West. "On the charge of murder in the case of the Crown versus Michael West, how do you find the accused?"

The foreman did not hesitate. "Guilty, Your Honour."

A murmur rippled through the gallery. Mick West closed his eyes for the briefest moment, then opened them again, his expression unreadable. His lawyer swore softly under his breath. Across the room, the prosecution team sat back in their chairs, their expressions smug but controlled. The lead prosecutor, Sarah Henshaw, folded her hands on the table, victorious.

Justice Grey adjusted his glasses and nodded solemnly. "Mr. West, please rise."

Mick stood slowly, his jaw tightening. He had known this moment was coming. There was no body, no eyewitness to the crime. But the weight of the circumstantial evidence had been too much. The bloody knife, the bloodstains on the tailgate of Young's LandCruiser, the damning will that left everything, over two point six million dollars, to Mick West. It had been enough.

The judge sighed, as though weary of the inevitability of it all. "Michael West, you have been found guilty of the murder of Samuel Young. While no body has been recovered, the Crown has demonstrated beyond reasonable doubt that you unlawfully took the life of the deceased. The evidence, though circumstantial, is compelling and overwhelming. The brutality of this crime, combined with the financial motive so clearly laid out before this court, leaves me with no alternative but to impose the maximum penalty."

He paused, his eyes hard upon the condemned man. "Michael West, I hereby sentence you to life imprisonment."

A collective exhale filled the chamber. There was no outburst from Mick, no protestations of innocence. He simply nodded once and allowed the guards to take him by the arms. As Mick West was led away to the cells below, he wondered, not for the first time, if they had truly beaten him, or if he had beaten them.

Because out there, somewhere, Samuel Young's body was still undiscovered.

"This crime," The Judge added, "is one of the most despicable known to man. A crime of betrayal, treachery, and greed. A crime so callous that a man would take the life of a friend, a friend who trusted him, who welcomed him into his confidence, all for the sake of wealth and personal gain."

Eric Phillip Simpson

It was a hot Tuesday afternoon when Eric Simpson pulled his Nissan Patrol to a halt about three hundred metres from the very camp where Sam Young had vanished thirteen months ago. The place was etched into local lore, a grim reminder of a tragedy that had rocked the outback and haunted the metal detecting community. Eric knew every contour of this rugged land from the news reports and whispered legends; he had chosen this spot for a reason.

Retired only four months earlier from Australia Post, Eric now lived in Innisfail, a small town in Far North Queensland, with his Italian wife, Leonora. Her father, a proud owner of a prawn trawler moored in Innisfail's harbour, had once sailed these waters with a hearty laugh and a steadfast spirit. But Eric's heart beat for another passion: fossicking. It was this yearning that had led him to purchase a gleaming new Minelab 6000 metal detector, a retirement gift that promised new adventures. Alongside it, they had splurged on a sturdy Nissan Patrol Ti-L and a Patriot Camper, dreaming of endless journeys across Australia's untamed wilderness.

Today, Eric was here not just to wander but to uncover secrets. He had devoured every scrap of news on the disappearance of Sam Young and the grim aftermath that had enveloped Michael West. In the hushed corners of metal detecting forums and Facebook groups devoted to fossicking, Eric had followed the discussions like a man chasing the ghost of a legend. Each post, each heated debate, added layers to the mystery of Sam Young, a man whose fate had become entwined with the rugged, unforgiving land.

With methodical precision, Eric began setting up camp. The air was heavy with the scent of eucalyptus and the distant murmur of the trees resting the breezes, a reminder of both the beauty and the brutality of the outback. As he cleared a small patch of ground, he couldn't help but feel the pull of destiny. There was an inexplicable reason he was drawn to this cursed spot, a sense that what had once been lost might yet be recovered, even if only in memory.

He laid out his modest belongings, a sleeping bag, a small stove, his trusty detector, each item a tool in the quest for secrets hidden beneath the red soil and ancient rocks. His hands, calloused from years of work and adventure, moved with the surety of a man who had learned to trust the land. As the sun dipped lower, casting long shadows over the scrub, Eric took a deep breath. He was ready to follow in the footsteps of those who had gone before him, to uncover the echoes of a story that had become legend in its own right.

Eric's mind was a forge of determination and wonder. From all he had gleaned from news reports and online chatter, it appeared that Sam Young had frequented this very spot, returning no less than six times in the year before his disappearance. To Eric, that was no random coincidence. It meant that Sam had been finding gold here; otherwise, why would he keep returning to the same rugged, unforgiving place? For Eric, it was a tantalising clue, a silent promise that the earth might still yield its hidden riches.

But when Eric shared his theory with Leonora, her reaction was as fierce as a tropical storm. In her strong Italian accent, she practically shouted, "What you are thinking, do you want to go on the missing list too? No fuckin a way we're going there!" Her eyes blazed with both concern and incredulity.

"Leonora," Eric tried to reason, his voice calm but insistent, "the man responsible for Sam's disappearance is locked up for life. There's no danger from him here. This is about gold, about what Sam found." He spoke with the quiet certainty of a man who had followed his heart and trusted the land.

Leonora's worry softened after much persuading. Eventually, with reluctant acquiescence, she agreed to join him on what he called a gold-seeking mission to the Mount Marian Ranges. It was a decision tempered by both love and fear, as the ghosts of the past mingled with the promise of riches hidden beneath the red soil.

Preparations began in earnest. Their Patriot Camper was nearly packed, its interior echoing with the promise of adventure, when fate intervened. Leonora's father, Carlos, who lived alone in his modest home on the Johnstone River and owned a prawn trawler, suffered a grievous fall. He fractured his foot and was left unable to walk without crutches. Leonora's maternal instincts flared, and she refused to leave him unattended until he was well enough to fend for himself.

Eric's heart sank as he realised that Carlos's accident would force the cancellation of their planned trip to Mount Marian. But Leonora, ever practical, insisted that if Eric truly wished to pursue the treasure hidden in those ancient ranges, he should go alone. "I won't be home much anyway, looking after Papa," she said, her tone firm yet laced with regret.

So on a cool Tuesday morning, with a resolve tempered by solitude, Eric set off alone. Instead of hauling the bulky camper, he opted for their self-erecting marque tent and a collection of lighter camping gear. Now, here he was, camp set up in the shadow of the rugged ranges. As the morning sun cast long, lean shadows over the scrub, he pulled out his MacBook Air, its screen glowing softly in the dawn light.

With meticulous care, Eric began to sift through the photos he had salvaged from the television search reports. He zoomed in on snapshots of the area, studying the gnarled trees and distinctive rock formations that marked the landscape. Every landmark was a potential signpost pointing toward the elusive campsite where Sam Young had vanished, where Mick West had last been seen.

His fingers danced across the keyboard as he annotated each image, piecing together a map of memory and mystery. Here, a twisted eucalyptus; there, a rocky outcrop like a sentinel watching over the land. Each detail brought him closer to the truth, to the hidden vein of gold that Sam had once followed.

Eric's heart pounded with the thrill of the chase, with the hope that somewhere among these ancient hills lay the key to unraveling the mystery of Sam Young's fate, and perhaps, in the process, uncovering the bounty the land had kept secret for so long.

It took Eric nearly an hour to pinpoint the precise location he'd been hunting for, a spot whispered about in the hushed forums and glinting in grainy television reports. With a determined set to his jaw, he began his ascent along the rugged incline, his new Minelab 6000 swinging rhythmically in his hand as he scanned the terrain. Every step stirred up red dust beneath his boots, and the wild outback seemed to whisper secrets of lost fortunes and ancient promises.

By the time he returned to camp, just before darkness swallowed the sky, Eric's heart was alight with anticipation. He pulled out his gold scales and, with trembling hands, measured the afternoon's yield: a whopping 37 grams of gold. The numerical value danced in his mind, a staggering three and a half grand. "You bloody ripper," he thought with a grin, already calculating that at this rate he'd repay the detector Leonora had gifted him in mere days.

Without delay, Eric stowed his newly acquired treasure and the scales into the Nissan's glovebox. The machine's interior was filled with the quiet hum of possibility as he set about heating a hearty meal of goulash that Leonora had packed for him. The aroma mingled with the lingering scent of eucalyptus and dust. With his stomach satisfied and his spirits buoyed by three stubbies of Great Northern Super Crisp, Eric retired for the night. Yet sleep eluded him; his mind was a cauldron of thoughts. The rush of three and a half grand earned in just a few hours filled him with both wonder and suspicion. He couldn't shake the thought that Sam Young must have known something vital to keep coming back to this very spot.

His thoughts drifted to Sam Young, the man whose fate remained a haunting mystery. Did Mick West really murder him? And why would a trusted friend betray another in such a savage manner? Or perhaps Sam had merely become lost in the unforgiving wilderness, a fate not uncommon in these parts. The possibility that Sam's body still lay hidden, perhaps mere metres away, gnawed at Eric's mind like a persistent ghost.

At dawn the next morning, Eric rose with the resolute determination of a man on a quest. He retraced his steps to the exact point where he had left off the previous day, his eyes scanning the landscape for his own markers. There, clinging to the trunk of a gnarled tree, was the yellow ribbon marker he'd placed, a beacon in the wilderness. From that mark, he set off in a north-easterly direction toward the end of the ridge where the terrain opened into a vast congregation of large boulders and rugged rock formations. There, he left another marker, a silent signpost for his own reference.

Standing amid the raw, ancient earth, Eric resumed swinging his detector. The machine's steady beeps punctuated the quiet morning air, a symphony of signals that spoke of hidden treasures and forgotten histories. This was where, he recalled, most of yesterday's targets had been found. Each ping from the detector was a note in a grand, untamed score, promising wealth and perhaps even clues to the enigmatic legacy of Sam Young. In that moment, beneath the vast outback sky, Eric was not just a fossicker chasing gold, he was a seeker of truth in a land where every rock and tree held a secret.

It was three o'clock on a sultry Friday afternoon when Leonora sat on the front step of their modest home, her eyes fixed on the dusty drive as if willing Eric to appear in the distance. She had spent most of the day at her father's house. Old Carlos, still as stubborn as the tides, was slowly recovering, though his grumbling was as ceaseless as the tropical rains. The impending wet season had already begun to lash the creeks, washing away prawns and leaving Carlos fuming at the thought of missing his daily chase after them. In a rare twist of practicality, Carlos had agreed to let his boats mate commandeer the trawler, with him merely observing, and a spare crew member would fill the void. With that settled, Leonora had returned home, heart heavy with anticipation for Eric's return.

By four in the afternoon, Leonora's concern deepened when her calls to Eric's mobile went unanswered, the device reporting that it was either disconnected or, more likely, out of range. The thought gnawed at her, for she knew Eric's phone was never off. As the sun sank lower and the day edged towards evening, the silence from his phone became an ominous echo.

By ten that night, the same message still glared from the screen. Anxiety now tight in her chest, Leonora's trembling fingers dialled the local police number, only to be met with endless rings before she reluctantly hung up, frustration mounting. At midnight, the worry had become unbearable. It was not like Eric to be late, nor to fall silent when trouble brewed. Desperation compelled her to dial triple zero.

After what felt like an eternity in the darkness, a voice finally answered. "Emergency, which service do you require?" the operator asked, his tone efficient and unyielding.

Leonora's voice wavered as she spoke, "My husband should have been home hours ago, I'm getting very worried."

The operator's tone remained impassive. "What service do you require? Do you want the police, fire brigade, or ambulance?"

Unsure and frantic, Leonora blurted, "I don't really know which one I should get. My husband, he's missing."

There was a brief pause, then the operator said, "What is your address, and I'll send the police."

"We're in the Cullinane area, just up from the hospital," she replied hastily.

"What is the street name and number?" the operator pressed.

Leonora's voice took on a hurried edge. "It's Eric Simpson's house, they'll know the house, okay?"

"Please give me your address, I need the address. What is the street name you live on?"

"It's Campbell Street, near the Leagues Club, you know where that is."

"What number on Campbell Street, and what town?"

Leonora's voice trembled as she answered, "Oh,..You're not in Innisfail? It's number 26, Innisfail. You know Innisfail."

"The police are on the way. Is your name also Simpson?" the operator inquired.

"Yes, I am Mrs. Simpson, Leonora Simpson," she replied, her voice quivering like a fragile leaf in a storm.

"Thank you, Mrs. Simpson. Please stay calm, the police will be there very soon," the operator assured.

Leonora clutched the phone, her heart pounding with fear and uncertainty as she waited, the oppressive night air thick with the scent of impending rain and the silent promise of resolution. The darkness seemed to echo her anxiety, each minute stretching out like an eternity until salvation arrived, or so she prayed.

The two police constables, cold and unyielding in the pale glow of the early morning, dismissed Mrs. Simpson's offer of coffee with curt efficiency. Their sole concern was to obtain the registration number of the Nissan Patrol that Eric Simpson had been driving. Leonora's brow furrowed; the car was new to them, and its registration papers lay tucked away in the glovebox. In a flurry of recollection, she suggested that perhaps the salesman at the Nissan dealership might recall the number, but the constable shook his head. At nearly two in the morning, such a man was unlikely to be at work.

Leonora recounted in halting phrases how Eric had left for an area near where, a year ago, a man had been brutally murdered. The police, however, pressed further, hinting that a town name would offer them a lead, after all, a year-old murder provided little direction without a proper location.

In that moment of desperation, a spark of memory flared within Leonora. She fumbled for her mobile phone and began flicking through her photos until she found it, a snapshot of Eric at the dealership, smiling broadly as he lifted the keys to their new Nissan. The photo was clear, capturing not only the sleek lines of the vehicle but also its registration number, boldly displayed on the plate. It was a moment of clarity in the chaos.

Holding the phone firmly, she passed it to the constable. He examined the image with a keen eye, then, with the deftness of a seasoned officer, activated the 'Airdrop' function. Within moments, copies of the photograph were sent to his own mobile and to that of his partner. With the registration number in hand, one constable hurried back to the police car to conduct a vehicle check and establish a lookout on the Nissan Patrol.

Meanwhile, the other constable continued his questioning of a distraught Leonora. "Which way did Eric go?" he asked, his tone low and inquisitive. "North or South?"

Leonora, still reeling from her anxiety, managed to reply, "It was... somewhere up past Cairns, some mountain where they find the gold. One of them got murdered, and the other ended up in jail, you know?"

"And how long ago was the murder?" the constable pressed.

Leonora's voice trembled as she answered, "About a year, maybe a year. And the murderer is serving life in prison."

The constable's eyes narrowed as he scrolled through his mobile phone, then he placed a quick call. Moments later, he returned, his voice taking on an air of significance. "Does Mount Marian ring a bell, Mrs. Simpson?"

Leonora's eyes lit up with reluctant recognition. "Yes, yes, it's Mount Marian," she confirmed softly.

With that confirmation, the police concluded their questioning. They left Leonora's house with stern instructions: keep your mobile phone close, and call us immediately if Eric turns up. As they departed, the dark night seemed to pulse with a renewed purpose, an unyielding hunt for a man who had vanished into the wilderness, and a mystery that would not rest until the truth was unearthed.

It was a grim Sunday afternoon when a patrol finally stumbled upon Eric Simpson's campsite in the rugged shadows of the Mount Marian ranges, not far from where Sam Young's ill-fated camp had once stood. The Nissan Patrol sat locked and silent, its metal frame glinting dully in the harsh light, while the self-erecting marque tent lay neatly closed, its flap tied secure as if its owner had only stepped away for a brief moment. Scattered around were small signs of life, a garbage bag holding three empty Great Northern stubbies and other bits of refuse, a nearby plate and utensils arranged meticulously on a folding table just outside the tent's entrance, and an Engel fridge, hooked to a solar panel, quietly storing pre-cooked food packages. Every detail of the camp exuded normalcy, an eerie testament to a man's careful planning, except for one glaring absence: Eric Simpson himself.

The camp was unnervingly pristine, as though its master had simply vanished into the wilderness, leaving behind only his carefully arranged belongings. The officers, their expressions grim and measured, decided to wait until dusk in hopes that Eric might return. As the sun slipped behind the horizon, casting long, sinister shadows over the scrubland, another police unit was summoned to secure the area, their presence a silent warning to the unforgiving land. It was now clear: Eric Simpson was missing.

The following day, the full force of police forensics descended upon the campsite. Specialists combed every inch of the area, examining the locked vehicle, scrutinising the neat array of camping gear, and inspecting the surrounding terrain with the precision of men determined to unravel a mystery. A joint search was mounted, with the State Emergency Services lending their rugged expertise to the investigation. It was eerily reminiscent of a search conducted a little over a year ago, a search that had yielded nothing more than whispered suspicions and unanswered questions. This time, too, the evidence led to a single, damning conclusion: Eric was nowhere to be found.

In the silent, unforgiving expanse of the Mount Marian ranges, the neat remnants of a once-vibrant camp stood as a ghostly testament to a man who had vanished without a trace, leaving behind only questions that would haunt the outback for years to come.

Search teams combed the rugged outback, and soon the yellow ribbons that Eric had meticulously placed in the gnarled branches of the scrub became clear markers of his passage. These were scattered along the trail where he had dug for gold, each vibrant strip a silent testament to his presence. Yet, aside from these ephemeral breadcrumbs, there were no further signs of Eric, no footprints, no discarded belongings, no hint that he had ever been there.

In a swift operation that matched the relentless efficiency of the outback itself, the entire campsite was packed up and hauled away by a tilt-tray tow truck to the Mareeba police station. Even the Nissan Patrol, standing like a sentinel amidst the desolation, was towed away. Mrs. Simpson provided a second set of keys, allowing the detectives to search the vehicle thoroughly. Every compartment was inspected; nothing was missing, except for one glaring absence: the Minelab metal detector.

The gold scales and a container holding a remarkable 37.2 grams of gold were found stowed safely in the glovebox, a silent promise of fortune amid the mystery.

The only item unaccounted for was the detector, presumed to be with Mr. Simpson himself. The only tracks discernible in the unforgiving terrain led from the campsite to the ridge. Beyond that, the ground turned too rocky and treacherous for any independent tracks to be distinguished. It was as if Eric had simply vanished between his neatly arranged camp and the rugged precipice where the boulders began their ancient, indifferent watch.

After six arduous days of search, the operation was gradually scaled down, and by the tenth day it was officially called off. Neither Eric Simpson nor his prized metal detector had been found. Forensic teams re-examined every inch of the campsite and the vehicle, but all yielded nothing more than the same sparse evidence, a ghostly reminder of a man who had vanished into the wild. The very same tracker, whose keen eyes had once unearthed vital clues in the case of Samual Young, could only locate the tracks around the campsite and two sets leading to the ridge. Yet, only one set of those tracks appeared on the return journey. In the rocky expanse of the ridge, the tracks were indeterminate, their origins obscured by the harsh, broken terrain, were they human, or the mere passing of an animal?

Tracker dogs were brought in, their sharp noses sniffing the air and the ground, but even they could not pick up Eric's trail. In Australia, a person is not declared dead until seven long years have passed, and so Eric Simpson remained an enigma, a missing man swallowed by the endless, unforgiving wilderness, his fate as murky and elusive as the desert mirages that danced on the horizon

It was about a month after Eric Simpson had vanished into the merciless outback when Mick West, haunted by the mystery of that disappearance and still reeling from his own wrongful conviction, decided to take a daring step. Determined to appeal his conviction on the grounds of new evidence, Mick managed to secure an appointment with a prison legal advice lawyer at Lotus Glen. The case of the missing Eric Simpson, with all its tangled threads of gold hunts and ghostly tracks in the wilderness, had caught the attention of those who knew the land well. They believed that something sinister was afoot among the fossickers in that remote region, and that Mick West, already behind cold, unyielding prison walls, had been wrongfully accused of a crime that was never his to commit.

Financially destitute and facing the bleak reality of his situation, Mick had no choice but to apply for legal aid. The system, as unyielding as the outback itself, demanded that any appeal be thoroughly vetted. His reason for appeal, cantered on the case of the missing Eric Simpson, had to be scrutinised by both legal aid and the prison legal advice lawyer. Only then would they refer him to the defence lawyer who had represented him at trial. This lawyer, if legal aid found the case viable, would be retained to take his appeal forward.

In hushed, somber meetings, the two lawyers poured over every scrap of evidence. They argued that the case of Eric Simpson was more than just a lonely mystery, it was a clarion call, a sign that something was deeply amiss in the remote fossicking regions. In their eyes, West must be entirely exonerated from any wrongdoing; how could a man confined within prison walls possibly have a hand in causing another to vanish into the wild? Yet, they conceded, the defence concerning the tracks left by West while searching for Young was too flimsy. The forensic evidence, the blood found on West's clothing, was claimed to have come from a minor cut suffered by Sam Young while preparing food, a scenario that had been dismissed as unfounded.

After long, bitter hours of deliberation, the verdict came down: there were insufficient grounds for an appeal. Mick was denied the right to challenge his conviction. The news shattered what little hope he had left. In a moment of raw despair, he confessed to his wife, Emily, that it seemed there was no hope of ever regaining his freedom, and that it would be futile for her to wait for him any longer.

But Emily was not one to surrender to despair. With a fierce, unyielding resolve, she looked into his eyes and declared that she would wait for him forever. "True justice will prevail, Mick," she vowed, her voice steady and full of a quiet power. "I don't know how, but I just know it. You are innocent, and one day, we will prove that to the world."

Her words, imbued with hope and defiance against an unjust fate, lingered in the air like a promise. Even as the cold machinery of the legal system continued its relentless march, Emily's unwavering faith shone like a beacon amid the darkness, a reminder that in the wild, untamed heart of Australia, the spirit of those who believed in truth could never be entirely extinguished.

Phillip James Laidlow

It had been just over a year since Eric Simpson had vanished into the unforgiving wilds of the Mount Marian ranges, a mystery that had long haunted the outback, when Phillip Laidlow, fresh from the crucible of the Queensland Police Academy at Belgium Gardens, Townsville, found himself transferred to the Mareeba command centre on general duties. For Phillip, who carried a quiet intensity and a relentless work ethic, the change of scenery was a welcome challenge. Whatever task was set before him, he attacked it with the vigour of a man determined to carve his own legend out of the rugged Australian landscape.

Mareeba suited Phillip perfectly. His parents still lived in Townsville, a place where his father, a proud Lieutenant Colonel stationed at the Laverack Army Barracks, had instilled in him a sense of discipline and adventure.

Townsville lay just over four hundred kilometres away, a five-hour drive that Phillip had come to cherish, if only for the rare chance to return home. To sweeten the journey, his parents had gifted him a Toyota SR5 Hi-Lux utility upon his passing out, a chariot worthy of traversing the harsh, red heart of Queensland. They had joked that he should visit them at least once a month, though ideally every weekend. Alas, the rigours of a 28-day roster, with only nine days off, meant such frequent returns were but a distant dream.

A solitary man by nature, Phillip had always found friendship elusive, and so he made the long drive to Townsville as often as he could, finding solace in the silent camaraderie of the open road. It was during a routine work lecture at the Mareeba command centre, a drab affair on missing persons, that Phillip first heard the name Eric Simpson again, and shortly thereafter, the tale of Samual Young. Yet what truly made Phillip sit up and listen was not the tragic vanishings themselves, but a brief, an almost offhand mention of the glinting bounty discovered in Simpson's Nissan: 37 grams of gold stashed away in a glovebox. None of the senior officers had spared a second glance at that detail, but to Phillip, it was like a siren's call from the depths of the earth.

Later that day, the oppressive heat of Mareeba gave way to a cooler evening as Phillip made his way to his rented unit in Cairns North, a modest refuge he'd chosen due to the scarce quality rental accommodations in Mareeba. The drive, a mere hour each way, afforded him the luxury of coastal air and a short walk to the vibrant hum of shops and clubs in Cairns City. Arriving at his Cairns North unit after the lecture, Phillip's mind buzzed with thoughts of gold. Sitting at his MacBook Air, he searched for the current price of gold, discovering that each gram fetched $97.68 on the market, with buyers willing to pay around $90 per gram. A quick calculation sent a jolt through him: 37 grams would be worth roughly $3,330.00. "Fuck me," he muttered, incredulous. Could it be that the lecture had misled him? Perhaps it was only 3.7 grams, not 37, that had been recovered, a trivial amount that explained the indifference of his colleagues. The discrepancy gnawed at him. For a moment, the spark of fossicking temptation lit within him, a wild, daring thought that he might take up the metal detector himself and delve into that same cursed ground. But the idea soon faded as reality reasserted itself.

With his mind still swirling with numbers and half-formed schemes, Phillip set aside his MacBook and headed out to the RSL. There, amidst the clink of glasses and the hum of evening chatter, he sought refuge in a few drinks and a hearty dinner, a temporary balm for the restless ambitions stirring within him, and a quiet promise that one day, the secrets of the outback would be his to uncover.

The following day at the station, Phillip sought to settle his restless mind on the gold matter without sounding like a fool. In the drab corridors of the police station, he approached a senior constable and inquired if there were any hard copies of the lectures available, anything that might clarify the details of that tantalising nugget of information. The constable, with a curt shake of his head, informed him that no printed versions existed; all the lectures were archived online on the police web portal, accessible only after logging in.

Frustration gnawed at Phillip, for the day's hectic events left him no time to log in. It wasn't until the following afternoon, during a rare 'study break', that he finally managed to connect to the site. There, scrolling through the previous lecture on missing persons, he found the moment that had set his heart racing: the part of the lecture that detailed how, in the glovebox of Eric Simpson's Nissan Patrol, a clear plastic container had been discovered holding exactly 37 grams of gold nuggets in varying sizes and weights.

His pulse quickened as he confirmed the details. It wasn't a typo or a misheard figure, 37 grams of gold, gathered in a matter of days. With renewed determination, Phillip quickly navigated the police web to locate the Eric Simpson case file. The recorded content was voluminous, but his eyes burned with focus as he sifted through every detail until he came upon the exact description of the search of the vehicle, again, 37 grams of gold nuggets, each one a glimmering secret from the earth.

Phillip's mind raced with questions. How long had Eric been prospecting out there? What lured him to that exact, seemingly enchanted spot in the Mount Marian ranges? And why, in the same vicinity, had Samual Young repeatedly visited, only to meet his grim fate? Phillip cared less for the tragic end of those men than for the mystery of their golden finds. In his mind, the numbers were the key, 37 grams in two days. Eric had left Innisfail on a Tuesday and was due home by Friday. In that brief span, he'd unearthed over three grand in pure, unadulterated gold.

The thought ignited a spark in Phillip, who had long harboured the quiet ambition of striking it rich himself. He recalled that the previous man to vanish in the area was no stranger to fossicking either, a seasoned prospector whose repeated visits to the same spot had become the stuff of local legend. Now, as Phillip pored over the details of the case, the gold found in Simpson's Nissan became more than just a number, it was a promise of the hidden riches that lay beneath the harsh red earth, a lure that had ensnared men and changed lives in the unforgiving outback.

In that moment, amidst the hum of the station and the sterile glow of his laptop screen, Phillip resolved to delve deeper into the mystery. He would learn everything he could about the case of Eric Simpson and Samual Young, not out of morbid curiosity, but to unlock the secret that had brought them both to that cursed place. For in the wilderness of Australia, where every rock and tree held a story, the gleam of gold was a beacon, and Phillip Laidlow was ready to follow its call.

Phillip had three rostered days off, and he spent them with an intensity that bordered on obsession. He scoured every scrap of media footage he could find on the search for Eric Simpson, pausing on grainy images of search teams combing the rugged terrain of the Mount Marian ranges. He studied the topography, memorising the gnarled trees and ochre-stained boulders that dominated the landscape. Every detail mattered. When he returned to work, he would need the exact coordinates of the search locations, data that he was certain lay buried somewhere in the police files.

At night, he turned his focus to the world of prospecting. On his fossicking Facebook page, he fired off a barrage of questions, quizzing seasoned prospectors about the best metal detectors for the job. The answers came thick and fast, and one reply stopped him cold, a man claiming that the top of the line detector, the legendary Minelab GPZ 7000, would set him back nearly $10,000. Phillip swore under his breath. That was a price tag he couldn't justify, not just for a detector. If he was serious about this, he'd need camping gear too, something durable, something that could withstand the harsh remoteness of the outback.

He spent the next day buried in research, his mind weighing cost against practicality, necessity against desire. By the time the sun dipped below the horizon, he had made his decision. He settled on a Minelab SDC 2300, a formidable piece of equipment, compact, powerful, and far more affordable at around \$3,500. He would need a hardtop canopy for his SR5, an investment of about \$4,000 to secure his gear in the unforgiving elements. And then there was the rooftop camper, another \$2,500, essential for those long, solitary nights under the stars.

Phillip did the math. Altogether, his plan would carve \$10,000 out of the \$14,000 in his savings. It would leave him with a cushion, enough for fuel, supplies, and whatever unexpected costs came his way. But most importantly, it would set him up to move. To act. To chase what had captured his imagination since that first moment in the station's lecture hall.

He leaned back in his chair, stretching his arms behind his head. A slow grin crept across his face. That will work, he thought. And it should be fun.

Back at the command centre in Mareeba, Phillip sat before the flickering glow of his workstation, his focus razor-sharp. He had located the full search file on Eric Simpson, combing through every detail with the keen eye of a hunter studying his prey. The coordinates were jotted down in meticulous order, precise waypoints leading to the last known whereabouts of the missing man. His iPhone brimmed with media footage, clips, images, and snippets of grainy news reports on the search effort. He had everything he needed to begin charting his own course into the Mount Marian ranges.

His next rostered days off would serve a dual purpose, equipping his vehicle for the rugged terrain ahead and spending time with his parents in Townsville. He had arranged to have a metal canopy installed on his SR5 Hilux, choosing a manufacturer in Townsville over the alternatives in Cairns. The reason was simple, Townsville had the heavy-duty steel model he wanted, while Cairns only stocked fibreglass.

The visit home was a welcome reprieve, a brief return to family life before he set off into the unknown. His father, the hardened Lieutenant Colonel stationed at Lavarack Barracks, was as sharp and disciplined as ever. His mother fussed over him, making sure he was eating properly, shaking her head at his latest obsession but offering no argument. They knew Phillip well enough, when he set his mind on something, there was no turning him away.

It wasn't until he returned to the canopy installers to collect his Hilux that he stumbled upon an unexpected boon. The company not only installed canopies but also supplied and fitted rooftop campers. Better yet, they assured him, installation would take little more than an hour. Phillip's grin stretched wide, one more item ticked off his list with hardly any effort. As he browsed the showroom while waiting, he found they also stocked a wealth of camping equipment, solar panels, storage units, and cooking gear. To top it off, they could fit a dual-battery system to his Hilux, ensuring he had power even in the remotest locations.

Within three weeks, he had everything he needed, his new Minelab SDC 2300 metal detector, the reinforced steel canopy, and the rooftop tent secured and ready for deployment. The transformation of his Hilux was complete; it was no longer just a vehicle but an expedition rig, a machine built for the wild.

Now all he needed was time.

His next three-day break was due the following Wednesday. It was tight, one day to get there, one full day to search, and another to return, but it was enough for a trial run. Each evening after work, he methodically stocked up on provisions, long-life food, bottled water, a gas burner, and a few cans of beer for the nights under the stars. By the time Wednesday morning arrived, there would be no delays, no hesitations.

The morning sun had already climbed high, casting long golden streaks through the thick humidity that clung to the land like an unseen hand. It was a typical December morning in the north, the air thick with moisture, the looming dark clouds more for show than storm. At 8:30 a.m., Cairns was already basking in 28°C, a heat that would only intensify as the day dragged on.

Phillip was far from the city now, his Hilux eating up the distance between him and the Mount Marian ranges. The road beneath him was a ribbon of dust and opportunity. He was eager, perhaps too eager, for what he hoped would be the first of many successful prospecting trips. His mind ran through every detail, every bit of research he had devoured, every fragment of information he had pieced together from the police files.

By midday, he had found it, the exact site where Eric Simpson had camped more than a year ago. It was a good location, well-chosen. Not too close to the river, sparing him from the nuisance of floods or mosquitoes, but near enough to fetch water when needed. The towering trees provided ample shade, their branches rustling in the restless breeze.

Phillip had never actually practiced setting up his rooftop tent before, an oversight, he now realised, but the instructions were clear enough. Step by step, he followed the guide, unfolding and securing the canvas like an old hand. Within minutes, it was up and ready, the small ladder leading up to his elevated refuge. He grinned. Easier than he'd thought.

His Engel fridge hummed softly in the rear canopy, the dual twelve-volt system ensuring a steady supply of power. He pulled out a can of xxxx Gold, the cold metal slick with condensation in his grip, and searched for somewhere to sit. It was only then that he realised his mistake, he had forgotten to bring a folding chair or table.

"Next time," he muttered, taking a long swig from the can.

The afternoon heat bore down on the land, the silence thick and unbroken. He finished his beer, wiped the sweat from his brow, and decided it was time for a quick reconnaissance. There was still daylight to burn, and he had come here to do more than just set up camp.

Slipping on his backpack, he slung his metal detector over his shoulder and began the climb up the ridge. The ascent was steep, but his determination was steeper. He reached the crest and pulled out the Minelab SDC 2300, flipping the switch to bring it to life.

The machine hummed, waiting to be tuned. He pulled the instruction manual from its carry bag, following the steps carefully as he ground-balanced the detector. The fine adjustments took only a moment, but in his focus, he placed the instructions atop a large rock and, without thinking, left them there as he moved on.

The silence was unnerving. The detector gave no signals, no beeps, no hints of hidden treasure beneath the earth. But Phillip pressed forward, his boots crunching over dry twigs and brittle leaves. Then, up ahead, something caught his eye, something that did not belong.

A flash of faded colour against the bark of a tree.

He approached and found a ribbon, its once-bright hue now dulled by the elements. It swayed slightly in the breeze, as if whispering a forgotten story.

Simpson.

Phillip knew the case well enough to remember this detail. Simpson had marked his route with two ribbons, both reportedly found and left untouched. This had to be one of them.

His pulse quickened. He was on the right track.

Tightening his grip on the detector, he pressed on, the hunger for discovery now a beast gnawing at his very core.

The sun had barely risen over the Mareeba Command Centre when the roster sheet for Saturday morning was checked. Among the names scrawled in neat black ink, one was conspicuously absent, Probationary Constable Phillip Laidlow had not signed in for duty.

The duty sergeant barely gave it a second thought. Young recruits often struggled to adjust to the rhythm of police life, and Laidlow was still in the early stages of his training. His role, at this point, was little more than an office shadow, learning how the machinery of the station functioned before being trusted with the streets. No doubt he had fallen ill or misread his schedule. Still, protocol dictated that an unexplained absence be noted. A brief entry was made in the logbook, a minor black mark on an otherwise unremarkable record.

By Monday morning, the story had changed. A different sergeant, reviewing the weekend's records, noticed that Laidlow had been absent since Saturday, without a single word of explanation. That was unusual. Even for probationary officers, discipline was expected. He flipped open Laidlow's personnel file and dialled the number listed on his contact sheet. The phone rang out. No answer. The sergeant made another note in the daybook, but now there was a shift in tone, a missing day was one thing, but disappearing entirely was another.

When Tuesday rolled around and Laidlow was still absent, the concern deepened into something more tangible. The sergeant, following standard procedure, tried his mobile number once more. Again, silence. A cold absence on the other end of the line.

This time, he took a different approach. He found Laidlow's residential address, a unit in North Cairns, and picked up the phone to the Cairns Police Station. Within minutes, a patrol car had been dispatched.

Twenty minutes later, the Cairns sergeant called back.

"There's no response," he said, his voice edged with a trace of concern. "We knocked. No movement inside, no lights on. If he's there, he's not answering."

A pause.

"What do you want us to do?"

The duty inspector at Mareeba was informed, and the matter was immediately escalated. Laidlow wasn't just missing a shift, he had vanished. The inspector made another call, this time to Townsville, to Lavarack Barracks, where Lieutenant Colonel Craig Laidlow, Phillip's father, was stationed.

The seasoned officer's reaction was immediate.

"What do you mean, he hasn't reported for duty?" Craig Laidlow's voice was sharp, filled with the quiet authority of a man unaccustomed to uncertainty.

"He hasn't signed in since Saturday morning," the inspector confirmed. "We've tried contacting him, checked his residence, nothing. We were hoping you might know where he is."

There was a long silence on the line. When Craig Laidlow spoke again, his voice had lost its edge, replaced by something colder.

"The last time we saw Phillip was three weeks ago," he said slowly. "He visited us in Townsville. We haven't heard from him since."

The inspector leaned back in his chair, a heavy weight settling in his gut.

Phillip Laidlow had disappeared.

The warrant was processed with the quiet efficiency of men who had done this many times before. Cairns Police wasted no time. Within the hour, a team arrived at Phillip Laidlow's apartment complex, the warrant in hand, their expressions unreadable beneath the brims of their caps.

The secure building presented little challenge. A uniformed officer, accompanied by the building manager, keyed in the security code, granting them entry. They moved with measured precision, their boots silent against the polished corridor floors. Apartment 6B, Laidlow's residence, stood before them.

A final knock. A pause. Then the officer in charge gave a nod.

The door swung open under the practiced force of the locksmith's tools, revealing a space that was both lived-in and undisturbed. There were no signs of forced entry, no disorder, nothing to indicate a struggle. A cursory sweep of the apartment told them what they already suspected, Laidlow wasn't here.

The lounge was neat, sparsely furnished, the air carrying the faint scent of detergent and aftershave. A half-finished bottle of water sat on the kitchen bench, the refrigerator hummed softly in the background, and a pair of running shoes were neatly positioned near the door. His bed was made, the sheets crisp. His police-issue notebook and standard-issue radio remained on the desk, untouched.

But something was missing.

His vehicle.

A check of the secure basement parking confirmed it, his allocated space was empty. Wherever Phillip Laidlow had gone, he had taken his vehicle with him.

The officers moved to the next stage of the investigation, speaking with the neighbours. A methodical door-knock yielded little. A handful of residents remembered seeing Laidlow in passing, a polite young man who kept to himself. None of them knew much about him. None had seen him in the last few days.

Not one of them knew he was a police officer.

As the officers closed their notebooks, one thing was clear, Phillip Laidlow had not simply overslept. He was gone, and no one had the slightest idea where he was.

At the Mareeba Command Centre, the walls of the operations room felt as though they were closing in. The general, internal notice had gone up, an open request for any information regarding the whereabouts of Constable Phillip Laidlow, but the response was nothing more than a void. A cold silence filled the air. Laidlow had only been at the centre for a matter of months, just enough time to gather a few acquaintances, yet not enough to form any meaningful connections. He was a solitary figure, a quiet observer of his surroundings, always focused on his work but keeping his distance. The nature of his absence, his sudden disappearance, raised more questions than answers, and the station seemed unsure whether to fear the worst or cling to the hope that Laidlow would turn up safe, albeit a little embarrassed by the concern he had caused.

As the days wore on, the search continued. An all-points lookout was issued, a 'missing person' alert sent out, but Phillip Laidlow's name did not generate any substantial leads. The matter was in the hands of the investigation team, but their efforts were hindered by the sheer lack of information. His parents, distraught and grasping for any thread of hope, were in constant touch with the acting duty inspector at the Mareeba Command Centre. They offered what they knew, however limited it was. They mentioned the recent installation of a metal canopy on Laidlow's Hilux, the rooftop tent they assumed he had planned to use for camping, perhaps an escape into the wild, something he had always wanted but had never had the chance to fully indulge in.

They failed to mention the metal detector, perhaps because they hadn't known about it, but this one omission would come to haunt the investigation, for it was the metal detector that would soon unravel a trail leading into the heart of the rugged wilderness. Despite this, the police made public appeals in the hopes that someone might have seen Laidlow, hoping to turn the tide of their investigation. The calls flooded in. Dozens of reports, each one seemingly leading to a dead end.

Then, four months passed. Time became a cruel adversary, and hope began to wither as the search for Phillip Laidlow grew colder with each passing day. That was, until two campers, weary and windblown from their trek, stumbled upon something that set the investigation in motion again, a vehicle, left alone on a stretch of dirt track in the Mount Marian Ranges.

The campers had come across the Hilux in a state that suggested it had been abandoned for a long time. A thick layer of dust coated the vehicle, the tires flat and caked in mud, but what struck them most was the eerie sense of desolation that clung to the scene. No one was around, the vehicle locked and empty, the rooftop tent neatly folded but untouched. There were no signs of human presence, no footprints in the dirt, no evidence of movement, just the forlorn vehicle and the quiet, oppressive stillness that hung in the air like a heavy fog.

The campers immediately contacted the authorities, and within hours, the police arrived. They confirmed what had been feared, the vehicle belonged to Phillip Laidlow. The registration was an exact match. A brief search around the vicinity yielded no immediate clues, so the site was secured, and a forensic examination was set to take place.

This would be the third time in nearly as many years that Mount Marian had played host to a forensic team. The area had earned a dark reputation, a place where mysteries and disappearances seemed to find their way. As the forensic team began their work, they noted the grim remnants of someone's time in the wilderness. A plastic garbage bag containing an empty can of beer, discarded without ceremony, lay near the vehicle. But the real discovery came when they opened the back door of the Hilux canopy.

The foul stench that hit them was overwhelming, a putrid smell that suggested the presence of something much worse than spoiled food. It was a smell that set their senses on edge, and their instincts screamed that something darker lay hidden within the canopy. They steeled themselves, expecting the worst, but as they uncovered the source, they realized that the smell wasn't the result of a body, but of rotten food in the Engel fridge, food that had been left behind, forgotten, as though someone had been interrupted in their preparations, abandoned in haste.

A thorough search of the vehicle began. The police dusted every surface for fingerprints, looking for any trace of Laidlow, any evidence that might tell them where he had gone, what had happened to him. The vehicle, locked and seemingly abandoned, held secrets, but it would take time to uncover them.

Once the search was completed, the Hilux was transported to Mareeba Police Station for further analysis. The forensic team would continue to work through the night, piecing together fragments of evidence in the hope that they could finally break through the thick veil of mystery that surrounded Phillip Laidlow's disappearance.

But deep down, both the police and Laidlow's family knew that this discovery, while significant, was only the beginning of a much larger, much more complicated search that would take them into the treacherous heart of the Mount Marian Ranges.

The early morning sun bathed the Mount Marian ranges in a harsh, unforgiving light. A sharp wind blew across the dry, parched earth, whipping up dust and debris, as the police and SES personnel gathered at the command post to begin the search for Constable Phillip Laidlow. The air was thick with the scent of earth and sweat, and the tension was palpable. Each man and woman, whether uniformed officer or volunteer, knew the stakes. Laidlow had vanished without a trace, and the discovery of his vehicle had raised more questions than answers. This was no longer just a search for a missing person, this had become a hunt for the truth, a search for something far darker than anyone had anticipated.

By dawn on the first day of the search, the teams were spread out, combing the terrain with the diligence of seasoned trackers. The air was thick with the sound of boots crunching against dry leaves and gravel. As the hours wore on, every inch of ground was turned over with meticulous precision. Then, around mid-morning, the first significant find was made. It was an unassuming object, a manual.

Lying next to a large rock, half-buried beneath the dried grasses and low shrubbery, the faded, almost indiscernible instruction manual for a Minelab SDC 2300 metal detector lay discarded in the dirt. It was clear that the document had been left in haste, perhaps even dropped in the heat of a pursuit. The discovery sent a ripple through the search team. The detector, an expensive and sophisticated piece of equipment, had been part of Laidlow's gear, a tool for prospecting, for finding the unseen treasures buried beneath the earth. But why had it been abandoned here, in this desolate place? The question lingered like the oppressive heat.

The search continued relentlessly, each day bringing more discoveries but fewer answers. On the third day, as the searchers expanded their grid, one of the SES members discovered something that sent a shiver through his spine. He had been combing through a cluster of tussocks, the dry, waving grass that dotted the landscape. It was there, among the blades, that he found something strange.

The grass had been disturbed, and as he moved it aside, he noticed dark spots scattered across the ground, small, irregular patches of a black substance. With careful hands, he gathered the grass and placed it into an evidence bag. As he stood up, his heart pounded in his chest. The substance was unmistakable, it was blood. But whose?

He immediately called for a supervisor, as protocol dictated. The supervisor, a seasoned officer accustomed to the rigours of the field, came over and inspected the find. He glanced at the bloodstained grass and, at first, dismissed it with a scoff. "Bullshit," he muttered, his voice tinged with frustration. "That's just bird shit, stop wasting our time."

But the searcher insisted, standing his ground. There was no mistaking it. This wasn't the result of a careless bird. The substance was blood, and it needed to be examined properly. With a reluctant sigh, the supervisor nodded, and the bag was carefully sealed, marked with its precise location for further investigation.

The search carried on, but now the team's focus shifted. The blood, found just below the tree where the second faded yellow ribbon had been placed by Simpson, was a chilling clue. The ribbon had been tied to a branch towards the end of the ridge, near where the rocky outcrops and boulders formed a natural barrier. The area had become a significant point of interest, especially since it seemed to link the Simpson case to Laidlow's disappearance in some obscure and haunting way.

The days blurred together as forensic teams worked tirelessly, collecting evidence and piecing together the fragmented story. Back at Mareeba, the forensic experts had their hands full, but their dedication never wavered. The blood sample from the grass tussocks was sent to the Queensland University of Technology for analysis. The sample was put through rigorous Raman spectroscopy testing, looking for any trace of blood type, DNA, or any other sign that could lead them to a conclusion.

The results came back swiftly, and when they did, they shook the investigation to its core.

The blood was identified as belonging to Phillip Laidlow, there was no doubt. The DNA matched perfectly with a sample that had been provided by Laidlow's father, Craig Laidlow, in the hopes of aiding the search. The blood type, too, was an exact match. But the most disturbing finding of all was the date, the blood was determined to have been released from a body between 12 to 16 weeks prior. That meant that, for months, Laidlow had been gone, his blood staining the land long before the vehicle was found.

The implications of this discovery were far-reaching. The question of Laidlow's disappearance was no longer a simple matter of a missing person, this was something far more sinister. How had he come to be here, so far from the safety of his vehicle, and what had happened to him in the weeks following his vanishing? Was he alive, or had he been caught in the ruthless embrace of the wilderness, unable to escape its grasp?

As the police continued to piece together the timeline, one thing was becoming abundantly clear, the search for Phillip Laidlow was far from over. But the discovery of his blood in such a remote and desolate part of the

Mount Marian ranges was a grim confirmation that he had been here, and whatever had happened to him, it had left a trail that no one could ignore. The question now was whether they could find him before it was too late.

The air hung thick with the oppressive weight of the heat as the search for Phillip Laidlow continued in the unforgiving terrain of the Mount Marian ranges. The sweat-soaked faces of the searchers mirrored the exhaustion of days spent combing the landscape for even the slightest trace of the missing constable. Despite their efforts, the answers remained stubbornly elusive. But now, the presence of a cadaver dog in the search zone brought with it a faint thread of hope, a glimmer of something more definitive. The dog, trained to detect human scent, was the team's last, best hope of uncovering the truth.

The handler, a grizzled man with sharp eyes and an intuitive connection to his dog, watched closely as the animal, nose to the ground, trotted forward with its head lowered. The dog's every step seemed measured, deliberate, until it stopped at the spot where the blood had been found, a patch of disturbed earth and scattered grass. The handler's heart skipped a beat. This was no casual sniff. The dog's reaction told them everything. The search was no longer a matter of finding a lost man. It had become a hunt for answers, answers that could only be found in the silence of the rocks and the dust of the land.

The dog, nose twitching, moved up the ridge, its paws surefooted as it ascended the jagged rocks. The handler followed, every muscle taut, every instinct alive with the knowledge that they were closing in on something significant. The dog paused near a large rock outcrop, the kind of massive stone formation that had been carved by centuries of erosion. There, beneath an overhang, barely visible to the naked eye, was a dark stain on the rock face, residual, unmistakable, a testament to something that had happened here, something that needed to be uncovered.

The handler moved closer, his breath catching in his throat. The stain was black, a sharp contrast against the pale rock. He signalled for the team, and together they moved to secure a sample. But the rock, as tough as the land itself, proved stubborn. After several attempts to collect the residue, the team was forced to break off a small piece of the rock face. The task was difficult, the stone resistant, but they persisted, knowing the importance of what was at stake. The sample was taken, sealed, and secured, but no further traces of blood were found in the immediate area. It was as though the land itself had swallowed up whatever had transpired here.

As the searchers fanned out once more, their gaze drifted toward the higher rock formations. They were close enough now to see the resemblance to another infamous spot, the Black Mountain rock formation near Cooktown. The landscape around them seemed eerily similar to the treacherous labyrinth of boulders that had plagued explorers for centuries. Black Mountain, an ancient, imposing cluster of massive rocks, had long been shrouded in mystery and dark tales. It was known as the 'Bermuda Triangle' of Queensland, and for good reason. The stories of early explorers, horses, and cattle disappearing into its rocky depths had been whispered since the late 1800s. No one had ever fully understood the secrets it held, but those who ventured too deep never returned. It was a place where the land itself seemed to conspire against those who sought to conquer it.

For now, the search was at an impasse. The blood sample, though confirmed to be Phillip Laidlow's, did not necessarily point to foul play. It could have been the result of a minor injury, something innocent, perhaps even self-inflicted in the wilderness. The inspector in charge of the operation, made sure to include this in his report to the media when the search was officially called off after ten days. The ambiguity surrounding Laidlow's disappearance remained, though the case had taken a darker turn, leaving a trail of unanswered questions.

Back in the world of bureaucracy and legal channels, Michael West sat in his dingy cell, absorbing the weight of his thoughts. The disappearance of Laidlow had ignited something in him, a deep curiosity, perhaps even an understanding that this mystery might hold the key to his own redemption. He had been following the media reports about the missing fossicker with growing intensity. The connection to the case, the possibility of a link to the strange happenings in the Mount Marian ranges, was too compelling to ignore. With time on his hands, he felt an urge to dig deeper, to uncover whatever secrets might lie buried beneath the dust and stone.

Frustrated by the lack of progress in his own legal battles, West submitted another request to the prison's legal advisor, hoping against hope that this time, someone might be able to offer him some guidance. Initially, he had thought that it would be another waste of time, another futile effort. But then, in the quiet of his cell, he realised that he had all the time in the world now. Time to probe, to ask questions, to seek out the truth.

To his surprise, the prison legal advisor agreed to reach out to Legal Aid on his behalf. It took a while, but eventually, West's previous defence lawyer was located, only to learn that the lawyer had passed away. His replacement was a much younger, inexperienced barrister, a woman whose fresh-faced enthusiasm might have been a blessing if not for the fact that she was completely unfamiliar with West's case. She requested a month to study the file, a delay that only fuelled West's growing impatience.

In the meantime, he had all the time he needed. The Mount Marian mystery had become his new obsession, and he would stop at nothing to uncover the secrets of the land.

Three weeks passed before the word finally came back to Mick, the legal experts having convened to consider his appeal. The momentum of the case had shifted, and now, with the added weight of yet another missing person, Phillip Laidlow, linked to the same strange circumstances as Samuel Young, the scales had tipped in Mick's favour. In addition to the compelling case of Laidlow's disappearance, the legal team had secured a crucial piece of evidence: an excerpt from the inspector in charge of the search for Phillip Laidlow. The report read, "The blood sample, identified to be from Phillip Laidlow, did not necessarily indicate foul play; it could have resulted from a minor injury." This nuanced assessment, suggesting that the blood might not be connected to any violent act, was to become the cornerstone of Mick's defence, a "general consensus," as they called it, that would cast doubt on the connection between the disappearances and the suspected foul play.

Mick, for the first time in months, felt a flicker of hope. The appeal was lodged with renewed vigour, and within weeks, it was accepted as legitimate grounds for revisiting his case. The prospect of freedom, long a distant dream, now loomed closer than ever before.

When the news reached him, Mick was a changed man. His weathered face, hardened by years of bitter confinement, broke into a smile that lit up the dreary prison walls. Emily, his wife, came to visit him soon after, and the joy on both their faces was unmistakable. For the first time in years, Mick was allowed to breathe easy, if only for a moment. The weight of his wrongful conviction, his time behind bars, and the suffocating injustice that had choked the life out of him was finally beginning to lift.

But Emily, ever the realist, cautioned him. She knew better than anyone the slow crawl of bureaucracy. "It could take a while before it reaches court," she warned, her voice both hopeful and anxious, as she placed a hand on his. "But whatever happens, Mick, we've got a future ahead of us."

But the court date never came. The unexpected happened. The appeal was accepted, and Mick's case was overturned. In one moment, Mick went from a prisoner to a free man. The very walls that had confined him for nearly three years were now a memory, fading into the past.

It was a homecoming like no other. When Mick was released, the joy of being a free man mingled with an undeniable sadness. He was a man without a home, without the life he had left behind. Emily, in an effort to cope with the years of hardship they had faced, had been forced to make difficult decisions. The mortgage had grown too heavy, and the strain of raising three children had been too much for her to bear on her own. She had sold their family home, bought a caravan, and parked it in her parent's backyard. It was a small, cramped space, but it was a home nonetheless.

Mick couldn't bring himself to care. All that mattered now was his freedom, the chance to rebuild what had been stolen from him. His obsession with regaining his family, with returning to some semblance of normalcy, overshadowed everything else. The years in prison had taught him harsh lessons. He had been as strong as he could be, but the weight of the experience had broken something inside him. His faith in human nature had been shattered, and his distrust of the Australian justice system ran deep, particularly when it came to the police force who had been all too quick to deem him guilty on the day he had tried to seek help.

But the world outside had changed, and so had Mick. His old boss, the one man who had always believed in him, welcomed him back with open arms, treating him like a son returned from the dead. It was a kindness Mick had never expected, a sign that even the harshest of times could breed moments of redemption. To Mick's surprise, his boss offered him a position as supervisor, a role Mick knew had been created solely to give him a second chance. His boss didn't truly need a supervisor, but Mick needed the work. He needed the steady income to support his family, even if that meant swallowing his pride and accepting a position that might be more about charity than merit.

Still, Mick accepted. He would make it work. He had no other choice. And in a strange way, the title felt like a small victory, a step toward reclaiming what he had lost. There was pride in it, even if it was tempered with the understanding that his boss was helping him in ways he couldn't yet fully appreciate. But Mick was no fool. He understood the fragility of his new life, the precarious balance between the past he had left behind and the future he was trying to build.

The world may have seen him as a man just beginning again, but for Mick, it was all a test. A test of his resilience, his will to live, and the strength to survive in a world that had broken him once before. The real battle was just beginning. But with his freedom in hand, Mick Laidlow was ready for whatever came next.

Mick had lived through enough hardship to know when to strike, and now, with his release from prison still fresh in his mind, he knew that the time had come to settle accounts, not with the law, but with his own shattered life. Legal aid had put together a solid case for compensation against the justice system, and Mick's legal team advised him to fight on, to take his case to court. But Mick was a man who had learned the bitter taste of patience, and he was done waiting. He couldn't afford to wait. His family had already paid too much, and he wasn't about to see them suffer any longer.

The offer came. Two point four million. A settlement that would spare him the years of legal wrangling and the bitterness of dragging everything back into the public eye. Against the advice of his legal aid team, who had urged him to hold out for more, Mick accepted. His family was struggling. Emily, his ever-loyal wife, had been carrying the weight of their misfortune, trying to keep the children fed, clothed, and safe. The payout, while not enough to right all the wrongs, would be enough to give them a fighting chance. Mick didn't have the luxury of dragging it out. He needed the money. They needed it.

The moment the cheque cleared, Mick found out that there was more he could have claimed. He could have also sought compensation for the inheritance he had lost when he was wrongly convicted. The fortune Sam had left him, the one that had vanished when Mick had been locked away, could have been included in his claim. But by the time the truth came out, it was too late. The system had robbed him once again. The thieves, the liars, Mick's hatred for the justice system burned like an open flame. "Thieving mongrels," he muttered under his breath, his fists clenched at his sides.

But there was no time for bitterness now. He had a family to care for. A future to build. And for the first time in years, Mick was free. Free to plan, free to dream, and free to give Emily and the kids a life that wasn't haunted by the shadow of his past.

The first thing Mick decided to do was buy a block of land. He had dreamed of owning a place where he could build his own house, something solid, something that belonged to him and his family. But as he scoured the land listings, he realised it would take time, time they didn't have. He needed to move fast. So, instead of waiting, Mick shifted gears. He would find a house, a place for Emily, and he would do it in whatever location she wanted. It wasn't about him anymore. It was about Emily, and the kids, and their future. Mick was ready to put his family first.

The next step was to get a new four-wheel drive ute for himself. A vehicle that screamed freedom, a machine capable of taking him anywhere he wanted to go, somewhere far away from the dark memories of the past. Emily, of course, would get a new car too. Something reliable, something that wouldn't break down on the side of the road like the old one had.

But there was one thing that weighed heavy on Mick's mind. One final loose end he had to tie up. His mate Sam. Sam, the one person who had stood by him when the world had turned its back. Sam, the one whose tragic disappearance had haunted Mick every single day he'd spent behind bars. Mick didn't know what had happened to him, but he was damn well going to find out. No amount of money or new possessions could quiet the ache of not knowing what had happened to his mate. Mick would get answers, no matter what it took.

As Mick surveyed the new world around him, he knew he was standing at a crossroads. The money had given him a fresh start, but it couldn't erase the past. His life had been ripped apart, and now it was time to rebuild. And while the house, the cars, and the land were the first steps toward a new future, the journey ahead would require more than just material things. It would require strength, resilience, and a reckoning with the ghosts of his past.

Mick Laidlow was free, but freedom came with its own burdens.

During his long years at Lotus Glen, Mick had refused to allow his mind to wither away behind the prison's cold walls. There was an education centre at the facility, one that offered a degree of intellectual escape from the monotony of prison life. The library was a sanctuary, a haven of knowledge, and it became Mick's refuge. He had never been one to shy away from learning, and this was a place where he could immerse himself in subjects he had always found fascinating. Mick devoured the books, each one adding to the complex web of knowledge that he began to weave around his thoughts.

Though Mick had always been a practical man, with his hands more accustomed to the dirt and sweat of hard labour, he had a particular fondness for geology. He found it challenging at first, the concepts of mineral formation and alluvial gold testing his patience. But the more he read, the more he saw the intricacies of the earth beneath his feet, and slowly, it began to click. His studies became an obsession, particularly the topic of alluvial gold, the rich deposits of precious metal that lay hidden in the earth's veins, just waiting for the right person to unearth them. But it wasn't just the science of it that fascinated him; Mick was also captivated by the history of it. He poured over old journals and stories of the great gold rushes, how the first explorers, miners, and prospectors had toiled in harsh, unforgiving landscapes, seeking fortune. It was the old ways of finding gold, in the desolate outback and rugged mountains, that gripped his imagination.

In particular, Mick found himself drawn to the locations where gold had been discovered over the years, and how those same terrains had shaped the lives of the people who had ventured into them. It was in these studies, as he poured over maps and geological surveys, that Mick began to form an unshakable conclusion: there was very little chance of finding gold in the area where Sam had taken him on those two fateful trips, the same place where Sam had vanished without a trace.

But it was more than just his studies of gold that kept Mick's mind sharp. The library at Lotus Glen was fully equipped, not just with books but also with audiovisual equipment and a vast collection of local newspapers. It was here, among the old headlines and forgotten stories, that Mick stumbled across a media report that would send chills down his spine. It was an article about a missing person, a case from two years before Sam's disappearance. As Mick read, the hairs on the back of his neck stood on end.

The location was eerily familiar.

The report detailed how a man had gone missing in the same area that Sam had taken Mick to, the same wild, unforgiving stretch of land that Sam had so often spoken about. This man, like Sam, had been out there alone, and, like Sam, he had vanished without a trace. The article, however, told a darker tale. This man's body had been discovered weeks later, wedged between two massive boulders at the end of a ridge, much like the terrain that Mick had trekked through with Sam. A search by the police and the State Emergency Service (SES) had turned up nothing until one of the SES searchers, scanning the ridge, had noticed a faint glint from the man's watch. It was that single reflection, the gleam of metal in the sun, that had caught the eye of the searcher. The body was found about ten metres below the surface of the top boulders, half-buried and wedged in such a way that it was almost invisible to the casual observer.

The details of the man's activities before his disappearance were sparse, there was no clear indication of what he had been doing out there. The report hinted that he might have been fishing, but nothing definitive was ever confirmed. The most troubling part of the story, however, was the chilling similarity to Sam's disappearance: the exact location, the rugged landscape, and the fact that the man's four-wheel drive had been found parked in the bush at what sounded like the very spot Sam had used as a campsite. Mick couldn't shake the feeling that fate had woven these two cases together, that somehow, this death was connected to Sam's, two men lost to the unforgiving terrain, both with their fates sealed by the same inhospitable wilderness.

Mick spent hours poring over that article, re-reading it until the words blurred before his eyes. The realisation hit him hard, there was something more at play here. Something sinister. The landscape that had claimed both Sam and this man held its secrets close, and Mick couldn't help but wonder what had truly happened to both of them.

Was it just an accident? A fluke of nature? Or had something darker been at work in that desolate stretch of wilderness? Mick's mind churned with unanswered questions, his thoughts racing back to the days when he had stood in the same place with Sam, unaware of the danger lurking in the shadows.

The case of the missing man was a haunting puzzle, one that added another layer to the mystery surrounding Sam's disappearance. Mick knew that somehow, those two stories were connected, and he was more determined than ever to find the answers. He wouldn't rest until he knew the truth. The more Mick studied, the more he realised that the wilderness wasn't just a place, it was a force, ancient and merciless, and if you weren't careful, it could swallow you whole, just like it had with Sam and this other poor soul.

And so, with his mind sharpened by the hours spent in the library, Mick's quest for answers began anew. He had learned much in those years behind bars, and now it was time to put that knowledge to use. The land had its secrets, but Mick was determined to unearth them, no matter what it took.

Mick had spent countless hours staring at the pages of those reports, turning the words over in his mind like precious stones, each one revealing something more unsettling than the last. Four missing people, all in the same vicinity, and each with a story that seemed to spiral into darkness, like a whirlpool pulling them under. The first man, the one whose name was never revealed in the article, though Mick had managed to dig up some information, had worked at a bank in Mareeba. But what was he doing up on that ridge? The article had claimed he was there to fish. That seemed to be the assumption, because his friends had spoken of his passion for fishing, he was apparently "ultra keen." And there, not far from the river teeming with Barramundi and Jungle Perch, they found his body wedged between the boulders.

Mick had never seen these particular boulders, but he had been to Black Mountain, and he knew how treacherous those formations could be. No sane person would willingly scramble over them, not unless there was something worth climbing for. But the river was right there, within reach, brimming with fish. So why would this man, an avid fisherman, leave the water to ascend the jagged rocks? Had he been chasing something more elusive, something buried deep in the earth?

Mick's mind, honed by years of study and reflection, churned through the possibilities. Maybe the man had been looking for gold. The idea felt right, somehow. After all, the area around the river wasn't known for its abundance of gold. Geologically, it was considered scarce in that part of the world, almost nonexistent. But Mick knew something about scarcity, it could drive people to extremes, make them desperate, make them blind to the dangers around them. And that thought, that nagging suspicion, wouldn't leave him. If gold wasn't supposed to be there, then why had this man been so far from the river, climbing up the ridge?

Mick's gaze fell upon the small stack of gold reports he had kept close since Sam's disappearance. The figures burned into his mind like a brand, 25 grams of gold, found by Sam in less than half a day, just after breakfast, before lunch. Mick could hardly believe it. In all his studies, he had never read about any rich veins of gold in the area, especially not in such a short time. Gold, by its very nature, was elusive, difficult to find, even in the most promising of terrains. But Sam had found it, 25 grams of it, glistening and pure, sitting there in the earth as though it had been waiting for someone to claim it.

And then there was the 37 grams of gold that had been found in Eric Simpson's glovebox. That was a curious thing. Mick had spent enough time with Simpson to know that he wasn't exactly the type to leave gold just lying around in his vehicle. Those two quantities alone, just 62 grams, were worth more than five and a half grand. A small fortune, considering how difficult it was to find even a fraction of that amount in the wilds of Far North Queensland.

The weight of it all was beginning to settle heavily on Mick's chest. Something was wrong, something about the whole situation didn't add up. The pieces were there, but the puzzle wasn't fitting together. How could Sam have found that gold? And why had the man from Mareeba, who was supposedly fishing, been found so far from the river, wedged between boulders as though he had been searching for something?

Mick's thoughts raced like a storm, each possibility more improbable than the last. He had learned enough in his years behind bars to know that nothing in the wild was ever as it seemed. Gold could drive men to madness, and the earth had a way of keeping its secrets buried, hidden from those who sought it. And maybe, just maybe, Sam had found something that had cost him his life. Maybe the man from Mareeba had found the same thing, and paid with his own life.

The question that lingered in Mick's mind now was simple: What was hidden up there, between those boulders, in that remote wilderness? The gold had to be more than just a lucky find. It had to be something more, something that had drawn these men to the edge of their own sanity. And Mick, for all his studies and all his knowledge of the land, was no closer to understanding what that something was.

But there was one thing he was certain of: he had to find out.

With that kind of money in gold, in an area where gold was supposed to be scarce, Mick couldn't shake the feeling that something was wrong. If 25 grams could be found so quickly, three hours, according to the reports, there should have been a gold rush, a mad scramble of miners and prospectors clawing over each other to get to the veins beneath the earth. But there had been none of that. It was almost as if the gold had just... appeared. Mick thought back to the day Sam had found it, just after breakfast, before the heat of the midday sun had begun to bake the ground. It was absurd, almost unnatural, there were places where gold was supposed to be, but this wasn't one of them.

And then there was Eric Simpson. The man had found his gold on his first day, no doubt about it, and it seemed he had stashed it in his car for safekeeping. But how had he managed to find it, so much of it, on ground that had already been worked over by other prospectors? Mick mulled over this, turning the problem over like a piece of uncut stone, looking for a flaw, a crack where the truth might shine through. Simpson had a better detector, sure. A much better one than Sam's. But 37 grams of gold? Over ground that had already been combed through by prospectors, including Sam Young? That didn't sit right.

Mick's mind wandered again, chasing after possibilities like a hound on the scent. He'd heard of a trick called "seeding," back in the old days of the American Wild West. When a man wanted to sell a worthless gold mine, he'd scatter gold dust and nuggets around the property to make it look rich, to lure in the gullible. Could someone have done the same here? Could the gold have been planted, to entice the men into the same trap?

The thought was absurd. Mick shook his head, muttering to himself, "Nah, that's crazy. Who the hell would put gold out there on the ridge, and for what? To what end?" The thought gnawed at him, but it still didn't make sense. No one would bother, not in a place like this, where gold was supposed to be so rare. But then again, if Simpson had found the gold on his first day, and it was near Sam's last known location, then they were both covering the same ground. Mick's stomach churned as he realised that Simpson's detector had been left behind, gone just like the man. Had he found the gold in the same area Sam had been? If so, how had he missed it the first time around? It all felt wrong. Too much gold. Too quickly.

"I need to talk to someone who knows detectors," Mick thought, his frustration bubbling over. But who in here would know about detectors? Who could he trust to tell him anything useful, locked in this hellhole of a place?

His thoughts spiralled downward. His mind kept returning to the Mount Marian ranges, their mystery, their hidden truths. The more he thought about it, the more it seemed like a puzzle that would never be solved. And it was maddening. What was going on out there? Was it just a mystery, or was it something darker? Something... sinister? Of course, it was sinister. Whatever it was. But was it human? Was it a person, hiding out there in the wilderness, watching these men disappear one by one? Or was it something else?

Mick stopped himself, suddenly realising how ridiculous he was sounding. He wasn't some fevered child, chasing after fairy tales. But then, in a flash of clarity, it hit him like a thunderbolt, maybe it wasn't a man at all. Maybe it was the gold itself. Luring them in, one after another, like lollies on a path for innocent children. The thought made Mick's skin crawl. Was that it? Was the gold itself the bait?

As Mick's thoughts returned back to his prison life, as it often would, where he would, easily slip into thinking about the mountain. But even as the thought settled in his mind, Mick felt the weight of it slip away again, like water through his fingers. It didn't make sense. It couldn't. He could feel his pulse quicken with frustration. The truth was out there, somewhere, but it was hidden under layers of dust and rock, behind a riddle that he couldn't solve. And all the time he spent studying the land, all the hours he poured over maps and reports, seemed to have been a waste. He would never get out of here to prove anything. He would never get the chance to return to that ridge, to stand where Sam had last stood, to answer the question that gnawed at him.

He recalled how prison life carried on, a monotonous blur of days that bled into each other. Mick's body had grown used to the routine, but his mind, his mind was a caged animal, restless and angry, caught in a cell of its own making. He would never get used to this place, not really. No one ever did.

But even as he struggled with the crushing weight of his captivity, his thoughts kept pulling him back to Mount Marian, to those strange boulders and the mystery that swirled around them like smoke. Was it a human hand that had caused these men to disappear, or something else entirely? The more Mick thought about it, the more the question seemed to slip through his grasp. There had to be an answer. There had to be. But what was it?

A nagging thought came to him then, just a flicker at the edge of his mind. Was it the gold? Could it be that simple? He told himself to stop, but he couldn't. He couldn't let it go. The gold. It had to be part of the puzzle. It had to be.

Mick had come to the harsh realisation that his newfound knowledge of geology and local history was little more than a distraction. The endless hours spent poring over maps and dusty tomes had been a futile exercise. It didn't matter how well he understood the alluvial gold deposits or the intricacies of mineral formation, the knowledge meant nothing here, behind these bars. It wasn't as if he could use it to unearth any answers, not when the truth was locked away, like a treasure buried under layers of secrecy and stone. The library had become a prison in itself, a cage of words with no key to set him free. So, Mick stopped going.

Instead, he took up chess. The game seemed like the perfect way to keep his mind sharp, to hold on to something beyond the monotony of prison life. But learning to play chess in prison was no easy task. The problem wasn't just the complexity of the game, the countless moves and strategies that required patience and concentration, it was the fact that chess was the most popular pastime behind bars. It was a game everyone played, and no one had time to teach. The seasoned players had no interest in helping a newcomer; they had their own games to win, their own rankings to uphold. It was a world of calculated moves and subtle victories, and Mick, a newcomer to it all, was a fish out of water.

But Mick was determined. He found someone, an old, wiry inmate with a sharp mind and a gruff demeanour named Srapovicz, who was willing to teach him the basics. Srapovicz barely spoke English and Mick found him extremely hard to understand, but he persisted in being taught how to communicate with Srapovicz and from there, he took off. Piece by piece, move by move, Mick began to learn.

He also learned that Srapovicz was a master of things other than chess. He had also taught Mick how to relax and go into a trance when things seemed to get on top of him. Mick's mind, so accustomed to solving problems in other ways, adapted quickly to the rhythms of the game. It wasn't long before he was playing against some of the best. But there was one lesson that stuck with him above all others.

It came during a match against a tough opponent, a man whose eyes never left the board, whose hands moved the pieces like a master. Midway through the game, the man paused, glanced up at Mick, and said, "To play good chess, you've got to be at least one step ahead." The man was Srapovicz, the man who had taught Mick how to 'win' at chess.

The words struck Mick hard, reverberating in his mind long after the game had ended. He had lost the match, distracted by the thought of those words. He wandered back to his cell, his mind racing, his thoughts tangled in the complexity of the game and, strangely, the mystery that had haunted him since the moment Sam had gone missing.

As he lay in his cot, the cool concrete beneath him, Mick replayed the words over and over again. "One step ahead." He muttered them aloud, and it hit him like a bolt of lightning. The person, or thing, responsible for the deaths wasn't just reacting. They were ahead of everyone else. One step ahead, always.

Mick stared at the ceiling, deep in thought, as the world outside his cell continued its endless march. It was a game, a cold, calculating game, and whoever was pulling the strings knew exactly how to play it. But then another thought struck him, were the victims even truly dead? Or had something else happened to them? Were they killed, or had something far more sinister been at work?

The questions piled up like stones in his mind, but no answers came. He thought of Sam, his old mate, his brother in arms, and wondered if there was a purpose to it all. Why had he died? What was the reason behind it?

The search for answers had been fruitless so far. No evidence. No witnesses. Nothing. The authorities had found little more than a trail of blood, a scattered piece of metal here, a discarded boot there. No solid leads. No clues to point them in the right direction.

Mick ran a hand through his hair, frustration building. "Why is there no evidence?" he asked aloud, as if expecting the walls of his cell to answer. And then, like a sudden gust of wind through a crack in a window, it hit him. The wet season. It was the wet season, the torrential rains that swept through the area like an unstoppable force, washing away tracks, hiding signs, covering up the truth. It was the perfect cover for something, or someone, to disappear without a trace.

The realisation sent a chill down Mick's spine. The first victim had disappeared in January. The wet season. Sam had gone missing in December. The wet season again. Eric Simpson had vanished in January, caught in the same downpour. And now, Mick thought grimly, it was his turn. His "ticket out" had come in February, right at the tail end of the season. It all fit.

Mick's heart raced as the pieces began to fall into place. The wet season wasn't just a natural occurrence. It was the perfect camouflage. It hid the truth, obscured the clues, made it impossible to trace the killers, or whatever they were, back to their lair. It was as if the land itself had conspired to bury the evidence, to keep the secrets hidden beneath layers of mud and water.

The search for Sam had been a rigged game from the very start. Mick could see that now, clear as the midday sun scorching the dry scrubland. It wasn't just bad luck or misfortune, someone had orchestrated this, played the board long before he'd even stepped onto it. And now, whether he liked it or not, he was caught in the web.

Walking away wasn't an option. Not without answers. Not without understanding what had really happened to Sam, to Simpson, and to the others. The missing men weren't just victims of chance or the wild, there was something else at work here, something unseen, but undeniable. Mick could feel it in his bones.

But how the hell did he fight back when he didn't even know who he was fighting? Who was pulling the strings? Why did the police treat these disappearances with such casual indifference, their investigations half-hearted at best? Mick had spent his life working the land, knowing that survival came down to being smarter, stronger, and always one step ahead. But this was different. This was a shadow war, where men disappeared and the world kept turning as if they'd never existed.

And the search, Jesus, the search itself had been a farce. Why weren't there more men out there? Why weren't they working in shifts, fresh searchers replacing the exhausted ones so the hunt could go on without pause? Mick had wanted to push on, twenty-four hours a day, through the night if necessary, but he had been met with tired eyes and half-hearted excuses. A day or two of searching, and then the urgency drained away, leaving only quiet resignation.

Mick clenched his fists, the muscles in his forearms tightening like steel cables. This wasn't just about Sam anymore. This was about exposing the truth, no matter what it took. And if no one else had the stomach to see it through, then damn it, he would.

Emily had fallen in love with the house at Brinsmead the moment they walked through the front door. Mick, on the other hand, had long since given up hope of finding the perfect home. It felt like an endless parade of houses, each one promising something better, yet all of them falling short. Mick had lost count of how many times they'd stepped over thresholds, his eyes glazing over with each new viewing. It wasn't until they reached the last house that something clicked, and Mick could see it in Emily's face, the spark of happiness, the warmth in her eyes as she took in the place.

The first home they'd seen had seemed like the one, but it had turned out to be nothing more than a fleeting hope. And now, after twenty more houses, they had finally found it. Emily was delighted, and Mick knew well enough by now, if Emily was happy, life at home would be good. It was a large, sprawling home with four spacious bedrooms upstairs, a fifth tucked away downstairs. The house boasted a massive rumpus room and a generous office that Mick immediately saw as the perfect space to launch his new business, 'West Homes.' The very name rang in his mind like a promise, an anchor for a future he was determined to build.

The double garage was ideal, and beside it, a carport large enough to house two more vehicles. Out back, there was a grand four-bay shed, perfect for a workshop, a haven for Mick's craft. The house sat on just under an acre, offering breathtaking views of Cairns City, its lights shimmering like a promise beneath the night sky. Of course, all this grandeur came at a price. But Mick had been planning for this moment for years. He could already picture the future, building homes under the banner of 'West Homes,' a business that would grow from the very foundation of this house. He even had a jingle in his head: The best homes are West Homes.

Moving into their new home was a smooth process, the caravan hitched to Mick's shiny new SR5 ute. It was a practical vehicle for the new life they were carving out. They had no furniture to move, of course, so a shopping trip around the Cairns furniture and electrical stores was the order of the day. The house, though, needed a bit of work, a few tweaks here and there, a workshop to set up in the shed. Emily had her eye on a new car as well. She wanted something that would comfortably fit her, the kids, and the weekly grocery run. After a few visits to the dealership, she settled on a Subaru Outback, a perfect choice for the family, with plenty of room and a smooth ride.

With the children still having two weeks of the Christmas holidays left, they decided to take a break. A week on the Gold Coast seemed like the perfect way to unwind, to enjoy some time together before the grind of real life set in. They packed up the Subaru and hit the road, the excitement of the trip making the long journey down feel like nothing. Mick found himself admiring the Outback's handling, its ability to glide through traffic and slip into tight parking spaces. It was a car built for practicality, and it had already earned its place as part of the family.

A week spent at the Gold Coast was a whirlwind, the theme parks and beaches blurring into one long, happy memory. Mick had never seen the kids so excited, their laughter echoing in the warm coastal air. It felt like the perfect break, a moment of peace before the storms of life returned.

But all good things must come to an end. As they packed up to head back to Cairns, Mick knew the wet season was waiting for them. The forecast had predicted a cyclone brewing, somewhere between Cairns and Cooktown. It wasn't anything out of the ordinary for the far north, but the timing was inconvenient. The storm had stalled his plans to head out to the Mount Marian region. He had kept his intentions to himself, knowing full well that Emily would not approve. The Mount Marian Ridge was a place steeped in mystery, a place Mick couldn't quite shake from his thoughts. But now, with the cyclone looming, he was forced to put those plans on hold.

The weather gave him the time he needed, time to sit back and reflect on the theories that had been running through his mind for weeks. The wet season, while a nuisance to most, would be his ally. It would give him the quiet he needed to study, to analyse, to consider all the pieces of the puzzle he had started to assemble. The mystery of the Ridge, the gold, the disappearances, it all seemed to fit together, but there were too many gaps, too many unanswered questions. The storm would pass, and when it did, Mick would be ready to take the next step. He would find the answers, even if it meant walking through the storm itself.

Mick's new home office was everything he could have hoped for, a sanctuary of sorts, tucked away in the quiet corner of the house, away from the rest of the world. The four walls that surrounded him felt different from the sterile confines of a prison cell. This was his space, where he could finally breathe, think, and focus. The sleek, modern iMac sat proudly on the desk, its high-speed broadband connection opening the doors to an endless sea of information. Mick knew that this was the key to unlocking the mysteries that had haunted him for so long. The Mount Marian Missing, he had dubbed it the MMM, and his mind raced with the possibilities. The answers were out there, somewhere, and he was determined to find them.

It didn't take long before Mick decided he needed to tell Emily what he was planning. He could feel the weight of the secret pressing on him, and the last thing he wanted was for her to become suspicious. The truth, however, didn't go down easy. He had expected as much.

"Just be happy you're out of prison and let it go," Emily said, her voice tinged with concern. "It's not going to help you now. What's the good of putting your life at risk? Let the police do their job, it's what they are paid to do. It's not your job."

Mick watched as the sadness crept into her eyes. She didn't understand. She couldn't. And yet, he couldn't help himself. The need to uncover the truth about Sam gnawed at him like a hunger that wouldn't be satisfied.

"I just don't understand what benefit it will have on you," Emily continued, her voice breaking. "Why can't you just be happy with what you have? You're just starting your own building business. You're setting up a new life. I think you'd be far better off focusing on that, instead of this other bullshit. How about thinking about me and the kids? We all thought we had lost you when you went to prison, and now we're all just so grateful to have you back with us. Please, don't destroy this now."

Mick's heart ached, but he knew this wasn't something he could walk away from. "Emily, I understand exactly what you're saying. I really do," he said, his voice firm yet gentle. "But you must also understand that I have no intentions of destroying our family. No way. And you should also understand that I want to find out what happened to Sam, and I want to completely exonerate myself from what I've been accused of. I have no intention of putting myself into danger. The minute I have any information on what's happening up on Mount Marian, I'll pass it on to the police. Believe me, I do not intend to become a hero."

Emily sat in silence for a long moment, the tension between them palpable. Finally, she spoke, her voice soft but resolute. "OK, Mick. Just no wild adventures, right?"

"Right," Mick promised, a faint smile tugging at his lips. "I promise. All will be safe. It's just an investigation, something that for some strange reason the coppers can't seem to crack."

With that, Mick turned his attention back to his research, knowing that the path he was walking would be anything but easy. To paint a full picture of what was happening in the Mount Marian region, Mick decided to start at the beginning. He needed to understand the history, to see the connections that others might have missed. The National Library of Australia's Trove website was a goldmine of information, and Mick wasted no time in diving into the back copies of The Mareeba Express.

It was there, buried deep in the archives, that he found the first article that spoke of a missing person, a man named Graham Eldridge. He had gone missing during a camping trip to the Mount Marian ranges, and while the article was brief, it held more information than any of the others Mick had come across. It mentioned that Graham was wearing a set of headphones when he fell, and the headphones were still attached to the body when it was found. The piece also named the bank in Mareeba where Graham had worked.

Mick, driven by the need for answers, reached out to Emily's mother, Peggy, who had once worked for the same bank, though in the Cairns branch, not the Mareeba branch. Mick needed to know if she had any recollection of Graham Eldridge.

Peggy's voice came over the phone with a slight quiver of uncertainty. "Graham Eldridge? The name rings a bell... I think a friend of mine transferred from the Cairns branch to Mareeba about five or six years ago. She might know him. Her name's Veronica Mitchell. She's retired now, lives at Speewah, but I don't have her address or phone number. I'm sorry, I wish I could be of more help."

Mick thanked Peggy for the information and answered a few questions about their new home, letting the conversation drift into familiar territory. He knew Emily's mother didn't have the answers he was looking for, but it was a start. He passed the phone to Emily, and as she began talking to her mother, Mick's mind raced.

The pieces were starting to come together, but the picture was still incomplete. Mick had more work to do, and he wasn't going to stop until he uncovered the truth about what happened to Sam. The Mount Marian mystery, the gold, the disappearances, it was all connected, and Mick knew he was the one who had to unravel it. The stakes were high, but for Mick, the reward was even higher: the chance to clear his name, find justice for his friend, and put the demons of his past to rest.

While Emily was still on the telephone with her mother, Mick felt the restlessness that had been simmering within him for days finally reach its boiling point. There were too many unanswered questions, too many pieces to the puzzle that needed to be found. He couldn't sit idly by while the mystery of Mount Marian continued to gnaw at him. He had to take matters into his own hands. Without a second thought, he decided to drive the thirty-five kilometres up the Kuranda Range to Speewah.

The road wound upwards through the thick, lush forest that dominated the area, the trees leaning over the road like ancient sentinels guarding the pass. As Mick drove, the anticipation grew in his chest, and the steady thrum of his ute's engine seemed to echo the urgency of his thoughts. He had to find Veronica Mitchell. She was the missing link, the key to understanding the strange and tragic disappearance of Graham Eldridge.

At precisely two in the afternoon, Mick pulled into the car park of the Speewah Tavern, the wooden building sitting quietly under the dense canopy of trees. It was a modest place, but it had the welcoming aura of a small-town watering hole where locals gathered to share their stories. Mick parked his ute and walked inside, an Australian Cattle dog observing his every movement as he did. The cool, dimly lit interior was a welcome relief from the heat outside. He ordered a beer, and as he took a seat at the bar, he noticed there was only one other person in the place, a solitary figure sitting at the counter, nursing his own drink. The bar attendant gave Mick a nod, acknowledging his presence with a quiet smile.

Mick took a sip of his beer, feeling the cool liquid slide down his throat. He set the glass down and turned to the bar attendant. "You wouldn't happen to know a Veronica Mitchell, would you?" he asked, his voice casual but edged with purpose.

The bar attendant paused for a moment, her eyes narrowing slightly as she processed the question. But before she could respond, the man at the bar spoke up, his voice gravelly from years of use.

"Barry's missus," the man said with a knowing glance. "You looking' for Veronica and Barry?"

Mick nodded, not wanting to reveal too much just yet. "Er... yes, I am. I don't have their address, though, but I know they live somewhere here in Speewah."

The man took another drink, then leaned back in his chair. "They sure do live here. Up at number four, The Glen. Just head up the main drag, then take the third turn to your left. It's about half a mile, and you can't miss it, I'll give Barry a call, see if he's home," the man said as he dialled on his mobile phone, the man mumbled something into it and ended the call. "He's up there, mate!"

Mick felt a surge of gratitude for the stranger' help. He thanked the man, finished his beer, and bid both the bar attendant and the drinker goodbye. Stepping outside and being watched again by the cattle dog, he climbed back into his ute and followed the directions, the anticipation mounting with every mile.

When Mick finally turned onto The Glen and found the house marked as number four, he felt an immediate sense of certainty. This was it. The gate was open, so he drove in and parked near the house. He sat there for a moment, watching the front door. More, Australian Cattle Dogs ran around in the yard, their tails wagging, as if they too had an inkling of what was to come. Mick could feel the weight of the moment settling on him, this was where he would learn the answers he sought.

It didn't take long before the owner of the dogs emerged from the house. A solid man, not particularly tall but strong in stature, with a face weathered by years under the harsh sun. He gave Mick a brief but welcoming nod. "What can I do for you?"

Mick stepped out of the ute, trying to keep his voice steady. "I'm Mick West. My mother-in-law, Peggy McMahon, worked with your wife, Veronica, over at the bank in Cairns. I was hoping you might be able to help me with some information about a fellow worker."

Barry, introduced himself to Mick and studied him for a moment, then gestured toward the verandah. "No worries, mate. Ronnie's here, I'll go fetch her for you." He disappeared inside, leaving Mick to stand in the warm air, the distant sound of the Cattle Dogs, still barking occasionally in the background.

Before long, a tall woman with a grey ponytail emerged from the house, a broad smile on her face. She looked every bit the picture of warmth and hospitality. "Mick, well hello! I've heard so much about you and Emily, and of course the kids. It's really nice to finally put a face to the name." She extended a hand to him. "How's Peggy and Gavin going?"

Mick shook her hand, a smile tugging at his lips. "Hello, Mrs. Mitchell. They're both doing well, thank you."

Veronica's smile softened as she led Mick to the verandah, where they sat down. She turned to Barry and nodded. "Barry, get Mick a beer, would you?"

Mick settled in, the conversation turning to more personal matters before he steered it back to the reason for his visit. "I was hoping you could help me with something. Do you remember a man named Graham Eldridge? He worked at the bank in Mareeba."

At the mention of Graham's name, Veronica's expression changed, her warmth replaced by a shadow of sorrow. "Oh, that poor, poor man," she said softly. "It was such a shame, and he was such a lovely man for that to happen to."

Veronica leaned back in her chair, the memory clearly weighing on her. "It was just after Christmas when he went camping all alone up in the mountains. He was really looking forward to going fishing and fossicking. His wife had bought him a metal detector for Christmas. He was still wearing the headphones when they found him." Her voice faltered slightly. "He had fallen into a hole, and his head was wedged between three boulders. The way the body was found... it looked like he had dived in headfirst. The impact was so brutal that it had removed his entire face. They could only identify him by a tattoo on his left arm."

Mick's gut tightened at the grisly details. "I remember hearing something about him finding two gold nuggets the month before," Mick said, his voice low. "He said they were small, but he was keen to find more."

Veronica nodded. "Yes, that's right. He was really excited about the metal detector, hoping to find more. The two nuggets he found weren't worth much, but he was sure there were more out there. He was so determined."

Mick's mind raced. Everything seemed to be pointing to something bigger, something more sinister. He pressed on. "I heard it was only by luck that they found him, though. Something about the flash from his watch being spotted by one of the SES searchers that was onboard a helicopter?"

Veronica nodded, her face solemn. "That's what I heard, too. It was the helicopter pilot who saw the flash from his watch. If not for that, they may never have found him."

Mick paused for a moment, lost in thought. "But I think that's not right. I heard that the SES searchers saw the reflection on the boulders while they were searching. It was that reflection that led them to him."

"No, definitely not," Veronica replied firmly, her eyes narrowing as she recalled the grim details. "The SES were told outright not to even try to walk over those boulders. It was too dangerous, too unstable. Everything was done by helicopter, even the retrieval of the body. They dropped a yellow paint bomb marker on the boulder near the tunnel, and that's how they pinpointed the spot." She paused, her face taking on a haunted expression. "The worst part, though… the way they had to get him out of that hole. A rescue man was lowered down into the narrow tunnel, right into the death trap. They had to strap Graham's feet with a sling, then hoist him out, inch by inch, away from the boulders. They lifted him high enough to clear the rocks, and then they lowered him to the SES crew waiting on the flatter ground. It was… just horrible."

Mick's stomach tightened, his mind reeling from the gruesome imagery. He had known the death was tragic, but this? This was a whole new level of horror. It made the story he had heard seem like child's play, far removed from the raw brutality of the truth. He couldn't help but feel sick at the thought of it.

"I agree," Mick said quietly. "That's beyond horrible. But there's nothing about this in the newspaper reports."

Veronica nodded, her face grim. "The newspapers weren't allowed anywhere near the recovery site. The authorities controlled the flow of information tightly, printed only what they were told. I remember, there was barely any coverage of the whole thing. Hardly a peep on the news, and the local papers had just a brief mention. The only reason I knew as much as I did was because I worked with one of the rescue guy's wives at the bank. She'd told me bits and pieces."

Mick took another swig of his beer, the taste now bitter on his tongue. He knew there was more to this than met the eye. He could feel it in the pit of his stomach, that sense of unease gnawing at him like a persistent itch. The pieces didn't fit right, and something about it all seemed off. The lack of coverage. The way the police had been so quick to label it an accident, a fluke. But Mick knew accidents. This wasn't one.

With the information Veronica had given him, Mick's mind was buzzing, a whirlwind of theories and half-formed thoughts. He finished his beer and stood up, wiping his hands on his jeans. "Thanks for your time, Veronica," he said, his voice quieter than before, as though the weight of the conversation had drained the energy from him. "I really appreciate it."

Barry, who had been quiet during the exchange, nodded with a warm smile. "No problem, mate. You're always welcome here. Bring Emily and the kids up sometime. We've got horses, quad bikes, plenty of room for them to run around. We'd love to have you all up."

Mick smiled back, though it didn't quite reach his eyes. "I'll make sure we do, Barry. Thanks again for everything."

He shook hands with both Barry and Veronica before stepping out into the warmth of the afternoon. The drive back down the winding Kuranda Range was a blur. His mind was a whirlpool, spinning with the new information, the eerie similarities between the cases, and the nagging feeling that something far darker was at play.

Mick gripped the steering wheel, his knuckles white against the leather, his mind a storm of tangled thoughts. The road stretched out before him, a strip of black ribbon cutting through the wilderness, but his focus was elsewhere, on the revelations that had just been laid bare.

The SES had been prohibited from walking on the boulders. That alone sent a shiver through him. Not advised against it, not warned of danger, prohibited. He could feel the weight of that word pressing against his chest. Why? What the hell was so important about those boulders that trained searchers were ordered to stay away?

And then there was Graham's watch, that tiny, flickering signal that had led rescuers straight to him, pulling him back from the abyss just before he became another lost soul swallowed by the mountain. The odds of that were staggering. A man could bet his life's fortune in a casino a thousand times and not come close to the kind of chance that had found Graham's body.

Mick's gut told him this wasn't coincidence. It was something far darker, something deeper.

How many others had disappeared into those rocks? How many bodies were hidden beneath the twisted maze of stone, their stories lost to time, their fates written off as accidents or misfortune? He thought of Sam. He thought of Simpson. Four men, all missing. Four lives that led back to one place.

Mount Marian.

The name carried a weight now, heavier than before, steeped in something ancient and malevolent. The mountain wasn't just an indifferent stretch of land, it was a graveyard.

And Mick couldn't shake the question clawing at the back of his mind.

Had the SES been placed under the same restrictions when they searched for Sam?

Because if they had, then the answer was as clear as the dust trailing behind his speeding truck.

No one had ever meant to find Sam Young.

Mick's jaw clenched, his pulse thundering in his ears. The pieces were shifting, clicking into place, but the picture they were forming was one he wasn't sure he was ready to see.

Yet, there was no turning back now.

He had to know.

Because buried in those boulders, among the dead and the missing, was the truth. And Mick West was going to dig it out, even if it killed him.

That's why the police were so quick to call it an accident, Mick mused, the thought striking him like a bolt of lightning. They didn't want to have to search the boulders. They didn't want to be digging around in those dangerous, black mountain-type rocks. Too risky. Too much potential for more bodies to be uncovered.

His pulse quickened as the realisation settled in. There was something incredibly wrong about all of it. Something wasn't right, and Mick knew that his instincts were telling him the truth. But where do I start? The thought swirled in his head as the road stretched out in front of him, a quiet, lonely path that mirrored the uncertainty in his mind.

He remembered the phrase that had floated into his mind when he first started thinking about the boulders. Black Mountain. The name of a notorious range, a place known for its darkness and hidden dangers. But why had it come to him now? What did it have to do with all of this?

Mick's fingers drummed nervously on the steering wheel. He needed to get back to his office, to sit down with the information he had gathered, and start piecing it all together. There were connections he had yet to make, links he hadn't even considered. But one thing was clear: Mount Marian wasn't just a random place. It was a land of secrets, of danger, and it had a lot more to hide than anyone had realised.

Mick's mobile rang, and his pulse quickened as he saw it was Emily calling. He reluctantly answered, knowing the tone of the conversation was about to shift from pleasant to stormy.

"Mick!" Emily's voice was tinged with frustration, "Where the hell are you? It's nearly six o'clock, and I've no idea when you'll be home. You disappeared without saying a word, and now I'm left here wondering if you've fallen off the face of the earth!"

Mick winced at the sharpness in her tone. "Sorry, Em," he said, running a hand through his hair. "I thought you'd still be on the phone with your mum, and I didn't expect to be out this long. I should've let you know."

There was a long silence on the other end before Emily sighed. "Well, you could have at least told me where you were going. I've been trying to keep dinner warm here, but I don't know if I'm supposed to wait or just eat with the kids. I'm just... a bit pissed off, Mick. That's all."

"I'll be home in about twenty minutes," he replied quickly, guilt tugging at him. "I'll make it up to you, I promise."

After dinner, which was awkward and heavy with the tension of unsaid words, Mick retreated to his office, where his mind raced with the information he had gathered. The phrase 'Black Mountain' was stuck in his head like a splinter he couldn't dislodge. He needed to know more about it, to understand the place, the danger, and the strange connection it seemed to have to the deaths and disappearances. He was no stranger to risk, but this felt different. There was something about Black Mountain that called to him.

Mick pulled out his mobile and began scrolling through his contacts, searching for someone he hadn't spoken to in years. It took a few minutes, but there it was, buried under a list of forgotten names, Brett. No surname. Just a number, and the address "Cooktown." It wasn't much, but it was enough to stir a memory, the faintest recollection of a man Mick had met years ago at tech college in Brisbane. Brett was one of those types, rugged, adventurous, always chasing the next thrill. Mick had always been impressed by the man's fearless attitude, though he'd never imagined that years later, he'd be calling him for help.

Mick dialled the number, heart pounding as the phone rang.

"Brett speaking," came the voice on the other end.

"Hello, Brett, it's Mick West," Mick said, trying to sound casual, though his mind was already racing. "Do you remember me?"

There was a short pause before Brett's voice crackled through with a chuckle. "Mick! Hell, I remember you. Yeah, I saw your name in the paper a while ago. Good to see you're out, mate. What a bloody mess you were caught up in. Those bastards, huh? They sure know how to pin things on people, don't they?"

Mick chuckled softly, but his mind was elsewhere, focused on what he really needed to know. "Yeah, it's been a hell of a ride. Listen, I'm looking for some info on something... Black Mountain."

Brett's tone shifted, sharp and curious. "Black Mountain? Well, that's a name I know well. What do you want to know about it?"

Mick took a breath, memories flooding back to their conversation years ago at tech college. Brett had told him stories about Cooktown, about climbing, about the dangers lurking in the shadows of Black Mountain. It had always intrigued Mick, the raw, untamed wilderness that surrounded the place.

"I was just thinking back to when we talked about it," Mick began slowly. "You and your old man were always climbing around the boulders up there. I remember you telling me how dangerous it was. But you said you had a way of doing it safely. What did you mean by that?"

There was a slight pause before Brett answered, his voice steady. "Yeah, that's right. When we climb those boulders, we're always careful. You've got to have the right gear, the right technique. It's not something you just walk into blindly, like most people think."

Mick leaned in, eager for the details. "What kind of gear? What do you use to stay safe?"

Brett's voice took on a more technical tone. "Well, the most important thing is the grappling hook. We've got one with two ropes attached. The standard single rope can be a pain, if the rope slackens, the hook can slip, and you're done for. But with two ropes, you can keep one attached to a tension block that's fixed to a 'climbing friend cam', basically a small device that locks into a crevice or crack in the boulder. That keeps tension on the rope, so it won't slip. The second rope is for climbing, and with both working together, it's a hell of a lot safer."

Mick was following along, impressed. "Sounds pretty complicated. But it makes sense."

Brett continued, his voice steady and confident. "It's safer, but it's still not foolproof. The big danger is that you don't know what's behind the boulder. You can't see what's on the other side when you're climbing. Sometimes, you get to the top, and there's a huge crevice or a tunnel between the boulders, and that can trap you. So, we use a drone to scout ahead, get a visual of the area before we even start climbing. It's made the whole process a hell of a lot safer."

Mick's mind raced as the pieces started to fall into place. A tunnel between boulders... a place to hide... The thought sent a shiver down his spine. Could this be what the police had missed? Could there be more bodies, hidden away in the crevices and tunnels, just waiting to be discovered?

He didn't speak for a moment, his mind churning with the possibilities. "Brett, you said a drone helps you scout ahead, right?"

"Yeah, that's right," Brett said, his tone matter-of-fact. "Why?"

Mick's grip tightened on the phone. "How close can you get with that drone? I need to know if it could help someone like me, someone who's looking for something… something up there, in those boulders."

Brett paused, thinking for a moment. "Well, you can get pretty damn close. We've flown it through some tight spaces, no problem. It's got a good range, and the camera is sharp enough to pick up details that a human eye might miss."

Mick's pulse quickened as he absorbed this new information. This could be it. This could be the break he needed.

"Alright, Brett. I'm going to need your help. I'm looking into something, and I need to get a closer look at Black Mountain. I'll be in touch soon."

Brett gave a low laugh. "Anytime, Mick. You know where to find me. Just don't get yourself killed out there."

As Mick hung up the phone, a feeling of resolve settled over him. The pieces were falling into place, and Mick knew that Black Mountain held the answers to questions that no one else was asking. The mountain wasn't just a place of danger; it was a place of secrets. And Mick was going to uncover them, no matter what it took.

Mick sat in the quiet of his car for a moment, reflecting on the long drive ahead of him. The road from Cairns to Innisfail stretched out before him, endless and straight, with only the occasional bend in the road to break the monotony. The day was hot, the kind of heat that clung to the skin and made every movement feel like an effort, but Mick was too absorbed in his thoughts to notice the discomfort. His mind kept drifting back to the strange series of disappearances, the eerie coincidence of the missing people, all vanishing in a rugged, unforgiving stretch of terrain. It was a mystery that seemed to coil tighter with every passing day, each new piece of information adding to the enigma, and it was one that gnawed at Mick's gut like a hungry predator.

The boulders in that area, their sheer size and jagged edges, reminded him of Black Mountain. That ominous place. The one that people spoke of in hushed tones, a place that held secrets no one dared to speak of openly. He had to know more. The way the bodies were found, the patterns, the twisted fate of the missing... It was as though the land itself was swallowing them whole. But Mick wasn't one to sit idly by, waiting for fate to catch up with him. He needed answers. And that's why he was here.

He'd found Leonora Simpson's address after hours of sifting through old media reports and the white pages telephone directory. It wasn't much, but it was enough to give him a starting point. It had been over a year since her husband, Eric, had gone missing, and Mick hoped, prayed, that she still lived at the address. The road trip from Cairns had taken him over an hour and a half, but it felt longer, every mile weighed down by the burden of what he was about to do. There was no telling how she would react, but Mick had a gut feeling that Leonora knew more than she was letting on.

He reached her home, a modest house tucked in a quiet street, and parked outside. The air was thick with humidity as he climbed out of the car, his boots crunching on the gravel driveway. He walked to the door, his heart pounding with anticipation. The knock on the door was gentle, yet it seemed to echo through the silence of the house.

When the door swung open, a woman stood before him. She was slender, her face a mixture of weariness and resolve, the lines of grief etched deep into her features. Leonora Simpson. The same woman who had been torn apart by the disappearance of her husband. She stood there for a moment, assessing Mick with a cautious eye, before speaking in a soft, guarded voice.

"Yes? Can I help you with something?"

Mick straightened himself, taking a deep breath before responding. His words came out in a measured tone, the lines he had rehearsed echoing in his mind as he spoke.

"Mrs. Simpson, my name is Mick West," he said, his voice steady despite the storm of emotions roiling inside him. "I'm looking for a friend of mine who went missing over two years ago at the same place that your husband disappeared a bit over a year ago. And I was hoping that you might be able to help me find him, or maybe even both of them."

It was the last words, the mention of "both of them", that seemed to hit her hardest. Mick could see it in the way her face shifted, the subtle tightening around her eyes. Without another word, she stepped aside and gestured for him to enter.

"Please come inside, Mick West," she said, her voice soft, but there was an unspoken weight behind it. "I'll talk with you."

Mick hesitated for only a second before stepping into the dimly lit house. It was quiet inside, save for the soft hum of a ceiling fan overhead. They walked into a modest living room, the kind of place that spoke of years of hard work and small comforts. Leonora motioned for Mick to sit, then herself took a seat opposite him, her posture rigid, as though bracing for what was to come.

Mick chose his words carefully, not wanting to push her too hard. "I understand if this is a sensitive subject, Mrs. Simpson. If you'd prefer, I can come back another time. I don't want to upset you."

But Leonora shook her head. Her gaze was firm, unflinching. "No, Mick. I've been living with this for too long, and I'd like to know what happened to my husband. If you're here to help, then I'm willing to listen."

Mick nodded, his heart heavy with the weight of his own story. He had never intended to drag someone else into the mess of his own troubled past, but he knew he had no choice now. He owed it to the missing. Owed it to Sam, and to the others. He cleared his throat, then began the story.

He told Leonora everything. About Sam's disappearance, how the police had accused him of killing his friend, and how they had painted him as the villain in a tale that was far from clear. He spoke of his acquittal and release from prison, the burden of the injustice still lingering on him like a shroud. But more than that, he spoke of his mission, his determination to uncover the truth, to set things right, not just for himself but for the families of the missing. For Leonora, for Eric.

As Mick spoke, Leonora's eyes never left his face, her expression unreadable. The air in the room seemed to thicken, as though the very walls were listening. When he finished, there was a long pause. The only sound was the distant hum of the fan overhead. Then Leonora finally spoke, her voice a soft whisper, but carrying the weight of a thousand untold stories.

"I've always wondered, Mick," she said quietly, "if Eric's disappearance wasn't just a random accident. Something didn't feel right from the start. And now you tell me your story... I think there's more going on here than anyone is willing to admit."

Mick leaned forward, his voice low but filled with determination. "That's what I think too, Mrs. Simpson. And I'm going to find out what really happened to your husband. Whatever it takes."

Leonora met his gaze, and for the first time in over a year, Mick saw a glimmer of hope in her eyes. It was faint, but it was there. She nodded slowly, as if making a decision.

"Then we'll do it together, Mick," she said, her voice steady now. "I want answers. I need to know the truth, for Eric's sake."

Mick's mind was already whirring with the new pieces of the puzzle as he sat across from Leonora, her teary eyes a silent testament to the grief she had carried for far too long. His next question slipped from his lips without warning, born out of curiosity and the gnawing sense that something wasn't quite right. "Why did Eric go to that particular area?"

Leonora wiped her eyes, her hands trembling slightly as she sat back in her chair. The question seemed to bring back a flood of memories, each one more painful than the last. "Eric had seen it on the TV, about the man who was missing," she began, her voice breaking slightly with emotion. "He watched the news about that man, and he kept saying how that place was where the gold was, where it had to be. Eric always believed that if someone kept going back there, they would eventually find it. He said, 'If that man keeps going there, then there is gold there, Mick. I know it.'"

Mick leaned in, his gaze unwavering as he listened intently. "And what did you say?" he asked quietly.

"I told him it was too dangerous," Leonora replied, her voice low and thick with sorrow. "I told him he wouldn't come back with any gold, that it was a fool's dream. But he didn't listen. He went anyway... and he didn't come back."

Her voice broke at the end of the sentence, and Mick's heart clenched. It was the same dangerous allure that had drawn so many before Eric, an obsession with gold, with finding something that could change everything. The wild, untamed pull of the land had claimed Eric, just as it had claimed the others. And now, Mick was determined to find out why.

Before Leonora could fall further into her grief, Mick shifted the conversation, asking a question that had been gnawing at him ever since he learned of Eric's disappearance. "Did Eric have headphones?" he asked. "Did his metal detector come with a set of headphones, do you know?"

Leonora blinked, as if surprised by the sudden turn in the conversation, but then her expression softened as she recalled the details. "No," she answered, shaking her head. "It didn't come with headphones. Those were extra. Can you believe it? Nine thousand dollars for the machine, and then you must pay extra for the headphones. But Eric, he wanted them. He paid the extra money because he wanted to hear everything, every little sound."

Mick's mind was already racing, absorbing every detail she provided. "So Eric did have the headphones," he muttered, more to himself than to Leonora. He had his answer, at least to one question. But now he had to piece everything together.

On his way back to Innisfail, Mick couldn't stop thinking about what he had learned. There were two things that stood out in his mind like a beacon in the night. The first, and most obvious, was that Eric had gone to that specific location because he believed there was gold there. Just like Sam had, just like many others before them. But this wasn't just about the treasure; it was about the lure of the unknown, the dangerous allure of the wild.

The second point, though less clear, was still vital. Mick now had strong reason to believe that Eric had been wearing headphones when he disappeared. And that, Mick knew, was no small detail.

It was a strange coincidence, but Mick couldn't shake the feeling that the headphones were more than just a trivial detail. He knew, for instance, that Graham Eldridge had been found with headphones still around his neck. And Sam, well, Mick had witnessed Sam's constant reliance on his headphones when he was fossicking. The speaker on his metal detector had been shot, rendering it useless without the headphones.

Now, three out of the four missing men had been wearing headphones when they disappeared. It was too much to ignore. The question was, had Phillip Laidlow been wearing them too?

Mick shifted uncomfortably in his seat. As much as he had tried to embrace the world of metal detecting, Mick wasn't entirely sold on the idea of wearing headphones himself. It was a choice that felt... disconcerting. When he used the detector, though he was an amateur, barely scratching the surface of the craft, he preferred to keep his senses alert to the world around him. The headphones, to him, were like a barrier to the outside world. They cut off the noise of the environment, shutting out the subtle sounds of danger, of movement. It felt like driving a car with the music blaring too loudly, blocking out everything that mattered.

No, Mick wasn't fond of headphones. And yet, it seemed that every man who had gone missing had been wearing them. The thought lingered in his mind like a dark cloud, the weight of it pressing against his chest. What was it about the headphones? Were they somehow part of the puzzle? Or were they just a coincidence? He wasn't sure, but he knew one thing, he needed to find out.

Leonora, sitting silently across from him, seemed to sense the change in Mick's demeanour. Her eyes were filled with a quiet understanding, the weight of their shared loss hanging heavily in the room. "You think the headphones have something to do with it, don't you?" she asked, her voice soft.

Mick met her gaze, his jaw set in a hard line. "I don't know, but I think it's something worth looking into. If Eric had them, and Sam did, and Graham too... then maybe, just maybe, there's a reason for it. A reason none of us have figured out yet."

Leonora nodded slowly, her face pale but resolute. "I hope you find out what happened, Mick. I really do."

Mick stood up, his mind a whirlwind of thoughts, and offered her a tight smile. "I will, Leonora. I'm not giving up."

As he walked out the door and into the blinding sun of the afternoon, Mick's thoughts turned back to the missing men, to the headphones, to the boulders, and to the dark secrets buried beneath the earth. There was more to this mystery than he had imagined, and he was determined to uncover it, no matter what the cost.

Mick sat back, the afternoon sun casting long shadows across the road as he looked down at the receipt. It was a piece of paper that, in its simplicity, could hold the key to a deeper mystery. But it was the line of thought that had been building in Mick's mind, the strange collection of disappearances, the oddities surrounding each of the missing men, that had brought him here. He had never believed in coincidences, not after what had happened to him. And this, whatever this was, had too many unanswered questions.

"Six grand on camping gear," Mick muttered under his breath as his eyes traced the numbers on the receipt. "And for a boy who hated fishing. Hell, he even hated fish."

Sean Laidlow was standing in the doorway to the kitchen, his arms crossed, a stern yet thoughtful look on his face. Libby had reappeared from the hallway with the receipt, her expression still one of quiet concern. Mick could tell she wasn't entirely comfortable with the situation. But then again, who would be?

"Is this all?" Mick asked, tapping the receipt gently with his fingers.

"That's it," Libby said softly, "though I'll be honest, we didn't really dig into it. It was all too much to handle at the time, and we were just so worried about Phillip. He was supposed to be on his own, finding himself, you know? Not spending that kind of money on a hobby he'd never shown any interest in before. I guess we all thought he'd come home with stories of the wild, not... not this."

Mick understood. The parents of a missing person rarely ever understood the oddities. It was like trying to decipher the behaviour of a man you thought you knew, but in the end, you were left with nothing but questions and regret. The thought of what they must have gone through, the uncertainty, the silence, the fear of the unknown, struck Mick in a way that was almost painful.

He looked at the receipt again, his mind running a thousand calculations. The total sum for the work, for the off-road modifications to the car, made it clear that Phillip Laidlow had been preparing for something. But it wasn't fishing trips or casual camping. No. There was something else at play here. Mick's gut told him that.

"Is there anything else, anything at all, that you can think of?" Mick asked, his voice taking on a more urgent tone.

Libby and Sean exchanged a long look before Sean spoke. "There's one thing... one small thing that might be worth mentioning."

Mick leaned forward, his instincts sharpening like a knife.

"We found a notebook in Phillip's car after he disappeared," Sean continued, his voice low, careful. "It was wedged behind the driver's seat. I don't know why he'd kept it there, but it had some strange notes in it. There were sketches, nothing elaborate, just quick drawings, but they were of some odd shapes, like... like rock formations."

"Rock formations?" Mick repeated, his pulse quickening. "What kind of rock formations?"

"It's hard to say," Sean muttered. "But there were a few that looked like something from a place near Black Mountain. Like boulders stacked together, but with these odd angles. And there were a few notes jotted down about 'coordinates' and something about 'climbing.' I don't know exactly what it meant. But I thought it might be worth mentioning."

Mick's mind was already racing, the pieces of the puzzle falling into place one by one. Black Mountain. The climbing. The mysterious notebook. His earlier conversation with Brett flashed through his mind, the grappling hooks, the ropes, the meticulous planning needed to climb boulders that could easily kill a man if not approached with care. It all tied together too neatly to be a coincidence.

"I need to see that notebook," Mick said, his voice taut with anticipation. "Do you have it?"

Sean hesitated, then nodded. "It's in the garage. I'll go get it."

As Sean disappeared into the garage, Mick turned his attention to Libby. "I know this must be hard for you," he said quietly. "But I think you're closer to the truth than you realise. Phillip's disappearance, Eric Simpson's, and even the others, it's all connected. I just need a little more to go on, and I'll find out what happened to him."

Libby's eyes met Mick's, the silent understanding between them undeniable. "I just want to know why," she whispered.

Mick nodded, his resolve hardening. "I'll find out."

It didn't take long for Sean to return with the small, weathered notebook in hand. Mick took it from him with a sense of urgency, flipping it open to the first few pages. As he scanned the pages, his heart began to pound in his chest. There, scrawled hastily, were the words that made his blood run cold: 'Coordinates. Climbing route. Black Mountain.'

Mick read the words again. This was no coincidence. It was the same area, the same dangerous terrain. The same obsession with the boulders, the gold, and the climbing. Phillip Laidlow had come to the same conclusion as the others, and now Mick understood what had drawn them all to this cursed place.

"I need to get to Black Mountain," Mick said, his voice low but resolute. "I think I know where Phillip is. And I think I know where the others might be, too."

Libby looked at Mick with a mixture of fear and hope in her eyes. "Do you really think you can find them, Mick?"

"I don't know," Mick replied, his tone grim, "but I have to try."

With that, Mick stood up, tucking the notebook into his jacket pocket. The weight of it was more than just paper, it was the burden of truth, and he wasn't about to back down now.

He had a long road ahead of him, one that would take him deep into the heart of danger, to a place where the earth itself seemed to swallow men whole. But Mick wasn't afraid. He knew the cost of finding the truth. He had paid it once before. And he would pay it again, if it meant bringing these men home.

Mick's fingers trailed down the invoice, each item written in neat black ink, but it was the cost that caught his attention. As his eyes scanned the list, the price tags seemed to jump out at him. "Well, it certainly looks like he was getting ready to do some serious off-road camping by the look of this," Mick muttered, but his words faltered as he came across a particular line, Minelab SDC2300 Metal Detector with Accessory Kit Special Deal - $4,300.00. His brow furrowed as the number registered in his mind. "Was Phillip into fossicking, Sean? I see here that he bought a fairly expensive metal detector."

Sean and Libby exchanged a blank look before Sean shook his head. "No, not that I know of," he said. "We had no idea what he was doing with it. The police did find some metal detector instructions during their search, but it didn't mean much to us at the time. We just thought it was another one of his gadgets."

Mick nodded, his gaze never leaving the line on the invoice. "The SDC2300 is a metal detector, Sean," he said, looking up. "And I'm telling you, that's a serious piece of equipment. Not something you'd pick up at a local hobby shop."

"Bullshit!" Sean's voice cracked with disbelief. "Forty-three hundred dollars for a metal detector? No way would Phillip spend that much on that kind of thing."

Mick's expression remained unchanged as he leaned back, a distant look in his eyes. "I'm not pulling your leg, Sean. That's about mid-range. The top-of-the-line detectors run closer to nine or ten grand. Trust me. This machine is designed for one thing, gold."

Libby and Sean stared at Mick, their faces a mix of confusion and growing concern.

"Amateurs, hobbyists, and the average fossicker, they wouldn't touch anything like this," Mick continued, his voice steady. "They'd be happy with a detector in the thousand to fifteen-hundred-dollar range. But this... this is a premium tool. If Phillip bought this, he wasn't out there looking for coins or old relics. He was chasing something bigger, gold. And that's something I know all too well."

Sean frowned, still processing Mick's words. "But Phillip? He never mentioned anything about looking for gold. He never said anything about fossicking. He was always talking about off-road camping, adventures, getting away from everything. Gold? I don't know, Mick. It's hard to believe."

Mick paused, letting the silence hang in the air before he spoke again. "It seems that Sam and Eric were chasing something when they went missing, probably gold, given the circumstances. They had the same kind of detectors, the same obsession with Black Mountain. Maybe Phillip was following the same lead."

Libby's eyes widened, a flicker of understanding crossing her face. "I... I never thought of that. It makes sense now. The camping gear, the new gear for his ute, all of it. We didn't make the connection. But now that you mention it, he was always one for opportunistic investments. If he thought something would pay off, he'd spend money without a second thought. Could he have been chasing gold?"

Mick gave a slow nod. "That's what I'm thinking. All the signs are there now, especially the way he kitted out his ute and bought that detector. It's no ordinary metal detector. And if he was up there, near Black Mountain... well, it's no surprise he's gone missing like the others."

The conversation left the air thick with unease, but Mick was already gathering his thoughts, his mind clicking over faster than the thoughts could catch up. He had to go back to the mountain. He had to follow the same trail, pick up the pieces left behind by the missing men, and discover what had really happened to them. There was too much at stake now, too much to ignore.

"Well, thank you both for your time," Mick said, standing. "I know this hasn't been easy, but I promise I'll keep you in the loop. If I uncover anything new, you'll be the first to know."

Libby gave him a small, tight smile, her eyes still clouded with concern. "Thank you, Mick. We just want to know what happened to him. Phillip, Eric, and all of them. It's... it's been so hard."

Mick nodded, his hand on the doorframe. "I'll find out, Libby. I'll make sure of it."

He stepped out into the late afternoon, his mind already elsewhere. The weekend climb was only a few days away, and he had a plan to finalise. Brett and his father would meet him at the base of the range on Friday for a weekend excursion, a chance to scout the terrain again, to look for new clues. Mick had a list of supplies to gather, swag, gas stove, esky. All the things he needed to be ready for the climb, but his thoughts were already with his own gear, the things he'd lost in the police evidence room. His detector, the $9,000 machine that had been taken from him, was still in limbo. He knew they claimed it could be used as evidence, but part of him suspected it would never be returned. And that pissed him off.

But Mick wasn't one to back down. Not when he was this close. He'd done the hard yards before, and he would do them again. If it meant getting his gear back or simply getting answers, he'd fight for it.

As he drove away from the Laidlow's home, he dialled Emily's number. "Still at the Rockpool?" he asked when she picked up.

"Yeah, just wrapping up. The kids are playing in the pool."

"I'll be there soon. We've got the weekend ahead of us, but I need to get some things together. A climb's planned with Brett and his father for Australia Day weekend. We're taking the Friday off for an extra day in the ranges."

Emily's voice was light, but there was a touch of concern beneath the surface. "That's great, Mick. I know you've been planning this for a while."

"I'll make it worth your while," Mick said with a small, grim smile. "But first, I've got some gear to pick up."

The road ahead was long, but Mick knew it would lead him to answers. And once he had those answers, nothing would stop him from putting the pieces together, no matter where the trail took him.

Emily's brow furrowed as Mick finished explaining his plans for the weekend. She wasn't exactly thrilled at the thought of him heading into the rugged ranges again, not after everything that had happened. She crossed her arms and shot him a look of mild disapproval, her voice low with concern. "You sure you're going to be all right, Mick? I mean, it's not like you're exactly a spring chicken these days, are you?"

Mick chuckled, brushing off her concern with a grin that didn't quite reach his eyes. "I'll be fine, Em. It's just a walk and a bit of climbing. Two experts to keep me from doing something stupid. You know me, I've got a bit of a knack for surviving these things."

But Emily wasn't so easily reassured. She eyed him warily, her lips pressing together in that familiar, worried frown. "Just promise me you'll be careful. Don't go acting like a hero up there. You've got two kids who still need their dad."

Mick met her gaze with a soft but firm smile. "I'm not going anywhere, Em. I'll be back before you know it."

That seemed to settle her nerves a little, but there was one more thing. Their eldest boy, Luke, had been adamant about joining his father on the climb. The twelve-year-old had practically been bouncing off the walls with excitement, practically begging to tag along. But Mick wasn't ready for that yet, he knew the climb was tough, the terrain rough, and he didn't want to risk anything happening to the boy.

It took a lot of convincing, some creative promises, and a few bribes to finally get Luke to agree to stay behind. He moped for the rest of the morning, but after a while, he relented. "Maybe next time, Dad," he muttered, not quite able to hide the disappointment in his voice. Mick gave him a rough tousle of the hair and a smile that was equal parts pride and regret.

With that out of the way, Mick was free to meet up with Brett and his father. He had arranged to meet them at the Marianvale Pub that Friday around eleven, just for a quick lunch and a beer before they made their way up into the ranges. As Mick stepped into the pub, the cool air inside offering a welcome relief from the midday heat, he spotted them immediately. Brett, tall, thick-set, and with his familiar dark complexion, was standing at the bar chatting with a man who looked like an older version of him, his father, Brian.

"Brett, mate! How's it going?" Mick called as he made his way over, his hand already reaching out to shake Brett's with a firm grip. The two men shared a moment of camaraderie, both grinning like old friends reunited.

Brian, who was slightly stockier than his son but just as broad-shouldered, gave Mick a nod. "Good to see you again, Mick," he said, shaking Mick's hand with a grip that felt as solid as a rock.

After a round of hearty greetings, they ordered beers and took a seat at one of the many empty tables. The time of day, just before noon, meant the pub was quiet, but the atmosphere was warm and inviting, the promise of a cold beer and good food lingering in the air.

Brian was the first to break the silence. "Sounds like you've had an eventful three years, Mick. You'll have to fill us in tonight at camp. But for now, how about we get a steak and a couple more beers before we head up the hill?" he suggested, his tone casual but welcoming.

Mick and Brett both agreed that it sounded like a solid plan. They perused the menu, and as luck would have it, there was a special on: T-bone and a schooner for $20. It was the perfect excuse for a proper lunch before heading out to the ranges.

Lunch passed in a haze of laughter, good food, and better beer. Brett and Mick reminisced about old times, catching up on life's twists and turns, while Brian chimed in with his own stories of the old days, keeping the conversation lively and full of life. By the time the plates were cleared, they were all ready to head out.

The drive up into the mountains was smooth, with Mick leading the way in his truck, Brett and Brian following closely behind in their Hilux ute. They arrived at the campsite just after four-thirty, giving them plenty of time to set up before darkness fell. The landscape around them was a mix of sparse trees and jagged rocks, but Mick loved it. The isolation, the stillness, this was where he felt alive, where the noise of the world couldn't reach him.

Mick had learned from Sam's tricks, and so, true to form, he'd stocked up on a whole rump steak, which he planned to carve into individual steaks as needed. But Mick being Mick, he'd gone one better. He'd also brought a whole porterhouse, just to cover all bases. He wasn't planning on letting any of the men go hungry, not on his watch.

He'd even found a new contraption for grilling that was far superior to the one Sam had put together years ago. Mick couldn't help but feel a little smug about it, but then again, Sam had always been more of a half-baked inventor when it came to these things. This new grill, however, was a work of art, solid, practical, and damn effective.

As they settled into the campsite, the air grew cooler, and the first stars began to twinkle above, the fire crackling warmly between them. There was something about being up here, away from the hustle of everyday life, that made all the worries fade into the background. They were all men of the land, in their element, ready to face whatever the mountain threw at them.

For now, though, it was just the fire, the beer, and the quiet companionship of old friends. Mick knew they'd have more to talk about tonight, once they were sitting around the fire, but for now, he was content. They'd have a good night, and tomorrow, they'd face the climb with fresh eyes, ready for whatever came next.

The air was warm as the evening sun dipped low behind the jagged peaks of the ranges, the warmth of the day refusing to let go. The fire crackled and popped in front of them, the flickering flames casting long shadows across the rugged terrain. They all sat in their folding 'squatter' type chairs, the fire's dance adding a sense of comfort, despite the wild surroundings. Another hearty steak meal had settled into their stomachs, the satisfying weight of it only adding to the camaraderie that hung thick in the air. And for Mick, there was a purpose to this gathering, beyond the shared meal and the alcohol that now flowed freely between them. He had a story to tell, and it was one that had been years in the making.

His voice, rough but steady, carried over the low hum of the fire. The narrative he wove stretched on for hours, the tale unfolding slowly, the weight of it sinking deep into their bones. Between long pauses and frequent sips of the cold gold stubbies, Mick took them through the entire sequence of events, from the first signs of trouble to the mounting questions that had plagued him ever since. The men listened intently, their expressions unreadable but their minds churning with the possibilities Mick laid out.

As Mick spoke, the firelight glinted off their faces, casting them in sharp relief as the tale deepened. "So, the first man to vanish was a keen fisherman," Mick continued, his voice steady but his eyes distant, as if seeing something far beyond the firelight. "He stumbled upon a bit of gold, purely by chance, and, like many before him, he couldn't resist. He came back with a metal detector, big mistake. That's how Sam came here, too. Sam wasn't a true fossicker, mind you, more of a fisherman, a bloke who found gold by accident, but it was enough to get him hooked."

Brett and Brian exchanged glances, the weight of Mick's words sinking in. They had heard bits of this story before, but now, hearing it from Mick's mouth, it felt different. Real.

"But then there's Eric Simpson," Mick went on, shifting in his seat as he spoke, the firelight dancing in his eyes. "His wife, she'd told me, said he'd heard about Sam's disappearance in the papers and figured that this place was a gold mine, no pun intended. He went out and bought a bloody expensive metal detector, nearly ten grand. And it paid off. The police found 37 grams of gold stashed in his glovebox when they found his vehicle."

The two men nodded, the pieces falling into place. "Seems like Eric was following a trail, just like Sam," Brian muttered under his breath, his fingers tapping the edge of his chair thoughtfully.

Mick gave a sharp nod. "Exactly. But then, there's Phillip Laidlow, he was in the police force, a loner by all accounts. Word's out that he knew about Eric's gold, did the math, and decided to get in on the action. So he came up here, set himself up for some serious prospecting."

The fire crackled louder, as if punctuating Mick's words. He took a long drink, letting the moment settle before speaking again. "And that's the mystery of it. Why did they all come to this place? What made them think that this was the spot? This whole range is littered with boulders and rocky outcrops. It's not exactly the kind of place you wander into without a damn good reason."

There was a pause, the conversation heavy on their minds. After a long moment, Mick cleared his throat and shifted. "Tomorrow, we fly the drone," he said, his tone shifting to business-like resolve. "We need to find the spot where Graham Eldridge was last seen."

The following morning came with the bite of early light and a coolness that hinted at the high-altitude chill yet to come. They gathered their gear, making their way to the ridge where they hoped the drone would provide answers. As they followed the rocky path, Mick couldn't help but notice the faded yellow ribbons that marked Eric's earlier trail. It was hard to miss them, now weathered and frayed, but they were the only clues they had.

It wasn't long before they reached the more treacherous part of the ridge, where the path narrowed, and the towering boulders loomed like silent sentinels, their sheer size intimidating. Mick had never ventured this far along the ridge before, and he could feel the weight of the unknown pressing in around them. The air grew thicker, cooler, as the boulders hemmed them in, creating a canyon of stone that made it feel as if the mountains themselves were watching them.

"This place..." Brett muttered under his breath, his eyes scanning the imposing landscape. "It's got the feel of Black Mountain, doesn't it?"

Mick could only nod in agreement. The sense of isolation was almost suffocating, the terrain unforgiving. But they had come this far, and they weren't about to turn back now. Brian led the way, moving with the ease of someone who had spent a lifetime climbing these rocks. He found the perfect flat area to set up the drone and started preparing it for flight.

The drone hummed to life, its small, efficient blades cutting through the air as the screen on Brian's mini iPad flickered to life, providing a wide view of the area around them. They all watched in silence as the drone floated higher, the rocky ridge unfolding before them like a patchwork quilt of stone.

And then, there it was, the yellow paint marker. Faint but unmistakable, the marker stood out against the sea of rocks below. Brian tried to manoeuvre the drone closer, but the hot air pockets coming off the rocks made it tricky to control. The drone shuddered slightly, buffeted by the shifting currents, but Brian's hands were steady. They had found it.

"We know where it is now," Brian said, his voice calm, but there was a note of urgency behind it. "We'll walk or climb out to it from here."

With a knowing glance, Brian began unpacking the grappling hook from his backpack. He handed it over to Mick. "You ready for this?"

Mick nodded, adjusting his climbing boots, Arbpro climbing boots, the ones Brian had insisted he get before the trip. They were lightweight, but the ankle support was impeccable, and the grip on the rocks was something to behold. Mick had to admit, they were perfect for this kind of terrain.

"Stay in the middle, Mick," Brian said, already heading up the boulders with ease. His movements were fluid, effortless, as if he had been born in the mountains.

Mick followed, doing his best to keep pace. The boulders were a challenge, each step a test of balance and strength, but the boots held fast, and with every movement, Mick grew more confident. It wasn't easy, but nothing worth doing ever was.

The rocky path seemed to go on forever, the boulders stretching out in every direction. But Mick didn't care. He was focused. This was the moment. They were close. And they wouldn't stop until they found the answers they were searching for.

The air was thick with the scent of the earth, hot and dusty from the morning's warmth. The landscape stretched out in front of them, a brutal, jagged wilderness that had remained untamed for centuries. They moved with quiet determination, the fire of their resolve burning brighter than any light they could carry. The yellow marker, now barely visible under the harsh sun and time's cruel passage, called them forward.

They approached cautiously, each of them mindful of the silent danger that seemed to pulse from the rocks around them. The boulders lay in front of them like a maze, a trap, as if the mountains themselves had crafted this place to hide something they wanted left undisturbed. As they neared the spot marked by the fading yellow paint, it was clear that they had reached the threshold of something that was more than just a dead end in the rocks. This was a place of death, of silence, of the kind of secret that nature doesn't want shared.

The ground beneath them was steep, so steep that it sent a ripple of unease through Mick as his boots scraped over the stone, sending small pebbles tumbling into the abyss below. They crouched at the edge, peering down at what they assumed was the tunnel where Graham Eldridge had been found, his body twisted and bent in an unnatural position.

Before them, the slope fell sharply, a ten-metre drop that led straight to a jagged cone-shaped formation made of three protruding boulders. They jutted up from the earth like the claws of some giant creature, the sharp edges almost daring anyone to get too close. The cone itself was barely wide enough to fit a man's head, but its diameter, about three hundred millimetres, was just enough to trap anyone who fell, forcing their head into the narrow space with terrifying speed. It was a natural trap, a cruel invention of nature.

Mick's gut twisted at the thought of what might have happened here. The realisation that anyone unlucky enough to slip in this treacherous terrain would be doomed was inescapable.

"Jesus Christ, if you go down there head first, you're done for," Mick muttered, staring at the cone. He couldn't help but imagine the terror of someone slipping, falling into that suffocating gap, the unforgiving rock rushing up to meet them. The coldness of the thought sent a shiver down his spine, and he shook it off, trying to focus.

To the right, a larger hole caught his eye. This was no mere crevice but a deep void, the kind that hinted at secrets buried far deeper than the surface of the earth. From their vantage point, it looked to be a far more dangerous path, one that led into the unknown.

"That's the one to look at, Dad," Brett said, his voice carrying the faint edge of anticipation.

Brian nodded, his face hardening with resolve. "We'll make an anchor at the bottom of this boulder," he said, gesturing to the one they were crouching on, "then you can abseil down on a single luff pulley and check it out, Brett. Thirty metres should be enough."

Brett nodded, already moving with the familiarity of someone who had done this before. He attached a LED light bank to his golf cap, a small but crucial detail that would illuminate the darkness below. Brian pulled a static lightweight rope from his backpack, its coils falling like a snake at their feet. Mick watched as Brian carefully lowered himself, slipping backwards over the boulder's edge to secure a crevice anchor with a sling and pulley.

"I'm good, Dad," Brett said, his voice steady as he adjusted his UHF headphones. The sound-activated microphone snapped into place, and he gave his father a thumbs-up.

Brian's voice came back through the static of the handheld UHF. "Got you, son. Loud and clear."

With that, Brett lowered himself over the boulder, his body disappearing from sight as he dropped past the cone formation, the rope unfurling smoothly behind him. For a moment, the only sound was the distant flutter of the wind and the subtle, unsettling creak of the rope. The minutes stretched on, a heavy silence falling over the three men as they waited.

It felt like an eternity before Brett's voice cracked through the static. "Dad, can you hear me? Can you hear me?"

Brian's voice was firm. "Got you, Brett. What's down there?"

Brett's words were urgent now, tinged with unease. "I've run out of rope, Dad. But I think there's something down here. I can smell it. There's something down below, maybe another ten to fifteen metres. I think it's a body, or at least... something."

Mick's stomach turned at the thought, but Brian acted swiftly, pulling on the rope, his hand steady as he brought Brett back up. When Brett finally emerged from the darkness, his face was pale, eyes wide with the haunting realisation of what he'd encountered.

"Jesus, Dad," Brett breathed, his voice shaking. "It stinks down there. Something's dead. I couldn't see what it was, but it's bad. I need a respirator to go back down there. It's not safe."

Brian's brow furrowed in concern, but he nodded, his instincts taking over. "No more rope, Brett. We're done down there for now."

The group moved swiftly, their minds heavy with the implications of Brett's discovery. They had seen enough for the day, but the mystery was far from over.

As they made their way back from the boulders, Mick caught sight of something that hadn't been visible from their previous route, a much easier access to their left. It hadn't shown up on the drone's feed, but now it seemed like a perfect opportunity to explore a safer route back.

"Let's take this way," Mick suggested, pointing to the new path. "It looks easier than what we came through, and we won't have to climb like we did before."

Brian took a deep breath and nodded. "You're right, Mick. This way is much better. Not nearly as challenging. Let's head back."

The three men moved through the easier path, their pace quickening as they left the foreboding boulders behind. The mountain seemed to hold its breath, the silence pressing in on them as they descended, but they knew the answers were out there still, waiting to be found. And they would return. They had to. There was no other choice.

By the time they had returned to their camp at around four-thirty, the sky had turned a deep, brooding grey. A fine drizzle began to fall, the rain cool and gentle against their skin as they sat around the fire, the light flickering off their weathered faces. The warmth of the flames cut through the chill, and they took comfort in their routine. Each man opened a beer, the hiss of the can punctuating the silence before Brett broke it.

"I don't really know, fellas," Brett muttered, staring into the fire as the smoke rose in thin columns. "But I reckon that's a dead body in that hole up there. The stink is just too strong for any animal. I've never smelled anything like it before. What do you think we should do? Go to the coppers?"

The question hung in the air, heavy with its implications. They all sat back in their folding squatter chairs, the weariness of the day settling into their bones, but the thought of what they had found up on Mount Marian was impossible to ignore.

Brian, never one to rush into decisions, took a long swig from his beer, his eyes narrowing as he considered the matter. "I think we should tell them," he said slowly, the weight of his words clear in his voice. "Whether they'll take it any further, I don't know. But at least we have to tell them. And I don't think we should go back up there until we do. Looking at that place, well… you wouldn't find a better place to hide a body. That's for sure."

The others nodded, grim faces all around. They knew it was the right thing to do. There was no going back. And yet, the thought of what they'd uncovered left a bitter taste in their mouths. They lingered a moment longer in silence, then cracked open another couple of beers, as though the simple act of drinking would steady their resolve.

Mick, always one to add a bit of humour when the tension became unbearable, grinned and said, "Tomorrow's Sunday, then a public holiday Monday, yeah? I reckon we should report it to the Marianvale police station tomorrow, just to stuff up that fat fuck of a sergeant's weekend."

Laughter erupted around the campfire, but the strain of their discovery still lingered in the air, palpable despite the humour. Brett, ever the one to cut to the heart of things, spoke again, his voice tinged with a dark realisation. "If it's a body, it's probably the young copper. He disappeared only about three or four months ago. The others would've been well past the smell by now, but him... he'd still be fresh."

The words settled between them like an uncomfortable truth. It was a horrible thought, but one that couldn't be ignored.

The next morning, they found themselves at the Marianvale police station, the air thick with anticipation and the smell of rain on the wind. The sergeant, a man whose face seemed carved from stone, sat behind the desk, his expression as unreadable as ever.

They took turns telling their story, how they'd found the body, how it had reeked, how the hole had seemed a perfect hiding place, a cruel trap that nature had set long ago. Mick spoke last, his voice sharp with an edge of frustration.

"And why the fuck are you back here?" Sergeant Kearns asked, his eyes narrowing as he glared at Mick.

"Because I want to find out what happened to my mate, Sam," Mick shot back, anger rising in his voice.

"You fucking know what happened to your mate. You fucking killed him."

The accusation hit like a slap, and Mick's face darkened, his fists clenching. "I have now been found not guilty," he said, his voice trembling with anger. "And I want to know what happened to him."

"You've been acquitted, not fucking exonerated," the sergeant sneered. "You're on thin ice, Mick West."

The tension in the room was palpable, thick enough to cut through with a knife. But Brian, ever the calm one, stepped forward, his voice even and composed. "You might be the one on thin ice, Sergeant," he said, his tone measured but firm. "Come on, boys. Let's report this to the Cairns police."

The sergeant's face twisted in a mixture of frustration and resignation. "Sorry," he muttered, his voice laced with fatigue. "I've had a bad day, fellas. I think what you've just told me has put me over the top. But Mick, I've always thought you killed your mate up there. And it'll take a lot to convince me otherwise. You'll need to stay here until I can get in touch with my boss in Mareeba."

The three men exchanged glances, then nodded. They had no choice. Mick, though still simmering with anger, agreed to stay. They told the sergeant they'd book into the pub for the night, as they weren't expected home until Monday, and that he could find them there.

When they arrived at the pub, Mick couldn't help but grin, a wicked smile curling on his lips as he sat down at the bar, a beer in hand. Brett, who had been watching him closely, raised an eyebrow. Then they all burst into laughter.

"Fat fuck is very apt," Brian said, raising his glass in a mock salute. The laughter echoed through the pub, the absurdity of the situation momentarily lifting the weight that had hung over them all.

At four-thirty, Sergeant Kearns walked into the pub, his shoulders slumped as if the weight of the world was on them. He walked up to Brian and, without preamble, asked, "Would you be available to meet a police team at your campsite around nine o'clock tomorrow morning?"

Brian looked at Mick, who was the one who had orchestrated the search for Sam. "It'll be up to Mick," Brian said. "He's the one who started this search, after all."

The sergeant, clearly embarrassed, mumbled an apology. Brian, with his usual calm demeanour, reassured him. "Don't worry about it. We'll be there at nine. We'll meet you at the campsite."

The sergeant gave a quick nod, his voice carrying a touch of sincerity as he turned to Mick. "Thanks, Mick," he said, loud enough for everyone in the pub to hear before he walked out.

"Huh," Brian said, his eyes twinkling with a mix of amusement and irony. "Looks like the sergeant's warming to you, Mick."

The three of them shared another laugh, the tension of the past hours easing ever so slightly.

"Nine o'clock tomorrow morning, back up the hill," Brian added. "They'll meet us at the campsite."

It had been a long, grim day. The mystery of what they had found on Mount Marian still weighed heavily on their minds. But, as they settled in for the evening, it was clear that the three of them were in for another difficult day ahead. Despite the strange, almost morbid nature of their discovery, there was a strange camaraderie between them, a bond forged in the fires of the day's events.

But for now, they would enjoy the night. There was no point in letting the weight of the mountain press them down too early. They would rest. Tomorrow, the truth would unfold.

The rain had poured relentlessly throughout the night, casting a dreary spell over Marianvale. By Monday morning, Australia Day, the sky remained a heavy quilt of cloud, with occasional breaks where the sun peeked through, only to be swallowed up again by the thickening humidity. The air was stifling, the temperature rising as high as the forties, and it clung to their skin like a damp cloak.

The three men stood in the same spot they had been the day before, where they'd launched the drone from, at the foot of the mountain that loomed above them like a silent sentinel. The police inspector in charge of the investigation was a stocky man, his uniform soaked through from the humidity, but his eyes sharp as he listened intently. Brett, Mick, and Brian recounted their findings to the inspector with precision, describing the easy track they had discovered on their return from the boulders. It had been an unexpected revelation, one that had changed the course of their search, and the inspector had asked them to pass this information along to the search and rescue team that was expected to arrive shortly.

The rescue crew arrived just after midday, their truck groaning under the weight of heavy equipment, though the furthest it could reach was the old campsite where they had parked their vehicles. No track led further, not through the dense bush or the rough terrain that bordered the mountain. With the equipment still packed tight in the truck, the crew chose to survey the area first, taking their time. It was a slow, methodical approach, and one that Brian found frustrating.

He had gone to great lengths the day before to explain the situation to the rescue captain, offering his thoughts on how they should approach the descent into the tunnel. He had suggested using at least fifty metres of rope, a double line with a single luff pulley, and, most importantly, the need for respirators. But the captain had only nodded, noncommittal, like he had already made up his mind. Brian could sense it, the captain's dismissive air. The man was the rescue leader, and in his eyes, he didn't need any advice from outsiders.

Brian bit back his frustration. It was their job, after all, but it felt as if the captain had dismissed their input entirely, despite the weight of their experience and knowledge of the area.

The police were now in charge, and after a brief discussion, they informed Mick, Brett, and Brian that their presence was no longer required. The site was to be closed off for the investigation, and the authorities would take it from here.

Mick shook hands with both Brett and Brian, their farewell heavy with the unspoken understanding that they had done what they could. The uncertainty of what was about to unfold hung in the air, thick and oppressive. But they had their own lives to return to, their own paths to walk, and the search, whether it ended in rescue or recovery, would take its course without them.

Mick arrived home around four o'clock that afternoon, his face drawn from the events of the weekend. Emily, ever anxious to hear about the outcome, waited with bated breath for any news. The television became their anchor, the flickering images offering the only insight into what had happened up on the mountain. They flipped through every channel, but there was no mention of the discovery. Nothing.

"It's probably because of the public holiday," Mick muttered, his frustration rising as the hours wore on. They both knew how these things worked. News cycles were fleeting, and unless something truly catastrophic happened, a disappearance, no matter how tragic, could quickly fade from the public's attention. Life moved on.

But nearly three weeks later, the local news finally carried a small, fleeting mention of the discovery.

"The body of missing Mareeba police constable Phillip Laidlow was found today in a rock formation near the town of Marianvale. It is believed Mr. Laidlow had slipped and fallen while bushwalking in the Mount Marian ranges," the newsreader said, his voice flat and devoid of any real emotion.

The report was barebones, almost clinical in its brevity. No further details were given, no mention of the efforts made to locate Laidlow, no recognition of the men who had spent their own time combing the mountain, piecing together the mystery of the disappearances. Mick's heart sank as he stared at the screen, the hollow feeling of injustice creeping up his spine. The words on the news didn't do justice to the effort they had put into finding the man.

Mick's anger boiled over as he picked up the phone and dialled Sean Laidlow's number, the father of the young constable. When Sean picked up, Mick immediately extended his condolences, but the conversation quickly turned into something much deeper.

The truth was raw, and Mick could hear the tension in Sean's voice when he spoke. Sean had not been told the full story of how Phillip's body had been discovered. The police had kept quiet about the men who had found the location. They had simply reported that a group of bushwalkers had alerted them to a body in the boulders.

"I wasn't aware it was you, Mick," Sean said, his voice thick with emotion. "I didn't know it was you and your friends who found him. They didn't tell me that."

Mick's frustration bubbled to the surface again. "They never do. It's the same thing every time. You'd think they'd at least acknowledge the people who do the work. Hell, if we hadn't been out there, they'd still be scratching their heads." His voice grew harder, more bitter with each word. "I've been saying it for years. There's no interest in the missing men. No real effort. Just the same old bureaucracy. It was a bloody shame."

Mick continued, telling Sean of the place where Phillip's body had been found, a place eerily familiar to Mick. It was the very same spot where Graham Eldridge's body had been discovered some months prior. The coincidence was chilling, and the realisation sent a shiver down Mick's spine.

"Strange coincidence, isn't it?" Mick said, his words hanging in the air like smoke. "Graham Eldridge... Phillip Laidlow. Same place."

The conversation stretched long into the night, the two men trading stories of their losses, their questions, their grief. Sean's voice had softened by the end of their talk, but the unresolved pain still lingered. Mick could hear it in the silence between the words. The police had given them answers, thin and unsatisfying, but the real questions remained. And with them, the ever-present feeling that the truth was being kept just out of reach.

For Mick, the weight of it all was too much to bear, but he knew he had no choice but to carry on. The past would always haunt him, as it did the others. The mountains held their secrets, and some things, it seemed, would never be uncovered.

Three days after the news had aired, barely a whisper about the discovery of Phillip Laidlow's body and the official story of his 'accidental' fall, Brett called Mick, his voice thick with frustration.

"Slipped and fell, my arse," Brett growled into the phone. "How the hell could he have been walking out there in the first place? The coppers didn't mention a damn thing about climbing gear. I'll bet anything he didn't have any. Me and Dad are going back for another look around. You in?"

Mick's pulse quickened at the suggestion, the excitement bubbling up before he even realised it. "Shit yeah, I'll go with you."

"I'll give you a hoy. Probably the weekend after next, if that suits."

"Anytime suits me, mate. Thanks," Mick replied, his mind already racing ahead to the mountains, to the rock-strewn hills where the truth still lurked, hidden beneath the earth and stone.

As Mick ended the call, a spark of suspicion flared within him. It was clear that Brett and Brian weren't buying the official line. Neither was Mick. The bodies, Graham Eldridge's, and now Phillip Laidlow's, had ended up in the same twisted place, and Mick couldn't shake the feeling that something far darker than a simple accident was at play. He wasn't the only one who thought so. Brett and Brian clearly shared his gut feeling, and that made Mick feel less like a lone wolf and more like part of something bigger, a hunt for the truth.

The days passed quickly, and by the time March arrived, the wet season had come and gone, leaving the land lush and green in the wake of the storms. The sun beat down with a fierce intensity as Brian made preparations to launch his drone. Today, they weren't going to retrace their steps from before, they were headed for the left side of the boulders, the area they had missed on their previous search.

It was a hot and sticky morning when they arrived at their old campsite, the air heavy with the smell of the bush and the promise of adventure. The fire crackled as they roasted steaks, the smoke rising in tendrils into the heavy sky, and as they ate and drank, their conversation turned once again to the search that was about to unfold.

"I'm no detective," Brian said, staring into the flames as if the answers were hidden there, "but two missing people, found in nearly the same spot... that doesn't sit right with me."

Mick nodded, leaning forward, his gut telling him that Brian's suspicions were spot on. "Exactly," Brian continued, his eyes narrowing as he thought aloud. "Maybe the first body, Graham Eldridge's, didn't fall the way it was supposed to, maybe it got caught between those three big boulders, stuck, like it was meant to follow down to the hole where Phillip's body ended up."

Brett, who had been listening in silence, spoke up, his voice measured and steady. "Well, there are no more bodies down that hole. I'm sure the rescue crew would've checked every inch of it. They wouldn't have missed anything like that."

Brian gave a slow, thoughtful nod, then turned his attention back to the drone. As it buzzed into the air, its tiny blades cutting through the thick humidity, they scanned the right-hand side of the boulders where they had been before. The sight that greeted them was the same as last time, rough, jagged rock faces, towering over them like ancient guardians. But then, something different caught Brian's eye.

He leaned forward, squinting through the monitor of the drone as it hovered over the terrain. There, behind the first three rows of boulders, was something that stood out, a large, dark hole, nestled just behind the chaotic mass of stone.

"That's it," Brian murmured. "I reckon we should check out that hole first, before we look anywhere else. But it won't be easy getting up there. Might be a tough climb."

Mick stood up from where he had been sitting, wiping his hands on his jeans, his eyes fixed on the area Brian had pointed out. The excitement in his chest grew stronger. "Hell, we've got to give it a shot," he said. "Last time, we didn't find the right track. But this time, we learn from that. Right?"

Brian smiled, a flicker of mischief in his eyes. "Exactly. That's what they call learning from your mistakes. Let's see if we can find a better route." He turned his gaze toward the far right, where a patch of dead, scrubby trees stood, scattered like forgotten sentinels in the harsh sun. His finger hovered over the controls. "Bonanza," he muttered under his breath.

The drone's camera zoomed in on the scene below, offering a bird's-eye view of the rugged landscape, the twisted trees, and the sharp, jagged edges of the boulders. Brian's heart raced as he adjusted the drone's angle, guiding it toward the dead trees. His instincts were telling him something. There was something more out there, something waiting to be found.

"I'll take the drone over there and get a better look at that hole," Brian said, his voice low and determined. "You guys stay sharp. We might not be alone up here."

As the drone moved steadily towards the right, Mick's mind raced. It was one thing to stumble upon a body in the wilderness, but two bodies in the same area? That wasn't coincidence. It was something else. A pattern. And patterns, in Mick's experience, never happened by chance.

The breeze rustled through the trees, the only sound breaking the heavy silence that hung around them. For a moment, Mick allowed himself to picture the past, the men who had gone missing, the ones who never came back. He thought of Sam, his lost mate, and the nagging feeling in his gut that the truth was much darker than anyone had let on.

"Stay sharp, lads," Mick said quietly, his eyes fixed on the drone as it flew higher, the world beneath it growing ever more distant. The search was far from over, and something told Mick that the answers were out there, hidden in the shadows of the mountains, waiting for them to find them.

In the distance, the boulders stood, silent and unyielding, as if daring them to uncover their secrets.

The early morning sun was beginning to beat down with the weight of summer as Brian led the way up the familiar ridge toward the boulders. The path, though rough, was passable enough. There were no cliffs to scale, no steep gradients to navigate, just a few scattered rocks, mere bumps in the otherwise gentle ascent. A well-worn animal track cut through the low scrub, the ground hard and dry beneath their boots. It was almost as though the land itself had decided to help them find their way.

The trio moved with the ease of men who knew the land, who had tread these paths before. Brett was carrying the grappling hook, his eyes scanning the landscape ahead, while Mick followed close behind, scanning the rugged terrain with a practiced eye.

Brian, always the first to find the way, slowed and pointed toward a gap between the towering boulders, a narrow passage barely wide enough to slip through. It was not much of an opening, but it was enough to promise a way forward. "Look," he said, "No need for the grappling hook, Brett. There's a passage through on the side here."

Brett's hands hesitated on the rope, the grappling hook still in his grip as he studied the narrow passage his father had pointed out. A mere crack in the stone, but with Brian's experience, it was clear that it was just wide enough to get through.

The gap led to a narrow ledge that wound around the side of the boulders, a ledge that eventually opened up to reveal a large hole in the rock face. The hole wasn't a sheer drop, but a sloping gradient of about twenty to twenty-five percent. It looked treacherous enough to make a man pause, but not enough to deter them.

Brian's voice was calm, but there was a quiet tension underneath. "Steep enough," he said, his eyes scanning the rocky terrain. "It could drop off at any point. Brett, put your harness on. Light and hookup rope too."

Brett had already started unpacking the necessary gear as his father spoke. He moved with the fluidity of someone who had done this before, too many times before. "I'm ready," he said simply, securing the harness around his waist and clipping the rope to his gear.

Brian's eyes sharpened, his gaze fixed on his son. "I don't have to tell you to go easy, Brett. Stay safe. Put on your UHF headset. Give us a full commentary. We'll be ready to haul you back the moment you say."

Brett gave a silent thumbs up, his expression serious but determined. He stepped toward the cave, his boots crunching on the gravel as he moved into the shadow of the boulders. The passage was tight, forcing him to twist and turn as he manoeuvred his way deeper into the cave, his path zigzagging between massive rocks, some of which seemed as though they had fallen into place centuries ago.

It had barely been a minute before the first crackle of static came through the UHF. Brian's voice was low but firm, his eyes never leaving the entrance to the cave. "Repeat that, Brett. Couldn't understand. Come back."

More static. Then, a faint voice. "Remains are here." The words were cut off abruptly, the static growing louder, drowning out the rest of what Brett was saying.

Brian exchanged a glance with Mick. They said nothing, but both men's jaws tightened. Time seemed to stretch thin, each second passing with agonising slowness.

Then, the UHF crackled back to life, clear as day. "Can you hear me, Dad? I'm coming out."

Brian exhaled a breath he didn't realise he was holding. "OK, son," he replied. "Take it easy."

Minutes later, Brett emerged from the shadows, his face grim. He didn't need to say much. His eyes, dull with the weight of what he had seen, said it all.

"There's two bodies down there, Dad," Brett said, his voice flat, almost emotionless. He didn't seem shocked, he was just stating a fact, as though it was something he had expected.

"Bodies?" Brian and Mick asked in unison, their voices a low rumble of disbelief.

"Well, they're skeletal remains," Brett clarified, his words slow, heavy. "And a couple of packs. Metal detectors."

Mick's face twisted in disbelief, his breath catching in his throat. "You're fucking joking, Brett?" he hissed, his voice barely a whisper. But as Brett shook his head slowly, the truth sank in.

"This is pretty sad, Mick," Brett said, his voice softer now. "This could be your mate Sam and the other missing guy, Simpson."

Mick didn't reply at first. He couldn't. The words felt like a punch to the gut, the weight of the realisation settling on him like a boulder. His mind raced, but there was no clarity, only a dark, gnawing feeling deep in his chest.

Brian, ever the leader, stepped forward and clapped a hand on Brett's shoulder. "Come on, boys," he said, his voice low but steady, pulling them back from the edge. "Let's pack up and get back to camp. We'll think about what we're going to do next."

The walk back to camp was silent, save for the sound of their boots crunching on the dry earth. Mick's mind whirred with a thousand questions, none of them with answers. Two bodies. Two missing men, lost in the wilderness, their skeletal remains now buried in the rock. It was almost too much to bear, but Mick couldn't help but feel the same sharp certainty that had gnawed at him before. This wasn't just an accident. This was something darker, something planned. And the truth, no matter how ugly, was finally coming to light.

As they reached the camp, the sun hung low in the sky, casting long shadows over the earth. The campfire crackled and popped, the flames dancing in the wind. But for Mick, the warmth of the fire did nothing to ease the chill that had settled in his bones.

The truth had been uncovered, but it only raised more questions. The only thing Mick knew for sure was that this search was far from over. And whatever lay ahead, he was ready for it.

The walk back to camp was a quiet one. The sun hung high in the sky, scorching the earth beneath their boots, but the heat seemed to barely touch their minds. They moved in a slow, measured pace, the sound of their footfalls muffled by the dry, cracked earth. It had only taken them a little over five hours to uncover what the police and SES had spent ten days searching for. But while the search had been carried out in the public eye, their findings came in the dead of afternoon, when the world was unaware of the grim discovery.

Brett, Brian, and Mick walked in a silence heavy with thought, their minds swirling with the implications of what they had just uncovered. No words were needed. The air itself seemed to speak volumes, the crisp, dry wind blowing in their faces, the distant hum of insects, the weight of the secrets buried beneath the earth.

As they reached camp, Brian cracked open a cold beer, the fizz hissing in the silence. The group sat around the fire, their eyes fixed on the flames as the warmth of the fire met the chill of realisation.

"Well," Brian said, breaking the silence, "we can't report this the same way we did last time. If we do, the cops will be on our backs faster than a cat on a mouse."

Mick nodded grimly, his fingers wrapped tightly around his own beer. "We need to consider how we report this," he said, his voice rough with the weight of the situation. "It's gonna become political, and the police are gonna look like fools. I can guarantee that."

Brian exhaled slowly, the tension etched deep in his face. "You're one hundred percent right, Mick," he said, taking a swig from his bottle. "I think we need a solicitor. We can't keep making asses of the local cops. It won't end well."

Mick's face darkened as he thought it over. "I'll contact my solicitor tomorrow," he said after a beat. "But first, let's pack up. We'll head back to my place, and we'll figure it out from there."

The decision made, they packed up their gear, the weight of their discovery still heavy on their shoulders. Mick called Emily as soon as he was within range of mobile service, his voice calm as he briefed her on what they had found. He assured her that they'd be there shortly, and that both Brian and Brett would be staying the night.

Emily's response was a mix of confusion and relief. She didn't know whether to feel shocked, saddened, or even elated. What she did know was that the mystery was over. Mick had done what he set out to do, and now, there was nothing left but the aftermath.

By the time they arrived at Mick's house, Emily had already begun preparing for their arrival, arranging the spare bedroom with both a queen-size bed and a single. A modest meal would follow, nothing extravagant, just the comfort of home after the heavy weight of the day.

The following morning, Mick set about calling his solicitor. However, the man was unavailable. Undeterred, Mick contacted a law firm with a city address, seeking an appointment. The receptionist assured him that they could fit him in by 10 a.m. and he agreed, the sense of urgency pressing in on him.

The three of them arrived at the solicitor's office, the weight of the morning's events still hanging over them like a storm cloud. For over two hours, Mick, Brian, and Brett took turns recounting the tragic story, their voices steady but heavy with the knowledge of what they had uncovered. When they reached the part of the tale concerning the discovery of the bodies, the solicitor called for one of the senior partners to join them. The solicitor and the Queen's Counsel (QC), a man with an air of authority and experience, listened intently to each detail, their eyes narrowing as they pieced together the grim puzzle.

When the QC finally spoke, his voice was calm but deliberate. "I suggest we arrange a meeting with the Cairns Crown Prosecutor this morning, and take his advice before proceeding further."

The solicitor pressed a button on the intercom, instructing his receptionist to urgently contact the Crown Prosecutor. The group sat in silence, each lost in their thoughts, as the minutes stretched on.

When the call finally came, the Crown Prosecutor's tone was mixed, somewhat empathetic, yet tinged with concern. When Brett described the discovery of Phillip Laidlow's body, it sent a ripple of shock through the prosecutor. The details seemed to throw the entire case into a new light, one that demanded immediate action. Without delay, the prosecutor called the assistant police commissioner, explaining the situation with urgency.

Within minutes, a plan was set into motion. The assistant police commissioner would be arriving at the office at 2 p.m. to discuss the case in person. The QC, the solicitor, and the others agreed to be present at that meeting.

The Crown Prosecutor listened to the entire story once again, his expression carefully neutral, though there was a flicker of disbelief in his eyes when the details of the skeletal remains were confirmed. When the prosecutor spoke again, his voice was firm. "This is no longer a case of missing persons. This is a case of homicide."

The assistant police commissioner arrived at the appointed time, and after hearing the testimony from Mick, Brian, and Brett, he agreed that they had done the right thing by coming forward. He immediately contacted the Chief Superintendent of the Cairns Police Department and ordered him to bring an inspector capable of leading the search and recovery operation for the remains.

The three friends were then escorted to separate offices, where stenographers took their statements, each question recorded in meticulous detail. When the statements were finished, they were ushered into the conference room where the senior officers were waiting. The atmosphere was tense, as the full gravity of what had transpired began to sink in.

The Crown Prosecutor, the assistant commissioner, the QC, and several other senior police officers sat at the head of the table. A court attendant read the statements aloud, and each of the officers asked their questions, probing for more details.

Afterward, the assistant commissioner requested that the three men assist in the search and recovery operation the following day. All agreed, though the QC spoke up, demanding that their legal fees and any other charges related to their assistance be covered by the Crown Prosecutor's office. The request was granted without question.

That evening, Mick, Brian, and Brett returned to the comfort of Mick's home. They had done their part, but the storm was far from over. As they sat around the table, the silence between them spoke volumes. They couldn't help but wonder what would have happened if they had reported the discovery to the local police immediately. It seemed clear now, heads would roll at the local police station.

The next morning, when they met with the search and rescue team, there was a noticeable shift in the way they were treated. The same captain was present, but this time, there was a newfound respect for Brian and the others. They led the search party to the cavern entrance, and this time, they were allowed to stay and observe the recovery operation.

But despite the careful movements of the officers, the remains were covered as they were brought from the cave, protected from prying eyes, hidden from the public.

Two days later, the local and national news carried a report that sent shockwaves through the community. The bodies of the two missing men had been identified through dental records as Samuel Young and Eric Simpson. The report, however, had a chilling addition. Both skulls showed signs of bullet entry wounds. The authorities were now treating the deaths as homicides.

In a final, shocking twist, the news stated that Phillip Laidlow's body, recently interred in Townsville, would now be exhumed for a full autopsy. The case was no longer one of tragic disappearances, it was now a web of murder, deceit, and mystery that was just beginning to unravel.

The autopsy report on Phillip Laidlow had confirmed the worst. Two projectiles had been recovered from his body, one embedded deep in the chest cavity, the other lodged in his skull, with a clean entry wound between the eyes. Cold. Precise. Calculated.

The forensic team compared them against the rounds extracted from the other two bodies, and the results were unsettling. They were identical, .22-250 caliber, .223 in diameter, and 40-grain hollow points. A military-grade round, devastatingly accurate at long range. A professional's choice.

It was becoming horrifyingly clear to the authorities, this wasn't a case of lost hikers, nor was it some drunken hunting accident. The pattern was forming.

A killer was at work, one who moved through the wilderness unseen, striking with clinical precision. A predator, methodical and remorseless.

The police had handled the earlier disappearances as routine search-and-rescue operations. Missing persons cases followed a standard playbook, assume they were lost, start from their last known position, and work outward in an ever-expanding grid. The searchers had been looking for exhausted, disoriented bushwalkers, not victims.

And certainly not prey.

The mistake had been made from the outset. In each of the last three cases, the missing had been known to be camped nearby. Their gear was still there, tents intact, fires doused but not abandoned. Their footprints told stories of casual movement, not fear or flight. But outside those immediate campsites, the ground had not been studied with the same scrutiny. The wider search area had not been examined for the signs of a hunter, an observer, a stalker.

A specialist police officer from Brisbane was brought in the head the investigation. From the moment Detective Inspector Chris Granger stepped off the plane from Brisbane, he carried the weight of three decades of hunting the worst humanity had to offer. He was a man forged in blood and violence, a predator of predators. For two years, he had walked the concrete canyons of Los Angeles, working side by side with their elite homicide unit, chasing killers who left bodies in alleys, motels, and abandoned cars. But this, this was different. The brutality was the same, but the setting had changed. Instead of neon-lit boulevards and urban decay, he found himself in the vast, untamed wilderness of North Queensland. A killer was out there, moving through the shadows of the bush. And Granger was here to hunt him down.

He wasted no time. His experience told him that murder, especially the kind of cold, clinical killing he was seeing here, was rarely random. There was always a pattern. Always a thread that, once pulled, unraveled the truth.

Granger's instincts pointed him to one certainty. This was the work of someone with skill. Military skill. The precision of the shots, the choice of weapon, the near-total absence of evidence, all of it pointed to a professional. Someone who had been trained to kill and knew how to disappear.

His first order of business was simple: identify a stranger. Not just any outsider, but someone who had a past soaked in war and blood. A man with military experience who had come to town and lingered. Someone who had made himself known, but not too known. A ghost walking among them. A stranger to the town who may have become a regular visitor

With that in mind, the hunt began.

Granger knew from experience that the most dangerous killers were those who had been trained to kill, not thugs or opportunists, but professionals. Men honed into weapons, capable of eliminating a target with precision and vanishing without a trace. This was not the work of some deranged drifter or a petty criminal. No, this was something else. Cold. Efficient. Military.

He sat in the small, stuffy office that had been set aside for him at the Cairns police headquarters, the walls cluttered with crime scene photographs, maps, and forensic reports. The brutality of the murders told him much, but it was the method that spoke the loudest. The choice of a .22-250, a sniper's round, capable of devastating damage at range. The controlled, deliberate execution of each victim. And most importantly, the absence of hesitation. These were the hallmarks of a man who had killed before, under orders, in places where death was just another part of the job.

Special operations. SAS, most likely.

Granger reached for his satellite phone and made a call to Brisbane. Within the hour, he had authorisation to begin a classified search. Every Special Air Service operative or ex-SAS man who had left the regiment in the past two decades was to be cross-checked against Queensland's recent arrivals. Then, that list would be narrowed down further, only those men who possessed the stamina, skill, and mental fortitude required to carry out such an operation.

"Start with the last two years," he instructed his contact in Intelligence. "Anyone who's relocated, visited, or spent significant time in the region. I want names, addresses, service records. If he bought a beer in a pub, I want to know about it."

He disconnected the call and leaned back in his chair, staring at the crime scene map on the wall. The killings had all taken place within a specific radius. A controlled hunting ground.

Granger exhaled slowly.

Somewhere out there, a ghost was walking among them.

The hunt was relentless, methodical. Undercover officers were scattered throughout the town, moving unnoticed among the locals, blending into the easy rhythm of country life. They drank in the pubs, swapped stories in the barbershops, and lingered at the small grocery stores, striking up casual conversations with shopkeepers and weary farmers. They listened, prodding gently, never pushing too hard. People in these parts were wary of outsiders, and suspicion could shut doors faster than a snake strike.

Beyond the town limits, the same quiet probing was taking place in neighbouring settlements. Small villages, roadside diners, even isolated cattle stations where men lived hard and spoke little. But for all their efforts, the officers had unearthed nothing of value, no whispered suspicions, no rumours of a stranger lurking in the bush, no drifters with military training and dead eyes.

What they did uncover, however, was a steady stream of grievances aimed at the local police sergeant. Complaints of corruption, of favouritism, of things not quite adding up in the way they should. A few even hinted at something darker, a quiet murmur that the man wasn't as straight as his badge suggested. Many had said that he seemed to be against visitors, or campers including fishermen, coming to the area. Many visitors complained of receiving speeding, parking, vehicle defects and other infringement notices. It was like no visitors were welcome at all.

When the reports reached Granger, he barely spared them a glance. He tossed the file onto his desk and leaned back in his chair. "That's a problem for Internal Affairs," he muttered. "I'm here to catch a killer, not clean up the local station."

His focus was unwavering. Somewhere in the vast, untamed wilderness of North Queensland, a predator was still at large. A ghost with a rifle and the skill to vanish without a trace.

Granger wasn't interested in petty police politics. He was after something far more dangerous. And he would not stop until he had his man.

Jonathan Reise Wagner

Jonathan "Jonty" Wagner had always felt the raw, unyielding pulse of South Africa in his veins. From the moment he had set foot on the dusty grounds of the SAPS Police Academy in Tshwane, Pretoria, he had known his path was set. He had spent ten months training in the rigorous and unforgiving world of law enforcement, and in those months, he had learned not just the technicalities of policing, but the very soul of it, the understanding that a man's duty was to the people, even when those people turned their back on you.

The training had been intense. Early mornings filled with drills that tested endurance and skill. Days spent learning tactics, forensics, and the intricate dance of law enforcement in a world teetering on the edge of chaos. It was a crucible, and Jonty had emerged from it unbroken, with a burning desire to serve. He had taken to his lessons with an almost preternatural ease. His sniper skills, taught by his father on their farm near Ventersdorp, became the stuff of legend at the academy. His ability to track a man through the bush, to read the land as if it were a living creature, was uncanny. These were the skills that marked him out as exceptional.

After the academy, Jonty had entered the "Phase Two" probationary period as a constable. For twelve months, he had proven himself in the field, handling difficult situations with the kind of professionalism that most seasoned officers would envy. By the end of that period, it was clear: Jonty Wagner was a force to be reckoned with. His focus, his unwavering discipline, his precision, they were qualities that set him apart.

It wasn't long before Jonty's skills caught the eye of his training officer, who recommended him for entry into the STF (Special Task Force), South Africa's elite counter-terrorism and rescue unit. A place where the best of the best came together to tackle the nation's most dangerous situations. It was here, in the heart of the STF, that Jonty's true potential would be unleashed.

But behind his rise in the ranks, the country around him was changing. His parents, Cornelis and Janine, had long since become disillusioned with the spiralling violence that gripped South Africa. The farm near Ventersdorp, once a place of peace and prosperity, had become a target. Countless break-ins had left them fearing for their lives. Cornelis, a man of great patience and iron resolve, had fought back one fateful night, shooting and killing seven of the armed intruders who had attacked their home. The court case that followed was a gruelling affair, one that almost saw him imprisoned for murder. But in the end, a shrewd lawyer and one of the last remaining sympathetic white judges had won the case for self-defence.

But even in victory, the shadows loomed large. The prosecution appealed the ruling, and Cornelis was warned that the new South Africa would not be so kind in the future. Fearing for his life and the safety of his family, Cornelis made the difficult decision to lease the farm to an African buyer. A year-long lease was signed, with an option for purchase after the term. With the future uncertain and the threat of legal troubles hanging over them, Cornelis and Janine made the decision to leave. They moved to New Zealand, a country with no extradition treaty with South Africa, seeking the peace and anonymity that had been denied them at home.

Jonty's relationship with his parents had always been strong. His father's lessons in marksmanship and tracking were some of the most formative moments of his life. Cornelis had been a man who lived by his own code, and Jonty admired him for it. But the truth was, Jonty had always known that the farm, the life they had built in South Africa, was no longer tenable. The violence, the instability, it had all come to a head, and his family had no choice but to leave.

As he rose through the ranks of the SAPS, Jonty's skill and dedication became more and more apparent. He made the rank of lance sergeant with remarkable speed, quicker than many of his colleagues had expected. His understanding of tactics, of the fine balance between law and force, set him apart. The STF recognised his abilities almost immediately, and he was accepted into their ranks without hesitation.

But not everyone was impressed by Jonty's meteoric rise. His African sergeant, an ambitious officer with his own dreams of promotion, saw Jonty's success as a threat. There was no denying that Jonty was fast becoming a shining star in the force, but his sergeant was determined to hold on to his own ambitions, even if it meant undermining his subordinate.

Yet, it wasn't just the sergeant who felt threatened. Jonty's captain, a man of considerable experience, viewed him with a mixture of admiration and suspicion. While Jonty was a model STF officer, a dedicated and skilled operative, his success unsettled the captain. The fact that Jonty was white only added to the tension. South Africa's political landscape had shifted dramatically in recent years, and the country's leadership had made it clear that the new South Africa would prioritise racial representation in its institutions. It was a time of upheaval, and Jonty found himself caught between his desire to serve and the weight of a society that was changing beneath his feet.

The captain's unease was palpable, but it was a silent rivalry, one that simmered beneath the surface, never fully breaking through. Jonty knew that his success would always be tempered by the reality of the world around him.

He had the skills, the determination, and the drive to be one of the best, but in a country so divided, even the most talented men could find themselves obstructed by forces beyond their control.

Jonty's rise to prominence was inevitable, but the path was not without its challenges. His father's influence, his own training, and the strength of his character had gotten him this far. But in the STF, where the stakes were higher and the enemies more deadly, Jonty would soon find that even the most gifted soldier could become a pawn in a much larger game.

Jonty Wagner, with his sharp mind and keen instincts, had wasted no time in understanding the delicate and often unsettling dynamics of the station near Cape Town where he had been posted. The pressures of the job, the shifting political landscape, and the ever-growing sense that things were becoming untenable had weighed heavily on him. He had been astute enough to recognise that something was off, something that spoke to the very heart of the challenges South Africa was grappling with. The law enforcement world, once a place where he could find a sense of purpose, had become riddled with contradictions. It was disheartening, to say the least.

Jonty's thoughts turned to his parents, who had already left for New Zealand. The idea of joining them in that distant, cool land did have its appeal, especially with the political turmoil raging across South Africa. But the reality of the climate in New Zealand gave him pause. The weather was simply too cold for someone like him, accustomed to the warmth of the Cape Town sun. The thought of trading the arid, sun-baked landscapes of South Africa for the chill of New Zealand was not an attractive one. After all, he had spent much of his life thriving in the warmth. It was then that an alternative idea began to take root, a thought that led him to Australia.

Australia's climate, much like South Africa's, felt familiar and welcoming. The idea of settling in a land where the sun still blazed in the sky, where the harsh winds of Africa were replaced by the steady breezes of the Australian outback, seemed like the perfect escape. Moreover, his parents, now settled in New Zealand, were just a short flight away, should he wish to visit. The prospect of living somewhere far removed from the violence and unrest of South Africa, where the sun shone brightly and the air was warm, proved irresistible. Jonty's mind was made up, Australia would be his new home.

Joining the Queensland Police Force was surprisingly simple. The need for officers was great; the ranks were thinning as many constables had chosen to leave due to poor pay and subpar working conditions. For Jonty, however, the pay was a significant step up from what he had known in South Africa, and the conditions were far more manageable. Crime rates were far lower, too, an undeniable relief after the constant tension he had lived with in Africa.

There, the criminal world was ever-present, a shadow at every turn. Here, in Queensland, it was a different world entirely.

Jonty was posted out to Marianvale, a small town nestled in the hills of Far North Queensland. The assignment came with the rank of Senior Constable, one rank below what he had held in South Africa. However, he was assured that, after two years of service, he would be promoted to Sergeant. That suited Jonty perfectly, he could settle in, learn the ways of his new country, and work his way up, just as he had done in South Africa. The pay was far better than what he had been accustomed to, and the promise of a more stable and peaceful life made it all the more appealing.

At first, finding accommodation in Marianvale proved to be more of a challenge than he had anticipated. The properties he looked at didn't quite meet his expectations or his lifestyle. The townspeople were friendly, but the accommodations were often a little too rustic or far from his ideal. Undeterred, Jonty rented a small, modest unit in Mareeba, a larger town not too far from Marianvale. It wasn't ideal, but it would do for the time being. The extra travel was a small inconvenience compared to the peace he found in the day-to-day rhythm of his new life.

But Jonty was a man who believed in the power of patience. And as he explored the area further, he found something that called to him, something that whispered of the kind of peace he had longed for since leaving South Africa. On the road leading up to Mount Marian, off the main thoroughfare, was a property that seemed to speak directly to his soul. It was a modest four-bedroom house set on two thousand acres, with a breathtaking view of the nearby mountains. The land, though wild and untamed, had an air of serenity about it. Jonty could see the road winding through the hills, leading past his property and beyond, where it disappeared into the rugged beauty of the Mount Marian ranges.

He knew at once that this was where he belonged. The land had a quiet majesty, a stillness that allowed for reflection and solitude, a place where he could finally put down roots. But to make it his own, he would need some help. His parents, ever supportive, had agreed to lend him the funds to buy the property. They transferred enough to cover the purchase, along with extra money to help him stock the land with cattle when the time came. But for now, Jonty was content. The work of setting up a cattle farm would come in time. For now, he savoured the solitude, the quiet peace of the land that stretched out before him, the kind of peace he had never known in his previous life.

Each morning, as the sun rose over the ranges, Jonty would stand at the window of his new home, looking out over the sprawling land he now owned. The air was warm, rich with the scent of eucalyptus and earth, and the sound of the birds in the trees filled the silence like a song. It was a different world, but it was one that Jonty had quickly come to appreciate. For the first time in years, he felt a sense of calm settle over him, a feeling that perhaps, just perhaps, he had finally found his place in this vast, sunburned land.

The days in Marianvale rolled on like the sluggish brown river that wound its way through the Queensland outback, slow, uneventful, and largely insignificant. Jonty Wagner had come to realise that police work in this part of the world was what the Australians so eloquently termed "fuck all." There was no crime to speak of, and if anything did happen, it was usually some petty disagreement between two sweaty farmers at the pub, sorted out with a few swings and a round of drinks. The only other officer stationed in Marianvale was the sergeant, a man Jonty quickly assessed as an absolute imbecile.

When it came to Sergeant Thomas Kearns, the locals had a lexicon of insults at the ready, each more colourful than the last. "Dickhead" was a staple, "fuckwit" was reserved for moments of particular disdain, but lately, "fat fuck" and "lard arse" had taken centre stage in the public's imagination. Not that Kearns cared. If he'd ever given a damn about what the people of Marianvale thought of him, he had drowned that concern in a tide of home-brewed beer long ago.

He carried himself with the bloated arrogance of a man who had long since mistaken his own delusions for reality. He saw himself as an enforcer of the law, a pillar of authority in this dusty, sun-bleached backwater. The truth, however, was far less impressive. His version of policing rarely extended beyond the walls of his own office, where he spent most of his days tinkering with his latest batch of beer, testing its colour, its aroma, its bite, while droning on about how he had been destined for greater things. Townsville, perhaps. Maybe even Cairns. But instead, here he was, Marianvale, where the most pressing crime was a stolen chicken or a punch thrown outside the pub on a Friday night.

Jonty listened when he had to, offering the occasional nod, but mostly, he let the sergeant's words wash over him like the droning of flies. Unlike Kearns, he was content in Marianvale. There was something about the slow rhythm of life here, the way the land stretched endlessly beneath the brutal Queensland sun, that suited him just fine. If the Queensland Police Force ever got the bright idea to transfer him, he already knew exactly how that conversation would go: Get fucked.

He didn't need this job. Not really. It was a convenient arrangement, nothing more. A bit of cash, a place to lay low, but nothing he was willing to trade his real interests for. And whatever the brass in Brisbane thought, he wasn't about to swap his quiet dominion here for some soulless bureaucratic posting in a city office.

Kearns, on the other hand, needed this job, or at least the illusion of it. Without his badge, he was just another washed-up drunk clinging to relevance. His mornings began with beer, thick and golden, sloshed into a heavy tumbler that rarely left his grasp. He drank steadily, methodically, never enough to bring him down, just enough to keep the warm fog around him at all times. It was a delicate balance, an art form in its own way, and he considered himself a master.

He wasn't stupid, though. When word came that the higher-ups might be making a visit, or that a fresh-faced inspector from Cairns was heading through town, he exercised restraint. He could play the role when he needed to, straighten his uniform, sober up just enough to pass for competent. That was the trick, never let them see the cracks.

His beer was weak by most standards, a modest three percent alcohol by volume, but that was the secret to its success. It allowed him to maintain his slow and steady intoxication without ever losing his grip entirely. Everything was kept in-house, as he liked to say. The brewing, the bottling, the drinking, it was a closed system, a self-sustaining cycle. And as long as he controlled it, the charade could go on indefinitely.

As far as Kearns was concerned, he had it all figured out. The town could laugh, call him names, roll their eyes behind his back. It didn't matter. He had his beer. He had his uniform. And as long as no one looked too closely, he could keep up the act for years to come.

Jonty had made it clear to Kearns that he knew about the brewing. He'd done it in that slow, deliberate way of his, letting the words settle like dust in the dry heat of the office. He hadn't needed to shout, hadn't needed to spell it out. Just a few carefully placed comments about the smell of hops lingering in the station after hours, about the way Kearns' hands were always sticky with malt and sugar, about the way his breath carried that unmistakable tang even in the mornings. Kearns had laughed it off at first, muttering something about a man's right to a hobby, but Jonty had seen the flicker of something behind those bloodshot eyes. A shadow of concern.

Because the brewing wasn't the real problem. It was the drinking. The steady, methodical consumption that started at dawn and barely let up before nightfall. Jonty had seen it before, men who thought they could control it, who convinced themselves they weren't drunks because they weren't staggering, weren't slurring, weren't making fools of themselves in the streets. But Kearns had another problem, a far greater one, and Jonty had uncovered that too.

It had started with a passing glance at the payroll records, a half-hearted curiosity that had sharpened into something else entirely. At first, the names had seemed unremarkable, just another cleaner, another office clerk, faceless public servants whose wages were drawn from the vast and indifferent coffers of the Queensland Government. But there was something off. Jonty had never seen them, never heard mention of them. In a town as small as Marianvale, that was impossible. You couldn't so much as fart without half the district knowing about it. Yet these two employees, this so-called cleaner and ancillary clerk, remained ghosts.

That was when Jonty had started digging. And it hadn't taken much. A few discreet inquiries, a little cross-checking, and the whole rotten scheme had begun to unravel.

There were no casual staff. No cleaner. No clerk. The names were fiction, but their salaries were very real, siphoned off month after month, funnelled straight into Kearns' account. It was a simple scam, crude even, but effective. The money paid for his beer, for whatever else he wasted it on.

Jonty had let Kearns know, just subtly enough to make the sergeant sweat. A throwaway remark about how government jobs were hard to come by, how funny it was that no one ever seemed to see these extra staffers. Kearns had gone very still then, his face an expressionless mask, but Jonty had caught the quick dart of his eyes, the way his fingers tightened ever so slightly on the rim of his glass.

It was a beautiful thing, watching a man realise how much trouble he was in.

Jonty hadn't said more, not yet. He was patient. He liked to let a man stew in his own paranoia for a while, let the fear fester and bloom. Kearns would know he had been found out. And that knowledge alone was enough to set the wheels in motion.

It was a fine bit of theatre, watching Kearns work when the auditors arrived at the station each year. The way he spun his web of lies with the ease of a man who had been doing it for so long he almost believed it himself. He would lean back in his chair, casual as you please, a hint of indignation in his voice, as if he were insulted that anyone would dare question the existence of his staff.

"Ah, Geoff McKillop," Kearns would say, shaking his head with a perfectly rehearsed sigh. "Bad luck, fellas. Just missed him. He was in earlier, picking up a jacket he left behind. Damn shame. He was looking forward to meeting you blokes."

Jonty would bite the inside of his cheek to keep from grinning. Geoff McKillop, the ghostly cleaner, was as real as a politician's promise, but Kearns played it well. He always had an answer, always had a story.

Then they would ask about Marge, the fictional office clerk. Kearns would rub a hand over his face, letting out another deep sigh, this one laced with just the right amount of sympathy.

"Marge? Ah, yeah, she's doing it tough at the moment. One of her kids got knocked over by a car. Poor little bugger. She's been down in Cairns every day at the hospital, keeping vigil, you know how it is. She gets in here whenever she can. Hopefully later this afternoon."

It was masterful. The tragedy was just vague enough to be unquestionable, just tragic enough to discourage further inquiry. Who was going to press a grieving mother about her work hours? Not some auditor from Brisbane with a clipboard, that was for damn sure.

Jonty had to leave the office, every single time. If he stayed, he knew he'd give himself away. The effort of holding in his laughter, of watching Kearns spin his ridiculous yarns, was too much. He would step outside, lean against the sun-warmed wall of the station, and let the laughter roll out of him in silent, heaving fits.

Kearns thought he was a genius. Thought he had it all figured out. Maybe he did. The Queensland Government, in all its wisdom, seemed content to let him carry on year after year, his imaginary employees faithfully drawing wages that found their way straight into his own pocket.

And Jonty? Well, he wasn't about to ruin the show just yet. Some things were just too damn entertaining to bring to an end.

What Jonty missed, though, with an ache deep in his gut, was the hunt. In Africa, he had hunted alone, stalking the great cats of the veld, the lion, the leopard, and the caracal. Each required a different set of skills, each a different approach, especially at night, where the darkness made the hunter and the hunted equal. He had mastered this art, honed it to perfection, and his reputation in his hometown of Ventersdorp had spread like wildfire. Before long, tourists had begun seeking him out, offering money for guided trophy hunts. It was then that Jonty had turned his analytical mind to the science of ballistics, to the study of rifle calibres and projectile weights, to the delicate balance between power and precision.

The cheetah, light-framed and sleek, was best taken with a .270 Winchester, fast, deadly, but clean. The lion, a beast of muscle and thick bone, demanded more, a .308 Winchester was popular among seasoned hunters, though those with less nerve favoured the brute force of the .375 H&H Magnum.

But the problem, Jonty had learned, was that most of these so-called hunters were nothing more than wealthy amateurs, men who had never truly faced danger, never truly known what it was to stalk a predator in its own territory. They bought their ammunition off the shelf, pre-loaded with standard weights and velocities meant for general-purpose shooting. And that, Jonty knew, was a mistake.

Different animals had different bone densities, different muscle structures, and a poorly chosen bullet could mean the difference between a perfect kill and a ruined trophy. He had seen it time and again, heavy calibres used on light-boned animals, the sheer force of the impact ripping through flesh and hide, leaving the pelt unusable. And so the hunter, in his foolishness, would take another life, hoping to preserve the next skin intact. It was senseless waste. It was sick.

A true hunter, a professional, did not rely on mass-produced ammunition. He crafted his own, tailoring each round to the game he pursued. The goal was always the same, a single, precise entry wound, and no exit wound to destroy the skin. Jonty had mastered this technique, refining it with a rifle that, ironically, had been designed for war.

The weapon had been engineered not to kill outright, but to wound, forcing enemy forces to divert resources toward medical aid, thus weakening their numbers on the battlefield. It was a simple but brutal strategy, one that exploited the very nature of warfare itself. Jonty had taken that principle and applied it to his hunts, utilising extreme projectile velocity but modifying the bullet itself, a light, hollow round that would enter the body and detonate inside before it had the chance to pass through.

The result was devastating. A clean kill, a perfect trophy. No wasted life, no unnecessary suffering. It was efficiency honed to its most lethal form. And Jonty, standing on his land in the Australian outback, staring out at the sprawling wilderness before him, felt the itch return. The hunt was in his blood, and no amount of quiet days in Marianvale could ever change that.

Jonty Wagner had always been a man who sought perfection in his craft. He had spent years honing his skills, first in the brutal landscapes of South Africa, then in the quiet but untamed lands of northern Queensland. He worked his own loads for his rifle with a meticulous precision that bordered on obsession, choosing a .22-225 military calibre and loading it with a 40-

grain hollow-point projectile of .223 diameter. He used the maximum propellant charge, ignited by a magnum primer, ensuring that his rounds left the barrel with blistering velocity. The only flaw in the setup was its sensitivity, its sheer speed meant that the light bullet could be deflected by even the slightest obstruction, a stray twig or a wayward leaf. It was a flaw he accepted, knowing that, in the right conditions, his shots were devastatingly precise.

But precision alone was not enough to keep a man like Jonty engaged. His position in the Queensland Police Service had quickly become a source of frustration. The job was dull, uninspiring. The crimes here were petty, uninventive, brawls between drunken farmers, the occasional stolen vehicle, a dispute over land boundaries. This was not the work of a warrior. It was the work of bureaucrats in uniform. Even the wilds of his property offered little solace. Kangaroos were too predictable, their movements sluggish and unchallenging. The wild dogs, while clever, stirred something in him that made him hesitate, he had always loved dogs. The deer and goats in the area might have provided some sport, but their minds were simple. What Jonty craved was the hunt of something truly cunning, something with instinct and intelligence. Something that could fight back.

It was on one of his long walks through the Mount Marian ranges that he first toyed with the idea. He had been moving quietly along a ridge when he spotted a lone figure by the Mitchell River, a fisherman absorbed in his task, oblivious to the world around him. Jonty raised his rifle, sighted in on a branch above the man's left shoulder, and squeezed the trigger. The shot was perfect. The branch exploded in a shower of splinters, and the man recoiled in shock, looking wildly around him. Before he could react, Jonty adjusted his aim and fired again, striking another branch to the man's right. This time, the fisherman abandoned his rod, his instincts overriding reason. He leapt into the fast-flowing river, disappearing beneath the surface as he swam downstream.

Jonty remained motionless, watching the water churn and froth where the man had gone under. He had not intended to kill him. It had been a test, a game. But the river was swift, and the man had been panicked. If he drowned, it would not be Jonty's fault.

Curious, he made his way down to the campsite. The fisherman had set up a decent spot, a large tent, a table with a folding chair, a small gas cooktop. There was an esky full of beers, and Jonty helped himself to one, leaning against the man's vehicle as he took a long drink. He recognised the truck. He had seen it before, coming up the road near his property. The man had been in his territory.

The rush of adrenaline still coursed through him, a high he had not felt since Africa. It had been exhilarating, a moment of pure, unfiltered instinct. And that was when the idea took hold. Hunting men was different. They were unpredictable. They would run, they would fight, they would try to survive. This had been a fluke, but if he planned it properly, it could be something far more thrilling.

Jonty smiled to himself as he finished the beer and moved off before the man returned, taking another beer with him, and the empty can.

The man who had been fishing reported the incident the next day at the Marianvale Police Station, to the officer in attendance the following morning. The man had suspected that the shots were not directed at him but just shots from a reckless shooter firing over the top of the hill behind the river where he was. The station officer, Senior Constable Wagner, had agreed with the fisherman that many of the recreational shooters were somewhat irresponsible.

Jonty had waited for the right moment, watching Sergeant Kearns with the patience of a lion stalking a wounded antelope. Timing was everything. A misstep, the wrong tone, and the man might panic, might do something stupid. But Jonty had a way with words. He knew how to press a man without setting off alarms, how to slip his will into the conversation like a dagger between ribs.

He leaned in across the cluttered desk, his voice calm, deliberate, carrying the weight of an unshakable certainty.

"Listen, Sarge. Listen carefully."

His South African accent curled around the words, each syllable clipped and precise, forcing Kearns to focus, to absorb. The sergeant's bloodshot eyes flickered, his thick fingers tightening around the beer glass he thought he had so discreetly nudged behind a stack of reports.

"I'm hunting two legged game on the mountain," Jonty said, his voice flat, as if he were discussing the weather. "And I don't want you worrying about it. Okay?"

A flicker of confusion crossed Kearns' face, but Jonty didn't give him time to interrupt.

"Because I will take care of the carcass's," he continued smoothly. "So they are never discovered."

Silence. The dusty ceiling fan groaned overhead.

Jonty watched as the words sank in, as realisation began to bloom in Kearns' dull, alcohol-addled brain. His lips parted slightly, but no words came. His mouth slackened, his breathing grew shallow.

Jonty allowed the moment to stretch, then went on, voice steady, unhurried.

"All you need to do," he said, "is to discourage any vigorous searching for lost people. That's all."

He gave a slow, easy smile. The kind of smile that belonged to a man who had already calculated every possible outcome and had no doubts about which way the wind would blow.

"You'll need to play it down, Sarge. With authority, with confidence. Speak as a man who knows these hills, these valleys. Convince them. No hope of survival. No point in sending search parties. The terrain is too rough. The weather too unpredictable."

Then, as if it were an afterthought, a mere flick of dust off his sleeve, he added, "Especially around the rocks."

A knowing pause.

Jonty's eyes remained fixed on Kearns, reading the man's reaction like a map. There was no need to threaten. The sergeant had spent his entire career bending rules, shifting the line between right and wrong wherever it suited him. A weak man who valued his comfort, his security, his routine of beer-soaked afternoons and fabricated payrolls.

Jonty had three days of leave ahead of him, and the prospect of a trip into Cairns filled him with anticipation. A night at the casino, the clink of chips, the scent of fine whiskey, and the dull hum of conversation against the background of the slot machines, it was all a welcome diversion from the mind-numbing dullness of Marianvale. But beyond the allure of relaxation, Jonty had a purpose. He needed to acquire a few game cameras, tools that would sharpen his instincts, elevate his sport, and give him the upper hand in what he had begun to think of as his new hunting ground.

The cameras were more advanced than he had imagined. Their sensitivity was extraordinary; even the distant movement of a car, six hundred metres away, was enough to trigger the recording function. He tested them meticulously, placing them at strategic points along the road leading to his property. Now he would know exactly when someone ventured too close, and more importantly, when campers settled along the river.

The next morning, he set out towards the familiar fishing and camping grounds, weaving his way through the scrub, his rifle slung over his shoulder like an extension of his own body. He found the perfect vantage point to install another game camera, its lens hidden beneath the natural camouflage of the bush. From there, he ascended the ridge, following its spine until he reached the great boulders. What he saw made his pulse quicken. It was a labyrinth of caves, deep crevices plunging into the earth, a place that exuded the raw power of nature and held the eerie silence of the unknown.

He ran his hand over the rough stone, feeling the heat that still lingered from the sun's embrace. Here was the perfect place. He could funnel his prey towards these jagged rocks, where escape would be impossible. It was an executioner's chamber fashioned by nature itself. Now, all he needed was a way to lure them in.

The answer came to him unexpectedly, as he watched a documentary on his laptop one evening. It was about a small town in Victoria, Wedderburn, where gold fever still thrived. Hundreds of hopefuls ventured there each year, scouring the land with metal detectors in search of fortune. That was it. That was the bait. Gold. The very thing that could turn an ordinary man into a desperate, single-minded beast, willing to follow the lure into the jaws of death.

Jonty grinned to himself. It was so simple. Just as he had once laid a trail of wheat on his father's farm to trap birds, he would now lay a trail of gold to ensnare men. From the riverbank, he would scatter nuggets, drawing them away from their harmless fishing and up towards the ridge, and then to the great boulders where he would be waiting. Too easy. Almost too perfect. The only concern was the cost. Gold was not cheap.

But then, why should that matter? The victims wouldn't be taking their gold with them. He would retrieve it from their lifeless hands, clean it, and use it again. A perpetual snare. An investment that would pay for itself in blood.

He turned to his computer, searching for places to purchase gold nuggets. Buying them outright proved impossible, but there were several dealers in Cairns who bought gold from prospectors. If they were buying, they must also be selling. The logic was flawless.

He checked his bank balance. His parents had wired him a substantial amount to purchase cattle for the property. A grin spread across his face. Cattle? To hell with the cattle. His hunt was far more thrilling than watching dumb beasts chew cud.

The next day, he strolled into the bank, exuding confidence. The teller barely raised an eyebrow when he requested to withdraw fifty thousand dollars in cash. He smirked as he signed the forms, giving a casual shrug when asked about the purpose of the withdrawal.

"Buying a new car," he said smoothly. It was close enough to the truth, except the vehicle he sought was not one with wheels, but one that would drive men to their doom.

With a thick wad of cash burning in his pocket, he set off for Cairns, his mind already calculating his next move. The hunt was beginning, and he could feel the slow, intoxicating surge of excitement coursing through his veins. He had found his game, and soon, they would come to him, unknowingly following the gleam of gold straight into the hunter's embrace.

The plan had unfolded with the precision of a well-laid ambush. The game camera near Jonty's house had captured the arrival of a vehicle, its driver heading toward the river while Jonty had been at work. By the next morning, the footage confirmed that the car remained at the campsite. This was good. This meant patience would yield results.

At the station that day, Jonty ensured Sergeant Tom Kearns was well into his afternoon routine of either guzzling his home-brew or stirring another batch of foul-smelling beer. He would be out of action for hours. That gave Jonty the window he needed. He took the police Landcruiser, its presence ensuring no unwanted questions if spotted, and drove up toward the campsite. Checking his second game camera, he reviewed the crisp footage: the fisherman moving to and from the river, unsuspecting, oblivious.

With the patience of a seasoned predator, Jonty began placing small gold nuggets in the scrub just beyond the campsite, each piece catching the light, tantalisingly visible. Just enough to stoke excitement. He knew it would take time. The fisherman would need several visits before he transformed from an angler into a gold-fevered prospector. That was fine. This was a long game.

Days passed. Then a week. Then two. The game camera revealed that the fisherman had left. Jonty made another trip to the site and reviewed the footage. There it was, the moment the fisherman had discovered the first few nuggets. The way he had stared toward the ridge, as if it held secrets yet to be uncovered. A smile curled at the edges of Jonty's lips. Hook set. Now, he only had to wait.

It was nearly a month before the fisherman returned. Jonty, as was his routine, checked the footage before work. The man was back. But more than that, he was on the move, metal detector in hand, heading toward the ridge. Jonty's blood surged, a familiar fire igniting in his veins. He drove to the site, parked discreetly, and retrieved his .22-250 rifle.

The fisherman had left a trail for himself, yellow ribbons tied to branches marking his path. Perfect. Jonty followed, his eyes scanning the footprints in the dirt, the deep impressions of boots eager for gold. The anticipation coursed through him like a drug, heightening his senses, sharpening his instincts.

Then, movement ahead. Jonty stilled, lowering himself into a crouch. The fisherman was a mere twenty-five metres away, tying another ribbon. He was entirely engrossed, focused only on his newfound passion, his hands working deftly at the branch. Jonty inhaled, exhaled, then squeezed the trigger.

The first shot struck a rock mere metres from the fisherman's head, sending shards flying. The man reacted instantly, leaping into the air, spinning, his face a mask of confusion and alarm. He turned blindly, his instincts betraying him, he ran straight toward Jonty.

Jonty didn't move. He calmly placed another shot, this time striking a boulder ahead of the fisherman. A jagged chunk of rock shattered and slammed into the man's chest, halting him mid-stride. A panicked wheeze escaped his lips as he staggered back, his body twisting toward the sanctuary of the rocks.

Jonty dropped to his belly, aligning the Leopold telescopic sight to the base of the fisherman's skull. The angle was perfect, an upward trajectory, straight to the brain. The shot cracked through the air like the snapping of a whip.

The fisherman crumpled at the entrance of the boulders.

Jonty estimated the distance, roughly two hundred and twenty metres. A fine shot. Clean. Efficient. No exit wound.

He slung his rifle over his shoulder and walked toward the body, retrieving the fallen metal detector and backpack along the way. The man's limbs were limp, the weight of death already settling in. Jonty bent down, grabbed the body beneath the arms, and began dragging him toward the concealed crevice he had discovered earlier.

The terrain was in his favour. He manoeuvred the body with ease, guiding it to the gaping maw of darkness between the boulders. With a final heave, he pushed the corpse forward. It should have been effortless. It should have been over. But something caught. The man's headphones, still looped around his head, snagged on an outcrop of stone, yanking his head violently to one side.

Jonty stepped back, observing the grotesque position. The body had veered off course, wedging itself into a narrow funnel where three boulders formed a crude, jagged cone. The head had been forced downward, almost compacted into the tight space. It was an absurd and unexpected end to what had been a flawless execution.

Jonty exhaled sharply, shaking his head. Nothing to be done about it now. He retrieved the man's belongings and tossed them into the chasm. The metal detector clattered somewhere in the darkness below, lost to the abyss.

Then, with the nonchalance of a predator having finished a meal, Jonty turned on his heel and walked away, the boulders behind him now guarding their latest secret.

Jonty knew that patience was key. He had no intention of rushing his next hunt, and so he let time pass, allowing the dust to settle from his last kill. Almost a year slipped by before another opportunity presented itself, and when it did, he knew he would have to be careful. This one had been returning frequently over the past two months, but each time, Jonty had been unable to act, work commitments, other interruptions, or sheer bad timing had kept him from taking the shot. But then, finally, the man returned, and this time he was not alone.

Jonty cursed under his breath when he saw the second man. It complicated things. A lone target was one thing, but two men meant double the risk. He considered abandoning the hunt altogether, but then he observed their routine. They didn't search for gold together; they split up and went their separate ways. That changed everything. He would just have to adapt.

The younger of the two took to the riverbanks, moving slowly along the water's edge, scanning the rocky shallows with his metal detector. The fast-moving current would mask the crack of Jonty's rifle. Perfect. He would wait until they had finished their midday meal and resumed their prospecting. Then, the hunt would begin.

It played out much like the first one. The man, oblivious to his fate, swept his metal detector in slow arcs, the headphones clamped over his ears making him deaf to the world. Jonty took aim and squeezed the trigger. The bullet smashed into the rock beside the man's head, sending shards of stone flying. But this one was different. Instead of panicking and running towards the boulders as Jonty had hoped, the man reacted swiftly. He threw himself sideways, rolling behind the very rock Jonty had targeted. A cold tendril of unease crept up Jonty's spine. The bastard wasn't behaving as expected.

"Fuck it," Jonty muttered under his breath. There was no time to waste. The man was too far from the boulder pit, and if he managed to gather his wits, he could cause trouble. Jonty exhaled, steadied himself, and took aim once more. The crosshairs of his Leupold scope settled on the exposed section of the man's skull. He fired. The shot was clean, precise. The dull, wet thud of impact confirmed the kill.

Jonty moved swiftly now, stripping the body of anything of value. The weighty gold nuggets came first. The metal detector and backpack could wait. He assessed the man's bulk and sighed. This one was bigger than the last, heavier. Carrying him would be a challenge, but Jonty had prepared for this. He hoisted the corpse into a fireman's carry, his muscles straining under the weight, and began the trek to the new location he had scouted months before, an easier, more convenient disposal site. When the body was safely stashed in the cavernous void between the boulders, Jonty returned for the detector and the backpack, placing them with the corpse like an offering to the gods of the hunt.

This one was different. More activity. More excitement. More risk. And it had only enhanced Jonty's thrill.

Then came the unexpected bonus, he met the second man, the dead man's friend. Jonty played his part masterfully, his expression a mask of concern as he spoke to the bloated fool of a sergeant.

"I reckon that fella might've had a bit too much to drink," Jonty suggested, rubbing his chin thoughtfully. "Maybe they had a fight. Maybe it got out of hand. Who knows?" He let the words hang in the air before adding with a smirk, "Wouldn't be surprised if that bastard killed his own mate."

Jonty almost laughed out loud when he saw the oaf of a sergeant take the bait. Arresting the poor sod, charging him with murder, it was almost too easy. The fat fool thought he had solved the case, and Jonty? Jonty had just pulled off another perfect hunt.

The next one had been almost too easy, which in itself was a shame. Jonty preferred the thrill of the chase, the tension in the moment before the final shot. But this one had simply wandered into his sights like a beast at a watering hole, oblivious to the predator in the long grass. Still, the bastard had managed to put a wrinkle in Jonty's plans, he couldn't find his gold.

After he had hauled the old bloke's body down into the cavern to join the others, Jonty returned to the campsite, methodically searching for the gold nuggets. The bastard had locked his car, and Jonty, in his satisfaction, had neglected to check the man's pockets before he sent him tumbling into the abyss. He stood for a moment, hands on his hips, staring at the locked vehicle.

"Fuck it," Jonty muttered. That old bugger had collected a fortune in gold, Jonty's gold, carefully planted to lure him in. No way was he getting it back now.

He had to be smarter next time. More methodical. The thrill of the hunt was intoxicating, but he needed to keep his wits about him. Now, it was time to watch the news and see how much attention this latest disappearance would stir. He had to admit, this was good hunting. The best he'd ever known.

It wasn't until he heard the report on the evening news that he realised the next victim had been one of his own, a fellow Queensland copper. A misstep, but shit happens. The young one, Laidlow, had been a fighter. He had led Jonty on a chase through the boulders, fast and unpredictable, darting between rocks like an animal with the instincts to survive. But instincts weren't enough. Jonty had fired six times before two bullets finally found their mark, one in the chest, the other a clean shot between the eyes. Even in death, he had an air of defiance about him. A tough kid, Jonty thought. Could have been a good copper, given the chance.

Jonty was at the station when three blokes came in, their faces pale, their voices edged with nervous excitement. They had found a body in the tunnel.

Jonty sat behind the desk, feigning nonchalance, watching the sergeant as the news sank in. He leaned back in his chair and scoffed.

"Well, there you go," he said, shaking his head. "I told you that bastard was no good. The one you let out. He's at it again."

The fat sergeant bristled at the accusation, his face reddening with the realisation of his mistake. He had been too quick to release the ex-con, too confident in his own judgment. Now he looked like a fool. Jonty suppressed a smirk.

By the time they had retrieved all the bodies, the authorities were still floundering in the dark. No leads, no evidence, no idea. The entrance wounds from Jonty's rifle were barely noticeable, small, precise, without the telltale carnage of an exit wound. Unless someone was looking for them, they would go unnoticed.

These Australian cops weren't so smart, Jonty mused. Not smart at all.

Jonty Wagner guided the police Landcruiser down the winding, treacherous bends of the Kuranda Range, the heavy vehicle tilting and groaning under the strain. The road was a bastard, an unforgiving ribbon of asphalt twisting through the rainforest like a drunken python. As he flicked on the high beams to cut through the mid-morning mist, he sneered to himself, thinking about the bureaucratic nonsense that kept them from building a decent road. Some limp-wristed environmentalists had decided that a bloody tree frog, of all things, was worth more than the safety of human lives. Christ, in Africa, they'd bulldoze the whole damn place if it got in the way of progress.

Jonty laughed, a low, satisfied chuckle, as he imagined Sergeant Tom Kearns writhing in agony in some sweat-stained bed, doubled over with gut cramps or worse. The fat bastard probably had it coming. It was almost poetic, really, a lifetime of sloth and excess finally catching up with him.

Not that Jonty gave a damn. If anything, Kearns being sick was a minor inconvenience. It just meant he had to take the weekly reports down to Cairns himself. He didn't mind, though. It was a good excuse to get out of that dead-end town, to feel the open road beneath him, and breathe air that didn't stink of stale beer and regret. Maybe he'd even stop for a cold one before heading back, stretch his legs, enjoy the sun.

But back in Marianvale, Kearns wasn't laid up in bed like Jonty assumed. No, Sergeant Kearns was in deeper trouble than he had ever been in his life.

Mick West and his crew had been making things too hot for him, too damn hot. And Kearns, soft and cowardly as he was, had finally cracked. For weeks now, he'd felt that gnawing fear burrowing into his gut like a parasite, growing stronger with every passing day. The moment Jonty Wagner had laid it all out for him, his voice calm, deliberate, that icy South African accent making murder sound like a matter of routine, Kearns had known he was in over his head.

For a while, he had convinced himself he could live with it. Pretend he hadn't heard. Drink until the voices in his head dulled into a distant hum. But the problem with knowing something like that, something monstrous, is that it doesn't go away. It clings to you. It changes you. And when Kearns looked in the mirror, he saw a man who was no longer just a corrupt little sergeant skimming cash off ghost employees and brewing his own piss-weak beer on government time. No, he was an accessory. An accomplice to what Jonty Wagner was doing up on that mountain. Killing innocent people for fun.

And that was a line he could no longer cross.

So, in the end, he did what weak men always do. He ran for help.

His cousin, the Assistant Commissioner of Police, was the son of Kearns' father's brother. Family. Blood. And when Kearns called him, when he finally let it all spill out in a desperate, shaking voice, the man listened. He didn't interrupt. Didn't ask for clarification. He just let Kearns talk until there was nothing left to say.

And then, in the calm, clipped tone of a man who had survived long enough to reach the highest ranks of the force, he said, "I'll handle it."

That was it. No questions, no outrage. Just cold, decisive action.

Rick Bird was the answer. A detective sergeant from Cairns, hand-picked for the job. He would be waiting in Marianvale, ready to meet Kearns. And it had been Bird's idea to get Jonty out of town, to send him to Cairns under the pretence of delivering the weekly reports.

"It'll be easier that way," Bird had said. "Away from his turf. Away from his weapons. Let's make this clean."

The cousin's final words to Kearns before hanging up had been just as calculated, just as ruthless.

"Don't say more than you have to, Thomas. Let Bird do his job. And for God's sake, don't breathe a word about your brewing or your ghost staff. This is about survival, not confession. Understand?"

Kearns had swallowed hard, nodded to the empty room, and wiped the sweat from his brow.

He understood.

And Jonty Wagner, well, he didn't know it yet, but his days were numbered.

He was now standing in the dim, dust-laden confines of Jonty Wagner's home, his expression grim, his thick fingers sifting through damning evidence. Sergeant Rick Bird from the Cairns police station stood beside him, holding up the sleek, deadly Sako .22-250 rifle, turning it slowly in his hands. The Leupold scope gleamed in the weak morning light. Kearns nodded, his suspicions confirmed. Alongside it sat a meticulously arranged kit, reloading equipment, canisters of ball powder, and a tin of hollow-point projectiles.

"He's been making his own rounds," Bird muttered, his voice taut with understanding. Kearns grunted in reply, stepping over to a shelf where a small, unassuming container sat. He lifted the lid and let out a slow breath. Inside, nestled in the soft folds of a cloth, were gold nuggets, dozens of them, varying in size and weight.

"Looks like our boy's been getting paid for his kills," Bird remarked.

Kearns didn't reply. He was staring at the next piece of evidence, a compact game camera, its SD card still in place. He popped it into his laptop and scrolled through the files. The images appeared, grainy but clear enough: Wagner, standing before the lens, adjusting the settings, his expression void of anything but cold calculation. Another camera was found at Wagner's so-called campsite, aimed strategically at the track leading up to the ridge. More SD cards, more images.

Kearns felt his pulse quicken. The bastard had been documenting everything, his obsession captured frame by frame.

By the time Jonty reached the Cairns police station, his mind was already on lunch. He dropped the reports onto the duty sergeant's desk with a careless nod and turned to leave when the officer behind the counter stopped him.

"Hold up, Wagner. Got some papers for you to take back to Marianvale."

Jonty sighed and was about to lower himself onto a bench in the reception area when two plainclothes detectives emerged from the corridor. One of them, a lean, hawk-eyed bastard with the bearing of a man who never joked, spoke first.

"Jonty Wagner?"

The voice cut through the warm afternoon air, steady, authoritative. It wasn't a question so much as a summons.

Jonty straightened, turning toward the source of the voice. Two men stood by his truck, dressed in plain clothes, but there was no mistaking them for anything other than cops. The way they carried themselves, the quiet confidence, the subtle weight of sidearms beneath their jackets, detectives, without a doubt.

"Yeah?" he answered, his voice even.

The taller of the two took a step forward, a smirk playing at the corner of his mouth. "Been waiting for you, mate. Couldn't get you on the radio for some strange reason." His tone was light, but something about it didn't sit right with Jonty.

The second man, stocky, built like a rugby forward, closed the distance, standing just a little too close. "We've got to head out to Mount Marian. More lost hikers. And Kearns is sick in bed, so…" He shrugged, a deliberate pause. "You're the man."

Jonty blinked, then gave a slow nod. He felt a flicker of anticipation stir in his chest. A bit of action at last. Something to break the monotony. He knew it wasn't one of his, which meant this could be interesting. A real search. A real mystery. Still, he would need to be careful, steering them away from his rocks would take some finesse.

"Oh… okay," he said, playing it casual. "I'll meet you up there then?"

The taller detective chuckled, shaking his head. "Nah, mate." His eyes flicked toward Jonty's truck. "Leave that heap of shit from Marian here. We need to get there today."

The two men laughed, and Jonty joined in, forcing a grin.

But somewhere, deep in his gut, an instinct honed by years of hunting, both animals and men, whispered to him.

Jonty strode onto the rooftop level, the wind buffeting him as the helicopter's rotors chopped at the humid Queensland air. He was still wary, a lingering uncertainty gnawing at him, but he masked it well. He turned to the smaller of the two detectives, the one who had yet to introduce himself, his expression questioning.

The man grinned, his teeth flashing white. "Polair, mate! Fuck driving." He clapped Jonty on the back, as though they were old friends sharing a joke.

Jonty found himself grinning too as he climbed into the front seat of the Bell 429, feeling the powerful machine hum beneath him. This was the way to travel. No bouncing over rutted dirt tracks, no choking dust, just raw speed and freedom. He ran his hands over the controls with something close to reverence.

"Way to go, fellas," he said, settling in. "Reminds me of Africa. We had the Iroquois there. Used 'em for hunting down gangs in the jungles."

He wasn't exaggerating. The memory burned bright, the thick, oppressive heat of the African bush, the rhythmic thump of rotor blades cutting through the sky, the adrenaline spike as they swooped in low on a target. His hands twitched on instinct, muscles remembering the weight of a rifle pressed against his shoulder.

This,…now, this was what he missed. Not the dreary monotony of small-town policing. This was where he belonged.

Jonty let out a low chuckle, still high on the moment. "What are the chances of getting into this full-time?"

The detective in the pilot's seat turned slightly, flashing him an easy smile. "Mate, if you're fair dinkum, we're desperate for guys to join Polair." His voice was light, but there was something measured behind it, something weighing Jonty's reaction. "I'll give you a transfer application when we get back. Remind me."

Jonty nodded, barely able to contain his excitement. This could be it, the escape he'd been looking for. The chance to leave the dead-end grind of Dimbulah behind.

He didn't notice the quick glance the two detectives exchanged.

Didn't see the silent understanding pass between them.

The Bell 429 banked low over Mount Marian, the landscape below a patchwork of dense scrub, jagged outcrops, and the skeletal remains of trees long since bleached by the sun. The rocks, Jonty's rocks, loomed ahead, their labyrinthine crevices yawning like the gaping mouths of ancient predators.

Jonty felt the shift in altitude, a controlled descent that set his instincts on edge. He glanced at the pilot, his brow furrowing. The man met his gaze through the intercom headset, his expression unreadable.

"Rendezvous with ground force," the pilot said evenly. "You can take off your earphones now."

Something prickled at the base of Jonty's skull, but he obeyed, peeling the headset away. He barely had time to register the movement in his periphery before the second detective, seated behind him, leaned forward, his hand steady, his grip practiced.

The Browning Buck Mark Bull pistol was already levelled at Jonty's head. A quiet phut-phut broke the drone of the rotors.

The first subsonic round punched through the thin skin above Jonty's right ear, mushrooming as it tunnelled through soft tissue, obliterating his brain before it could even register the impact. The second followed an instant later, a cold insurance policy.

Jonty Wagner was dead before his body sagged sideways, before his final exhale left his lips.

There was no arterial spray, no gruesome explosion of bone and matter, just a pair of neat, unremarkable entry wounds. The ICC subsonic rounds had done their work, expanding lethally inside the skull but never exiting. Quick. Efficient. Clean.

The detective in the backseat holstered the suppressed pistol and exited the aircraft, moving with deliberate precision. From the cargo compartment, he retrieved a webbing sling, the lanyard already clipped to its release system. The pilot, still silent, reached across the cockpit and unlatched the passenger door. With a casual shove, Jonty's body slid from the seat and crumpled to the dirt below.

The detective crouched, looping the sling beneath Jonty's lifeless arms, securing it snugly across his chest. His uniform remained pristine, his duty belt still fastened with the regulation Glock and handcuffs, a dead policeman dressed for duty.

With practiced ease, the detective climbed into the front seat, gripping the lanyard attached to the quick-release mechanism.

The Bell lifted off once more, Jonty's body swinging beneath it like a carcass strung for butchery. The helicopter rose higher, the landscape shrinking below until they hovered over a narrow ravine, an ancient scar in the earth where four massive boulders had settled together, forming a deep and bottomless grave.

The two men exchanged a glance. No words were needed.

A sharp tug on the lanyard.

Jonty's body dropped soundlessly into the chasm, swallowed whole by the shadows below.

The Bell pivoted in the air, banking smoothly toward Cairns, its passengers already leaving the past where it belonged, buried in the rocks.

Back in Cairns, the two detectives moved with the cool efficiency of men who had done this sort of work before. The helicopter was handled with quiet precision, wiped down, secured, and logged as though it had never left its hangar. There was no need for words between them. The job wasn't finished just yet.

Jonty Wagner had come to Cairns in a Queensland Police Land Cruiser Troopy. That detail needed to be erased just as thoroughly as the man himself.

One of the detectives climbed into the Troopy's driver's seat, the engine rumbling to life beneath his steady hands. The other followed in a Land Cruiser Wagon, keeping a measured distance as they rolled out of Cairns and headed west, toward the rugged emptiness of Marianvale.

They drove in silence, the endless Queensland bush stretching out around them, the shadows lengthening as the sun dipped lower in the sky. They had already chosen the spot, a place well beyond the usual tracks, far from the prying eyes of hikers or station workers. Few came this way, and those that did weren't the type to ask questions.

The Troopy left the main track, bouncing over rough terrain, swallowed by the thick scrub. They pushed deeper into the wild, weaving through gnarled ghost gums and ancient termite mounds that stood like silent sentinels in the dust.

At last, they reached the predetermined site, an isolated pocket of land west of 'the rocks', where nature would conspire with them to keep secrets. The Troopy was guided into position, its tires sinking slightly into the dry, cracked earth. The detective behind the wheel cut the engine.

The bush swallowed the silence, leaving only the whisper of the wind through the trees.

The men moved quickly. The Troopy was wiped down for prints, the interior checked over. A final sweep to ensure nothing had been left behind, no careless mistake, no loose thread. Satisfied, the detective locked the doors and stepped back, surveying their work.

It looked like any other vehicle left behind by some unlucky traveler, abandoned in the vast indifference of the outback.

Without another word, they climbed into the Wagon and turned back toward Cairns, the dust settling in their wake, covering their tracks as if the Troopy, and Jonty Wagner, had never existed at all.

Sergeant Tom Kearns sat behind his battered old desk, drumming thick fingers on the armrest of his chair, staring at the untouched mug of homebrew beside him. He wasn't drinking this morning, his gut was a mess, a twisting knot of unease. He knew what it was. Instinct. The same instinct that had kept him one step ahead of trouble all these years.

Senior Constable Jonty Wagner had failed to report for duty. That in itself was odd, Wagner was cocky, reckless, maybe even dangerous, but he was never the kind to simply vanish. Not without a reason.

Kearns leaned back, exhaling through his nose as he scanned the duty roster again. Wagner had taken the police Land Cruiser Troopy, JG667R, out the previous day. That meant he was out in the field somewhere. But where?

By midmorning, Kearns had made the first call, punching Wagner's number into his mobile. The call rang out, unanswered. No voicemail. No response. He tried again an hour later. Nothing. A slow, unpleasant feeling began to crawl up his spine.

At midday, he switched tactics and called Wagner's home phone. The silence that met him on the other end told him everything he needed to know.

That afternoon, with no word and no sign of Wagner, Kearns typed up a formal report and sent it up the chain to the Officer in Charge at Mareeba. He worded it carefully, professionally, making no mention of his own creeping suspicion. He had been told by Rick Bird to "Just act naturally" and impressed onto him how important it was to do that.

The following morning, Mareeba's response came through, short and direct. A search was approved and organised.

Kearns set the radio handset down with a heavy sigh. He had been around long enough to recogniseHe had been told when things were going to get messy.

Jonty Wagner had walked off into the scrub and disappeared.

And Kearns had the feeling that nobody was ever going to find him.

Mick West was about to have dinner with his wife, had heard the report on the news about the missing constable.

ABC Far North Queensland News Bulletin – 6:00 PM

"Good evening, I'm Sarah Montgomery with ABC Far North Queensland News. Authorities are ramping up their search efforts after a police officer was reported missing west of Marianvale."

"Senior Constable Jonty Wagner, stationed at Marianvale, was last seen on duty two days ago. His marked police vehicle, a Land Cruiser Troopy bearing registration JG667R, was discovered abandoned earlier today along Mitchell's Road, approximately twenty-three kilometres west of Marianvale."

"Police and emergency services launched an immediate search after Wagner failed to report for duty and could not be reached via radio or telephone. Search crews, including officers from the Mareeba station, SES volunteers, and PolAir, are currently scouring the rugged terrain surrounding the area where his vehicle was found."

"Inspector Greg Matheson from the Queensland Police Service says they are treating the disappearance with utmost urgency."

"'At this stage, we are following all leads and maintaining hope for a positive outcome,' Inspector Matheson stated. 'We urge anyone who may have seen Senior Constable Wagner or his vehicle in recent days to come forward with any information that could assist in our search.'"

"The area west of Marianvale is known for its dense bushland, rocky outcrops, and unpredictable weather conditions, making the search operation particularly challenging. Local residents have expressed their concerns, with some assisting search crews in combing the difficult terrain."

"As the search enters its second day, authorities remain tight-lipped about possible leads or concerns for foul play, but stress that no theory has been ruled out. Anyone with information is urged to contact Crime Stoppers or their local police station."

"This is Sarah Montgomery for ABC Far North Queensland News. Stay tuned for further updates as they come to hand."

Mick and Emily had both fallen silent, the low drone of the ABC news bulletin still murmuring from the old radio in the kitchen. The words Senior Constable Jonty Wagner had caught Mick's attention like a fishhook to the gut.

"Did you know him? Jonty Wagner?" Emily asked offhandedly, her voice laced with the indifference she reserved for anything related to the police. She had lost all faith in them after what they had put Mick through.

Mick, however, wasn't so quick to dismiss it. His mind had already begun sifting through old memories, reaching back to the day he'd first met Wagner. The name hadn't registered at first, but now it came back to him with clarity.

"Yeah," he murmured, his voice tinged with something close to regret. "I remember him. South African bloke. Probably the friendliest copper I ever had to deal with."

He leaned back in his chair, staring past Emily, beyond the walls of their little house, as the memory unfurled itself in his mind. That first morning at the Marianvale Police Station, Mick had been half-asleep on the holding cell's cot when Wagner had come in, rapping on the bars with the back of his knuckles. Unlike the others, Wagner hadn't barked orders or thrown his weight around. Instead, he'd unlocked the door and "Morning," the constable said, his voice smooth but with a distinctive accent. "Breakfast?" he asked, his hand motioning toward the table beyond the cell. "Best eat up, mate. Those boffins will be here soon."No sense facing the day on an empty stomach," Wagner had said with an easy smile.

Mick had been suspicious at first. A decent cop? In his experience, those two words didn't belong in the same sentence. But Wagner had proved to be different. He wasn't some puffed-up arsehole swinging a badge around for power. No, Wagner had been a straight shooter, someone who treated a man like a man, no matter which side of the bars he was on.

Mick let out a slow breath, shaking his head as if trying to dislodge an uneasy thought. "Yeah… he was a good bloke. Isn't it always the same, though?" He glanced across the table at Emily, his expression dark with something unspoken.

Emily barely looked up from her dinner, her knife scraping against the plate. "It is. Always the innocent ones," she muttered, her voice heavy with that same weary cynicism that had settled over her since Mick's own run-in with the law.

Mick didn't reply. He just stared past her, his mind turning over the news report. He didn't know what kind of trouble Wagner had landed in, but he had a bad feeling about it. A copper didn't just disappear, not out there.

Three days passed before they found Wagner's police vehicle. It had been parked well off Mitchell's Road, a lonely stretch of dirt track cutting through the scrub twenty-three kilometres west of Marianvale. It was locked, no signs of struggle, no indication of foul play. Just sitting there, as if Wagner had pulled over, stepped out, and simply vanished.

The searchers had something tangible now, an anchor point to begin their hunt. The rugged wilderness of Mount Marian stretched out before them, vast and unyielding, filled with gorges, caves, and thick, tangled bushland that could swallow a man whole.

But Mick knew that country. And he knew that a man didn't just disappear without a trace unless someone had made damn sure he did. But, there was nothing he could do to help.

Chris Granger was seething.

His credibility among the ranks in Cairns and Mareeba was slipping fast, and now he was being sidelined with what felt like a pointless errand, finding Jonty Wagner. It was an insult, a task unworthy of a man with his experience. He had hunted down psychopaths before, walked through the carnage they left behind, smelled the blood in the air, and pieced together the twisted logic behind their brutal acts. And now, here he was, standing in the sweltering heat, staring at an abandoned police vehicle that had been trampled by every clueless fool who had set foot on the site before him.

He clenched his jaw as he surveyed the damage. Any trace evidence, footprints, tire tracks, a stray fibre, had been obliterated by careless boots. The scene was worthless. He had fired off an angry report to his superiors, demanding answers, and had been met with little more than empty assurances. "It won't happen again," they had promised. He knew better.

Frustrated, he turned his attention to Wagner's home. If the man had vanished, then his house might hold the key to his movements. But when he arrived at the Marianvale Police Station, he was met with a solid, immovable wall in the form of Sergeant Tom Kearns.

"I need to get inside," Granger said bluntly.

Kearns, a seasoned officer with years of small-town law enforcement under his belt, didn't flinch. "You'll need a warrant for that, sir."

Granger frowned. "Sergeant, I outrank you."

Kearns folded his arms across his broad chest, unfazed. "Being of superior rank doesn't mean you can flaunt the law. No warrant, no search." His voice was steady, resolute. "With all due respect, sir, I suggest you head back to Cairns and do this properly."

Granger's hands balled into fists at his sides. He knew that Kearns was right, legally, at least. But this wasn't about protocol. This was about finding out what had happened to Wagner. About getting ahead of the storm that was coming.

Instead, he found himself stonewalled, forced back to Cairns with nothing but wasted time and growing doubts. Wagner was still missing, and with every passing hour, the weight of it pressed harder on Chris Granger's mind. He had seen cases like this before, men who vanished, leaving behind only questions and the stench of unfinished business. But this one felt different. There was a hand in this, a force working behind the scenes to keep the truth buried. Someone didn't want Wagner to be found.

As he sat in the dimly lit confines of his office in Cairns, staring at the growing pile of reports on his desk, a name surfaced unbidden in his thoughts, Thomas Kearns.

Granger's jaw tightened. He had dismissed the murmurs about Kearns before from his undercover men, brushing them aside as petty grievances from locals who always had something to say about the police. But now, the man's name carried a different weight. He reached for the file that he had, at the time, ignored and now flipping it open with a measured deliberation. The report detailed complaints, whispers of corruption, unexplained incidents that had been swept under the rug. And an abundance of minor motor vehicle offences that had been written around the town in the recent years. It wasn't concrete, nothing he could pin Kearns to, but it was enough to make Granger pause.

Kearns had been too quick to shut him down, too firm in denying him access to Wagner's home. That could have been nothing more than a man following the rules, or it could have been something else entirely. A delay. A stall. A means to ensure that whatever truth lay hidden in Wagner's house stayed hidden a little longer.

Granger leaned back in his chair, rubbing a hand over his face. He had been looking in the wrong direction, chasing ghosts in the wilderness when the answers might have been standing in front of him all along.

Perhaps it was time to take a closer look at Sergeant Thomas Kearns.

Kearns was confident, almost certain, that he and Rick Bird had stripped Wagner's home of anything incriminating. They had been thorough, methodical. Every scrap of evidence that could tie back to them had been removed, every loose end neatly clipped.

But almost certain wasn't good enough.

Something gnawed at him, a whisper in the back of his mind that refused to quiet. Had they missed something? A document tucked away in a forgotten drawer? A note scrawled in the margins of a ledger? He couldn't afford mistakes, not now.

Granger was gone, back in Cairns, sulking over his own incompetence, most likely. He wouldn't be back for hours, if he returned at all today. That meant Kearns had time. Plenty of time.

He glanced at his watch, then made his decision. A quick look, nothing more. Just enough to be sure. He had last been at Wagners home accompanied by Detective Sergeant Rick Bird. Rick Bird was a professional police officer. Kearns did not for a second, consider that Bird would not have double checked everything, before closing the door on Wagner's home.

He grabbed his keys and headed for Wagner's house.

There exists a huge difference between these two officers;

The police force has always been a dichotomy of personalities, those who see it as a job and those who see it as a calling. Thomas Kearns and Rick Bird epitomised these two extremes.

Thomas Kearns: The Opportunist

To Kearns, the badge was merely a means to an end. It was a stable pay check, a uniform that carried weight in a small town, and most importantly, a position he could manipulate to his advantage. He wasn't driven by duty or justice but by self-preservation and personal gain.

He worked just hard enough to avoid scrutiny, never going beyond what was necessary. If paperwork could be ignored, he ignored it. If a crime didn't demand his attention, he let it slide. When an opportunity arose to exploit the system, be it through small favours, bribes, or overlooked transgressions, he seized it without hesitation. The law, for Kearns, was a flexible thing, bent to suit his needs.

He wasn't corrupt in the traditional sense, he didn't run criminal enterprises or take money from syndicates, but he was corrupt in spirit. He knew the game and played it well, skimming off the edges of power without ever stepping over the line that would bring real consequences. He made sure to keep his hands clean, at least on the surface. To the people of Marianvale, he was just another cop, one who didn't make waves, one who didn't ask too many questions.

And that was exactly how he liked it.

Rick Bird: The True Believer

Rick Bird was cut from an entirely different cloth. If Kearns saw policing as a job, Bird saw it as a mission, a way of life. There was no clocking in and clocking out for him. The job didn't end when the shift was over because it wasn't a shift, it was who he was.

Bird didn't just enforce the law, he embodied it. His standards were uncompromising, his expectations of himself and those around him unrelenting. He viewed men like Kearns with open contempt, lazy, self-serving parasites who had no business wearing the uniform. To Bird, the badge wasn't just authority; it was responsibility, a sacred burden that demanded everything a man had to give.

He was ruthless in pursuit of justice, methodical in his investigations, and unyielding in his belief that the law was absolute. His dedication made him feared by criminals and resented by colleagues who found his intensity exhausting. He had no patience for incompetence, no tolerance for weakness.

While Kearns manipulated the system, Bird fought for it, upheld it, and at times, was consumed by it. It wasn't just a job. It was his identity.

Two Sides of the Same Coin

Men like Kearns ensured the system functioned with minimal friction, allowing the world to keep turning even if justice was compromised along the way. Men like Bird ensured that justice was served, even if it was 'out of the book', and meant making enemies within their own ranks.

Kearns would retire one day, wealthier than he should have been, slipping quietly into obscurity. Bird, on the other hand, would likely burn out before he ever got the chance, leaving behind a trail of broken friendships and unfulfilled potential.

They would, and certainly did bend the rules, but the difference was that Bird was a professional and it was extremely unlikely that he should ever get caught.

It was exactly for this reason that Sergeant Thomas Kearns walked into a trap when he had gone to double check Wagners home. Sergeant Thomas Kearns had always believed himself to be a step ahead of the game. He operated in shadows, manoeuvring through the police system like a seasoned politician, never outright corrupt, but always finding ways to bend the rules to his advantage. And yet, for all his cunning, it was his own arrogance that led him straight into the lion's den.

Detective Inspector Chris Granger, a man weathered by decades of hunting predators far more cunning than Kearns, had grown tired of the sergeant's deliberate obstruction. Kearns had stalled the investigation, dragging his feet when asked for files, conveniently forgetting requests for information, and outright refusing to grant access to Wagner's home without a warrant. It was as if he was daring Granger to lose patience.

Granger, however, was not a man easily provoked. If Kearns wanted to play games, he'd oblige, but on his own terms. That was why he had arranged for Wagner's house to be placed under quiet surveillance. A single unmarked car parked at a distance, its occupants watching in shifts. The house itself was still sealed, officially untouched, but Granger was not a man to trust paperwork alone.

And now, just as he had suspected, Kearns was walking straight into his web.

The sergeant had waited until darkness cloaked the town, slipping out of the station with all the confidence of a man who had done this sort of thing before. The streets were empty, the night air thick with humidity, but Kearns barely noticed. His focus was singular, he had to make sure there was nothing left behind, no overlooked clue that could tie him to whatever it was that had happened to Wagner.

He parked his car a block away and moved on foot, keeping to the shadows. It was second nature to him, an old habit from years of knowing how to stay unnoticed. Approaching Wagner's front door, he produced a key, one he had acquired when he was with Bird, and let himself in, careful to close the door silently behind him.

He never saw the movement across the street.

In the unmarked car, the officer on watch grabbed the radio.

"He's inside."

The trap was sprung.

Within moments, another unmarked vehicle pulled up at the far end of the street, silent as a predator in the wild. Granger himself emerged from the shadows, a grim smile playing at the corner of his mouth. He had been right about Kearns.

Now, it was time to see just how deep the rot went.

The two unmarked police cars glided into position, their movements precise and coordinated. Kearns' police Cruiser was effectively boxed in, pinned between the vehicles like a beast caught in a well-laid snare. The officers moved swiftly, four shadowy figures stepping from the cars, boots silent against the pavement, weapons holstered but hands poised, ready for action if necessary.

Inside, Sergeant Thomas Kearns froze for the briefest of moments, a fraction of hesitation that would have gone unnoticed to an untrained observer. But these men were not untrained. Chris Granger saw it, that flicker of shock, the calculation behind Kearns' eyes as his mind scrambled for an escape route.

Then, like the seasoned survivor he was, Kearns recovered. His face rearranged itself into an expression of casual surprise, his lips curling into that easy, almost arrogant smirk he wore when he believed himself untouchable.

"Well, well," Kearns said, slipping his hands into his pockets as though this were nothing more than an unexpected social call. His voice was smooth, his tone even. "I figured you'd be back soon with your warrant, Granger."

He reached into his jacket pocket and pulled out a key, holding it up between two fingers.

"So I thought I'd save you the trouble," he continued, his smile never faltering. "Jonty left a spare at the station. Thought I'd meet you here and hand it over personally."

A masterful lie. Delivered with precision, no hesitation, no stutter.

But Granger wasn't buying it.

The detective took a slow step forward, his gaze never leaving Kearns' face, studying the man like a seasoned tracker reading the landscape for signs of deception. Kearns was good, very good, but Granger had spent decades staring down men who thought they could outsmart him. And they had all made the same mistake.

Granger allowed the silence to stretch, a tension so thick it pressed into the space between them.

"Thoughtful of you," Granger said at last, his voice quiet, measured. "Funny thing, though…" He took another step, close enough now to see the sheen of sweat beginning to form on Kearns' temple. "If that key was at the station, what exactly were you doing inside before we arrived?"

For the first time, Kearns' mask slipped, just a fraction, just enough.

Granger smiled.

Granger had him.

"You've just committed break and enter," he said, his voice casual, almost conversational, like a man commenting on the weather.

And just as smoothly, without raising his tone, he turned to one of his men.

"Arrest him and take him back to Cairns."

It was then that Kearns' instinct took over. His hand moved automatically toward his Glock, fingers brushing against the holster. A fatal mistake.

"Don't," one of Granger's men warned, his own weapon already unholstered and trained on Kearns. The voice was level, calm, but there was no mistaking the steel behind it. One more inch, one more second, and Kearns would be nothing more than a corpse cooling on Wagner's living room floor.

Kearns hesitated, then slowly lifted his hands in a show of reluctant surrender. He exhaled through his nose, jaw tightening as one of Granger's men spun him around and snapped the handcuffs into place with the efficiency of a man who had done it a thousand times before.

"Break and enter, my arse!" Kearns spat, shaking his head as they secured his wrists. But now, he was thinking again, the initial panic washed away by the cold, calculating part of his mind that had kept him alive and on top for years. "I knew you were coming back with a warrant," he continued, his voice regaining its familiar smugness. "Now get these fucking cuffs off me!"

Granger watched him for a long moment, then simply turned away as though Kearns were no more than an inconvenience.

"Get him into the Cairns watch house," he said flatly to his men. Then, as an afterthought, he added, "Oh, and while you're down there, get a search warrant for this place too."

He didn't need to look back to know Kearns was fuming. The Sergeant had played his game well, but the house of cards was starting to crumble.

Can of Worms

The forensic team combed through Senior Constable Jonty Wagner's house, moving with the meticulous patience of men who had learned that even the smallest fragment of evidence could crack a case wide open. They found little, but what they did find was telling.

In the kitchen, wedged deep in the hairline crack of the linoleum-covered floor, were three tiny granules of extruded stick gunpowder. The chemical analysis identified it as 'Varget', a propellant commonly used in precision rifle cartridges. It was a name familiar to anyone who reloaded their own ammunition, a powder favoured by long-range marksmen.

Further evidence lay beneath the kitchen's uneven skirting board, tucked under a raised section where the masonite walls met the floor. The find was small but damning, a Hornady .223 projectile, 40-grain, with its distinctive copper-jacketed tip. The bullet lay waiting in the dust, as if forgotten, as if overlooked by whoever had tried to scrub this house clean.

But it was in the garage, a separate structure behind the house, that they found the most intriguing clue. On a shelf, half-buried beneath a tangle of tools and old rags, sat a solid steel block, rough-edged and unremarkable at first glance. Eighty-five millimetres long, twenty-five wide, twenty-five thick, its weight was deceptive, heavy for its size, dense, deliberate.

One end had an irregular boring, a cylindrical cut drilled into its face, sixty millimetres deep and precisely eleven millimetres across. The forensic technician turned it in his hands, frowning, before recognition dawned.

"A full-sized reforming die," he murmured. "For resizing .223 casings."

The implications were clear. Someone, perhaps Wagner, perhaps someone else, had been handcrafting their own ammunition. Precision loads. Carefully measured. Carefully prepared.

The physical hunt for Senior Constable Jonty Wagner had been officially called off. The scrublands had been scoured, every dry creek bed and dense patch of bushland west of Marianvale walked and rewalked by search teams, but there was nothing, not a trace of him.

With no new leads, the investigation into the triple homicide that had shocked the region, the brutal murders of Samuel John Young, Eric Phillip Simpson, and Phillip James Laidlow, began to stagnate. What had started as an urgent manhunt had now turned into a slow, suffocating wait.

All focus now fell squarely on one man, Jonathon Reise Wagner.

His disappearance was no longer treated as that of a missing person. Wagner was now the case.

From across the Tasman Sea, his parents arrived. Cornelis and Janine Wagner, weary and heartbroken, stepped off a flight from Whitecliffs, New Zealand, a quiet town nestled in the Canterbury region, some seventy kilometres west of Christchurch. The journey had been long, but it was nothing compared to the anguish of not knowing.

The Queensland Police Force, despite their growing unease about their missing officer, had publicly held their ground, Wagner was an outstanding policeman, they maintained. His record was clean. His performance had been exemplary. There was no reason for him to have vanished.

For two weeks, Cornelis and Janine Wagner stood in front of news cameras, pleading for answers. They made public appeals, offered rewards, did the rounds of radio and television. They were dignified, composed, but their pain was unmistakable.

Yet the silence remained unbroken.

With no fresh developments, no new clues, they could do nothing but return home. Two weeks after arriving in Cairns, they boarded a flight back to New Zealand, back to the cold emptiness of Whitecliffs.

But they left with more questions than answers. And behind them, the shadow over Wagner's name only grew darker.

Chris Grainger leaned back in his chair, the dull hum of the air-conditioning in his Cairns office the only sound in the room. The report on Senior Constable Jonathon Reise Wagner lay open before him. It was thick, compiled from multiple agencies, including Interpol, the South African Police Service, and Australian Immigration.

His eyes moved swiftly through the dense pages of official jargon and operational history, until they landed on three letters that sent a slow, burning surge of adrenaline through his veins.

STF.

His fingers tightened on the edge of the report.

He knew what those letters meant. He'd trained with men like Wagner before, ghosts, predators, warriors. STF wasn't just any police unit. It was South Africa's elite Special Task Force, the men who stepped into the shadows of war and handled the jobs no one else could.

They were the best of the best.

Grainger's own military background at Lympstone, the gruelling Commando Training Centre in Devon, England, had introduced him to men cut from the same cloth. Special operations. Counter-terrorism. Hostage rescue. A breed apart.

And now, Grainger knew, without a shred of doubt, this was no ordinary missing persons case.

Wagner was the killer.

Samuel John Young. Eric Phillip Simpson. Phillip James Laidlow.

Three confirmed kills. But Grainger wasn't fool enough to believe it stopped there. There could be more.

His eyes flicked to a name scrawled in the margin of an earlier report, one that had been nagging at the edge of the investigation for weeks.

Graham Eldridge.

A case that had gone cold, dismissed as a disappearance.

Maybe Wagner had been cleaning up loose ends. Maybe Eldridge had known something he shouldn't have.

Grainger exhaled slowly. The hunter had become the hunted.

Grainger tapped his fingers against the desk, his mind working through the puzzle. Wagner had owned a .22/250 at some point, of that, there was no doubt. The forensic team had confirmed the presence of Varget powder in the kitchen, and the resizing die found in the garage had been custom-machined for .223 casings, a near-perfect match for a .22/250 round.

But that raised three critical questions.

Where was the rifle?

Where was the rest of the reloading equipment?

And most pressing of all, where the hell was Wagner?

Grainger had been in this game long enough to know that the presence of reloading gear in Wagner's house meant more than just a passing interest in precision shooting. It meant Wagner was meticulous, careful, and, most importantly, he was planning something.

A man like Wagner didn't just vanish. He had a plan. A destination. An objective.

Grainger pushed back from his desk and stood, his jaw tightening.

Somewhere out there, in the wild expanse of North Queensland, Wagner was watching. Waiting. Preparing.

And Grainger was going to find him.

Grainger felt a surge of frustration rise in his chest as he walked through the sterile corridors of the Cairns watch house. He had been sure he was closing in, certain that Sergeant Thomas Kearns would be the loose thread that, once pulled, would unravel this whole tangled mess. Now, it seemed someone had cut the thread before he could even take hold of it.

He reached the charge desk and addressed the watch house sergeant, a stocky, tight-lipped officer who looked as though he had seen it all and cared for none of it.

"Bring Kearns to an interview room," Grainger ordered, expecting to see the man led in, still in cuffs, still rattled from his abrupt fall from grace.

Instead, the sergeant gave him a blank stare. A bad sign.

"Kearns?" the man echoed.

Grainger's impatience flared. "Yes, Thomas Kearns. The sergeant I had arrested last night. I want him in here, now."

There was a beat of silence.

"He's gone, sir."

Grainger's eyes narrowed. "Gone? What do you mean, gone?"

The watch house sergeant shifted uncomfortably. "He was released."

Grainger's jaw clenched. "On whose authority?"

"Detective Sergeant Rick Bird."

For a long moment, Grainger simply stood there, the weight of the revelation settling over him like a gathering storm.

Rick Bird.

Grainger had barely paid the man any attention before now. He had been too busy chasing Kearns, Wagner, and the ghosts of the past to consider who else might have their hands in this dirty game.

That changed now.

Grainger walked down the second-floor corridor, his boots echoing on the polished linoleum. Something didn't sit right. He had been in enough stations, enough offices, enough war rooms to know when something was out of place. And this was out of place.

A Detective Sergeant with an office on the executive level? Next door to PolAir? That was unheard of. The proximity to the police aerial unit made some sense, but a sergeant in a space usually reserved for high-ranking brass? That stank.

He reached the frosted-glass door with Detective Sergeant Rick Bird etched neatly into the panel and rapped his knuckles against it.

The office beyond was even more out of place. Large. Spacious. Almost luxurious by police standards. It had a receptionist, a receptionist?, stationed at a sleek desk. Detective Sergeants didn't get receptionists.

She looked up immediately, her expression smooth, professional.

"Inspector Grainger," she said.

Grainger hesitated. How the hell did she know who he was?

"I need to see Sergeant Bird," he said. Then, after a pause, "Rather urgently."

The receptionist gestured toward a chair. "Please take a seat."

Grainger's patience was wearing thin, but he sat anyway. He had barely settled when another door opened, and Rick Bird himself strolled out like a man without a care in the world.

"Chris! How are you?" Bird said, extending a hand in greeting. "I was just about to call you, actually."

Grainger didn't take the hand. Instead, he studied Bird, his mind racing.

What the hell was going on?

A few minutes ago, he had been ready to tear into a sergeant for overstepping his bounds, for undermining his investigation, for releasing Thomas Kearns without so much as a courtesy call. And now, here he was, standing in an executive-level office, facing a sergeant who somehow outranked his own damn pay grade?

Grainger opened his mouth to demand an explanation, but Bird was already waving him inside.

"Come in, come in," Bird said, lifting a hand in a calm down gesture.

Before Grainger could speak, Bird picked up the desk phone and started talking. The words were meaningless background noise, but Grainger caught the tone, casual, confident, controlled.

Grainger lowered himself into a chair, still trying to figure out which way was up.

Then the side door opened.

And in walked the Assistant Police Commissioner.

"Good to see you again, Chris."

The Commissioner strode forward, extending a firm hand, his face a mask of official warmth. Grainger shook it out of instinct, his mind already scrambling for answers.

"I'm here to congratulate you on your magnificent job," the Commissioner continued, smiling.

Grainger's frown deepened. Congratulate him?

"With all due respect, sir, I haven't concluded my task," Grainger said. "There's still a hell of a way to go yet."

The Commissioner's expression didn't change.

"Chris," he said, his voice lowering slightly. "I'm going to need you to listen to me carefully. This investigation is now officially over for you."

Grainger's back straightened. "The hell it is."

"Just hear me out," the Commissioner interjected, raising a hand. "Please. One minute."

Grainger's jaw tightened, but he gave a slow nod.

"This case, your case, is part of something bigger. Something far-reaching, something that extends beyond this jurisdiction. We're working alongside the federal police on an ongoing operation, and at this stage, your investigation can proceed no further."

"And why the hell not?" Grainger snapped.

The Commissioner exhaled through his nose, his tone sharpening.

"Because that's all I can tell you. And that's all I'm going to tell you."

Silence hung in the room, thick as storm clouds before the first crack of lightning.

Grainger stared at the Commissioner, then at Bird, then back again.

He had just been shut down. Hard.

And that only made him want to dig deeper.

End....

Other Books By Max Barrington

Woolgar River Park

Task

Rétrograde Justice

Dying To Find Gold

The New March

Bad Company

The First Ten Years in Australia

Fifty Five More Years

You Couldn't Make This Stuff Up

The Writer & The Written

What's Mine is Yours

The Darkie's Gold

The Intrusion

The Premonition

Revelation at Narern

King to Spare

The Telephone

Going Backwards

www.ingramcontent.com/pod-product-compliance
Lightning Source LLC
Chambersburg PA
CBHW050108120726
47904CB00004B/1266